To the person/peop[le]
read this book.
first book from
wrote during the

know there **SHADOWED**
are a few
mistakes
Dark Moon Rising

and they Sam Kettle and Natasha Slee
were edited when we re-released
them. we hope you enjoy the
trilogy. Best wishes Natasha
and
Sam.

N. Slee

1

When the Dark Moon meets its peak,
There's a brother who is your destiny
Hide, my child, safe and sound,
As in this brother, your destiny is found

In the Moonlight, she will show you,
All the questions, that were kept from you,
Go in search until she's found,
Resist the evil all around.

When the Dark Moon meets its peak,
There's a sister who is your destiny
Hide, my child, safe and sound,
As in this sister, your fate is found.

In the Darkness, he'll show you,
All the answers, that were kept from you,
Go in search until he's found,
Resist the liars all around.

Yes, you will speak to those who'll hear
And in your words a sadness flows
But can you brave what you most fear?
Can you face what the Dark Moon shows?

When the Dark Moon meets its peak,
There are the siblings, and their destiny
Come, my children, homeward bound

When all is lost, then all will be found.

Amelia;

I sat upright and looked around the darkness of my room, my heart slamming hard against my breast plate. My breaths were coming short and fast and I felt as though I was about to pass out. I had, had *that* dream *again!* What did it mean? I wish that I understood the words that had been plaguing my dreams for as long as I could remember. I closed my eyes and focused on controlling my breathing once again; just like I had taught myself after years of being tormented by this nightmare. After a few minutes, I rolled over to my bedside table, scooping my phone from the cabinet top and swiped at the screen awakening it from its slumber. I stared at the time and huffed loudly, dropping my phone back down onto the bed beside me.

It was that time of year again. The one time of year that I dreaded more than anything. October 31st. My birthday. I know that this should have been a special day. One that we should have been celebrating in style, especially as it was my eighteenth birthday, but this was also a painful reminder that this was the eighteenth anniversary of my mothers' death.

A time of year that became a taboo subject, one that no body other than me acknowledged. Even my father and grandparents ignored today and always had done. I had lived with them since the day I was born. The moment I was born my father left me here. Every year I would light a small candle and sing happy birthday to myself, as no one else was going to. It was a lonely existence, and it hurt, but this is just the way that my life must be.

I understood that everyone was in pain, I understand that this is a constant reminder of the loss of a wonderful woman, it was a horrible day to celebrate when your hearts were full of grief and loss. *But I was in pain too*, and no one seemed to care, not one bit.

My mother was never spoken about. No matter how many questions I asked, no matter how much I pleaded with my grandparents to tell me anything about her, I got shut down immediately.

The only two things that I knew about her was that she died a couple of hours after my birth, and that her name was Molly.

My two older brothers weren't left like me. They went with my father back to the mansion. I guess that was because they didn't bring painful memories every time my father looked at them like I did, they were the ones full of happy reminders. A time when their lives were perfect and complete. My two older brothers, Charlie and Eddie, were the apple of our fathers' eye. He literally couldn't be any prouder of them. Eddie; the youngest of my two siblings, was the only family member that liked me. He was never mean to me, and his eyes weren't full of hate and loathing when he looked at me. We would always laugh and joke together, and he was the only one that took the time to find out about how I was doing. But this time with Eddie was rare, I only got to see them once a year.

Charlie the oldest, was a whole other kettle of fish; he hated me. He blamed me for our mother's death and made sure that I knew about it. He once told me he wished it was me that had died all those years ago; I was only seven years old at the time. I grew up thinking he was right, and the pain of his words never went away. I started believing that maybe it should It have been me, but then again, maybe it shouldn't have been either of us.

I turned to look in my bedroom mirror for the last time, and caught sight of my red, swollen eyes; all I had done since I woke was cry; just like I did every year, the redness had emphasized my green eyes, a stark contrast to one another. I gulped down a deep steadying breath and stared at myself for a few more seconds in silence. This was it; this would be the very last time I would stand here, in this room, the room that I had lived in my entire life. After today everything was going to change. I glanced around slowly at my surroundings, taking in the blue paint that had faded over the years, and the white carpet, now yellowing with age and sighed. I was terrified. I didn't know what was waiting for me beyond these walls, but I knew that it must have been better than this existence that I had been living.

I never needed to worry about packing anything to take

with me. All that I had in here was a wardrobe, mirror, a bed and a photograph of my parents and brothers before I "*killed*" her. I would stare at it for hours, desperately trying to find a similarity to my family, anything at all, but there wasn't one. I looked nothing like any of them, my mother had red hair and brown eyes. My father and brothers are naturally tanned, and they are all tall. My dad has long blonde, nearly white hair and Icy Blue eyes, he is 6ft 4 and is built like a brick shithouse; *a phrase that my grandad liked to use whenever he spoke about his son.* My brothers have my dad's build, Charlie looking nearly identical to my father, except with our mum's brown eyes and Eddie who was the spitting image of my mother had my dad's icy blue eyes. And then there's me? 5ft; and a half, my hair is dark brown, and my eyes are an Olive-green and skin so pale that I could give snow white a run for her money.

I gulped down a deep breath, trying my hardest to compose myself. This was something that required my full attention. There was no time for me to sit here, allowing the sadness of today consume me. I smiled softly to myself and looked at my reflection once more.

'*Happy birthday to me, happy birthday to me, happy birthday to meeee, happy birthday to me*' I whispered sliding my white converses out from under the bed and pulling them on. I was getting ready to go for a walk, a walk that was normally forbidden because I was never allowed to leave the house. I wasn't sure exactly where I was going to go. If I was honest, I didn't even know where in the world I was, other than England, but all I did know was that I was going to walk and walk, and never turn back. I chose today because I am now officially an adult. That means that technically I don't have to answer to anyone other than myself.

My life was all one big mess, I was never allowed to leave the little cottage that I lived in unless it was with my father and that was only once a year a few days before my birthday. My grandmother who was a strict woman had home schooled me, teaching me all the ways of pack life as well as other lessons that I was going to need in life; not that I ever got to put that in practice. I was made to study for hours at a time, with no breaks in between, and she would test me on subjects over and over until I got the answers to her questions correct; if I didn't, I would get hit with her slipper. My grandfather was a silent man, I could see the sympathy in his eyes whenever he looked at me, but he never said a word to defend me. Was this because he just wanted a more peaceful life? Or was this because he truly didn't care? Either way, I suffered a lonely and painful life and I was desperate for an escape. I gasped and closed my eyes as that ghostly sirens call filled my mind once more. It used to only be heard in my dreams, but lately I was hearing it everywhere. *Was there no escape from this madness?* I sighed, pulling myself together once more and slowly opened my bedroom door a crack before slipping through it.

I crept down the wooden staircase, taking care to avoid the steps that would creak when my watch let out a single beep. It was 7am, my grandparents wouldn't have been up for another half an hour, I had a 50 minutes head start before anyone would come looking and I planned to not waste any time. I stepped out into the cold October air and felt the bitter winds blow across my skin. Although I was still yet to have my first shift, luckily, I still had the werewolf's tolerance to cold temperatures. I drew in a deep ragged breath, feeling the sting on my lungs and my cheeks turn cold and smiled.

'Freedom at last' I whispered to myself, noticing as my breath clouded the air before my eyes. I glanced up at the front window of the small two-bedroom cottage; my grandparent's curtains were still closed, that means that I still had time to use the cover of the dim dawn to make my escape. I quietly hurried down the cobble stone path and carefully opened the small white gate, praying that all the rain we had had lately hadn't turned the hinges rusty; I was in luck, it opened silently. My lungs suddenly burned as I realised that I had been holding my breath and exhaled closing the gate silently as I stepped through. I stood for a moment unmoving, fear rippling through me, this was the furthest I had ever made it on my own, and I fear of someone out there in the dense woodlands watching me prickled at the back of my neck. I waited a few seconds more, then I ran.

Straight ahead from the cottage was a dirt path which led down to a field that stretched as far as the eye could see, which was always filled with beautiful wild horses. I used to admire them from my bedroom window, watching the way they would gallop around. I always believed them to be such beautiful animals. I always dreamt of owning my own horse, wished that a rich man would imprint on me and buy me stables of them. But then, the fact that all animals hated werewolves being too close to them was another reason that I knew that that dream would never be fulfilled.

Although I am a werewolf, deep down I knew that horses were my spirit animals. To me they represented freedom without restraint; basically, everything I did not have. They would travel for hours and go on for miles, going as far as they dared to go; that's exactly what I wanted to do. No, what I needed to do. Living in the middle of nowhere was going to become a challenge for me though, other than a field which backed onto a woodland, all there was, was a road. A road that was rarely ever used. Running down the road was too risky; I would almost certainly be seen. I needed to get across the other side of the field and into the woods. That wasn't a problem, but getting there quickly, was where my problems lay.

I slowly inched forward, stepping out onto the dirt path, holding my breath and listening for any unseen threats that may have been lurking around the dense woodlands surrounding me. After a few moments pause, I released my energy, pushing forward, one foot after the other, refusing to stop or even glance back. I knew that the sound of my feet hitting the dirt was enough to alert any werewolves nearby, but I prayed that if my grandparents were woken by the sound, they would be too dazed to rush out after me.

I got to the large iron gate that separated my grandparents land from the fields and leapt over it in one smooth action; surprising myself at my agility. I landed on the balls of my feet and rolled forward, before springing back up to my feet and dashing through the field. I wasn't sure how long I had been running for, but allowed myself to glance back, watching as the small cottage grew further away with every step that I took. I continued looking back, watching as it got smaller and smaller, until I couldn't see through the windows any longer. However, I knew that if anyone was to look out of one, then they would see me.

I hadn't even got halfway, and I was exhausted, my heart was racing, and I was out of breath, if I could have shifted into a wolf at that moment, I would have. But I had never shifted, I was never allowed to, every time I asked, I was always told I had to be 18 and I had to have had my first period. Normally female were-wolves don't bleed until they turn 18, but I had been having periods since I was 12, it was all so confusing for me. There were still so many questions that had been left unanswered that I had begun to wonder if maybe my family were as confused as me. I just assumed they were making everything up so that I didn't shift. Perhaps they thought that once I knew how to I would try to escape. I giggled to myself, oh the irony.

I could feel my momentum slowing and my legs had begun to throb. I wasn't used to this much physical activity. My calves hurt and my throat was dry. I slowed my pace and glanced around at the wild horses surrounding me. Although I wasn't within arm's reach of them, I was shocked that they seemed to be unphased by my presence; I remember looking out of my bedroom window one full moon as my pack family had gone out on a hunt. The moment that they were within a mile of the beautiful creatures, they bolted. And the same was said of when they were in their human form. These horses didn't seem to be bothered when I walked past or near them, which was surprising. I tried to keep my distance as I didn't want to panic them, not only did I not want to scare these beautiful creatures, I didn't need them to make enough noise to alert the en-tire pack that I was attempting to make my escape.

I slowed my pace even more as I neared the horses, holding my breath in fear of scaring them when one horse caught my eye; and apparently, I had caught hers too. She was beautiful, her mane was a silvery grey that appeared to glisten in the morning sunlight, but her coat was ice white; so pure that it almost looked as though she was coated in a thin layer of ice. *I could have sworn that I even saw her coat shimmering like diamonds every now and again when she moved.* She turned her face slightly and looked into my eyes stopping on the spot for a moment before she slowly started walking towards me. I didn't feel scared of her and was thrilled that she never seemed to fear me either. There was something special about her, something different. There was an aura about her that just seemed to make me feel that much calmer. She stopped right in front of me and gently nudged my head with her beautiful face, nuzzling into me softly, while exhaling through her nose softly. Slowly I placed my hand on her nose and started stroking her.

'You are such a pretty girl' I whispered, smiling as unshed tears stung my eyes. She knelt herself down and moved her head to the side, gesturing for me to climb up on her back. But I was scared. *What if I was getting this all wrong and she threw me off?* I would have a broken back and be stuck back where I started, and not to mention a majorly pissed off father. I thought about it for a second and decided the latter would be a lot worse to deal with 'Okay, here its goes' I said in an unsure tone. I stepped forward and hesitantly reached out for the horse when the siren's call rang through my mind once more. I gasped and stepped back, closing my eyes and pressing the palms of both hands to the sides of my head. *What the fuck was happening to me?* I opened my eyes and stared into the beautiful mares' hypnotic eyes, and a sudden calmness washed over me. I stepped forward once more and gently ran my hand down her neck. She shook her head and neighed in delight.

I slowly climbed up onto her and felt as she waited for me to be seated properly before lifting herself back up and shifted slightly under my weight. We both stood motionless for a second and then she was off, galloping towards the woods.

'So, you are a clever girl too?' I asked grinning, I knew this horse could understand me; I didn't know how I knew; I just did. I put my arms around her neck and allowed myself to slip into my day-dream. I thought about keeping this horse and owning my own little cottage away from everyone, free from the prison that my family had made for me. Free from the laws of the pack. We could go on long rides and camp out under the stars in the middle of nowhere, and then I could just enjoy mother nature and all her beautiful creations. My Pretty Girl by my side through it all.

The horse; or Pretty Girl as I had decided to name her, picked up speed as soon as we were closing in on the woods. I held my breath as the shadow made by the canopy of the trees engulfed me, the scent of the damp musky wood filling my nostrils. I looked at my watch, it was now 7:33am. My grandparents would have just woken up as they did every morning for as long as I could remember. They wouldn't notice I was gone for another 12 minutes, 7:45 was always when my grandfather would get me out of bed to shower and eat before I would either do schoolwork or chores. I was just so glad I was away from the life of being a prisoner. I closed my eyes and tightened my grip slightly around Pretty Girls neck, feeling the soothing warmth of her body radiate through me, as the rhythmic thudding of her hooves resounded around the wood like a lullaby.

It had felt like we had been riding for ages, but Pretty Girl seemed to be determined to keep going; and it seemed that she knew the direction she wanted to take me, like she had done this run many times before. I didn't care where we ended up, just as long as it wasn't back home. I didn't care where we went, what direction, or how far. I looked at my watch it was now 8:59am. How had I been riding on her back for nearly an hour and a half? Where had the time gone? I leant back slightly and looked around at our surroundings. I had no clue as to where we were, and all directions appeared to look the same. I glanced down at my horse and gently stroked my hand down her mane.

'Do you need a bit of a rest pretty girl?' I asked, as she slowed down slightly. She snorted and looked around, but still trotted forward slowly. Her muscles tensed under my palm and I knew instantly that she was becoming anxious.

'What is it girl?' I asked softly; stroking her mane, as fear slowly began crawling up my spine. We both froze; behind us a twig snapped and instead of assuming it was another wild animal, like any normal person would do, I had become a paranoid wreck. *Fuck! they have found me!* I panicked, thinking my grandfather had raised the alarm. I turned my head towards the direction of the snapping twigs just as a light brown wolf slowly made its way from the shadows and slowly began walking towards us, snarling. The sirens called rang out in my head once more, this time I didn't stop to give it a moment's thought.

'Run' I cried, gently jabbing Pretty Girl's sides with my heels. The horse started running as fast as she could; which was hell of a lot faster than I thought possible. I was struggling hold on to her, but I wasn't ready to die. I didn't need to look behind us to know whether the wolf was giving chase or not.
I could hear it panting and snarling behind us. I knew horses could run for miles, but she hadn't even had any water and I knew she was thirsty and that she needed a rest. We were not going to outrun it, but she ran as fast as she possibly could refusing to give up.

'Today isn't the day we die' I called to her, hoping that my words would ease her panic. She turned her head slightly and picked up even more speed. But the wolf did also. I could see it closing in on us from the corner of my eye. Moving at speeds that would go unnoticed to any mere mortal. I turned my head to face it just as it leapt towards Pretty Girls flanks with its jaws wide open, saliva dripping from its razor-sharp teeth. I closed my eyes and allowed instinct to take over, kicking my right leg out, and catching it in the throat before he had a chance to reach my horse.

The wolf let out a frustrated snarl, catching itself before it hit the ground and taking off after us once more. I shook my head looking at Pretty Girl once more; it wasn't fair to put this innocent animal in danger, I needed to get off without having her stop. I looked up straight ahead and noticed a tree which had started tilting, thick branches still securely attached sloped over to the left, the side we were heading for. I slowly loosened my grip on the horse and raised my hands above my head, just as the branch passed over us. The forced my palms hit the rough bark caused me to cry out as it bit into my flesh, but I closed my fingers around the branch and felt as I was yanked from Pretty girl. I noticed her hesitate slightly as I came off her and shouted to her;

'Keep going! Don't stop!' She had already got me further than I could have got myself. I knew the wolf that was behind me was a werewolf, I hoped it would shift into human form and leave the horse alone. I tightened my grip on the tree's thick branch and swung my legs forward pushing my feet onto the tree's trunk, hoping to be able to pull myself up higher into the tree.

I could hear her galloping getting quieter as the top of the horse's head disappeared through the line of the trees. I didn't need to look down to know that the wolf wasn't following her, I could hear it snarling and jumping up at the tree, snapping its jaws in attempt to reach me. I pulled myself up onto another branch until I reached one that could take my weight. I looked down. I didn't recognise this wolf, and its scent didn't seem to be from one of ours back at the mansion.

'Shift and I will talk' I screamed; my whole body was shaking. I had never been this scared in my whole life. The wolf was banging into the tree repeatedly trying with all his strength to knock me down. I was losing balance and could feel myself slipping. 'Please, stop' I begged trying so hard to hold on. I glanced down to my right to see if the tree had a hollow hole that I could put my foot into, but it was too late. The branch I was on snapped, causing me to drop down onto the ground below. The second my feet hit the ground my ankle gave out a sickening crack, and red-hot pain radiated through my ankle, causing me to feel sick. This was it. My life was over.

I turned back to look at the light brown wolf, who was now slowly inching closer to me, it had a look on its face that said it was enjoying causing me fear. Tears stung my eyes, but I refused to show this beast that it was scaring me. If I was going to die, then I was going to die with dignity. I turned my face to stare deep into the wolf's black eyes, clenching my teeth in anger. I drew in a deep breath, attempting to stand when out of the corner of my eye, a black wolf pounced, leaping over my head and hitting the light brown wolf with a thud. I let out a small gasp and scurried backwards, watching as the two started fighting. The ghostly lullaby rang out around me, this was the first time that it had been more than just a calling, it was the lullaby from my dreams. *But what did this all mean?*

I'm dead I thought, trying not to cry. I just wanted to get away and now two wolves are fighting over who will kill me first. I struggled to my feet and attempted to put weight on my ankle, but it was no use, the pain caused me to cry out. At my cries, the black wolf glanced over to me, a strange look in its eyes. But apparently that was the opportunity that the other needed. It leapt forward and clamped its jaws down around the black wolfs neck, throwing it over its shoulder like it was nothing more than twig. I scurried backwards, dragging my injured foot, reaching out for anything to hold on to. Just as the wolf pounced, the sound of galloping hooves filled my ears and a flash of brilliant white blurred across my vision. Pretty Girl!

'Oh my gosh' I squealed my eyes widening as tears fell from them freely. 'You came back?' I watched as the horse reared up on its hind legs, before spinning around and kicking the brown wolf in the face. The sound of cracking bones sang out around the stillness of the forest, as the wolf fell backwards, skidding across the dirt. I watched in awe for a moment, holding my breath and praying that it wasn't getting up again. And it didn't. At that moment all the tension that I had been holding left my body, causing me to topple over, I felt I had been saved by an angel and I could breathe a sigh of relief. Pretty Girl moved with speeds that didn't seem possible for a wild horse, catching me. In one swift movement, she flipped me up, causing me to land on her back softly.

Pretty took off once again, galloping through the wilderness, taking me further away from the danger that I had been in. And just for a moment, I found myself imagining what it would be like to be happy, me and my wild horse on our own, roaming around the English wilderness, away from the all the secrets that plagued me my entire life. But my joy was shortly outlived. I could hear the thumps of someone or something running behind us, the panting seemed to be getting closer.

'Oh no, no, no, no.' I cried turning my head to look behind us. It wasn't the brown wolf though; this time it was the black one. Why could I not just run away in peace? Why was everyone so hell-bent on getting in my way? He was faster than the last wolf, but Pretty girl wasn't about to give in to him. I didn't think she could run any faster, but she did. I noticed this wolf wasn't growling, or snarling like the other, this one was just chasing us.

I turned my head to look at him once again, he was the deepest of blacks and one of the biggest werewolves I had ever seen.

'Shift' I shouted but he wouldn't. I didn't know what to do, I had never been in a situation like this before, I knew he would chase us until the horse got tired. And I wasn't sure how much further Pretty Girl would be able to go.

'Pretty girl, slow down' I called softly, as I leant my head down towards her neck, but she didn't hear me, she just carried on running, she wasn't going to slow down anytime soon. I pushed myself back up, sitting up a little straighter when a sharp pain throbbed across my forehead causing me to be wrenched from the horses back once again. I landed on my back, smacking my head as I dropped onto the hard dirt. I screamed in pain and could feel the warmth of blood as it started running down my face. This is it, I thought staring up at the grey sky, this was the end, this was how I was going to die.

I silently started to weep, stifling back sobs, maybe everyone was right, I should have never left the house. Everyone had wished that it was me that had died instead of my mother, and now it looked as though they were finally getting their wish.

I watched in fear as the black wolf towered over me, the edges of my vision darkening.

'Please no' I whimpered, starting to feel dizzy. I was waiting for his big jaws to clamp down on my throat, but he just leant his face forward, inching it closer to mine. I looked up at him and stared into the beautiful golden-brown eyes I had ever seen; on man or beast, and they were warm, not menacing at all. He nudged me in the face lightly, sniffing at the blood as it dripped down onto the dirt. I tried to open my mouth to speak, but I couldn't keep my eyes open any longer. I gave in to the darkness. And then everything went black.

2

Amelia;

Come, my children, homeward bound
When all is lost, then all will be found.

I opened my eyes with a start, my heart pounding in my chest. _Those words… again. What did they mean?_ I strained my eyes, trying to adjust to the bright lights around me. I was in a bed, but it wasn't my bed, the air smelt different. My room didn't usually smell of anything, this room smelt of spiced pumpkins. I knew the smell well; my father would always give a spiced pumpkin candle to my grandmother every time he visited us at the cottage. My eyes widened and my heart skipped a beat, I was back at the cottage. _No, no, no. This couldn't be happening!_ I tried lifting my head to look around, but it was agonising; the room felt as though it was spinning. My stomach tightened as a sudden wave of nausea washed over me.

'Hey, hey, hey' a female voiced hushed. 'Try to get up slowly, you have had a nasty fall.' It wasn't my grandmother, but it was a voice I recognised.

'M-Marie?' I croaked.

'Hello darling girl' she whispered, smiling as she leaned over the bed and gently ran the back of her finger over my cheek. I waited for a moment as my blurry eyes focused on her face, her blue eyes sparkling under the bright lights, and the soft wrinkles that framed them. I blinked rapidly, fighting through the dull ache in my head and allowed my eyes to travel over to sandy blonde hair which was now beginning to grey and smiled up to her weakly.

Marie was the Alpha's mother and the packs recently retired Luna. She would sometimes join my dad and her husband; Tristan on their annual visits to the cottage. She was always kind to me and would show interest in what I was doing whether that would be me playing with my toys, doing chores or studying; she was the only woman that had been in my life that showed me a mothers love; although she had aged slightly, that warm smile remained the same, full of love as always.

'My dad?' I asked trying to lift my head, this time a bit slower.

'Can wait poppet.' She smiled putting one of her arms under my back and gently lifting me as to sit me up.

'Where am I?' I asked looking around the room, I wasn't back at the cottage. This was a bedroom, it's walls were painted a dark green, gold wall lamps lighting it up. The floor was wooden with gloss painted over it a large green rug lead from the door to the bed.

'You are at the pack mansion.' Marie said pulling the green duvet off my legs. I started crying, I didn't want to be here as much as I didn't want to be at the cottage, I wanted to be away from everyone, I was supposed to run away and be free, start a new life up somewhere away from everyone and now I was in the pack mansion, my father probably making plans for me to go back to the cottage.

'Shhhh, it's okay, you aren't going back to the cottage, this is your home now sweety.' I put my head down and started to un-controllably weep.

'I don't want to be here either.' I said in between sobs.

'Amelia, I can promise you this. You will not have the same life that you had with your grandparents. You are part of our pack and you will be treated as such. I can't promise complete freedom as there are always rules to follow, but that will come in time.' Marie soothed, as she carefully helped me to my feet. I put as little pressure on my ankle as possible as I could still feel the throb, but luckily my werewolf genes had already started the speedy healing process.

'I don't understand. Why now? Isn't it a bit convenient that I try to run away and then I am suddenly moved into the pack mansion?' I snapped. I closed my eyes, instantly regretting the way that I was talking to her; but it was as though, I had no filter stopping the words from coming out. I sighed softly and shook my head, trying my hardest to fight back the tears that were threatening to spill before continuing. 'I thought that I was free. I thought that I was going to escape the prison that was my life.' I whispered, my voice wobbling with the raw emotion clogging my throat.

'Sweetheart, there is more to this than any of us know or understand. I wish I could give you the answers that you need. But I am certain that they will come in time.' Marie answered, not seeming to be bothered by my sudden outburst.

Marie started walking me over to a white door and grinned proudly, gesturing to the room around her.

'This is your bedroom. Arlo allowed me to choose it for you, not that he had much say in the matter anyway; so, I chose one with an en-suit. Every lady deserves her own bathroom.' She continued with a beaming smile. She paused for a moment before opening the door we had come to stop at; my bathroom was bigger than my room back at the cottage. There was a toilet, sink, bath and a shower, with still so much room to walk around. It was lovely admittedly, but nothing was going to change my mind. *I was breaking out again, whether anyone liked it or not.*

I watched as Marie closed the door once more and slowly led me over to the large bay window that looked out over the grounds of the mansion. There were acres and acres of land surrounding us and a little kids park in the front garden; it reminded me of a community town as everyone either lived in the mansion or houses and bungalows around it. I glanced over to the other side of the meadows and could just about make out the cemetery at the back, small carved wooden totems representing each pack member that had passed. Just visible through the line of the trees; I assumed it would be for fallen pack members, I wondered if my mother's totem was there, but was too wary about asking anyone, *I had always been shut down as soon as I mentioned her name, so why would that have changed now?* I realised that I had been quiet for a few moments too long and pulled myself from my mental rant. I forced a smile and sighed softly.

'So, what are these rules that I need to follow?' I asked, hoping that Marie couldn't see through my small talk. The more that I learnt about the life of the pack, the easier it would be for me to make my second escape; I just needed all the details. The more I followed the rules, the less noticed I would be. That would make for an easier escape! Marie clucked her tongue and shook her head.

'My sweet girl, there is plenty of time for all that. For now, let's get you down to the kitchen for something to eat. I bet you are famished.' She replied, placing her hand gently on my back and guiding me from the room.

We stepped out into the long hall and I looked across at the red and gold décor that framed the walls. I never imagined the inside of this building reminding me of some fancy hotel, but what else did I expect? Marie slowly walked forward, making sure that I was able to keep up; even with my limping. We continued down the hall and I glanced backwards.

'Why are there only two rooms on this floor?' I asked, curiosity getting the better of me. Marie chuckled and shook her head again.

'I guess that, that is just the way that this building was designed.'

'Oh, right. I just assumed that there would be more of us, I guess. I always assumed this place just looked like a giant fancy hotel on the inside' I responded. I glanced over my shoulder once more and took in the two doors that stood together when we stopped once more. I turned my attention back to what was in front of me and couldn't stop the awe-struck gasp that escaped my lips. We had paused at the top of the grand staircase that curved around to the left which led down into a large main hall. The giant, crystal chandelier sparkled like diamonds above our heads, casting prisms of light across the grey marble floor. *Yep! Definitely a fancy hotel on the inside!* I turned back to look at Marie who was smiling kindly to me as she held her arm out for me to hold on to. No one had ever been this caring over me, as nice as it was, I was still finding it a little strange. Kind of like this is all some elaborate trick and this is just the build-up.

Slowly we descended the stairs, taking them one step at a time making sure as not to put too much pressure on my still swollen, black ankle. I could hear the faint whispers from the other werewolves that were dotted around the main hall. I didn't know these people, and they didn't know me, but that didn't stop them from judging me anyway. We finally made it to the last step and Marie continued leading me away from the others.

'Darling, pay no mind to the others. It has been a while since we have had someone new come into the mansion. I am sure they just don't know how to react to your presence. Things will even out in no time. You'll see.' She whispered comfortingly, reaching down and taking my hand in hers. I bit the inside of my lip and nodded, not sure whether I could trust my voice to come out sounding strong and confident. As much as I wished that this could be my new home with my new family, I still knew that I didn't belong here. I wasn't one of these people. And, I never would be! The sting of unshed tears burned my eyes and I turned my face away from Marie and looked out one of the floor-length windows that covered the entire wall. To my surprise, it led to a room that held a huge swimming pool, covered over with a greenhouse-like dome allowing the sunlight to pour in from above. I focused on the way that light glistened across the crystal-like surface of the water and found that it had already started to soothe me.

'This room here is the games room. It's a place that all the youngsters such as yourself likes to hang out. Maybe you could stop by in there later and meet some of the others that are your age?' Marie asked softly. I forced a smile and nodded not wanting to come across rude, but it was all so much for me to take in.

We stopped at a pair of large wooden doors with long thin windows and I peered inside. We had made it to the kitchen. I hadn't realised up until now how hungry I actually was. I hobbled forward and peered in through the glass and took in the sight of the black marble work surface and the white tiled floor. This kitchen was huge. There were a few other members of the pack dotted around the large room, all wearing white and black; the girls wore white blouses with black skirts, and the guys wore white long-sleeved shirts with black trousers, their look finished with a small red apron tied around their waist.

'They are the servers.' Marie said, answering my unasked question. I turned my attention back to her with a look of confusion crossing over my face. She smiled down to me and looked back at the workers. 'Some members of the pack work here. It's their way of earning some money while they are here. This is their way of making a living so that one day when they leave, they have a little bit of money to help them out while they make a new life for themselves. I nodded and turned back to look at the servers and was shocked to see a girl hurrying over to us.

I took in her beautiful auburn hair, all pulled up into a bun on the top of her head. Her pale skin was dusted with freckles across the bridge of her nose and under her light brown eyes, and she had a smile on her face that would make even the most miserable person smile. Before I had a chance to prepare myself, she pulled the door open and smiled out to us.

'Oh, my goodness, I heard that we had someone knew in, I just thought that it was rumours! Hi. I am Piper. What's your name?' She asked, still smiling down to me. I opened my mouth to reply but no words came out. Piper stepped backwards and gestured for us to walk towards the kitchen. 'So, how are you finding it here at the mansion? I bet this is a lot to take in, right? I guess we are all just used to this life, it's all we have ever known.' She continued. I turned my stare to Marie who just smiled back at me.
'Piper, we have come to collect the order that I placed.' Marie said softly. Piper froze, turned her smile to me and then nodded, disappearing out the back and hurrying back to us with a large cupcake cradled between her hands.

'Here you go. I made sure that they had everything prepared for when you needed it.' Piper rambled. I nodded and forced another smile and stepped back. Was this cupcake for me? No one had ever really given me cake *on* my birthday. 'Well, if you need anything else you know where to find me.' Piper said one last time before disappearing back out into the kitchen. Marie chuckled lightly to herself before turning and guiding me out of a side door that led us out into the courtyard.

Marie and I stepped out into the grounds and I turned back to look at the building. The Pack Mansion was just as I imagined it, a tall elegant grey stoned building with colour stained windows that glistened in the dusky twilight. If I hadn't felt like I was being held prisoner against my will, then this building would have been a dream house. She led me over to a wooden bench off to the side and handed the cupcake to me.

'I hope you like it. It's a salted caramel fudge brownie cupcake. I just figured that you should have something to mark it being your special day.' She whispered, planting a soft kiss on the top of my head. *Is this what it felt like to be loved by a mother?* I thought to myself. I could no longer contain the tears that had been threatening to spill. Marie pulled me into her arms, and we sat there for longer than I cared to remember. We sat and spoke about the way that life was going to be here in the pack, she explained the things that would be expected of me, and that I was still yet to meet my alpha.

Seconds turned to minutes, then minutes into hours, and before I knew it, we were seated beneath a velvety black sky littered with twinkling stars. Marie helped me back to my room and said that she was having some food sent up to me so I could just focus on resting for this evening. We said our goodnights and then went our separate ways. I watched as she slowly disappeared down the hall before closing my bedroom door and collapsing against it. This was going to be a whole new experience for me, but I still didn't want this life. I needed to plan. So that was exactly what I was going to do.

I had been there for two days and I still hadn't seen my father or my brothers, nor had I seen the new Alpha; Arlo. Charlie was his Beta, Arlo's right-hand man. They had been best friends since they were toddlers, so it wasn't surprising Arlo had chosen him. Marie turned back to me and smiled sweetly.

'Let's get you back up to your room. Get bathed, get in a pair of the new pyjamas that I sent for and you can recuperate for a couple of days.' I nodded, this was all so much to take in, and I think I needed a few days to get my head around everything.

I spent all day and night in my room, I didn't know anyone else other than Marie and didn't really want to integrate with anyone else; I was more interested in making sure I was healed enough to make my next escape. I was too shy and not used to being in social situations; and If I am honest, I was terrified of seeing my dad. I knew he was going to go batshit crazy at me for trying to run away and I had a sneaky suspicion that Marie had been the one keeping everyone away from me to give me some peace. But this day was to be different, I was told by Marie; who had come to visit me with a hanger of clothes concealed under grey wrappings, that Arlo had requested that I came down for dinner and that I had to meet my pack, this time I could not argue. I had to obey my Alpha; that was rule number one; but not for long. I had plans to run away again. This time I was going to wait until I had shifted for the first time, I had more of a fighting chance then. Plus, I suppose that I should have learnt everything there is to know about our kind before I go on the run. *Not understanding the changes that I would be going through would be awful!* I would get what I could from these people and then I will be gone!

Marie had chosen for me to wear a red tight-fitting dress which had sleeves that went down to my elbows, the dress went just above my knees. I think my father would have a fit if he saw me in anything shorter. I had a wardrobe full of brand-new clothes still with tags on them. They were expensive and fashionable, but all I owned were joggers and T-shirts. I thought that Marie had given me someone else's room at first. However, she was very proud to tell me they were all mine; she had bought them all, as well as all the shoes, stocked my bathroom with the most luxurious toiletries I had ever seen; which smelt divine by the way, and filled the vanity unit with makeup. I guess she was trying to do anything to make

SAM KETTLE & NATASHA SLEE

me stay. I followed Marie down the large purple carpeted staircase into the main hallway. I watched as she walked with confidence, her long sapphire blue dress shimmered against the light from the chandelier. She was a beautiful and elegant woman, the once upon a time young bride of an Alpha 14 years her senior.

She led me into a hall, which was massive; much bigger than any of the others that I had seen so far, just like beauty and the beasts dancing room only this was full of tables and chairs. A long white marbled table was placed in the middle of the room, it had 22 marbled chairs neatly tucked in, one at each end and 10 on each side. The other tables were not as long but still seated around 16 people each. I knew I was part of a big pack, but I didn't realise how big. It was the first time I had seen anyone other than Marie for the past two days. Everyone stared at me as I followed her to the biggest table, whispers filling the large room and following me like a wild-fire, I put my head down and stared at my feet.

'Enough!' a man roared, slamming his fist down onto a table causing me to flinch. Arlo Blakeley, the Alpha was standing by the front entrance with his father Tristan; my father, a young man I had never seen before and my brothers. He was extremely tall; around 6 foot with black curly shoulder length hair, his eyes were a light yellowy brown; I knew I had seen those eyes somewhere before. 'As you all know, Amelia Hunt has now officially joined our pack, she is your Beta's sister, so I expect you all to be respectful and kind.' he said in a clear, authoritative tone. Charlie turned his face away from the pack, looking more than a little embarrassed at being associated with me and that Arlo had announced that I was his sister; he looked at me like he wanted me to just disappear. It was clear to me in that moment that nothing had changed, I was still loathed. He had never joined my dad on his visits to me, Eddie would always come along though and we both get into trouble continuously, but not Charlie. He let me know that I was nothing to him, and that was just the way that it was always going to be. Eddie was a natural funny person but he was also a menace, I remember once he had placed a whoopie cushion under my grandmothers favourite cushion, it made a terrible noise and she went as red as a beetroot, telling my father he needed to *"control that boy"*.

Arlo sat at the top end of the table, his father was next to him one side and Charlie on the other. Next to Tristan was Marie, then my father and then me. Next to Charlie was Eddie and next to him was another of Arlo's friends whose name I had yet to learn. Other important pack members filled the rest of the table. It was so daunting being sat around all these people who either didn't know me, but knew of me, or they simply despised me. For once me and Charlie agreed on something, because at that time I just wanted to disappear.

Everyone sat chatting amongst themselves while I stared down at my hands refusing to make eye contact with any of the others. Although, every now and again I would feel the burning hot stare of Arlo boring into me. I was too nervous to look up. The main doors to the hall flew open and the most amazing smell filled my nose, causing my stomach to growl.

We were served a beautiful hog roast, with all the trimmings, crackling, steamed veg, roast potatoes, parsnips, fennel infused gravy and to finish off there was the largest selection of fresh fruit, cakes and other pastries for dessert. It was the best meal I had ever eaten in my life. I ate with my head down the entire time, not talking to anyone or risking eye contact with my brother's.

Sitting next to my father was horrible, I felt his eyes on me every now and then, his angry, disappointed eyes tearing into me like lasers. I knew after the meal I was in for it; Marie may have managed to keep him away from me while I was hidden away, but now there was no hiding. This man was determined to keep me locked away for the rest of my life, I was sure of it.

'Excuse me Miss Hunt, would you like a glass of wine?' A gentle female voice said. I looked up, the red-haired girl with a soft freckly face was holding a tray full of glasses of wine, red, white and Rose' I had never had alcohol before, and I knew my father and Charlie would certainly not approve.

'Piper, right?' I asked with a soft smile. The girl nodded,

looking happy that I remembered her. I turned my attention back to the glasses on the tray and nodded. 'Yes, that would be lovely, thank you. Could I have some of that one please?' I asked pointing to the Rose', she placed the glass of wine in my hand and smiled.

'That isn't a very wise thing to do Amelia' my father hissed leaning towards my ear so no one else would hear.

'Nothing I ever do is very *wise* according to you father.' I replied, rolling my eyes, before taking a large sip of the pink liquid in my cup. I looked up at him and fluttered my eyelashes, he was extremely pissed off, and I was loving it.

'We will talk after this meal'. He growled through clenched teeth. I rolled my eyes and took another sip of my drink this time a bigger mouthful, Eddie was grinning at me. He clearly found me annoying our father funny. Charlie on the other hand, looked furious with me, he slowly shook his head at me and then glanced up at the father and widened his eyes as in, *'well are you not going to stop her?'* I'm not entirely sure why me having a glass of wine seemed to be such an issue, I was well within my rights to drink. *'What?'* I mouthed at him before taking another mouthful of wine. His face went bright red, steam may as well have been coming out of his ears. This time I looked at Arlo, he was smirking at me, clearly very amused at our family disagreement, his sipped his red wine as he looked at me, unblinking. My eyes met his. I knew those eyes. Why did I know those eyes? I sat for a minute. Why did I know those eyes? I allowed myself to get lost in thought for a moment; not understanding how I could recognise someone when I had never been here before, when it suddenly hit me!

The eyes! I *had* seen them before! He was the black wolf in the woods. My stomach did somersaults, and I thought I was going to throw up. My Alpha was the one who saved me?

Could my life get any worse?

3

Amelia;

I picked through the food and tried my hardest to eat, but sitting in the room like this, knowing that everyone was whispering about me in some way had me a little on edge. I never realised how intense and close nit pack life was going to be. I shook my head and noticed one face at the table that wasn't staring, glaring or whispering about me; Marie. I offered a gentle smile in return, before dropping my stare back down to my lap, where my hands were folded. *How long did I have to sit through this torture?* It might have been different if I had a friend here. But the only friend that I have ever had in the world was my Pretty Girl.

I turned my gaze to Arlo and stared at him, watching as he tried not to look bored at the conversations that were going on around him. There was a look upon his face that made him seem so much older than what he was. A look that said he had the weight of the world resting on his shoulders, and at any minute he may succumb to the pressure. I took in his curly shoulder length black hair, and the way it moved as he shook his head, clearly getting into a bit of a debate with Charlie.

The sound of a shrill and over enthusiastic laughter cut through the chatter, drawing his attention to her side of the table. A look crossed his face that was hard for me to place. It looked like a mixture of curiosity and desire, with a hint of something else. I turned my stare from Arlo to the girl and watched the embarrassing scene playing out before me.

I took in the sight of her perfectly straight, platinum blonde hair that seemed to hang all the way down her back, and the way that her blue eyes shimmered whenever she thought that Arlo was actually looking at her. The way that her cheeks flushed crimson as she was fluttering her sea blue eyes and flipping her long hair over her shoulder. I know that I had no social skills so to speak, but even I could pick up on her desperate attempts to flirt with our Alpha. I rolled my eyes and turned my stare back to the glass in front of me. I didn't know very much about the pack lore; being kept in the dark all your life has that effect on people, but even I knew that the Alpha had to be extremely careful when it came down to choosing his Luna. And if she was the type of girl that was destined to rule our pack alongside him, then things in this mansion were going to take a drastic turn for the worst.

I turned my attention back to the girl and her friends; who were all whispering something to her, causing her to giggle loudly once more. It was obvious why she had picked these two girls as her sidekicks. They were pretty, but they paled in comparison to her. Their brown and black hair seemingly making them blend into the background. I sat and watched the three girls; or the 'bitches of Wolf wick' as I had now decided to call them, and quickly downed the rest of my rose'. This time I didn't even need to look up. Piper reappeared, seemingly from thin air and placed a fresh glass in front of me. I no longer bothered checking for my dad and Charlie's reaction. I don't know if it was the wine or not, but I honestly didn't care right now.

There seemed to be a break in the eating, as people left the table for a bit, going off in little groups, talking amongst themselves. To my surprise, Piper dropped down into the empty seat beside me and smiled.

'So, how are you finding it here at the mansion?' She asked, placing her circular golden tray on her lap. I sucked in a deep breath and blew out dramatically.

'Well, is pack life always like a prison?' I muttered, causing Piper to bark out a laugh that was in competition with Lori. She clasped her hand over her mouth and cleared her throat.

'Sorry. It's just strange to hear someone talk so bluntly about the pack. Usually all we ever hear is how this is the place to be. And how people would literally kill to get in here.' Piper replied, tucking a lose strand of her red hair behind her ear. I bit my lip and closed my eyes. I was supposed to be trying to make a good impression on my first time with the pack, and here I was, insulting the one person that is being nice to me. I cleared my throat nervously and turned my stare to Piper once more.

'So, do you live in the mansion too?' I asked, hoping my swift change of subject was enough to get out of the awkward situation that I have just put myself in. It was Piper's turn to look uncomfortable.

'Um, actually no. This is reserved for the highest members of the packs. I live out in one of the little houses with my mum. Just out there.' She whispered, pointing out through the large windows that led out to the little village that was within the mansion grounds.

'What do you think you are doing?' Came a sharp voice from behind us. I turned to see what was happening, and locked eyes with the blonde girl across the room, glaring daggers at us. I looked back to the person that was stood over us with her arms folded behind her back. Piper jumped to her feet and looked as though she was about to cry.

'A-Adela... I... I'

'What makes you think that you can sit down while you're working. Let alone sit at the table with the higher members of the pack? Do not make Lori have to report this!' Adela snapped, flipping her lightly curled black hair.

'N-No. There's no need for that. I-I'm sorry.' Piper stammered, her eyes widening in fear as she glanced around the room, obviously looking for Arlo.

'Who do you think you are speaking to someone that way?' I snapped, rising from my seat and glaring at the black-haired girl standing before me. Her eyes blazed with anger and her jaw flexed.

'You may be new, but that is no excuse to talk to your superiors this way.' She snarled, stepping so close to me that I could feel her breath on my cheek. I widened my eyes and stepped back. Adela smirked and looked me up and down. 'At least you know to back down in the presence of the higher ranks.'

'Oh, no. Please don't think that I was cowering to you. It was just the strength of your dog breath that nearly knocked me over.' I retorted, my tone sounding bored. Adela's eyes blazed once more, and she turned her stare to the blonde girl; Lori; who was watching our show.

'Why you little-'

'Ok everyone. Please take your seats once more. The kitchen has just informed us that the dessert trolly is on its way up.' Arlo called, gesturing for the rest of us to do as he commanded. The whole time that our alpha was talking, I never broke my stare from the bitchy girl standing before me. Her eye twitched with anger as she flicked her hair over her shoulder and in my face before she stormed away.

'Are you ok?' I asked, turning back to face Piper once more. She stood motionless in front of me, her eyes and mouth open wide. She nodded quickly before scurrying away back out into the direction of the kitchen. I dropped back down into my seat and took a huge sip of my wine. The sound of the main doors opening drew my attention across the room. The servers all came in with trollies full of cakes, pastries and every other type of dessert you could think of. I always have had a bit of a sweet tooth, so now I finally had something to focus my attention on. On the plus side, werewolves apparently had a higher metabolism than most others, so we didn't have to worry about putting on weight. The moment the servers had left the room once more, I watched as the others rose from their seats and hurried over to the trollies, filling their plates with more food than what seemed necessary. Shaking my head, I rose from my chair and made my way to the trolly furthest away from anyone. Seeing all these desserts at a distance was incredible but seeing them up close was in a whole other league entirely. The kitchen staff should have been proud of themselves; these desserts could have put even the most famous chefs to shame. I completely lost all focus of everything else around me and allowed myself to be lost in my own sweet heaven.

Until. I was rudely snapped from my happy place as someone barged past me, almost knocking me to the floor. I whirled on the spot and came face to face with intense sea blue eyes surrounded by a head of platinum blonde hair. I rolled my eyes and turned to face her fully.

'Watch where you are going next time! It would have been such a shame for you to make a fool of yourself in front of your entire pack now, wouldn't it?' Lori asked sarcastically with a smirk. I felt the anger bubbling up inside my chest and closed my eyes. As much as I hated to admit it, she was right. If I lost my cool now then that would be me making a fool of myself, and my family in front of everyone. So, I did the next best thing. I smiled.

'I am so sorry Lori. I really must pay more attention to my surroundings.' I paused and leaned in a little closer. 'I know that it must be hard for you, walking, breathing and looking where you are going all at the same time. Blondes struggle with even the simplest of tasks.' I continued smugly. I stepped back and leant across her, scooping a large slice of hot chocolate fudge cake onto the cake slice and slipping it on to my plate. As I began to turn away from her, Lori flicked her arm out at a speed that was even hard for me to see coming. She clipped the edge of my plate, causing it to drop from my hands and clatter to the floor loudly before smashing. The entire room fell into silence and all eyes turned towards me.

'I think someone has had a few too many wines with dinner.' Lori called loudly, looking around the room and giggling as if we were friends. She turned her smiling face back to look at me and her smile fell for a moment, a look of pure hatred crossing her face, before she put the smile back on.

I dropped to the ground and began gathering up the broken pieces of plate, before searching for something to clear up the mess of cakes that were now smeared all over the floor. The sound of footsteps rushing towards me had me holding my breath, the image of my father flashing through my mind rushing at me in anger causing me to feel sick.

'Here. Let me do that.' Piper said, dropping down to her knees and sweeping up the mess into a dustpan. 'I am so sorry Amelia. This is all my fault.' Piper whispered without looking up.

'What are you talking about? This isn't your fault; you have nothing to apologise for. Some people just need to be put in their place.' I growled quietly, glancing over my shoulder and locking eyes with Lori once more. The smirk that crossed her face filled me with so much rage that it took everything inside me to not run over to her and knock it off her face.

'If I hadn't of sat down to talk to you none of this would have happened. I am sorry, I should have known my place!' Piper continued, still refusing to meet my eye. I reached out and placed my hand over hers, causing her to flinch.

'Piper, please don't think that you have to feel that way around me. I am not like these people.' I said softly. I may have not had much experience with people, but even I knew that there was a right and wrong way to treat people. And the way that this girl was treated was despicable. Piper smiled over to me and I could see the unshed tears shimmering in her eyes when she dipped her head back down to the floor and continued sweeping.

'Hey, you better go back to your seat. Please, I really don't want to make anything worse for you.' She mumbled, keeping her eyes down. I rose to my feet and turned back to face the pack, noting that most people were still staring in our direction. I suddenly had no interest in eating. I hurried back over to my seat, swiping a bottle of rose from the counter as I did. I dropped back down to my seat and poured myself another glass.

I sat in silence, refusing to meet anyone's eyes for the rest of the meal, and trying my hardest to ignore the whispers that were still about me flowing around the room. Arlo announced that dinner was over and without a moment's hesitation I pushed up from the table and downed my fifth glass of rose; I have never been drunk before but I definitely felt a little woozy. I shook my head in attempt to clear my slightly blurred vision and made my way towards the main doors; I suddenly felt extremely hot and needed the comfort of my own room. I placed my hand against the wall and slowly made my way forward. The sound of the chattering around me grew louder until it almost reached a level of intolerable. I closed my eyes and continued stumbling forward, covering my ears with my hands as I went.

I felt my foot scrape along the floor and knew too late that I was going to fall; and there was nothing that I could do about it. I fell into something hard, followed by the sound of sloshing and a frustrated growl. Before I hit the ground, I felt a strong pair of hands wrap around me, holding me in place. I opened my eyes and stared up into the golden-brown eyes sparkling down at me. Arlo.

'I-I...' I stammered, scrabbling in my mind to find the right words to say, but my mind had turned to mush. Arlo pulled me back up onto my feet and for a moment I was lost in his gaze. The angry sound of a girl behind him brought my attention back to the room.

'What the fuck!' Lori exclaimed, clenching her teeth and balling her hands into fists. I looked from the angry girl to a smirking Arlo; who was obviously trying his hardest to not smile, I bit the inside of my mouth to keep myself from laughing. 'What the hell is wrong with you, you stupid bitch!' She growled again. I turned my attention back to Lori and fought to find the words when Arlo interrupted.

'I am sure that Amelia is very sorry. It was clearly an accident.'

'No! She...'

'Lori, I think that Amelia can be forgiven. This is her first time with the entire pack, and I am sure that she was more than a little intimidated about the entire situation.' Arlo interrupted, giving me the chance to break free from his grasp and make my second attempt at fleeing the room.

Before I could escape, a firm hand slapped down onto my shoulder causing me to freeze. I didn't need to look around to see who it was. From the tightness of the grip it could have only been one person. My father.

'Amelia please come with me; I need to talk to you.' I froze on the spot and shuddered, by the tone of his voice I knew that he was far from happy with me; but what was new there? I was led to a reasonably sized room, it wasn't big, but it was certainly four times the size of the living room back at the cottage. I looked around and realised that it was some sort of an office. It had four dark blue crushed velvet sofas. Just in front of them was a round dark-oak coffee table. Then it suddenly dawned on me. I was in the Alpha's office! I glanced around the room and took in the sights surrounding me.

It was clean and tidy; just like the rest of the mansion, painted portraits of all the past Alpha's and their Lunas lined the walls; each looking sternly at the artist, showing their intimidation in their image. I ran my eyes along the wall, taking them all in until I finally got to the last one. Arlo. I looked at Arlo's one, he was on his own, obviously he hadn't found his Luna yet. It was a very recent portrait, I knew this because he had only just become the pack's Alpha; I assumed that the portraits were something that happened fairly early on, he wasn't smiling, he had a serious expression on his face just like the others, except a little less intimidating. He was wearing a black suit with a red satin tie. He really was a handsome guy, and it was a nice painting, but it was a shame that he wasn't smiling, I still hadn't seen him look happy yet.

The sound of my father closing the door behind us brought my attention back to what was happening, and I crossed the room quickly and dropped down into the softest sofa I had ever sat on. The minute that I was in it, I felt as though I was in heaven. I regained my composure and braced myself, waiting for world war 3 to start. And as soon as he closed that door, he turned to me with his disapproving eyes burning into my soul.

'What the hell were you thinking, Amelia? Why the fuck did you go out by yourself?!' He growled, crossing the room in three large strides, just stopping inches from my face. I rolled my eyes, surprised by my lack of fear that I usually held of him.

'I just wanted to go for a walk.' I lied trying not to make eye contact with him, he always had a way of knowing if I was lying to him or not. I still wasn't sure that I knew how he could tell, I just assumed it was something to do with looking in my eyes.

'You know full well that you never go out without anyone else. We have been over and over this.' He said grabbing my shoulders and shaking me. I shrugged free from his grasp and gulped down a deep breath.

'But I am 18, it was my birthday, I just wanted a bit of

freedom. Especially now that I am legally an adult' I said quietly looking down at the floor. I was so fed up of looking down at the floor like it was me who should have been ashamed. Why should I have to keep doing it? I didn't do anything wrong, I never had. I could feel myself getting hot as my anger rapidly began to bubble to the surface, this was going to end badly.

'Freedom?!' he cried 'You cannot have any freedom. It is not safe for you out there! You know nothing of this world, the dangers and th-' I cut him off before he could say anymore. Why wasn't it safe for me?

'And why is that dad? Why do I not know anything of this world? Hmmm? Because you have kept me prisoner for my whole life? You have done this, not me! And what do you mean it isn't safe for me?' I cried standing up and accidently knocking him backwards. He steadied himself and looked stunned; I had never stood up to him before.

'I have tried to protect you, you un-grateful bitch.'

'Protect me from what?' I shouted back in frustration. He turned away from me as he let out a low guttural growl in anger. I waited silently for a moment before I continued. 'Answer my question!', but he didn't acknowledge me. It looked as though he had decided to ignore me and pretend like this situation wasn't happening, his back still turned away from me. I clenched my teeth once more and balled my hands into fists before continuing.

'You know what? Fuck you! I hate you. All of you, just as much as you all hate me. Actually no. I probably hate you all more. Why don't you just let me go?' I spat barging past him and walking towards the door.

The man who is supposed to be a father to me and yet is a stranger, grabbed my arm and threw me to the floor. He had thrown me with such force that I skidded forward until I slammed into the door with a bang.

'I am so sick of this.' He muttered, almost to himself. He shook his head before turning back to look at me. 'What has gotten into you? You are acting like a spoilt little girl and I will not stand for it.' He said through gritted teeth. 'I will not have you embarrassing

me in front of my pack. There may be many things that I will toler-
ate, but that is not one of them!' He hissed. I turned my face away
from him for a moment and closed my eyes, pushing back the tears
that had been threatening to spill. There was no way that I was
going to show weakness in front of him. Not this time. In one swift
movement, he lunged forward, grabbing my wrists and yanked me
to my feet.

'Why did you come here you horrid little bitch? I don't want
you here but now your grand-parents do not want you back at the
cottage.' He snarled, staring down at me with a look of disgust
burning in his eyes. I struggled lightly against his hold, but his grip
was getting tighter and tighter the angrier he got.

'Get off me' I whimpered, tears beginning to fill my eyes.

'No, you will listen to me. You can hate me as much as you
want, but you will obey me. You will not leave here unattended,
you will not drink alcohol, and you will be respectful to me at all
times, especially in front of our Alpha.' I could feel his spit hit my
cheeks as I tried my hardest to turn my head away from him.

'Fuck you' I hissed tears rolling down my cheeks, I pushed
all my body weight into him making his grip loose enough for me to
get away. The moment that his grip loosened, I wrenched my arms
free and threw open the door, so hard that it slammed against the
grey stone wall, and ran through the halls, heading in the only direction I could. I needed to be free from this worthless life. No way
was I staying here. Screw shifting, I was leaving right now. And this
time I didn't care if I lived or died.

4

Amelia;

I ran through to the main doors, not bothering to pay any attention to the people that were standing in the hall, watching me as I ran past them. I know that I wasn't as fast as anyone here, I hadn't even come into my full werewolf abilities yet, but I didn't care. I was ready to take on anyone that was going to try and get in my way. The tears in my eyes blurred the faces of everyone around me and it was a relief when I finally reached the main doors; I shoved them with both hands, not stopping for a second. The minute the cold evening air hit me it seemed to fill me with a renewed strength. The muscles in my legs had begun to throb and my lungs were starting to burn. I stopped, placing my hands on my knees in attempt to catch my breath. I straightened and glanced at my surroundings, happy at the fact that no one had appeared to have been following me. I turned back in the direction I had been running and started to walk.

I walked through the gardens of the mansion, tears still streaming down my face. I was so hurt emotionally; I was never going to escape my father and his controlling ways, and I was probably never going to gain "*my*" packs approval. But I really couldn't give a fuck. My father kept saying I was in danger but wouldn't say why or how. But the only dangers that I could see were the ones residing in that damn mansion.

I thought back to the werewolf in the woods, the one that Arlo had saved me from, was that who he was referring to? Or was that just an unlucky coincidence? There was only one way to find out, if my father wasn't going to tell me, then I would go and find that wolf myself and question him and demand the answers I knew I deserved. The first of which would be *"why the hell did you try to kill me?"* But who was I kidding? I didn't know my way back to those woods, a tree branch knocked me off a horse and I had to be rescued by my Alpha. I was pathetic, and a useless individual. Just like everyone had always told me.

I continued walking through the grounds until I came across some stables, I had no idea there were even stables at the pack mansion, especially since animals didn't tend to like werewolves, something about them being able to sense the beast that lived deep within us. It was strange, I lived in this beautiful big building but knew nothing about it and all of the stuff that filled the land that belonged to our pack.

A horse whinnied and started banging against one of the stable doors, causing me to stop and look around. I froze. I would have recognised this beautiful face anywhere.

'Pretty girl!' I cried, rushing over to the stable door throwing it open and letting her out. For the first time, the tears that fell from my puffy blood shot eyes were tears of happiness. I didn't think that I was ever going to see her again. She was as happy to see me as I was her.

I put my hands on either side of her face and pressed mine into hers.

'I missed you so much, but why did you let them bring you here? You need to be free, not locked in stables.' I said softly, gently running my hands down her soft nose. 'Let's set you free pretty girl. No one deserves to be kept against their will'. I took off my high heel shoes allowing my bare feet to sink into the dry soil and took the clip out of my hair letting it fall back down to my hips. The look in her eyes showed that for once, someone understood me and wanted to care for me, my beautiful big friend, my wild horse. It was strange, we understood each other, and I didn't know how. I was a werewolf and she a horse, she should have been petrified at the mere sight of me, yet we had already built an unlikely bond. I cared for her so much and I wished that I could keep her, but she wasn't a tame horse. I took her from her friends, a life she was happy in and now she had been locked in stables for a couple of days, most probably terrified by the monsters that stalk around the grounds.

Pretty girl knelt ready for me to climb onto her back, turning her face slightly, watching as I climbed on.

'Let's go' I called stroking her mane. We rode through the dark woods, my hair flowing as the wind brushed past me, again I felt free. For the first time in days I finally felt that I was able to breathe. I wished I could live a life with my wild horse, just me and her, riding all around England, I could find a home with a large stable so she could walk about and not feel like a prisoner and then we could live in peace.

Pretty Girl started slowing down as we got to the other side of the woods, and there was no trace of the sun in the sky. I was cloaked in a veil of darkness and it made me feel at ease. She stopped a few feet away from a cliff and started eating some grass. It appeared that we had been running for hours, and the poor thing hadn't stopped to eat or drink once. I slowly climbed off her back and stood staring into the distance. I had never been able to stop and just look at the nights sky before, not like this. In the middle of nowhere everything seemed so much more... magical.

I listened to the owls hooting in the distance behind me, the light wind blowing, gently caressing my bare skin, and Pretty girl chewing on grass. This was perfection to me, the sound of animals and mother nature, this was heaven. How could anyone be kept away from something so amazing? Anger bubbled up within me at the thought of missing out on all the wonders of nature over the past eighteen years. That was time that I was never going to get back. Time that my father had stollen from me. And that was something that I would never be able to forgive him for.

I glanced down the side of the cliff and noticed the little lights that twinkled from the ground below, I assumed that they were from houses and streetlights from a world that had no idea about the monsters that roamed within it. I shook my head, dislodging all the negative thoughts and focused on the twinkling once more. It reminded me of looking at night sky, and that thought was strangely calming.

'Beautiful isn't it?' a deep voice said from behind me causing me to flinch and topple forward. There was a flash of black and pinkie white as two warm hands grasped my shoulders, stopping me from falling over the edge.

I whirled around and came face to face with the man behind the voice and glared.

'Oh my gosh you frightened me half to death' I gasped, not quite being able to contain the rage that was swirling within me; Arlo smiled, not the full smile I wanted to see, just a half smile. I shook my head and clenched my teeth. I actually thought that I was free of that damn pack, for a minute I thought that I had outrun them. I guess I should have known better.

'I'm sorry, I didn't mean to startle you.' He admitted as he stood staring at me. I wriggled free from his grasp and turned away from him, looking out in the distance once more. I felt him shift closer to me, turning to look out in the same direction that I was, his hand folded behind his back. He also seemed to be at peace, unfortunately the same could not be said for me any longer. This was supposed to be my time, my time for freedom. My time for release. But here I was, being reminded that it didn't matter how far I went, I was always going to belong to the pack.

Don't get me wrong, I totally understand. I could only imagine what it would be like to have the responsibility of a large pack and he had only just taken over from his father, everything was still new to him. Add that to the fact that he was so young, I am sure there are other pack members that would feel belittled to have someone younger than them in charge. It must have been daunting. But that was still no excuse to now become my new stalker. I understand that the alpha had a responsibility, but he didn't own me. As of today, no one did!

We stood near the edge of the cliff in silence for a while, strangely it wasn't awkward, I didn't feel uncomfortable around him, which was strange, but then I just put that down to him being the alpha. Did that mean that the alpha had some natural *charisma* that made his pack feel calm around him? Either way, that was still a little creepy. I closed my eyes and drew in a deep breath through my nose, trying my hardest to understand the situation that we were currently in. I didn't feel like he was angry with me for leaving the grounds, but then, would I have really been able to tell as we were stood here in silence, not looking at one another? I exhaled loudly and looked at him from the corner of my eyes. *Damn this boy is good looking!* I shook my head, trying to dislodge the thoughts of Arlo from my brain before turning to look at him a little more.

'Did my dad send you?' I asked breaking the silence.

'No, he didn't. I saw you run from my office and told every-one to give you some space.' He paused for a moment, seemingly trying to gauge my reaction; or lack thereof. He cleared his throat before continuing. 'I told them that I would come and find you after you had some time to clear your head.' He admitted. My face flushed and I started feeling irritated once again. How dare he put me in this situation. Allow me to cool off? I grit my teeth once more and shook my head.

'I don't need you to come and find me and I do not plan on going back to the pack mansion, so you needn't have bothered. And I don't care what you all think you know about me and my fam-ily, because you don't know anything, so just back off.' His stare into the distance didn't break as he put his hands into his trouser pockets and sighed; although there was a hint of a smile tugging at the corners of his lips.

'I know you don't' I looked at him.

'You know I don't what?' I snapped in reply. He finally turned to look at me, an unrecognisable gleam in his eye. *Did he find all this amusing?*

'I know you don't plan on coming back to the mansion. But that still doesn't mean that I do not have a responsibility to make sure that you are safe.' He answered, his voice soft and calm, and surprisingly, caring. I tilted my head to the side like a dog who didn't understand its owners' commands.

'So why have you followed me?' I asked, this time my voice a little less aggressive. *Was this his way of diffusing the situation?*

If it was, he was annoyingly good at it.

'Because I am not the only one who has followed you here.' My stomach turned in knots when he said that. I looked at pretty girl she was still eating grass, she wasn't alarmed at all, was he lying to me? Was he trying to scare me? A ploy to make me go back.

'Who has followed me?' I scoffed, my face showing how annoyed I was.

'The same one as last time' Arlo declared. I looked around, the woods were dark and silent, I couldn't see anything moving and I couldn't smell anything. Arlo followed my gaze. 'He has gone, he ran when I started following you. But he will be back, and next time he will get to you. You need to understand he is relentless and is determined to get you alone, I won't always be able to save you Amelia,' I clenched my teeth once more, feeling instantly infuriated at his words *Excuse me? Save me?* I didn't ask to be saved, how dare he.

'I never asked you to save me!' I shrieked in frustration, turning on the spot and sulkily walking over to my horse. Arlo's face changed; he was now looking angry

'Why are you being so reckless? Why do you have a death wish? Do you want to be killed?' He snapped, his words causing me to flinch as though he had physically hit me. I was taken back by what he said, and I knew that there was no way I should argue back to my alpha, but that wasn't going to stop me.

'No, not at all! I just want to be free. Free from a life that I am forced to live. I don't belong with your people. You know that. I know that. So, just let me go?' I pleaded, closing my eyes and forcing myself not to cry. Arlo sighed and then walked towards me.

'You will be free, one day. And I know that you think that you don't belong with us. But deep down I know that you do. And my father has always taught me that an alpha should follow his heart. If freedom is the thing that you truly desire then I shall grant it to you, but first, we need to stop this wolf that is currently out to get you.'

'Who? Who do you need to stop, Arlo? Why won't anyone

tell me who he is? I feel like I am being shadowed, kept in the dark from my own life.'

'If I tell you, you promise me, you will come back to the mansion and do as your told?' Arlo coaxed. I sighed and rolled my eyes, was this information really worth me forcing myself back there? I nodded to myself, I guess the longer that I am there, the more I can try to learn to shift. And once that happens, I can be free. I let out a growl of frustration before answering.

'You tell me, and I will come back to the mansion, but I won't be dictated to by anyone.'

'You forget who your Alpha is' he smirked with a playful glint in his eye. *Did he actually find this amusing?* I seriously hated this guy! I mean, he was hot as hell, and when he spoke to me, he made my insides turn to jelly, but I still hated him. I was lost for words for a few seconds and then I looked into his eyes.

'I might do what you ask, within reason.'

'I tell you what, how about we make a compromise? You don't go wandering off by yourself and I will personally go for walks with you, that way I can show you everything this place has to offer, as well as ensuring your safety.' He paused for a second and then said, 'you can leave the mansion, but you must stay on the grounds, no further than the stables and if you want to ride you're horse, we have a field...' Arlo moved a strand of my hair away from my face, his soft fingers brushing against my cheek. I suppressed the shiver of ecstasy that burned across my skin wherever his fingers touched; he was so handsome, and his golden eyes were just drawing me in.

'I don't have a horse.' I stammered still lost in his eyes.

'You have a unicorn over there.' Arlo proclaimed.

'A unicorn? Pretty girl is a wild horse I took from a field.' I said turning my stare back towards her in confusion.

'No, she is a wild unicorn.' he stated calmly. Was he being sarcastic, taking the piss out of me or did I actually steal a unicorn? I mean, unicorns didn't live in England! Did they?

'Why are you being so nice to me?' I asked him as he helped me up onto Pretty Girl's back.

'Because I like you.' He admitted. I narrowed my eyes and

considered his words for a moment. I watched as that annoying amused smirk crossed his face and I watched as he circled Pretty Girl before gently placing his hands on her face. Wait. He's a were-wolf. Animals are supposed to be terrified of us. He couldn't have been serious about her being a unicorn? She didn't even have a horn. I shook my head in attempt to clear all the confused thoughts from my mind before answering him.

'But you don't even know me. How can you say you like someone without even knowing them?' I watched as he shook his head and chuckled… *chuckled!!* He wandered around the side and I felt as he climbed onto the back of my horse and leant into my ear.

'Maybe I know more than you think. Or, maybe I see the person that you are destined to be?'

'You only know what you have been told, that doesn't mean that you know me.' I replied bluntly. Arlo didn't move his face from my ear as he sighed.

'Do you know how difficult you are?' He asked, seemingly waiting for me to answer him. He laughed softly and leant in a little closer. 'You're right. I apologise. I guess the only way to truly know someone is to learn about them. So then let me get to know you, the real you.' He whispered, his breath brushing against my ear and sending a wave of desire rushing down my spine. I bit my lip and smiled to myself.

'Tell me what you know of this man who is out to kill me first, and then I will think about it.' I retorted smugly. Arlo rested his head against my back and growled playfully.

'Deal. But you owe me.' I smiled to myself and rolled my eyes, *seriously, I owed him?* Who did he think he was? Although I wanted to be mad at him, something deep inside me longed to know more about him. Arlo reached around from behind me, placing his hands on my hips, causing jolts of electricity racing over my skin wherever he touched. I closed my eyes and tried to focus on anything other than how much I wanted him to touch me more.

'So, what is it that you know about this wolf? I am assuming that he isn't someone from our pack?' I asked, turning my head slightly and talking over my shoulder, praying to anyone who would listen that my blush would go unnoticed.

'No. He is most definitely not someone from our pack. And if I am honest, I don't know where he comes from, or who he is. All I do know, is that our pack has been picking up his scent for years. And although he always comes back, we never manage to trace his scent back to where he came from.' I bit my lip and tried as hard as I could to suppress my disappointment. I really had hoped that I would get some more answers than just that. I reached up and tucked a loose strand of hair back behind my ear and allowed his words to sink in for a moment longer.

'How is that possible? I mean, someone can manage to evade the entire pack for so many years. And, how many years are we talking?'

'If I am honest, I don't know. It shouldn't be possible. We have some of the best trackers in the world in our pack, and even they struggle to follow it. It's as though someone if purposely throwing the scent off. Whoever it is, is clearly getting help from someone.' Arlo paused for a moment and sighed softly. 'And as for how long, well, apparently my father had the same trouble back when he was alpha. So, I would say that this guy has been coming back frequently for just over eighteen years.' I gasped at his words and shook my head. *Surely this wolf hasn't been looking for me all my life.* Why would he do that? There was nothing special about me! I couldn't even shift for goodness sake.

'Does your father have any ideas of what it could be that it is looking for?' I asked, my voice barely that of a whisper. Arlo shook his head and rested it against my back.

'That's the thing. No one knows. Whatever it is, it must be extremely important. I mean, why else would someone risk coming onto an elite packs' territory? If an outsider is found within our lands' then the penalty is death.' I nodded once more and tried my hardest to calm my thumping heart. I knew my next question was going to be risky, and I wasn't even sure that I wanted to know the answer, but I asked it anyway.

'What do you think he will do if he ever catches me?'

'That's never going to happen.' Arlo replied, a little too

quickly for my liking.

'But, what if it does? What do you think will happen?' I asked again, this time irritation causing my words to be short. Arlo let out a small growl, a sound that should not have turned me on as much as it did.

'Are you always this argumentative?'

'Do you always avoid questions by asking another?' I retorted. Arlo chuckled and I felt the tremors from its deep notes reverberate up my back, sending a rush of heat into my stomach that begged for him to touch me. His chuckling stopped and a sudden tenseness clouded the atmosphere.

'Amelia, if I am honest, I don't know what that wolf would do to you. And I really don't want to think about it.' His honesty and the tremor in his voice caught me off guard. The way he sounded was as though it pained him to think about something bad happening to me. But why would he care? Like I already told him, he doesn't even know me. I figured that this was just an alpha thing. They are supposed to be extremely protective over their packs after all.

We rode the rest of the journey home in silence, neither of us knowing what to say. All humour and good feeling had gone the moment he answered my question and all I could think about was how I just wanted to be back in my room hiding away from the pack. We finally reached the wrought iron gates of the mansion and before I knew it, we were back at the stables.

I had locked Pretty girl safely away for the night, making sure to give her plenty of kisses before I had left. It was horrible leaving her behind. She was so close to the woods, the place where so many dangers lurked, and I was frightened that something would hurt her. I know that pack lore states that other packs cannot trespass on other pack territory. But that doesn't mean anything. If someone really wanted to break into our turf and hurt Pretty Girl, then they would. The thought of losing her caused a pain in my chest to ripple through my entire body, I was supposed to set her free, but I couldn't bring myself to do it.

She was the only friend I had in this world; the only friend I have *ever* had, and the thought of her being hurt or frightened made me feel sick, I just wished the stables were closer to the mansion. Maybe this was something that I could have suggested to Arlo *if I had planned on staying here.*

'You really do love her, don't you?' Arlo asked, snapping me from deep in my thoughts and bringing me back into the here and now. I turned my dazed stare back to my alpha; who hadn't taken his eyes off of me, from the moment that he had climbed up onto Pretty Girl's back, until now. Arlo had decided to stay with me; just so he could walk me back to the mansion. I had told him I was more than capable of getting back myself, but he just would not take no for an answer. *Was he doing this out of protection? Or was he doing it because he was worried that I would try to run away again?*

I hated how much he was acting like my father; I felt like everyone thought I was incapable of doing anything by myself. All of this "we need to protect you bullshit" was not cutting it anymore, I still didn't believe him when he had said that someone had followed me to the woods; surely Pretty girl would have reacted to the other wolfs scent? *Why didn't she react to Arlo's scent? Was it because he had saved me; more than once? Or was there something else about him that Pretty Girl liked?* I realised that I was so lost in thought that I hadn't answered him. I nodded,

'I guess I do; she is really special to me.' Arlo smiled at my words.

'When you're with her you look so happy. It's nice to see that. You always seem so... sad' I paused for a moment at his words and turned to glare at him. Arlo chuckled *again!* And shook his head. 'I didn't mean anything by it. It was just an observation.' I exhaled softly through my nose, telling myself that there was no need to always be so angry with everyone, before answering.

'She makes me happy, it must sound really silly, but when I am with Pretty Girl, it's almost as if she understands me, like she can read my mind' *Why was I being so open and honest with him?* I expected him to laugh at me, tell me how ridiculous I was being, but he just nodded along and smiled sweetly.

'It is strange though. Normally animals don't like us were-wolves. Although she is a unicorn, they are usually worse. They have their heightened senses, just like us. We scare the crap out of them. And then there's you. She must sense that you are special, that aura that you give off to everyone around you.' I couldn't help but smile at what he had said. *Finally*, I was the odd one out but for a good reason. I would rather be loved by animals then by my so-called family.

I couldn't suppress the grin that was plastered on my face. It was an unusual sight, me smiling like the Cheshire cat. This was the first time in my life that I had felt happy. I knew that this feeling wasn't going to last forever, but right here, in this moment, I allowed my happiness to consume me. I had the cheesiest grin on my face, it was actually really embarrassing but I couldn't help it.

'What?' Arlo asked a smile creeping across his face. I shrugged,

'I like being special to someone.' I replied, averting my eyes from his and looked out into the darkening scene surrounding us, I glanced at my alpha from the corner of my eye and was shocked at what I was seeing. Arlo eyes lost their familiar happy shimmer and for a moment looked almost sad at what I had said.

'Hey, it's not just Pretty Girl that your special too, my mum adores you.' I nodded, Marie did seem to really care about me, I am not entirely sure why, but she was definitely one of the nicer higher pack members and it was obvious that Arlo was more like his mother than his father.

'Your mum is lovely, she has made me feel so welcome, it's made this somewhat a little easier. If it wasn't for her and her kindness, I don't know where I would be right now.' I admitted.

'Has she told you, how she became the Luna?' Arlo asked, his voice picking up as a smile tugged at the corners of his lips.

'No, she hasn't. But I would love to know?' I said intrigued.

'Well as you know, an Alpha can only imprint on someone with high ranking in packs, *"royal blood"* if you like, and somehow my dad Imprinted on a young girl; my mum who was of lower ranking in the pack.'

'Wait? Are you telling me that your mother is not an elite?' I asked, cutting him short and staring at him with wide eyes. Arlo shook his head and smiled.

'Things are a little more complicated than that with this story.' He replied, raising an eyebrow before continuing. 'An Elite and a Mutt imprinting, well, this is extremely rare and there is normally an explanation for it. And, in my mum and dad's case there was. My mum was abandoned as a baby and taken in by one of our pack members who couldn't have children of their own. They raised her and lived in one of the houses.'

'I would never have known that your mum grew up as a Mutt. That's insane!' I whispered, my eyes glistening with fascination. 'So? What happened next?' I asked, leaning in a little closer, eager for the story to continue.

'She became a waitress, and of course my father was the Alpha at that time. He imprinted on her the moment that he laid eyes on here. Imprinting doesn't always work like that. Sometimes; Selene; the Moon Goddess, makes us wait. She knows when the time is right for us to imprint and she knows who is meant for who. However, with my parents, there was uproar! My grandfather; the elder at the time was furious. How could his son imprint on a Mutt, especially one who wasn't originally part of this pack?'

'Is being a non-Elite really that bad? I thought that it was just my family that acted like that.' I whispered. Arlo nodded.

'Unfortunately, some werewolves still live in their old traditions. I am one of the lucky ones. I don't know if it was because of my mother being raised the way she was or not but, my father is quite relaxed when it comes to the traditions.' Arlo paused for a moment and turned to me before adding. 'I am sorry for the way that you have been brought up. It's sometimes hard to remember that not everyone is as lucky as I am.' I hesitated for a moment, taken aback by his kindness.

'You have nothing to apologise for. I guess this is just the way that Selene had my life planned.' I replied softly, pausing as we reached the door to the mansion. Arlo pushed it open with one hand and gestured for me to enter first. I smiled over to him, waiting for him to close and lock the door behind us.

'So, what happened about your parents? I am dying to know!' I pleaded. Arlo's smile broke out across his face, causing him to look child-like for a moment. *Was he genuinely this happy that I was interested in his parents' story? Why wouldn't anyone want to know?*

'Well, as it turns out my mum, is the blood of an Elite pack member. There are many packs here in England; but only three of Elite bloodline, and my mum is of blood of a pack called Shadowfang. Her mother; my biological grandmother was the youngest daughter of the Alpha and she fell in love with a Mutt. She got pregnant by him and when her father found out who the child's father was it was sentenced to death. If it hadn't been for my grandmother running away and abandoning my mother here, then my parents wouldn't have imprinted, and I would never have been born.'

'Wow. What a story. Do you believe that the Moon Goddess had something to do with all that?' I asked. Arlo nodded as he clasped his hands behind his back.

'I think that everything happens for a reason. And when we feel that something is bad for us, we simply must try looking at it another way. And realise that this was just something that was placed in our path to test us.' I raised an eyebrow and smirked at him.

'Really?' I asked sarcastically.

'What?'

'How long did it take you to come up with that speech? Is it something you have to use often as Alpha?' I asked with a chuckle. Arlo rolled his eyes and shook his head.

'If you must know, I only use it in the very extreme cases where the persons soul is lost.' He retorted with a wink and a cheeky grin. I dropped my mouth open with a look of mocked hurt on my face and lightly punched his arm.

'Rude!' I giggled. Arlo wiggled his eyebrows suggestively causing me to bark out a laugh. For the first time in as long as I could remember, I was actually enjoying myself. We both walked giggling with one another and before I knew it, we were standing outside my bedroom door. I glanced around in confusion before smiling over to him sweetly.

'Thank you, Arlo. For everything.' I whispered. I turned my glittering green eyes down to the door handle and unlocked it, I paused for a moment, turning back and planting a soft kiss on his cheek before hurrying through my door and closing it behind me.

A kiss; Amelia! What the hell is this man doing to me?

5

Amelia;

I sat in my green velvet crush armchair reading a book on Unicorns that I had snuck down to the library to find in the middle of the night. I still wasn't sure if Arlo was messing around with me or not, if Pretty girl was an actual Unicorn wouldn't I know? For a start she doesn't even have a bloody horn. It sounded farfetched, I mean, I knew they were real but really? They weren't the myths people believed them to be. But I am just Amelia-May, there wasn't anything special about me, especially nothing that would warrant me finding a Unicorn. Although it would be pretty amazing if she was one. Unicorns are an endangered species; they are a myth to the human world and it's safer that way. If it ever came out that they did exist, they would be killed because mankind pretty much kills everything they don't understand.

It was 7:30 Am, and my eyes stung. I had spent the first half of the night thinking over the conversation between Arlo and myself, and then the argument with my father. It was around that time that I realised sleep was not going to be coming to me any time soon and I decided to go find the library. I remembered Marie telling me that there was one here; all I had to do was remember where she had told me it was.

Once I had found it, I searched every shelf until I found the book that I was looking for. I needed to know more about these creatures. I needed to know if Arlo was just tormenting me, or if he was telling the truth. After getting back to my room, I spent hours sitting here in my chair, reading. Who knew there was so much to learn about these beautiful creatures? The one thing that stood out the most was the fact that Unicorns were terrified of werewolves. So surely that meant that Arlo was lying to me? But why would he have done that? After opening up to me, I genuinely thought that we were having a special moment.

As much as I tried to forget about the way my father reacted, I couldn't. It didn't matter how much I tried to push it from my mind, that argument with him plagued me. I couldn't believe he put his hands on me, he hurt me. In my whole 18 years that man never once laid a finger on me, maybe I had pushed him too far? Or maybe he has pushed me too far and he can't cope with the fact I am finally done with cowering down to him and my brothers. Being here has changed me, I am finally able to be myself. I know that I am a lot stronger than what I thought. And there is no way that I am going to let fear control my life any longer. And although being in the pack mansion is a far cry from the freedom I crave, it is admittedly better than the cottage.

I dropped my book down onto my chest and tilted my head back over the arm rest, I thought back to mine and Arlo's conversation on our walk back to the mansion, all of the stuff he had told me about Marie, and how she came from nothing, being found as an abandoned baby to becoming Luna of the pack, talk about a Rags to Riches story. In a way it made me like her more, she was an unwanted child too, maybe that why she was so nice to me. He said that I was special to her, but I am still not sure why that is. Did she know about the way that my father and brothers had treated me all my life?

I had eventually got out of bed at 5, giving up on trying to sleep, I was exhausted, but my mind just would not shut down. I knew there was no point in trying to fight it any longer and decided to wake myself up with a cold shower. It certainly did the trick! I threw on a pair of grey joggers and a white T-shirt with Freddie Mercury singing on it. It was too early to go down and have some breakfast so that was when I decided to continue reading my book. I must have been totally engrossed in what it was reading because the next time I looked at my watch it was 8:15am. The time the pack joined for breakfast. I leapt from the chair and slipped into my white converses; neatly tucking the book under my pillow, I would continue reading it again later, now for food and answers. And there was no way I wanted to find out how my father would react if I was down late for breakfast. Was he still in his foul mood? I don't suppose that anything had happened to change his mind over night. But then again, did he even think of me when I wasn't around? I would bet that I was further from his mind than he ever was from mine. I bolted from my bedroom and dashed down the hall, hoping that no one had noticed that I wasn't there. I was also silently praying that Arlo wasn't already in the dining room. It was another of the pack Lore's' that the Alpha and Elders were to be the last in the room. I guess that was just some ancient Alpha's way of displaying his authority. I guess that some people needed to make others feel small so that they would feel better about themselves. Lori!

I approached the closed dining room doors and hesitated for a moment. I could hear the distant chatter as people were talking amongst themselves, but I couldn't hear Arlo. His voice was enough to be recognised in any crowd.

'You're late.' Came the familiar voice. I closed my eyes and turned around slowly. There, standing behind me was Arlo and his parents. I wished that I would be swallowed by the ground, I was so embarrassed. When I opened my eyes, I noticed Marie and her kind smile, her eyes darted from Arlo to me.

'I-I am so sorry. I had a bit of a late night.' I replied, dropping my stare to the ground. Arlo reached forward and tipped my chin so that I was facing him once more.

'Luckily, the rule only states that all pack members must be there before the Alpha. I am here. You are stood in front of me. I guess that means that you were here before me.' He answered with a smile. I tried to fight the smile pulling at my lips, but it was useless. The more that I was getting to know my alpha, the less I hated him. The sound of the doors opening behind me had me whirling around on the spot. I let out a small squeak of surprise before locking eyes with a shocked waitress. Without another word, I slipped around our server; I seriously needed to learn people's names and scurried to my seat.

The moment that I entered the dining room I was met again by whispers and stares, I didn't put my head down this time, I had no reason to, I would not let these people make me feel uncomfortable, I had as much right to be here as they did; even if Lori and her silly little friends didn't think so. I was still so pissed off with how she thought that her and her friends could treat people in the way that they did, she shouldn't be looking down on me, she shouldn't be looking down on anyone. I don't care about the pack order; everyone should be treated equally. In my eyes no one pack member is better than anyone else. Mutt or not. I seriously hated that word!

'Don't worry about them.' A familiar soft voiced said. It was Piper, today her auburn hair was down, she wasn't in her waitressing clothes; she was wearing a pair of jeans and a bright pink vest top instead. 'It's my morning off' she blushed realising I had noticed her change of attire. 'I would say come and join me for breakfast, but you know the rules.' she said disappointment filling her voice, pointing to the table that was full of Non-Elites, who were patiently waiting for their breakfast.

'But I think you are wanted here' I followed her gaze to my father and brother's; they were all standing by the table waiting for Arlo. No one was to sit down before he did

'Oh' I mumbled.

'It's okay though, we can meet up later if you want. Maybe we can go for a little walk and then I can tell you about these rumours' I rolled my eyes, these rumours were obviously something to do with me. I suddenly realised what Piper had just said. She wanted to go for a walk with me, like a friend. I smiled and started to nod when an angry voice stopped me.

'Amelia' My father called nodding towards Arlo, he had just walked into the hall and everyone but me and Piper were at our tables.

'Oh shit' Piper mumbled turning on her heel, without a moment pause I turned and rushed to the seat beside my father, refusing to meet his angry stare.

'Sorry' I mouthed at my father as he gave me a disapproving look.

'You need to be at your table standing behind your chair before he enters the room.' He said quietly. Really? Did all these people think that he was some kind of king? How am I supposed to get used to this?

Breakfast looked and smelt amazing as usual, I was desperate to go up and get some pancakes but had already decided that it was best to wait for Lori to get hers first, I didn't really fancy dealing her stupidity again today. I turned my gaze to my hands that were folded in my lap when a voice caused me to flinch.

'Amelia, would you like to come up to the serving table with me?' Arlo asked appearing beside me. I was taken back, everyone on the table went quiet and I could feel my father and brothers' eyes burning into my forehead, and I could practically feel Lori's anger wrapping around me. I bit the inside of my cheek to stop myself from laughing and nodded slowly.

'I would be honoured' I said in a sincere voice, but he knew I was being sarcastic, a smirk escaped his lips. He offered out his arm to me and I hesitantly placed my hand on it.

'Thank you.' He whispered, keeping his stare locked on the food table.

'Should I bow to you next time?' I Chuckled as me and Arlo started walking towards the serving table.

'Ha, ha.' He replied narrowing his eyes in a mock anger, still smiling. 'I knew you couldn't be polite without adding a bit of sarcasm in there' he joked. We were trying to talk quietly, knowing the main pack members were trying desperately to hear what we were saying, everyone was talking. I quickly glanced up at Lori, her face was bright red. Almost purple. she was angry. Was that anger directed at Arlo? Or myself? Either way, it brought me pleasure knowing that something involving me was bringing her discomfort. I allowed the small smile to show as we walked past her, and I could have sworn that I heard her growl. I waited a few more seconds until we were a good distance from the bitches of Wolf wick and turned my head slightly towards Arlo.

'Why the invitation?' I whispered looking up at his handsome face, he looked down at me and smiled

'You said that I only know what I have been told about you, so I plan on getting to know the real you.'

'Yeah well I think you may have really pissed your girlfriend off' I replied, nodding towards Lori. Arlo quickly glanced over at her and I noticed the pleased smile that he allowed to show briefly. He gave a small shrug.

'She isn't my girlfriend and I don't care if she is pissed off.' He said frankly and then he turned to look at me, his eyes twinkling.

'How about after breakfast we go for a walk, then I can show you what we have here in this incredible home of ours.' I looked at him curiously and nodded.

'That would be lovely. Thank you.' We stopped at the breakfast trolleys and loaded our plates with so much food that we could have fed a family; thank goodness for our fast metabolisms, before turning and walking back to our seats. By the time we had reached our table, Marie had already moved along so that there was a place for me in between her and her son. I smiled kindly to the woman as she gestured for me to sit beside her. For the first time, I felt as though I was being accepted. I didn't have to pretend to be something that I wasn't. All I had to do, was be myself who-ever that was.

We ate in silence, only glancing at one another occasionally out the corner of our eyes, both of us seemingly eating as fast as we could so we could get out of the dining hall and go for our walk. We finished eating and Arlo rose from his chair, before pulling mine out and helping me to my feet. The rest of the pack stared at us with wide eyes; and I didn't care. We exited the room in silence and hurried down the hall, before pushing open the main doors.

'Has my mum shown you much of the mansion at all?' Arlo asked me as we stepped outside, although it was a very bitterly cold day, the sun was shining and the skies were a pale blue, it was the first time since me being here that it hadn't rained or been cloudy.

'She has shown me the swimming pool but not much else

from outside.' I said looking around.

'Well this place is like a little village so there is much more than just the mansion and houses.' He said leading me down the gravel pathway.

'What else do you guys have here then?' I asked pretending to be interested in what he was saying, I was just happy to be out of the mansion and I was really happy to be with him.

'We have our own little pub' he winked.

'Oh really?' now he had piqued my interest.

'Fancy going there quickly. I want you to meet my best friend.' I stopped in my tracks and screwed my face up, Arlo realised what he had said and chuckled. 'No, not Charlie! My best mate Matt' How many best friends did he have?

'I would love to.' I smiled following Arlo to the pub, he said it was small and it most certainly was not small, I raised my eyebrows and sighed. *Oh, to be rich!*

Once in the pub; Arlo walked me towards a pool table, a boy around my age, maybe a little bit older, was leant over with a pool cue in one hand and under his arm, he was concentrating, trying to get one of the balls in the pockets.

'This is Matt' Arlo grinned. Matt shot the ball in the pocket he was aiming for and slowly stood up turning to look at us, his serious expression still didn't leave his face. His dark short hair was side swept with a perfect parting to one side, he was nearly as tall as Arlo, standing at around 6 foot.

'Hi' I mumbled putting my hand weakly up. His brown eyes looked me up and down and then he looked at Arlo, he didn't even acknowledge me. Just like the rest of them, clearly, he would be another who hated my guts.

'Matt; this is Amelia, the one I told you about.' Arlo chuckled nervously, glancing over at me with wide nervous eyes. He was nervous? Our Alpha? Woah. Matt nodded to me and then turned back to the pool table.

'He is really shy' Arlo whispered taking my hand and walking me to the bar.

'Matt? The usual?' he called over to his friend. Matt nodded and put a cigarette behind his ear.

'Yeah, I'm going to go and have a quick smoke, be back in 10.' I looked at my watch, it was 10 Am and they were going to drink? Now?

'Fancy a drink?' Arlo asked pulling out a thick black leather wallet. I looked up at the pub clock and Arlo shrugged at me. 'It's 5 o clock somewhere in the world, right?' He beamed. I couldn't help but smile back.

'I have only ever had Rose, so, I guess I will have a glass of that please?' Arlo nodded to the man behind the bar who had clearly been listening, and I watched as he hurried around getting our order. He returned with the wine and rapidly filled two tall glasses with beer before handing them across to Arlo. He reached for his wallet and the bar man shook his head, waving him away. Arlo smiled kindly at the man and grabbed the glasses before directing me back over to the table where Matt had clearly been sitting.

'I think you and Matt will get on.' Arlo said before taking a large sip of his beer.

'Oh really? I don't.' I mumbled.

'Trust me, once you get past the shyness, you will see what a top bloke Matt is. In fact, your both alike. He is very blunt... like you, he doesn't take and crap from anyone... like you.' I shook my head smiling.

'Okay, okay I get it.' I laughed, picking up my glass and sipping at the cold liquid slowly. Matt came back in; his serious face was now red, and he look really aggravated.

'That little Trollope and her mates are outside.' He grumbled sitting opposite Arlo.

'What's she done?' Arlo sighed rubbing his fingers across his forehead.

'Just Lori being a nasty piece of work again, apparently she is going to kick the crap out of your new bird.' He replied, nodding his chin towards me. I creased my brow in frustration and rolled my eyes as he continued. 'I told her to piss off, but apparently she wants you or she wants Amelia outside now.' Matt looked concerned for me; I wasn't too sure why.

I rolled my eyes, this girl really hated me, and I had absolutely no idea why. I put my wine glass on the table and stood up from my seat.

'Where are you going?' Arlo asked also standing up.

'Apparently to get the crap kicked out of me.' I said as I walked towards the pub door. Both Arlo and Matt jumped up.

'Amelia don't' Arlo said gently grabbing my hand, why didn't he want me to go? I wasn't scared of her and her bitch pack.

'Why?' I asked. 'I'm not scared of her. I haven't done anything wrong and she seems to have a major issue with me.' I turned myself back towards the door before correcting Matt. 'And by the way Matt, I am not Arlo's bird.' I said bluntly, reaching for the handle.

'Amelia please, just leave it, she isn't worth the trouble. I will deal with her; Matt, can you go and sit with Lia please?' Lia? Only Eddie had ever called me Lia. It was strange hearing Arlo say it, that's normally something friends do isn't it? Shorten your name as sort of a pet name. I look at Matt and he looked straight back at me, we both stood facing each uncomfortably for a few seconds. I paused and glanced over at Arlo once more.

'I will be fine. Just don't come and be a hero. Just stay in here and let me fight my own battles. Ok?' I said before pulling the door open and stepping outside.

'And here she is.' Lori hissed as I stepped out into the garden, she and her two friends were standing at the pub benches, all looking like they could smell shit.

'Here I am Lori.' I smiled forcefully. 'What the hell do you want?' I asked, sounding more than a little bored. 'Or, should I just ask what it is that I have done wrong this time?'

'More to the point, what have you done right? I think that it is time that someone put you in your place around here!' Lori retorted, snarling angrily. I rolled my eyes and took a slow step towards her.

'Lori, seriously, what is your problem? Do you have some underlining mental issue? Or is it purely the fact that that blonde hair of yours has cut off the blood supply to your brain?' I asked sarcastically. Her eyes widened and her nostrils flared, I knew that I was getting under her skin, and that thought just pleased me.

'You can't talk to Elites in that way Mutt!' Adela snapped, smiling spitefully, turning her hopeful stare to Lori. The blonde werewolf rolled her eyes and forced herself to smile at her friend.

"Mutt? Lori, is your friend backward? My brother is the Beta... or has she forgotten that?' I retorted. Lori turned a disgusted look at her friend and shook her head. I folded my arms across my chest defensively and waited for the onslaught of abuse that I was undoubtedly about to receive. Lori motioned with her head for her two friends to slowly circle me, acting like they were sharks who had just scented fresh blood in the waves, as she strolled closer to me.

'Like I said, you need to be taught a lesson. And as it happens, I am in a teaching mood.' Lori said, laughing nastily to herself. Before I had a chance to react. Adela leapt forward and latched on to one of my arms. I swung my free hand forward, hitting her in the side of the head with the palm of my hand. She let out a short yelp moments before the other girl pulled my free hand behind my back. Lori continued walking towards me, rolling her sleeves up to her elbows and finally released the first blow.

She punched my nose and I heard the crack of bone, swiftly followed by a torrent of warm blood gushing down my chin. Lori's eyes blazed with excitement and she pulled her leg back and kicked the side of my knee, dropping me to the ground. The moment I was down, Adela and Harper; the other of Lori's pack rats, pressed their knees firmly into my elbows, causing a wave of fire to rush up my shoulders. My hands were beginning to tingle, and I saw that my pain was only egging them on further. Lori raised her foot above my face and brought it down repeatedly, causing my eyes to burn.

I tried with everything that I had in me to throw my fist out as hard as I could, but it was no use. I was sorely outnumbered. I closed my eyes and tried my hardest to ignore the pain that radiated out from each blow that the girls took. I was not going to cry in front of them. They could do what they wanted, but there was no way that would get the pleasure of seeing my crumble. Another wave of pain washed through me as Lori kicked my stomach with all her might. What sort of a coward was she? She couldn't fight her own battles. She needed tweedled dumb and tweedled dee to pin me down so I couldn't fight back. It was in that moment that I decided, I was going to get her. It might not be today, but one day, she was going to get what was coming to her. And it was going to be me who did it.

An alright growl ripped out through the air around me and the sudden squeals of the three frightened girls. I felt their grips loosen and I curled myself into a ball. I tried to open one of my eyes, but it was already so swollen that it was useless. I could feel the thick sticky blood running down my face.

'Enough!' Arlo roared, turning his anger filled eyes on the three girls. I looked on with blurry eyes and saw Lori continue to glare at me. 'Back to the mansion. All of you' He shouted, standing inches from Lori, his face turning a shade of red that I didn't even think possible. Lori huffed and folded her arms across her chest before turning and storming off, back in the direction of the mansion. I couldn't see her, but I could hear the tantrum with every footstep that she took. I dropped my head back down onto the ground as a wave of nausea washed over me.

'I'm going to fucking kill her.' Arlo roared, I heard as the birds left the tree's frightened by the sudden growl they had just heard.

'Are you ok?' Matt asked, dropping down at my side and checking me over, I tried to speak, but no words would come out. 'I think she is going unconscious.' Matt cried with panic in his voice. The last thing I saw was Arlo's golden eyes, coming into view as I lost consciousness and fell into the darkness.

6

In the Darkness, he'll show you,
All the answers, that were kept from you,
Go in search until he's found,
Resist the liars all around.

Amelia

That song. It was back. I thought that I was free of this nightmare since leaving the cottage. I guess I had thought wrong. I hadn't heard it since being in the mansion, yet here it was filling my mind once again. I woke up and tried to move but was taken aback by the intense pain that was rippling through me. I tried to open my eyes, but they were still swollen, and pain bolted through my head as though someone was stabbing my brain. I gasped loudly and struggled to find my breath; every inhale felt like someone was tightening a rope around my chest. I braced myself and forced my eyes open, fighting through the feeling that I was about to pass out, but I did it. I stared up at the ceiling above and waited for a moment to regain my focus. A bright, long white light was above my head; it was the kind of light that you would normally see in a hospital. *Wait, am I at a hospital?* I tried to sniff, to see if I recognised the smell of where I was, but my nose ached, and my sinuses were so swollen that it was impossible to breathe through my nose.

'She is awake.' A voice I didn't recognise said. An old man in a long white coat looked down at me. 'Amelia, my name is Benjamin Bailey. I am just going to check you over quickly. Please let me know if you feel uncomfortable at any stage.' He paused for a moment as though he was allowing me to take in his information before continuing. I felt his shadow pass over my face and then blinding light. He shone a light into each of my eyes and wrote something on his clipboard, nodding his head. *He's a doctor, I must be at a hospital.*

'C..ca…can I sit up?' I croaked lifting my head slightly. My voice didn't sound like my own. It was rough and hoarse and completely alien to me. Before I had a chance to actually sit up, I felt two sets of hands hold onto each of my arms and gently lift me, making sure that I was stable before letting me go. Now that I was sitting up, I was overcome with the feeling that I was going to be sick. I wasn't in a hospital, it was more like a medical centre, I recognised the brown double doors. *The mansion has a medical centre, what else does this place have? A dentist? Opticians?*

'Hello sweet girl.' I recognised the soft female voice immediately; Marie. I strained my eyes a little harder to get a better look as she stepped closer to my bedside. She looked like she hadn't slept at all. Her normally perfectly styled hair pulled up into a loose ponytail, instead of wearing one of her posh dresses she was wearing an over-sized deep red jumper and black leggings. 'You are healing extremely well.' She smiled, stroking my hair gently. At the slight touch I forced myself not to cry out. Even the simplest of actions hurt.

'H-How long have I been here?' I stammered, trying my hardest to remain calm. Marie was silent for a moment and dipped her head.

'Three days sweet heat.' She replied solemnly.

'But, what about my first shift?' I asked, my voice weak. A look of sadness passing over her face. 'What? What is it?' I added, my eyes wide.

'I'm so sorry darling. You were not in any condition to shift. We had to keep you here, heavily sedated. It was too much of a risk to put your body through the extra trauma.' She whispered, unshed tears shimmering in her eyes.

'I am going to kill that bitch.' I muttered, wincing as I moved my head. And I meant it, I would kill Lori, one day she would get what was coming to her. That wasn't a threat. It was a promise that I was making to myself.

'Get in line darling, she is in a lot of trouble.' Marie nodded; her face now twisted and full of anger. 'I cannot believe she would do such a thing. I always said she was a piece of work; but Tristan would never listen to me.' Marie folded her arms across her chest and dropped into the chair beside the bed. 'Once Arlo and Matt brought you here, I know he summoned Lori. She will face some serious consequences; I can assure you.' I nodded at what Marie had said. *Not if her pathetic daddy has anything to do with it.*

I glanced over to the table beside my bed and took in the sight of the most beautiful flowers that I had ever seen. They were an assortment of roses in all sorts of colours, some that I didn't even know existed.

'W-Who are they from?' I asked weakly, jerking my chin towards the vase. Marie climbed from her chair and picked the label from the centre of the flowers and read the tag aloud.

'Amelia, I just wanted to give you these, so you had something as beautiful as you to look at when you opened your eyes. Love, Ethan.' I paused for a moment as my heart sank a little. For a moment I thought that they may have been from Arlo. But either way, these flowers truly were beautiful, and I needed to find the person who sent them to me.

'Who is Ethan?' I asked softly. Marie smiled softly and glanced over her shoulder. He is the son of Benjamin. The doctor that was treating you.' She replied. I nodded, trying my hardest to think back to if I had met him before, but I was coming up blank. 'I am going to get some coffee quickly; I think Matt is waiting outside to see you.' Marie whispered, stepping away from the flowers, before pausing as she looked down at me lovingly. 'Can I get you anything sweetheart? Some coffee perhaps?' I tried to swallow and felt my throat was dry and scratchy. I nodded lightly, ignoring the pain and hoping that it would ease the more I moved. *That's what we were all told as children right? Keep moving it so it doesn't tense up!* I hope to the moon goddess that that was true.

I watched as Marie left the room and Matt walked in, his face a mixture of concern and anger. Marie's words suddenly dawning on me. Matt was here, to see me. Why? I twisted around in my bed and tried to sit myself up a little more and cried out in agony. Matt crossed the room quickly than the average human and was there helping to prop me up.

'You are one crazy girl, you know that?' he said sitting in the chair that Marie had occupied moments before. I nodded at him wincing as I did. 'Me and Arlo got you here as quick as we could. I can't believe Lori! She went too far.' He was now clenching his fists, his dark brown eyes darkening; *if that was possible*, in anger.

'It's okay, I am fine, and Marie said I am healing well.' I croaked gently stroking my now healed nose. 'I will get revenge though.'

'Oh, I don't doubt it, but first we need to teach you to fight. I will do everything in my power to see you put that bitch in her place.' Matt said rubbing his big hands together. 'You are really brave though; brave...and stupid.' I looked over at him and attempted to narrow my eyes playfully; *Not that easy when they are practically already shut*.

'Maybe, but I am not going to back down from anyone, I don't care who they are, I don't deserve to be treated like I am a piece of shit. No one does!'

We sat in silence for a while watching the as the two nurses changed sheets on some beds that had previously been used; the doctor was sat on a chair in the corner of the room still writing things on his clipboard. I sighed and lent back on to the two pillows that were recently placed behind my head.

'Where is Arlo?' I asked glancing over at Matt.

'At a pack meeting, he said he will be over to see you afterwards.' Matt said walking over to the water machine. I watched as he put a white paper cup under a plastic tap and pressed a blue button for cold water. He filled the cup up and then smiled at me. 'You know, Arlo will only do what the elders tell him and even that is tough for him, but he actually listened to what you told him to do. I think he really likes you.' He passed me the cup and sat back down before continuing. 'And, I am beginning to see why.' He said with a kind smile.

'Thank you.' I said weakly taking a sip of the ice-cold water,

I felt as it rushed down my throat and landed into my empty stomach, my god I was so thirsty. I raised the cup to my lips once more and drained it of its contents. Marie came back into the room and grinned at me, glancing over her shoulder shiftily, she opened the door and in walked Piper, her pale freckly face full of a mixture of concern and anger.

'Oh my gosh! I have been so worried about you!' she gasped jogging over to my bed. She knelt beside me and looked as though she was about to cry. 'I am sorry you are going through this.' Tears filled her eyes and she sniffed, pulling a tissue from her pocket. Me, Piper and Matt looked up as Marie and the doctor stood at the bottom of the bed.

The doctor smiled. 'You have healed very well; you might still be sore for a day or two, but I don't see why you need to stay here any longer. I am discharging you but please do not hesitate to come back and see me if you have any concerns.' With that he walked away putting his blue pen behind his ear.

I climbed from the bed with some assistance from my three friends and Matt turned his back while Marie and Piper helped me back into my clothes. As stiff as I was, I was determined to carry on, and try to do everything with as little assistance as possible. *I failed!*

Marie, Matt and Piper all helped me up to my room, they didn't need to, but it was obvious they all felt sorry for me and I hated it. Its Lori they should be feeling sorry for, once I had regained my strength, I was going to do whatever I could to make her life hell. I suddenly smiled to myself. It looked as though I had finally given myself a reason to stay here. That and the fact that I was genuinely beginning to care for some of the people that lived here.

'Can I stay with Amelia?' Piper asked as they all helped me sit on my bed.

'That's up to Amelia.' Marie smiled nodding her head towards me. I didn't mind, it would be nice to have some company for a while and Piper was always full of gossip. Maybe she could tell me how Arlo dealt with Lori and her Bitch Pack. I was seriously hoping that it was going to be some brutal, medieval style punish-ment. I doubted it, but a girl could dream. I nodded *yes* and Marie and Matt left my room. Matt pausing one last time and smiling over to me with saddened eyes.

'So, what do you want to do?' Piper asked pacing around my room, something was bothering her, I could tell. She wouldn't stay still, beads of sweat forming on her head every time she tried to wipe it away.

'I don't mind.' I shrugged, 'but first, I think you need to tell me what is bothering you.' I watched as she froze on the spot.

'What makes you think that something is bothering me?' She asked nervously, I held her stare for a moment and she put her head down, she looked as though she was going to cry again. 'Piper; tell me what is wrong.' I said in a stern voice, my heart was picking up speed and I felt sick. It was clear that whatever she was going to say, wasn't going to be good.

Piper sat down beside me, making sure not to look at my face, she sighed and then started speaking.

'So, Lori has been telling everyone; that Arlo summoned her last night to talk about her punishment and they had a huge row' she said before pausing.

'Go on?' I urged.

Piper nervously licked her lips and looked at me, her eyes full of sadness. 'They slept together. Lori hasn't stopped going on about it.'

I was stunned. I felt as though I had been kicked in the stomach by that bitch all over again. So, whilst I was in the hospital bed that Lori had put me in, the man I had started to fall for fucked her. I had just started to let my guard down and he did that? My heart sank and I thought that I was going to be sick. An intense heat washed over my body and I felt sweat beading down my back. I stood up despite the pain I was in and walked towards my bath-room. I could feel a lump form in my throat and did not want any-one else to see me cry. I was done with this pack.

'Lia' Piper cried walking towards me. I put my hand up to make her stop and turned my head.

'Thank you so much Piper for telling me, I appreciate it, but I just need to be on my own.' I said swallowing back the lump that was desperate to escape my mouth. Piper dipped her head once more and nodded. Without another word she crossed the room, closing the door behind her. The minute that she was gone, I hurried into the toilet and threw up.

I sat against the now closed bathroom door sobbing, my heart hurt, I felt so betrayed. Was this all a setup to hurt me? Was everything an act? Was Arlo pretending to like me this whole time? Did Matt know? Did Marie? *Of course, they all did, heck even the doctor and the nurses probably knew.* I thought to myself, finally standing up. I could never trust anyone again, how could they all look me in the face knowing that Arlo practically led me to believe he actually liked me and then went a fucked his ex; someone he protested he hated? *Fuck the lot of them.*

I stormed over to the shower and turned the faucet, watching for a moment as steam gathered on the ceiling before crawling along it. I stripped my bloodied clothes off and threw them to the ground and stepped under the hot torrent of water. The minute the water hit me I felt refreshed and renewed. I pretended that all the hurt, lies and deceit was being washed down the plug hole with the dried blood from my hair.

After my shower I hurried back into my bedroom and rummaged through the drawers, finally deciding on some baggy lounge pants and a super baggy yoga t-shirt. I wandered over to my window bench and sat staring out as the sun slowly sank down behind the trees. I sat in silence and watched as dusk turned to night, the sky turned from blue, to orange, to pink, then to purple, before the sky was turned inky black and dotted with magnificent stars. I don't know how long I had been sitting there in my trance, but I somehow felt as though all my problems had disappeared while staring out into the black abyss. It was 8pm when I heard a knock on my bedroom door. I knew it was him. Although I had been waiting for him all day, I also didn't want to see him. But I needed answers. I was done with the lies.

'Come in.' I called trying to sound normal. Arlo came into

my room with my dinner on a silver tray. He smiled weakly and looked at me with sad eyes. *Was he being serious right now?*

'I have brought you some dinner.' He said placing it on my bedside table.

'Thanks.' I mumbled looking down at the casserole, it smelt delicious, but I just couldn't stomach any food right now. I couldn't even stomach looking at Arlo. 'I didn't realise that room service was in the alpha's job description.' I mumbled sarcastically, Arlo laughed to himself for a moment and paused.

'How are you feeling?' He asked putting his hands in his jeans pocket, he was studying my face, seeing how well I was healing.

'Dandy.' I replied sarcastically and then I stood up and faced my Alpha, my arsehole of an Alpha, my eyes burning into his. He screwed up his face and then went as white as a sheet. He knew then that I knew about him and Lori. 'Did you have a good time last night; Alpha?' I snapped, ignoring as my muscles and bones protested under each movement. Arlo closed his eyes momentarily and then sighed.

'It's not what you think happened.' He stuttered; his eyes now full of desperation. I laughed at him.

'It's exactly what I think happened, no, no, no! It's exactly what I know happened. You led me into a trap, let me think you actually liked me, let me start really liking you and then you threw me to the wolves.' *No pun intended.* I took a step closer to him. And jabbed my finger into his chest. 'You fucking had sex with her whilst I was beaten black and blue in a hospital bed below you, you acted like you hated her and then slept with her! How could I have been so stupid to have believed you?'

'Please Amelia; I never planned for that to happen. I do like you, so fucking much and I had every intention to punish Lori, I hate her, but I was stupid, and I allowed her to manipulate me, I am so sorry.' He put his hands on his head and ran his fingers through his hair. 'Please forgive me, I didn't set you up, I swear.' I didn't believe a word that came out of his mouth. And I wanted to make sure he knew that.

'I hate you.' I whispered allowing a tear to fall down my cheek. 'I really do hate you; you are a liar and just like everyone else. I should have known better, no one else could actually care for me; no one.' Tears were now falling uncontrollably from my eyes and Arlo took a step forward touching my arm. I jumped back and picked up the glass of orange juice that was next to my dinner. 'Don't touch me.' I hissed, but he didn't listen, he lightly tugged my wrist to try and get my attention, he was desperate for me to listen, but I lost it. 'I said don't touch me.' I screamed, the windows shook with my scream and I threw the glass in temper, allowing it to smash against my wall. 'Get out.'

'No, listen to me Amelia, please listen to me goddamit.' He shouted. *If he wouldn't leave, then I would.* I pushed past him, barging him with my shoulder as I went, *an action I instantly regretted,* and threw open my bedroom door, it made an awful bang, I am sure I had probably dented my bedroom wall. Arlo followed me as I stormed down the stairs. Lori and her bitch pack were standing at the bottom grinning from ear to ear.

'It was such good sex, he was so angry with me at first, but you know what a man is like when he is angry, he just needs a release and I knew he wouldn't be able to resist me.' Lori laughed, her stupid friends both giggling with her. I narrowed my gaze at her, and I saw the tiny hairs on her arms stand on end. In that moment I knew that she was scared of me. And I liked it.

I stopped on the bottom step, I had, had enough of her shit.

'That's all you will ever be; Lori, a fuck… because you have absolutely no self-respect, just like your precious little Alpha.' I said watching as the smile fell from her face. 'I am so glad you enjoyed being his *little release*, he must have been desperate.' I concluded sarcastically.

'Darling he could have had anyone in this mansion, and he chose me. Ask anyone in here, yeah admittedly he has been known to fuck a Mutt or two, but he always comes back to me.' She replied trying to make herself feel better. I heard Arlo growl loudly behind me, Matt and Piper were now standing by my side.

'Because Lori; he knows how easily you will spread your

legs, most of the other females here have some self-respect, unlike you. And like you said, he was angry. I guess he just wanted something easy and used. Looks like he got it.' I was now done arguing with this girl, she was getting on my nerves and if she said one more thing, I would seriously hurt her. I know she got the best of me yesterday, but I wasn't anywhere near as hurt as I am now. I was done.

'Face it; Amelia, you will never be good enough for him, you're an unwanted mutt and you do not belong here with us.' Lori chuckled flicking her blonde hair over her shoulder, her friends both laughed and then they froze. They were staring at me wide eyed.

I lost it; I flew off of the stairs slamming myself into her knocking her onto the perfectly polished floor. All I could hear were gasps coming from the pack members who had gathered round to watch 'the show'. Matt and Arlo pulled me away before I could stamp on her face just like she did to me.

'Get the fuck off of me.' I growled, breaking away from their grip and rushing back over to Lori who was trying to climb back to her feet. I swung my leg out and kicked her arms from under her, causing her to smack her face down onto the cold, polished marble. A sickening crunch filled the air followed by squeals of pain. I never bothered hanging around to find out the damage I had done. I ran out of the mansion, blocking out Piper and Matts calls to me. I rushed through the grounds and headed to the only place that I could think of. The Howlers Arms. The pub that *he* took me to. I pushed Arlo from my thoughts and marched forward. I needed to get shit faced.

'Um, excuse me... Miss Hunt...' Came a nervous voice from behind me. I whirled around on the spot and growled angrily.

'What?' I snapped, causing the guy rushing towards me to flinch and cower slightly. I knew immediately from his stance that he was a non-elite. My stomach dropped and I suddenly felt sick. *Great. Now he was going to think that I was just like the other Elites in this goddamn place!* 'I am so sorry. Is everything ok?' I asked, stepping forward and smiling kindly. The guy shifted a little nervously in front of me before turning his blue eyes up to meet mine.

'Um... my father asked me to bring this to you. I mean... he was going to do it, but I volunteered. I hope you don't mind. I was going to talk to you in the main hall but then you and Lori...' He paused mid-sentence and lowered his stare to his feet. He cleared his throat and held out a white box. I stared at it hesitantly for a moment as he raised his stare to meet mine once more.

'What is it?'

'Oh, sorry, I forgot that you didn't know who I was. I am Ethan Bailey. My father is Benjamin Bailey. The doctor that was treating you in the medical ward.' He replied, standing up a little straighter and grinning proudly. *The smile he held while mentioning his father melted my heart.* I reached out and took the box from him before placing my hand in his.

'Oh, so you're Ethan!' I said excitedly. 'Thank you so much for those beautiful flowers and your lovely note. It's really nice to meet you.' I replied sweetly.

'N-no... the pleasure is all mine Miss Hunt.'

'Please Ethan, call me Amelia.' Ethan's eyes widened, reminding me of a deer caught in the headlights of an oncoming truck.

'S-Sure thing Miss... I mean, Amelia.' He stammered nervously. I giggled lightly and shook my head.

'Hey Ethan... what are you doing right now?' I asked, tucking the medication in my back pocket before turning back to look at him. He offered a slight shrug and shook his head.

'Well, I have just finished my shift with my father, so now I was just going to go home. W-why's that?'

'Would you like to join me at the pub?' I asked sweetly. His face paled slightly, and I thought that he was about to pass out.

'I-I can't' He stammered once more. My smile faltered a little and his eyes widened even more; *who knew that that was even possible?* 'No... I mean... I really would love to but... it's frowned upon. I'm a Mutt. We aren't really allowed to socialise with Elites.' I clenched my teeth and shivered.

'Firstly, please do not refer to yourself as a Mutt. I hate that terminology. And secondly... my best friend is a Non-Elite. So why can't I be friends with another one?' I asked plainly. Ethan hesitated for a moment and ran his hand through his shaggy blonde hair and blew out a breath through his mouth glancing over his shoulder. *He really was a handsome guy. I was surprised that someone that looked like him was this nervous around girls. He could have literally been one of those shirtless models that they hang on posters to make girls want to buy whatever it is that they are selling.*

'I am sorry for offending you… but I will make you a deal… you promise that you are going to take your medication properly, and I will come out with you now.' He responded coolly. I rolled my eyes playfully and held my hand out in front of me.

'Deal' I said confidently. He slipped his hand into mine and I felt the slight tremble that they held but he nodded and kept eye contact with me.

'Deal! But… if you're going out drinking tonight then maybe you should start taking them in the morning? I'm not too sure that they are compatible with alcohol.' He said with a small smile. I rolled my eyes once more and nodded.

'Ok. I can do that. But… that just means that we have to get really, really drunk.' I added with a giggle and started running in the direction of the pub. I didn't need to look behind me to know that he was following.

I don't know how long we had been in the pub, but I was starting to feel the buzz from the alcohol. I sat on the bar stool, my arms rested on the counter with the stem of the wine glass pinched between my fingers, gulping back my third glass of wine. I was completely healed and ready to get drunk, I needed to block out all of the pain I was feeling. *How did I miraculously become healed? Was it the wine? Did it have healing properties? Or was it just that I was getting a little tipsy?* Either way, I didn't care.

'Another one; Amelia?' the barman asked.

'Yes please,' I smiled weakly. 'Put it on Arlo's tab, I'm sure he won't mind.' The barman nodded and smiled at me, it was the same one that served us before, I was glad he hadn't been at the mansion when everything kicked off with me and Lori, he would have probably called his Alpha to tell him where I was.

'So, is it only wine that you drink?' Ethan asked, propping himself up against the bar beside me. I pushed my empty glass across the counter so that the barman could reach it easily just in time for him to slide a fresh, full glass over to me. I sipped my wine and turned back to face my new friend.

'Well, wine is the only alcoholic drink that I have ever had so... I don't know if I like anything else.' Ethan's eyes flew open in amazement and he called the bar man over again.

'Hey Pete, can you get us 4 Jagerbombs?' He asked politely. *Ahh so that was the bar man's name... Pete. I made a note to remember that!* Pete hurried back over with a small tray containing 4 shots of brown liquid and a large glass filled with a fizzy yellowish liquid. A strong smell of liquorice and aniseed washed over me. It was so strong that it stung my nostrils a little; swiftly followed by a sweeter scent that blended the two smells together. Ethan reached into his pocket and pulled his wallet from within.

'Hey! What do you think you are doing?' I asked, glaring at him playfully. Ethan turned to look at me with a confused expression on his face.

'Um... paying?'

'No, you're not. Pete. Can you please put these drinks on Arlo's tab please? Oh, and any other drinks that this guy here buys!' I giggled, spinning around on the bar stool and fluttering my eyes to the man behind the bar. Pete hesitated for a moment before nodding.

'Of course, Miss Hunt.'

Ethan smiled to our new friend and turned back around to face me placing the shot glass and the tumbler on the counter. I looked at him in confusion as he picked up the shot glass and dropped it into the yellow liquid, causing it to fizz up slightly.

'Here. Try this. The trick is... you need to knock it back in one.' Ethan said with a proud smile. I creased my brows suspiciously for a second and watched as he followed his own instructions, gulping the entire contents of the glass in seconds. I mimicked his actions and swallowed in one go. The sweetness of the energy drink fizzed through me as the burn from the shot was like lava touching the back of my throat. I coughed lightly and Pete chuckled, handing me another one. This time I didn't hesitate, I repeated the process and swallowed it in one.

'I think I have found my new favourite drink' I giggled; my words slightly slurred. I waved Pete back over, ordering another round of Jagerbombs, as well as a beer for Ethan and a bottle of Rose for me. Just as Pete was turning away, I reached out and touched his arm, causing him to flinch. *Seriously, what did the Elites do to these guys to make them so jumpy around us?* 'Make sure you get a drink for yourself too, ok. It's on Arlo.' I giggled. Pete smiled over to me and nodded once. *I was pretty sure that he was just being polite. But I appreciated the smile.*

'Amelia, thank god you're here!' Piper gasped, bursting through the doors and running over to me, she sat next to me, trying to read my blank expression.

'What?' I asked looking at her desperate eyes.

'I just want to make sure that you're okay?' she whispered sadly.

'I am fine.' I grumbled picking up my fresh glass of wine. None of this was her fault and yet she probably felt like it was, I softened up and weakly smiled at her sad face. 'Shall we dance?' I asked, my speech only slightly slurred. Pipers face twisted in confusion for a moment before lighting up and she pulled me over to the juke box.

'What song?' she asked going through a list of romantic songs. I raised my eyebrows.

'Definitely not any of those.' I found a song perfect for my mood. 'This one.' I laughed dragging my friend onto the dance floor. I looked up at Ethan who was still sitting at the bar and nodded for him to join us. As the music started the barman dimmed the lights and put on bouncing spotlights, the colours went from Blue to Yellow to Red and then to Green. I downed my wine and put my glass on another pack members table, the alcohol had well and truly hit me, giving me a newfound confidence.

I felt Ethan's hands on my hips, as his swayed in sync with

mine in time to the music. *Wow, he really was an excellent dancer. And he was a gentleman. No matter how drunk he was, his hands never moved higher or lower than my hips.*

'Is it hot in here or is it just me?' I asked Piper, fanning my face. She nodded and watched in shock as I took my baggy jumper off throwing it over to the barman. Now all I was wearing was a belly top and comfortable lounge pants that were riding danger-ously low on my hips. But I didn't care.

Piper laughed and took my hands, we both took other pack members hands and pulled them up to dance with us, we were the only females amongst ten males, a recipe for disaster? *Who cares…? not me.* Another song came on, it was a bit more seductive then the recent ones, I climbed up onto the bar stool and placed my bare feet on the bar and pulled Ethan up to join me.

'A bottle?' I mouthed to the chuckling barman. Piper and the other pack members were all watching me with their jaws prac-tically on the dance floor. 'Come on, dance.' I squealed opening the fresh bottle of wine.

Matt walked into the bar and looked at Piper.

'What the fuck?' he mouthed his wide eyes full of amuse-ment. Piper shrugged and took her shoes off, glancing over to me and Ethan once more.

'Come on.' She called to Matt who was now sitting in his usual spot, he laughed and shook his head.

'Are you kidding? Arlo will kill me. He is probably going to hit the roof if he finds out that I am here, and this is happening.' He laughed. Piper shook her head and hurried back over to where I now stood on the bar; *Coyote Ugly style!* and joined me. We started singing at the tops of our voices. I noticed all the male pack mem-bers dancing in front of us, they were having such a great time and I was glad. *Fuck you Alpha.* I thought.

'Drink some water.' Piper said giving me a clear glass of icy water. She took a large gulp of hers and smiled. 'Go on' she nodded glancing at the pub door. I looked over and realised that Arlo had just walked in. No one else had seemed to notice; *why was I the only one?* I turned away from him and looked at the men who were all still dancing, drunk out of their faces and I poured the tall glass of water down my chest allowing it to all fall down into my bra and down my bare belly, I squealed as the water soaked my lounge pants and underwear and started jumping up and down. I turned to Arlo and sang to him, quoting a verse from G.R.L's Ugly Heart. He did not look happy with me at all, but I didn't care. He lost all of my respect when he slept with Lori and although he was my Alpha, I refused to answer to him and maybe then he would banish me from the pack, and I could be free. I jumped down from the bar and ran over to Matt, falling into his arms drunkenly, waiting as Ethan followed me and stood behind me at all times.

'Can I have a cigarette please?' I asked politely, he didn't know what to say, he just slowly pulled one out of his pack and picked up his lighter and handed them to me, looking over my shoulder at Arlo. 'Thank you.' I walked past my Alpha without even looking at him and stepped into the pub garden. I glanced over my shoulder and noticed that Matt had placed his hand on Ethan's shoulder, holding him in place. I looked at the faces of both men and they seemed to be ok. I shrugged to myself and stumbled over to the bench and dropped down onto the seat. I leant backwards and stared up at the stars above me and was taken in by their beauty. I leant further back, trying to get a good look at them when the ground came rushing to my face. *I have no idea how... who knew the earth could move like that?* I sprung up from the ground and patted the dry dirt from my clothes and stared down at my broken cigarette and shrugged. I pinched the broken part back together and smiled proudly to myself. *Who needed a man?* I tucked a stray strand of hair behind my ear and giggled to myself.

It was silent outside, and I should have been cold, but I was too hot from all the dancing I had been doing. I lit the cigarette and took in a long pull, I had smoked before, I used to steal my grandmother's cigarettes, but it wasn't a frequent thing. I sat on the pub bench and leant back on the wooden table, listening as the music inside was still thumping, slightly muffled by the brick walls.

I turned around on the spot and came face to face with an extremely angry Arlo.

'What?' I asked before taking another pull from the cigarette and blowing my smoke into his face.

'What are you doing; Amelia?' he growled.

'Smoking....' I replied knowing exactly what he meant. He clenched his jaw and took a big breath in, trying to control his anger.

'No... I mean... who the fuck falls from a bench like that?'

'What? Who did?' I asked, turning around to glance behind me feeling more than a little confused. I turned back to face him. 'Who fell'd?' I asked, his words not processing in my head. He closed his eyes and exhaled loudly.

'Fell'd isn't even a word!' He grumbled, more to himself but I answered anyway.

'Then why you say it?'

'What the fuck was that in there?' he snarled, baring his teeth at me like an angry dog. I mimicked his actions and growled pathetically.

'See... I can do that too!' I beamed proudly. His expression never changed, and I sighed. 'I was having fun; you should try's it sometime and I don't mean with your willy.' I hissed. I paused and threw my head back in laughter, giggling uncontrollably. 'Willy. Who says that?' I continued chuckling.

'Are you trying to piss me off, pay me back for what I did? This isn't you.'
I laughed at what he said.

'Wait... if I am not me... then who am I? Do you know me, *Alpha*;' I asked in confusion. I looked down at myself and noticed my white belly top that was now see through and giggled to myself. 'I think I spilled something.' I said with a slurred giggle and took another drag of my cigarette. Arlo growled once more and came storming over to me, throwing his jacket over my shoulders. I turned away, so he was facing my back, something that is very disrespectful to an Alpha and threw his jacket from my shoulders, and started walking back towards the pub.

'Do not walk away from me.' He roared grabbing my wrist. I spun around so we were toe to toe, his eyes now black.

SAM KETTLE & NATASHA SLEE

'Get off me.' I grumbled pushing against him, but he just tightened his grip.

'Please, would you just listen to me.' He begged finally loosening his grip. 'Please; Amelia, hear me out and then you can go, you can go and drink some more, you can fuck which ever man you want, just listen.' I pulled away from him and he let my wrist go.

'Fuck which ever man I want? I will have you...kn... know I am not like you. I am not Lori or your other whores you know... How many no... n Elites have you slept with...Alpha?' I said slurring my words as I poked his chest, trying my best to not fall over again.

Arlo sighed and then looked annoyed.

'The way you were in there.' He said pointing to the pub. 'You may as well have thrown yourself at them.'

I raised my eyebrows and crossed my arms sulkily.

'I was dancing! I wasn't opening my legs or giving them any reason to be... lieve I would sleep with... them; I am not you; *Alpha!* I was having such a great time, with my new friend Ethan, we were all just dancing to music and drinking and then you come and ruin it. I would never have sex with just anyone.' I turned my head to the side. 'Why did you come here? What do you... want from me? A fuck? Is that what you want Arlo? I know that is obviously all you see women for. Come on then, you want to fuck me... let's do it...now...here.' I then stopped and looked him in the eye, I had never seen him so angry. 'I hate you for what you did; leading me on to believe we could be friends, flirting with me and making me think that maybe there was something more. So, go and sleep with whoever you want, but do not pretend to be my friend, do not pretend to like me, I trusted you and I am so fucking stupid for doing so.' He was taken aback; I am not sure if it was the fact that I said I hated him or if it was because I told him that I had thought that we could have been more than friends or that I managed to say a whole sentence without slurring my speech, but a pained expression spread across his perfect face.

'All I want is for you to hear me out.' He said sternly.

'And I do not care for your explantation. I don't care that you shagged your ex, that's you're prerogative' I lied. 'What I do care about is, that you made me feel like you cared about me, you made me care about you and I don't want to care about you, it just leads to me hurting and everyone mocking me.' I bit back the tears; I would not let him see me cry. 'Go home Alpha; your whore is waiting for you.'

He looked upset and put his head down, he was ashamed of himself.

'I do care about you... a lot. I have never felt like this for anyone ever, not even with Lori and we were together for two years.'
I rolled my eyes, why the hell did he have to say her name, I hated it, I hated her, and I hated this whole situation. I shook my head and almost felt sad for him.

'I don't want to hear it; I don't believe anything you say. I don't want you near me. And I *definitely* don't want you "ruling" me as my alpha!'

'Hey, is everything alright out here?' Ethan asked, appearing in the doorway of the pub and looking between Arlo and Me.

'Go back inside Mutt, this doesn't concern you.' Arlo growled, his golden eyes flashing as he used his full force alpha's influence.

'Don't you fucking speak to him like that!' I snarled, raising my face to meet his. He leant forward and his eyes flashed with the alpha's influence once more.

'Get back to the mansion and go to bed!' He ordered. I froze on the spot for a moment as he stared down at me and his golden eyes swirled hypnotically. I leant in a little closer to him, so close that I could feel his body heat rolling off of him in waves; raising my hand and pointing in his face.

'Oh woooow... I never knew that they did that. They look like glitter! Do it again.' I squealed excitedly jumping up and down on the spot. Arlo pulled back a little and stared down at me in confusion, the glittering glow fading from his eyes. 'Hey! I said do it again... not stop it!' I said with a pout.

'Get back to the mansion. Now!' He growled. I turned on

my heel and started stumbling back towards the pub. He lunged forward and grabbed my wrist once more, twirling me around back in the direction of the mansion. I let out a growl of frustration and started staggering back to the mansion. And then the ground did that thing again. *It met my face once more.*

I hopped back up to my feet with a loud "Woo hoo" and giggled to myself before stumbling backwards once again and falling on my arse. Arlo closed his eyes and stomped over to me, shaking his head. Before grabbing my arm and flipping me over his shoulder and began carrying me back to the mansion. The world around me began to spin and a strange feeling built up in the pit of my stomach. I opened my mouth to warn Arlo what was about to happen, but it was too late. I puked all down his back causing him to stop in his tracks. *It wouldn't stop.* The river of vomit gushed from my mouth, coating his back and the backs of his legs. I stopped and slowly raised my head.

'Lovely.' Arlo grumbled, before continuing his trek back to the mansion.

'I feel sick.' I slurred, before flopping back over his shoulder.

No, you've been sick.' he mumbled. I felt the world begin to spin once more and this time I gave in to the darkness.

7

Arlo;

I scooped Amelia up from the ground and threw her over my shoulder. *I knew that I shouldn't have spoken to that Mutt in the way that I did, I would have to apologise to him in the morning.* Amelia kicked her legs out and slapped my arse in attempt to break free. I tightened my grip on her slightly, so I didn't drop her. She shouted something behind my back, but I couldn't make out the words. *Seriously, how much had she had to drink?* Her whole body tensed, and she fell quiet. I was just about to ask if she was ok when she threw up all down my back. I stopped walking and stood still, waiting for the seemingly endless river of vomit to stop, feeling the warm watery substance run from the small of my back down my legs.

'Lovely.' I grumbled to myself closing my eyes and trying my hardest to block what was happening from my mind. Amelia sat up a little and slurred.

'I feel sick.' *No shit sherlock!* She flopped back down against my back and fell still once more.

'No, you've been sick. Lia… a-are you ok?' I asked, still unmoving. I waited a few more seconds for her to answer and when she didn't, I asked again. 'Amelia! I said are you ok?' Still… nothing. I flipped her from my shoulder and laid her in both arms. She was out. Her gentle snores causing her chest to rise and fall lightly. *She really was the most beautiful woman I had ever seen… even if she has just emptied the contents of her stomach down my back.*

I stared down at her sleeping form for a second and a swirl of anger ripped through me. *I was such a fucking fool;* she didn't believe me when I told her I cared about her and I don't blame her. I had broken her trust, and apparently her heart. I tilted my head back and stared up at the waning moon.

'Selene, what have I done?' I mumbled, anger bubbling in my chest as I refused to look away from the glowing beauty overhead. No matter how hard I tried, I couldn't get over seeing her in the pub, standing on the bar dressed in next to nothing, she didn't see the excited looks the pack members were giving her, the way that they were watching as her body moved to the music, wondering which one would take her home, she was just so innocent. And then there was that Mutt, he had his hands all over her. *I would definitely be speaking to him about this when I apologised for the way I spoke to him.* That was not the appropriate way for one of them to interact with an Elite!

I shook my head at myself remembering her painful words *I hate you.* It stung because she had every right to hate me. I; her Alpha, had let her down, she wouldn't even call me by my name now, it was just *Alpha.* No body called me Alpha, I hated them calling me that. *But still, there was something in the way that she said it that just left me… weak.*

The rest of the walk back to the mansion was quiet, and solemn. I hated feeling this way. But I deserved it. As bad as I am feeling now, I knew that she was feeling worse, and that was all down to me. *And if she thought that she was feeling bad now, she will soon learn the effects of drinking in the morning!*

I paused at my bedroom door and rummaged in my pocket for the key before carefully pushing the door open. *There was no way that I could leave her alone while she was in this state.* I hurried over to the bed, kicking the door closed behind me and carefully laid her on top of it. I stared down at her soaking wet see through belly top and her muddy lounge pants. I plucked one of my clean t-shirts from the drawer behind me and pulled it over her head, and then carefully slipped her wet top off, weaving it through the neck of my tee and over her head. I then removed her lounge pants. I scooped Amelia up in my arms once more and placed her in my bed. The alcohol had succeeded in knocking her out, it was 3am, she needed to sleep, something I knew I wouldn't be doing at all. I strolled over to my bathroom and pulled my vomit-soaked t-shirt over my head and dropped it to the tile floor with a wet *smack*. I reached into my shower and turned it on before sliding my jeans off and kicking them over to where the t-shirt lay with a slight shudder. I stared at the water running from the shower head for a few moments and sighed, hoping to wash my sins away under the hot, running water.

After washing, *four times, why did I still smell of puke?* I hurried back out into my room and threw on nothing but my loose tracksuit bottoms and paced my room, trying to think of something to do; some way to make it up to her, it was no use, I wasn't going to be able to find the right answers without speaking to her.

I opened my balcony doors and stepped onto the concrete foundation barefoot, into the cold nights air. I heard quiet, muffled sobs and whimpers and glanced back through my open door; it was Amelia, she was tossing and turning in my bed. She was hurting. And it was all my fault. Sleeping with Lori was not my intention, it was far from it. I was furious that she didn't give Amelia a chance to defend herself, only a weak wolf needed the help of others in a fight, and they pinned Amelia down so Lori could do damage. It was pathetic and dirty.

After me and Matt rushed Amelia to the health centre, I collared Adela and Harper, threatening that if they ever pull a stunt like that again, they would be out of the pack for good and they would have to live as Deviants; but getting rid of Lori? Well that would cause an uproar. Her parents were not only Elite's, but they were important to the Packs running, we needed them more than I cared to admit.

I called Lori into my office, she was so proud of herself, grinning from ear to ear until she saw my face.

'Is everything ok daddy wolf?' she asked playing dumb and fluttering her eyes lashes at me.

'Are you fucking kidding me Lori, you beat the shit out of her! You didn't even give her a chance to fight back, using your stupid friends as restraints so that she was defenceless against you. What sort of wolf uses others to pin someone down just to over-power them? Its dirty. And that is *not* how this pack runs!' I watched as she started sulking, crossing her arms and narrowing her eyes at me. I could tell there was about to be one of Lori's famous tan-trums, but I honestly didn't care.

'She started it!' She hissed through clenched teeth.

'How? What did she ever do to you?' I roared clenching my fists, I wanted to hurt her, show her what it felt like to be over-powered. But I couldn't, a good Alpha would never do that to a pack member, no matter if they were the scum of the earth or not.

'She has taken you away from me, as soon as she came here you have been different. You stopped coming to my bed, stopped caring about me.' Lori looked hurt but she was twisting everything.

'How could she take me away, when I was never yours? I told you I didn't want to sleep with you anymore, that there is nothing there for you. I don't love you. How many times do I have to say it? But you just won't take no for an answer, *'It's okay Alpha it's just sex, I know there is nothing in it.'* It's my fault, I shouldn't have been so thick to believe you actually thought that.' I sat in my chair and stared at Lori, she was once a nice girl, a shy girl and then, she came into her shifting abilities and her true colours came out. She became obsessed with becoming Luna, convincing herself that I would imprint on her. *As if it worked that way!*

She slowly dropped her arms down from her chest and walked over to me, unbuttoning her pink dress; she had nothing on underneath, no bra and no panties. *Was this girl serious?*

'Stop Lori.' I growled as she slowly placed her bare bottom on my crotch, she looked at me seductively, but it wasn't working, I was just getting even more pissed off. 'Stop' I shouted knocking her to the floor. There was nothing I could do to stop it. I felt myself harden beneath my trousers and Lori's eyes widened with excitement.

She pathetically rolled over onto all fours and slowly began crawling back over to me, *this bitch is mental.*

'Come on Alpha; do it, I know you want to, she ran her fingers up my legs, gently massaging my thighs, before slowly pulling down the zipper on my fly. As ashamed as I was to admit it, the mere action caused me to pulse. I needed release and I needed it now. I watched as she slowly dragged her long nails over the bulge in my trousers, before undoing the button and slowly pulling them down to my knees. The minute she saw me stood there in my boxers her face flushed, and her eyes flared. I knew that she wanted it. She turned her eyes up to meet mine and slowly began kissing up my legs and then standing up so that we were eye level.

I literally wanted to smash her head against a wall. Anger ripped through me and my inner wolf emerged, I grabbed her shoulders, spinning her around and pushing her over the desk, I pulled my throbbing dick out of my trousers and shoved myself inside her, I had been completely taken over, I couldn't control myself. But I should have.

Lori was wet the minute that I entered, groaning loudly, she pretended like the sex was good, faking an orgasm as loud as she could. It was off putting, looking at her and I couldn't even see her face. She made me feel sick, I couldn't cum, I just wanted her gone. I pulled out and turned away.

'That is the last time I ever do that.' I mumbled putting myself away and turning away from her in disgust.

'Yeah, we will see.' She cackled, scooping her dress up from the floor before putting it back on.

'Don't you get it? You're just a fuck, a lousy one at that. Get the hell out of my office now.' I snapped, not caring about the brief look of hurt in her eyes. I shouldn't have slept with her. At the time it was kill her or shag her to just get her away from me, both options were wrong. It wouldn't have been a problem for me to just pick her up and throw her out of my office, naked or not. I wish I had done it. But I was stupid!

I stood staring out into the darkness until the sun started rising, the sky filled with beautiful shades of purple pink and orange, I wished Amelia could see it too. Amelia's whimpers stopped at around 4:30 am, but my heart hurt. I wished I could have made her feel better, have her listen to how sorry I was, but she *hated* me. *And I didn't blame her.*

The faint sound of thunder rumbled in the distance and I stood there for a moment, watching the forked lightning streak across the top of the trees. I felt a rain drop land on my foot and then it was as though someone had turned the taps on. Water fell from the black clouds above me, falling harder than I had ever seen before. I stood in the downpour for a moment and realised that I was drenched. It was freezing, even for a werewolf; usually the cold never bothered us. I growled in frustration to myself and turned, heading back into my room. All this pacing was pointless. I knew that I needed to get some sleep. I couldn't let the pack see me looking worn out. They need an alpha who is strong and alert. I tugged off my soaking bottoms and tossed them into my bathroom, listening as they plopped on the tiled floor, before climbing onto the sofa on the opposite side of the room from Amelia and flicking off the light, I laid there in darkness staring up at the ceiling until sleep finally claimed me.

I opened my eyes and glanced over to my bed. Amelia was still sleeping soundly, and at least now she looked a little more peaceful. I hurried from my make-shift bed on the sofa and threw on some clothes before hurrying down to the dining hall to meet my parents by the door. *As tired and worried as I was about Amelia, I still had my pack duties and rules to follow.* I would be sure to send someone up to come and check on her. *Possibly that Mutt, Piper.*

By the time that I reached the dining hall my parents were already standing there glaring at me impatiently. I threw them a casual smile and run my hand through my ruffled black hair, pushing it out of my eyes. My mother wouldn't even look at me, she had obviously heard what had happened. I should have expected it but; I kept glancing over to her to catch her attention, but it was no use.

'Morning.' I mumbled, trying to act normal. They both turned away from me and stood back to face the door. *Oh shit. They knew!* The dining hall doors opened, and I noticed the way that my mother kept looking at Amelia's empty chair and knew in that moment that that I had royally fucked up.

Breakfast dragged; it was so weird not having her sitting their bedside me. It took everything in my power to not just walk out and go and be with her. But I knew that I did not have that choice. The moment that breakfast was over, I hurried over to Piper and pulled her to the side.

'Hey, would you do me a favour and go and check on Amelia please?' I asked, pulling my bedroom key from my pocket and offering it out to her. Pipers eyes widened and she glanced around anxiously. It was extremely unusual for a Mutt to be in the Elites living quarters; *especially the alpha's*, but I knew that Piper was one of the only people in this place that Amelia trusted, and right now, making sure that she was comfortable was my main priority.

'B-but... I have to work.' She replied, her voice quiet and nervous. I flashed her a smile and shook my head.

'Honestly, it's fine. I will tell them that you are doing a job that I have requested.' Piper nodded and carefully took the key from me before turning and rushing from the room.

I watched as the auburn-haired girl rushed from the dining hall; it was so hard to focus on anything other than Amelia, and I knew that that wasn't healthy. Why had I suddenly grown that attachment to her? It wasn't like we were imprinting. If we were, we would both know it. I had known this girl for not even a week and yet it was obvious there was something between us, how is that even possible? There was just something about her, something intriguing and luring me in.

Amelia;
I opened my eyes and stared up at the ceiling. What the hell had happened last night? I sat up and felt as the room danced around me, causing a wave of nausea to hit me. I dropped my head into my hands as I fought the urge to be sick and attempted to quell the pounding behind my eyes. *Why was it so bright in here?* The last thing that I remembered about last night was dancing with Ethan on the bar and then... *Oh shit!* I looked at the room around

me and blinked a few times before glancing down at myself. *Whose clothes am I wearing? And who's room am I in?*

I looked around the room once more in attempt to figure out where I was and then I spotted the family photo hanging on the wall. *Arlo!* I dropped back onto the pillows and closed my eyes. *Please do not tell me that I had sex with him last night. How did I even end up in here?* I wasn't ready to talk to him yesterday and I still wasn't ready today, all I wanted to do was go to see Pretty Girl, I had so much to tell her. I climbed from the bed as carefully as I could and searched for my clothes. I stumbled into his bathroom and glanced down at the vomit-soaked clothes on the floor. *Oh god! Was that me?*

A knocking at the door snapped me from my thoughts and I started to panic. *What if it was Lori coming back for round two?* My stomach clenched and I thought that I was going to be sick. *Again.* When the sound of the key turning in the lock had me holding my breath and standing completely still.

'L-Lia…' Came a friendly familiar voice. I threw open the bathroom door and hurried over to my best friend pulling her further into the room.

'Oh thank goddess it's you.' I cried, with a heavy sigh. Piper screwed her face up in confusion and looked me up and down. 'Don't ask!' I muttered, tugging the bottom of the t-shirt a little lower, suddenly feeling very exposed.

'Ook. Um… Arlo asked me to come up and check that you were ok…' She paused for a second and glanced over to the un-made bed. 'Um… Lia… did you two…' She paused and offered an uneasy smile.

'Pipes… I have no idea! I don't remember anything. What the hell happened last night?' I asked, hoping that she would be able to fill in some of the blanks. She offered an unsure shrug and helped me find my clothes before hurrying back into my room. 'I need to know what happened, what did I do?' I asked glancing at Piper who was rummaging through my wardrobe.

'Well you and Ethan went to the pub, I met you there and then Matt turned up and th-'

'No I remember all of that, but what happened after I was dancing on the bar? That is literally the last thing I remember.' I croaked putting my head in my hands. *Man my head ached so bad.*

Piper sighed and turned to look at me.

'Arlo turned up and he saw you on the bar with Ethan... he was furious.' I looked back up at my friend in confusion. *Why was he furious? He had no right to be after what he did.* 'If I am honest Lia, I think you need to talk to Arlo about what happened. You went outside and he followed and then after a while me and Matt went and checked on you both, but you had gone.' I sighed heavily; I didn't want to talk to him. He was a complete idiot and everything about him infuriated me! *But... he was still the alpha and there were rules that had to be followed!*

With the help of Piper; I made an effort with my clothes today; I would do anything in attempt to make myself feel better. After going through my entire wardrobe we settled on black skinny jeans and a lose fitting Grey jumper, I pulled on my blue glittery wellies and waited as Piper did my make-up; anxiously trying to cover the bags under my eyes, but decided to go with an overly large pair of sunglasses that covered the majority of my face to complete my look... *and shield my eyes from the incredibly bright lights.*

Creeping out was a lot harder than I thought it would be, the staff were in and out of the dining area and kitchen continuously, the smell of the waffles was filling the air and making my stomach churn, I couldn't face food and I would have rather died than go in that room and seeing all the pitiful looks that I was undoubtedly going to get. Finally, I stepped outside, I had missed Pretty Girl so much, I had felt bad that I hadn't seen her for a little while, she must have been so sad in those stables by herself.

I walked towards the stables; my bright blue wellies were squelching in the wet mud as I took each step. I guess that it must have rained pretty hard sometime between my falling asleep and waking up this morning. I looked up at the sky, dark grey clouds were heading towards the mansion grounds, it looked as though it was going to pour down. I reached the stables and instantly saw

Pretty Girl's head, peaking over the stable door.

'It looks like me and you will be chilling together in the stables today; Pretty girl' I called walking towards the dark brown wooden gate. I heard a happy *neighhhhhhhhhh*, as I unlocked the rusty bolt. 'Hello, my angel' I whispered, walking through the fresh hay and throwing my arms around my horses' neck. Pretty girl seemed to be happy, the stables here were big enough for her to walk around without her feeling too trapped and the back of them led onto a seemingly endless field of grass. She had a lovely home, but I knew deep down, that it wasn't enough. *Was I referring to myself or Pretty Girl now? Possibly both?*

I've missed you' I whispered placing my head against her long soft neck, taking in her softness against my skin. She nudged her head towards me as if to say she had missed me too. Her grey eyes twinkling in the dim sunlight. I had never noticed her eyes before; they were very unusual but so beautiful. 'So much has happened.' I said sadly. I slowly wandered over to the large hay bales in the corner of the room and watched as Pretty Girl laid down on the ground beside me.

I sat and told her everything, she was silent the whole time, but I felt as though she was listening to me, I am sure she was listening to me.

'So basically; Arlo is a prick, I should have never trusted him... and I am never drinking alcohol again!' I finished, laughing as she nodded her head up and down. 'I am glad you think so too, would you like to go for a run in the field?' Pretty Girl hopped up onto her feet and reared backward gleefully. I wandered over to the open back of the stables and watched as she dashed back and forth in the field.

She looked so happy; it must have been so nice for her to stretch her legs. I started daydreaming again, I had the perfect opportunity to run and if I was going to do it, now would have been the time, but something was stopping me. I couldn't bring myself to leave, why? I don't know but the thought of it this time hurt.

A rumble of thunder filled the grey sky, snapping me abruptly out of my thoughts, I looked at my watch, it was 9:30,

Pretty girl had been running around for an hour but she didn't stop when the storm hit, it never bothered her at all, which was unusual because I was sure horses were scared of storms.

I let her run around for a bit longer, but the rain had just gotten too heavy; and I could have sworn that I noticed her coat was sparkling, as though she was coated in some form of glitter; although I was sure that it was just my eyes being tricked by the rain and the occasional flash of lightning. I ran out into the field, the rain falling so hard that it stung my skin whenever it hit, within seconds I was saturated and so was she. I hurried over to her and took in the gleeful look that was on her face. She was loving every minute of this. I placed my hands on her slick mane and she turned to look me in the eyes. The minute she looked at how wet I was she shook and galloped back over to the stable. I stood there motionless for a moment and smiled to myself, before running after her, heading back into the shelter of the stable.

The sound of the stable gates opening had me spinning around on the spot and staring at the entrance. My chest tightened as anxiety filled me. *Please Goddess, do not let that be Arlo!* I pleaded silently.

'Hello?' Came a familiar male voice as his silhouette filled the door frame. With a heavy sigh I felt my entire body relax.

'Ethan! How are you?' I asked, dropping down onto one of the hay bales and folding my arms across my chest.

'More to the point, how are you?' He asked with a chuckle. I glanced down at myself and realised that I was completely soaked from head to foot, and my hair was hanging down around my face like rat tails. With an embarrassed chuckle, I scooped my hair over one shoulder and tried my best to hide the blush that was creeping across my face.

'I am good… I think. Although, I thought that I was dying this morning.' He chuckled once more and offered a wry smile.

'Sorry, I guess that is my fault. I should have warned you about the way that those Jager's just hit you.' He paused for a moment and his smile faltered and a sadness filled his eyes. 'Hey, I um… I just wanted to apologise about last night. You know… when you and Arlo were arguing outside the pub. I wanted to come and help but... I couldn't... especially once he had ordered me to do something. I tried to fight it; I really did... but...' He paused and dropped his stare to the hay covered ground. *Oh, I remember now. Arlo and I were arguing, and then he shouted at Ethan... then... the glittering eyes!*

'Ethan... you don't have to apologise! The only one that needs to apologise around here is Arlo! He had no right to speak to you in that way!' I said, the irritation in my voice causing my words to come out short and sharp. I leapt to my feet and stepped towards him but was distracted as my phone clattered to the ground. We both paused for a moment, glancing at one another before both dropping to the ground to retrieve it. The moment that we both leant forward, our heads collided causing up both to flinch backwards.

'I am so sorry!' We both cried in unison, looking up and staring into one another's eyes. I never noticed how there were so many different flecks of blue in his eyes. He really was beautiful. I felt the burn of desire rush to my cheeks and turned my face away from him and busied myself drying pretty girl off with a towel I noticed was hanging nearby. I then made sure that I fed her some corn and oats. We both stood in silence as I worked until I turned back around to see him staring at me.

'Lia... I...' He started taking a step towards me. I held my breath as he closed the distance between us and raised a hand to my cheek. His touch was warm against my cool wet skin, and I felt the corners of my mouth twitch up into a smile. A loud crack of thunder had me flinching and stepping back from his touch. I closed my eyes as a war raged inside my own head. *Everything in me in that moment wanted him to kiss me.*

'I... I better get back.' I stammered, hurrying past him and back out into the torrential rain. I fought back the tears as they threatened to fall from my eyes. *At least in this weather no one would be able to tell that I was crying.* When a strong hand gripped my wrist and spun me back around to face them. I looked up into Ethan's kind eyes as he slowly ran his hand up my arm, not stopping until he reached my neck. We stared at one another once more and this time we didn't try to fight it. A flash of lightning illuminated the greyness for a second, just as our lips crashed together. The kiss was soft, passionate and full of desire, and I gave myself over to the happiness that I was feeling in that moment. I ran my hands through his soaked, shaggy hair and tangled it in my fingers, pulling his lips down onto mine harder. Every bit of darkness and sorrow that I had felt was gone in that moment. Just like someone turning off a tap, the rain stopped and the first glimmer on the mid-afternoon sun peeked out around the black thunder clouds that had been there only moments before.

We stepped back from one another and smiled awkwardly, as our cheeks flushed. I tucked a tangle of stray hair behind my ears and glanced over my shoulder to the stables once more.

'I better get going, I need to get the rest of these deliveries sorted for my dad. I just wanted to make sure that you were ok.' He said still smiling.

'Thank you, Ethan… for everything I mean.' I stepped forward and placed a kiss on his cheek before turning and walking back to the mansion. On my way there I noticed Lori walking in my direction; no doubt going to the pub to get the gossip on me. Her blonde hair was tied up in tight ponytail, and she was wearing a Mustard yellow dress with black tights and brown boots, with a large umbrella held over her head. As we got closer to each other I noticed the dirty look she was giving me, was she going to start another argument? I did not have the energy nor patience for her bullshit today, thankfully she walked straight past me, I noticed her bitch pack weren't with her this time. Surprise, surprise, she had nothing to say when they were not around. I also noticed the swollen nose and two black eyes; I had a feeling that was something to do with me. *Good!* She stormed passed me and never bothered looking back. Wherever she was going, she was determined to get there in a hurry. Either that or she really was just a coward.

I rolled my eyes and smiled to myself. *Now that is the true definition of a bully. When they are on their own, they are nothing!* I continued walking towards the mansion to be greeted by Marie, opening her arms and pulling me in for a hug.

'Sweetheart, you are soaked to the bone! How are you feeling this morning?' She asked giving me a knowing smile. *Oh shit. She knows about what happened last night!*

'I am ok thank you. A little… tender I guess… but other than that I am fine.'

'Did you see that those beautiful flowers were sent up to your room? I had Arlo take them up for you.' She paused for a moment and took a step closer to me. 'I was hoping that it would teach him the way a man should act when a young woman is unwell.' She said with a beaming smile. I chuckled, her words taking me by surprise. 'Anyway, don't let me keep you out here, go and get yourself warmed up and into something a little warmer.' Marie leant forward and kissed my cheek softly and then stepped aside allowing me to pass her by.

The hallway was silent, it took me back to mine and Arlo's argument and everything that had happened, I wished I could change rooms, but I knew he wouldn't let me. I wondered how Matt was doing, I left without saying goodbye to him last night although I was a little worse for wear! I turned to my door and put my hands in my pockets. I couldn't find my key.

'Oh shit' I mumbled looking down at the red carpeted floor, I searched my jeans pockets again, but my key wasn't there.

'Looking for this?' I jumped and turned around.

'Would you stop doing that!' I scolded glaring at Arlo angrily, he was holding my gold key in his left hand, his right hand was in his trousers pocket.

'Doing what?' he asked looking confused.

'Creeping up behind me and then saying something' I hissed staring at him angrily through my sunglasses.

'Would you rather me creep up behind you and stay silent?' He asked sarcastically. I stomped forward and snatched my key from his hand ignoring his stupid question.

'Anyway, shouldn't you be in a meeting?' I snapped. Arlo put his hand through his hair.

'Yeah, I should but I am too tired today.' He answered with

a shrug, acting like nothing was wrong. I rolled my eyes and turned to open my door, but I felt his warm hand on my waist, and I froze.

'Wait, can we talk?' he asked.

'Not really no, I am soaking wet, freezing cold, and we have nothing to talk about. You did what you did, there is nothing more to say.' I mumbled before pausing. 'Actually...there is something I wanted to talk to you about... last night?'

'What about it?' he asked smirking slightly. *How dare he smirk, this wasn't funny! I had alcohol induced amnesia and he had the cheek to smile about it.*

'You know what! Why am I so sore and why was I in your bed? And how did my clothes end up on your bathroom floor? Did we... have... you know... *sex*?' I asked looking down at the floor in embarrassment. His eyes widened in shock for a moment before he laughed once more stepping closer to me. *Did he seriously think that this was funny? He was sick!*

'Amelia... if we were going to...' He paused and leant in a little closer to me and in a mock whisper added; '*have sex*, I would much rather the recipient be fully aware and remember it!' He said with a dry laugh. I narrowed my eyes and never said a word. Arlo let out an exasperated sigh. 'You are sore because you "fell'd" ...' Arlo said trying to contain a chuckle.

'Fell'd? That isn't even a word.' I snapped crossing my arms across my chest.

'Well according to you last night; it was.' He sighed and lent against his bedroom door. 'You fell over; a couple of times actually... in your drunken state.' I rolled my eyes at him and then started rubbing my shoulder, it still ached a little...well that explains that, but it didn't explain why I was in his bed.

'So... are you going to tell me how I ended up in your bed?' I asked feeling even more embarrassed, *damn it; Amelia.*

'You were in my bed because I was worried you would choke on your own vomit in the night; not that I think there would have been much left in you... especially after how much you were sick down my back.' He said, his face showing his un-amusement. I tried to stop the smile from escaping my lips.

'I threw up on you?' I giggled, *I wish I had been half conscious for that, especially after the way he spoke to Ethan! Why was I remembering all the bad bits but not the good bits!*

'So that is why you were in my bed and no we didn't have sex.' He sighed, he looked so angry that I laughed at him. I breathed out a sigh of relief.

'Thank goddess for that!' I blushed as I looked up at Arlo. 'I am going to go now but thanks for finding my key.' I muttered, turning away from him and slotting the key into the lock.

I entered the room without saying another word and pressed my back up against the door, listening as he went into his room. I felt guilty and I didn't really know why, I had nothing to feel guilty about and yet the awful feeling wouldn't go away. Was it because I cared about him, that I could see through my anger and pain, was I willing to forgive?

I must have fallen asleep still sitting with my back against the door because a loud *tap, tap, tap* woke me from my sleep.

'Who is it?' I croaked forcing myself to stand up, I yawned and stretched my arms out, I still hadn't got changed. My clothes were still damp, and I was frozen to my core. It felt as though my bones had turned to ice.

'Its Matt.' A familiar voice called.

'And me!' piper said softly. I opened the door to my two new friends and forced a smile at them. They were both holding silver trays, one had a cup of tea and biscuits on it with a note and the other had pancakes and waffles. My stomach grumbled begging me to eat, I stepped aside letting them come in my room.

'How are you feeling?' Matt asked taking the old tray still with my dinner from yesterday on it and putting the new one down.

'Like shit.' I replied before taking a sip of my tea. It was sweet and hot, and just the thing that I needed after being still in my wet clothes. Matt reached forward and twiddled a clump of my wet, rat-tail hair between his fingers and raised his eyebrows questioningly. I offered a wry smile and a shrug before turning my attention to Piper, who had automatically started picking up the glass off of my carpet. I had intended on doing it myself when I got back, but then I guess I just was overtaken with exhaustion.

'Leave it; Piper, I will do that in a minute.'

'It's okay, you eat. You must be famished; its midday and you haven't eaten since yesterday morning.' She was right, I hadn't, and I was starving.

'Piper; please leave it, I will do it once I have eaten. Both of you take a seat, you don't need to stand up.' I smiled reassuringly, both Matt and Piper sat on the settee and looked at me with saddened eyes. I picked up the note and looked at the little message scribbled on it. *I am sorry. Xx* When would he just give up? I glanced back up at my friends, reading the expressions on their faces; I know they both had things to say. 'Go on.' I said looking at Matt.

'I am sorry I didn't tell you about Arlo and Lori, but he begged me not to say anything, he wanted to tell you himself.' He said running his fingers through his dark hair. Piper went as white as a sheet and started chewing the inside of her cheek. I wouldn't tell anyone that she had told me; she was my friend and it meant a lot that she did.

'It's okay, Arlo is your best friend, I completely get it and I respect you for it.' I smiled before snatching up one of the waffles coated in melted chocolate and nibbling on the edge; *I was trying to force myself to be civilised while I had guests. If they were not there, I probably would have been eating it like a beast.*

'Do you think you will talk to him again?' Matt asked raising his eyebrows.

'I don't really have much choice, do I? After all he is the Alpha and I have to live alongside him until he lets me leave.' I said before drinking down the rest of my tea.

'I think you should hear him out; Lia. He really is sorry; I know Arlo, and I have never seen him like this. He hasn't eaten all day and even cancelled a meeting, which he has never done before. I know he has hurt you, I would be gutted too, but Lori is a malicious and calculated bitch, she knew what she was doing. He actually came to the pub to talk to you and apologise last night but you were so drunk that it just wasn't the right time.' Matt said, desperation on his face, it was so clear to see how much he cared about and valued Arlo, not just his Alpha but his best friend too.

Piper finally spoke out. 'Yes but, Arlo isn't all that innocent, he did think with his ding dong and he really didn't need to.' I laughed at her choice of words before I could stop myself. *Ding dong.*

'Yes, he did.' Matt agreed 'But I spoke to him and it wasn't the romp she is making it out to be. Trust me. And I would like to point out that, he wasn't leading you into a trap; Amelia, none of this was planned.'

'Yes, but that's not the point; Matthew, he shouldn't have even entertained the idea and plus god knows who else she has been with and what diseases she might have.' Piper screwed up her face in disgust at the thought of what she had said. Matt bit his lip, obviously trying to keep a straight face.

'All I am saying, is that Amelia needs to talk to him and listen to what he has to say, rather than being so stubborn.' Matt glared at me nodding his head towards my bedroom door.

'She can't go and talk to him looking like that! We need to get her to look amazing and re do her makeup and hair first.' Piper squealed clapping her hands in excitement.

'Piper.' Matt grumbled.

'Yes?' she replied.

'Don't ever call me Matthew again.'

'Hey! I am sitting here you know!' I snapped, glaring at my two friends. They both turned their faces back towards me and sat like two deer caught in the headlights of a speeding vehicle.

I burst out laughing, *something I didn't think that I would be able to do again*, these two crazy friends of mine lifted my mood without even meaning to. They both had valid points and Matt was right, I should hear Arlo out and Piper was right, I shouldn't go looking like I had been dragged through a hedge backwards. Matt watched as Piper went through all my clothes, he was pulling faces at everything she held up.

'Move over, you deal with the hair and makeup and I will deal with the outfit.' He said jumping up and playfully nudging her out of his way with his hip. I watched Matt for a moment, seeing a side of him that I hadn't noticed before. There was something different about him, I just hadn't quite worked out what it was yet. I shook my head and cleared my throat.

'And I will pick up this glass.' I said getting on my knees, trying to find little pieces that would be easily missed. I managed to find nearly everything before I cut my hand. 'Fuck!' I yelped standing up, I still had loads of glass in both hands, and a large shard sticking out from my palm. Blood was pooling around it and collecting in my palms. *Oh man, this was a deep one.* Matt and Piper both rushed over to me.

'Put the glass in the bin and then we can have a look at how deep it is.' Piper said running into the bathroom. I did as my friend instructed and dropped the remaining glass into the waste basket, trying to stop blood from going all over the floors and walls. I turned back to face Piper as she hurried over with some tissue and inspected my wound.

'Ooh. This is a nasty one!' She whispered to herself. She turned her worried stare to meet mine and sighed. 'Lia, I think that you should go down to the medic ward. This looks pretty nasty!' She added, looking over my shoulder to Matt. I shook my head and pinched the large piece of glass between two fingers and sucked in a deep breath. *1, 2...* I yanked on the glass, dislodging it from my hand, causing burning pain to shoot up my wrist. I clenched my teeth and gulped down air through the pain.

'Lia!' Piper exclaimed, rushing forward and holding the tissue tightly against my open wound. She lifted the tissue slightly and gasped. I pulled my hand free from her grip and watched as the muscle, tissue, and sinew stitched itself back together. *What the fuck?*

'I-Is this normal for werewolves?' I asked with a nervous chuckle. Matt and Piper glanced at one another and shook their heads, speechless.

'Um, no. That's not normal at all.' Matt whispered, still staring down at the now scar-like mark on my palm. Piper wiped at the still tacky blood that was sitting in my hand and shook her head,

'Lia, why don't you go and have a shower? Maybe warm

yourself up a little? I think that I am just going to hoover up the rest of the glass.' She said, her voice flat and stunned. Matt rushed over to the wardrobe once more and pulled some clothes from within.

'I'm going to see if Arlo is alright.' Matt said laying an emerald green long sleeve belly top and a pair of dark blue ankle grazer jeans on my bed. I watched in silence as my two friends fled from the room like I was about to infect them with a terminal illness. *What the actual fuck? What is happening to me?*

By the time that I had had my shower, my two friends were back, sitting on the edge of my bed and talking in hushed whispers to one another. The moment that they heard the bathroom door open, they leapt up from the bed and turned to smile at me awkwardly.

'Ok, seriously guys, what is going on? Why do you keep looking at me like that?' I asked. They glanced at one another and plastered their faces and shook their heads. I narrowed my eyes at the pair of them as Piper hurried over to my vanity table, grabbing my hairdryer and gesturing for me to come and take a seat. I sighed softly and did as she instructed.

Piper blow dried my hair and did my makeup. And I had to say that she had done a really good job. Being a waitress for the pack wasn't fair on her, she had a talent, they should allow her to leave for a while and go to college. Give her a chance to have a dream. Why should she be forced to work for people that thought that it was ok to call her a Mutt?

Matt left the room once more as I got dressed. I pulled the top and jeans on that he had picked out for me and slipped on a pair of green dolly shoes. My nerves were playing havoc with my bladder.

'Go on.' Piper grinned, ushering me out of my door, Matt had just come back to my room.

'I told him you were coming to speak to him.' He said knocking on Arlo's door. Before he could answer they locked themselves into my room, leaving me to stand awkwardly waiting for Arlo to answer; *alone!*

'Cheers guys' I muttered.

Arlo opened his bedroom door and the minute that he laid his eyes on me they popped open wide. Without saying a word, he stepped aside, allowing me to go in. His room was much bigger than mine, he had a king-size bed with the headboard against the wall, on the other side of that wall was my settee. His room was decorated a dark purple, a diamond chandelier in the middle of a white painted ceiling, then my eyes fell to the picture of his bedroom wall. Two wolves were sitting on a cliff howling up to the moon Goddess, Selene. One was Sapphire blue; which represented the nights sky, dotted with stars and one was a pearl white which represented the moon. It was stunning.

'Thank you for coming to talk to me.' Arlo said breaking the silence and smiling weakly. He looked exhausted, why was my not talking to him, bothering him so much? I wasn't anything special, I didn't understand it.

'It's okay.' I said looking at his toned and bare chest. All he was wearing were black jogging bottoms that were riding dangerously low on his hips, revealing the perfect V of his toned body. My eyes travelled down the length of his body and I felt myself getting hot. *Now why would he do that? He knew I was coming in to talk to him.* I sat down in his big green armchair practically sinking into it, my god it was the comfiest chair I had ever sat on. Arlo sat on the end of his bed and sighed.

'I am sorry, for hurting you; Amelia, it wasn't my intention I swear to Selene it wasn't.' He whispered, his voice sounding just as broken and tired as he looked. I smiled weakly at him.

'I accept your apology.'

'Please can I explain everything to you?' He asked still looking sad.

'Arlo. You don't have to explain any-'

'I know I don't. But I want to.' He cut in. I paused for a moment and exhaled softly. I nodded yes and listened to everything he had to say.
And I replied truthfully to him.

'I do understand it; I honestly thought that you pretended to be my friend...I thought that you and Lori...and Charlie had planned for her to hurt me but you are my Alpha; we shouldn't even be having this conversation, you should not be explaining yourself to me. Yes, I was hurt and after thinking about everything, I knew that I was in the wrong too. I over reacted.' I paused before I said the next thing, wondering whether it was the right thing to say. 'I really did like you; more than a friend and I thought something was going to happen between us but once I had heard that you and she…I… I realised I was just being stupid; it was never going to happen. I guess I took your kindness as something else and that…' I gulped down a deep breath and struggled to keep my tears at bay before carrying on. 'That's on me not you.' Arlo looked surprised, I guess he thought that I was going to shout at him, he most certainly did not expect an apology.

'Amelia; why the fuck are you apologising to me? You had every right to go mad at me, I deserved everything you said. I get why you would think there would be something between us, I haven't exactly been innocent, I have flirted with you and told you I liked you, I introduced you to my best friend and broke your heart by having sex with my ex. I know I am your Alpha and I can promise you this, I would never be having this conversation with anyone else and I would never allow anyone to speak to me the way I allow you too, but it is because you are different, I can't put my finger on it. Your stubborn as hell, you argue back with me like no one ever has done before, you push my buttons and it drives me crazy. But you are kind, sweet, honest and you treat my pack how they should be treated; like equals; Elites and Mutts alike. And you make me laugh. Plus, my mum and best friend love you. And Matt hates everyone.'

Everything he said hit me like a ton of bricks. Did he just admit that there is nothing between us and it was all in my head? Or did he mean something completely different? I was so confused and yet so touched, no one had ever said such lovely things to me, and no one had ever been this honest. All I managed to say was 'Thank you.' Before standing up and walking towards his bedroom door.

Arlo jumped up and lightly touched my hand.

'Where are you going? I told you that I like you and then you just get up to leave? Honestly Amelia; you are so fucking complicated.' I turned around baffled at what he just said.

'I am so confused, I thought you admitted to leading me on.' Arlo crossed his arms and looked me in the eye. 'No Amelia; I like you, like, I really like you.'

I didn't know how to reply, my heart was pounding, *he likes me?* I knew I shouldn't have said it, but I did anyway, because it was the truth.

'It's not my fault that you have no communication skills and your wording is shit.'

'Shit? Shit? I just told you how amazing you are and now my wording is shit?' he cried in frustration.

I shook my head trying not to laugh at him, he was looking and acting so offended and yet, I was still so confused. He said that I was complicated, but he was more so! I licked my lips and looked up his beautiful face, his golden-brown eyes trying to read me.

'Yeah, your wording is shit. But I appreciate everything you said.' I smiled still trying not to laugh.

Arlo's face was still serious. 'Did you really think something would happen between us?' he asked taking a step closer to me.

'Yeah, I honestly did, at first I didn't want to admit it to myself. I guess that I am not the greatest person at reading people, I guess that, that is thanks to the way I was brought up in seclusion. But you grew on me, even your annoying way of creeping up on me.' I admitted plainly.

Arlo studied my expression, his eyes flicking back and forth across my face; taking in every feature and then he put his hand softly underneath my chin.

'I did too, you're such a pain in my arse but I like that... sometimes.' I smiled at him

'Baby steps eh?' I whispered, my voice trembling as he slowly inched a little closer to me. He nodded in agreement

'Baby steps.' He pulled my face gently to his and we kissed, both pulling away in unison, seemingly checking the other for moment. We looked into each other's eyes, neither of us could hold back much longer, Arlo pulled me into him and lifted me up, I ran my hands through his hair, and we kissed again, this time our tongues met and electricity zapped across every inch of me that he touched, and we couldn't pull away from each other, it was as though he was a human magnet drawing me in. Arlo placed me up against his door, slamming me into the wood hard causing me to groan in pleasure, still holding me up neither of us wanting the kiss to end.

'Halle-fucking-lujah.' Matt shouted from the other side of the door.

'Shhhh.' Piper hushed. 'They will hear us.'

'You're talking louder than me.' Matt hissed.

'For Selene's sake Matthew, now they know we have been here listening to them.'

'I swear Piper; you call me Matthew one more time I will throw you out of the nearest fucking window.' Arlo and I froze for a moment, listening to the argument happening out in the hall. Our kiss turned into big grins, before we broke out in laughter. Those two really knew how to ruin a moment. But they were my best friends.

And I wouldn't change them for the world.

8

Amelia;

I awoke with a start, blinking my eyes open and groggily took in my surroundings, the first thing I saw was the stunning framed painting on Arlo's bedroom wall, I was so intrigued by the legend and wanted to know more, I just couldn't get over the two beautiful wolves howling solemnly. The colours of them were incredible, I assumed the blue one was a male; he was slightly bigger than the other one; who was a shocking white, I had a feeling she was a female. I guess it was just something to do with the energy that I sensed from them. *What the fuck? Where did that come from? Their energy?* I shook my head as the reality sunk in. I spent the night in Arlo's room.

Although I stayed in here, nothing happened between us. We just spoke all night until the early hours. I don't really remember falling asleep, the last thing I do remember is laying my head on Arlo's chest and listening to the rhythmic thumping of his heart. I noticed the way that our hearts were beating in perfect unison, and then... it was morning.

I turned my head over to my left; my handsome Alpha was still fast asleep, his body facing me; one of his arms was lightly resting above his head and the other gently placed over me. I took in all his features; stubble was beginning to grow across his perfect jaw line and around his pale pink lips. I had never seen anyone look so hot while they slept. I had the urge to reach out and touch him. I stroked his cheeks with the back of my fingers and smiled when his eyes fluttered open.

'Morning.' He whispered sleepily smiling, his yellow eyes taking in my face.

I returned his smile.

'Good morning.' I replied, slowly sitting up and looking down at the purple satin duvet, that rested over our bodies, I was still wearing my clothes from the night before. Arlo reached up and pulled me back down so that I was facing him once more and threw the duvet over our heads. I laid there facing him, the tips of our noses touching as we stared into one another's eyes. I giggled and dropped my eyes down away from his stare.

'Sorry. I am just not ready for this moment to be over.' He whispered, shuffling closer to me and pulling my face into the crook of his neck. We laid there in silence; I don't know how long, it could have been minutes, it could have been hours, all I knew was that it was not long enough.

Arlo pulled back, kissed the top of my head and ran his eyes up the length of my body, before smirking gleefully.

'What?' I asked, trying *and failing* not to return his smile. He shook his head and threw the covers off of us. The minute that we were exposed I felt the cold wash over my bear arms.

'Do you want to have a shower here?' Arlo asked also sitting up and taking my mind off of the emptiness that now lingered where his touch had been.

'I have to go back into my room to get my clothes for today and sort out this face of mine.' I replied wondering what a mess my face probably was; I could feel the dried mascara flaking onto the tops of my cheeks. Arlo looked at me with one eye closed; clearly, he was still in the process of waking up. He shook his head, causing his wild black hair to dance crazily around his head.

'You still look gorgeous to me.' He whispered, leaning in and kissing me softly on the cheek. I pulled a face and glared at him playfully. Arlo rolled his eyes and nodded before climbing from the bed, his jogging bottoms still riding down his hips 'Meet you out-side the rooms in an hour?' he asked looking at his watch.

'Yeah okay.' I agreed finally getting out of the most com-fortable bed I had ever slept in. As I walked to the door, I heard Arlo come up behind me, he lent his face into my neck and gently kissed it. I turned myself around looking up at his smirking mouth. Why did he have to do this to me? Every time he touched me and every time, he kissed me sparks flew, my heart fluttered, and my legs went weak. I had never had feelings like these before, he always made me feel like it was just us, alone in this world. Arlo put his hands on my hips and pulled me closer to him leaning down towards my face, I looked up and kissed him. *Baby steps* I thought to myself. Baby steps was going to be easier said than done.

An hour later; just as we agreed, we met in our hallway; Arlo was dressed formally, something all the elite pack members did when they were to attend a pack meeting, he was wearing black trousers with a white shirt tucked into them with a blood red tie. He certainly looked better than me today, all I was wearing were high waisted skinny jeans and a white low-cut top tucked into them. My Alphas eyes fell to my chest and his jaw clenched, he took a breath in and then out again,

'Shall we?' he asked pulling his eyes away from my cleavage and blinking rapidly. I smirked at him.

'We shall.' I replied with a wink and a giggle. We were met at the dining room doors by Marie and Tristan; Marie's face lit up with a giant smile, showing her perfect white teeth. She looked at me and then back at Arlo, trying to read our straight faces.

'It is lovely to see you this morning; Amelia.' She said giving me one off her famous warm smiles. 'You look much better than yesterday and you have healed extraordinarily well.' Her face was now full of amazement, gazing at my now healed eyes as she stepped forward and pinched my chin between two fingers, gently turning my head from side to side as she inspected the lack of wounds that were on my face.

'Incredible.' She whispered. She then turned towards Arlo. 'May I talk to you after breakfast?' Her voice had turned to that of a serious note. Arlo nodded at his mother and glanced at me from the corner of his eye. Tristan finally said something, after staring at his son the whole time Marie was talking with me.

'Amelia had better go in now before the pack starts talking.' *Awkward!* I opened the dining room doors choosing not to look back at Arlo and his parents.

I felt everyone's eyes on me as soon as I stepped foot in the dining area, some pack members were gasping and all muttering to one another; '*How has she healed like that already?*'

I kept my head down and continued towards my seat, only looking up to meet those beautiful baby blue eyes sparkling back at me. Ethan was the only one that was not whispering or pointing at me. He just stared at me smiling. *He really was handsome.* I tucked my hair behind my ear and turned to look over at my father; who was tapping his wrist as though he had a watch implying that I was late. I stood behind my chair and waited for Arlo and his parents to enter the room. Those few minutes seemed like an eternity. *Why did I have to start to feel like this for him? Was I going to be pining over him forever?* The doors opened and the moment he and his parents entered our eyes met instantly. We never broke our stares the entire time that he walked through the dining hall until he was stood behind his seat. He motioned for all to sit down and the doors flew open. And in came the magnificent breakfast trollies. It was in that moment; while still staring at Arlo that I was hungry for more than just breakfast. *I was hungry for him!* I closed my eyes and fought through the emotions swirling within. *How could I be so attracted to two guys at the same time, who were the complete opposites of one another?*

Breakfast was going reasonably well, Marie insisted I sit with Arlo again; much to Charlie and my father's annoyance. I felt both of their eyes burning into my soul as well as Lori's. She had realised that she hadn't succeeded in pulling me and Arlo apart and I could tell it was eating her up inside. *Good!*

'So, Amelia; I see you have made some friends.' My father said dryly, pretending he was interested in my life. This was the first time he had spoken to me since our confrontation, he hadn't rushed to my bedside at the medical centre; like any normal father would. I wouldn't have been surprised if he was part of the reason that it all happened. *Did he really hate me enough to be a part of something like that?* He obviously didn't care, so why was he acting like he did now? I cleared my throat and twisted in my seat so that I could turn to face him fully.

'Yes, I have, thank you.' I replied bluntly, looking over at him.

'Yeah, with a Mutt.' Charlie sniggered. I stared at him, feeling my blood boil. I clenched my teeth and felt every muscle in my body twitch. *How fucking dare, he!*

'And your point is what exactly; Charlie. What is wrong with me being friends with; as you call them; *Mutts?*' He pulled a face at me and sniggered before glaring at me.

'Well there has always been something wrong with you. I guess you need to hang out with creatures like them to make yourself fit in somewhere.' He spat; his eyes wild. *Had he always looked this insane?* I gasped as my mouth fell open. I tried my hardest to breathe slowly and begged the Goddess to give me strength to not to jump over the table and wipe his ugly and evil smirk off of his face. He mistook my silence for weakness, so he continued. 'We don't socialise with them. They are beneath us. Nothing but the runts of the litter; as I said, just like you. You need to sort your life out *Amelia*. You are bringing shame to this family, no wonder why nan and grandad didn't want you back at the cottage. You are a disgrace to this pack!' Charlie snapped, his eyes growing wider, his nostrils flaring with anger, and spit flying from his mouth with every word. Arlo growled, a sound unlike anything I had ever heard him make. It was enough to cause the hairs to raise on the back of my neck; was *this his Alpha authority in action? If so, I could see why he was in charge. He was terrifying when he needed to be.* The entire hall fell into a stunned silence and took in the way that Arlo was glaring at his Beta. I felt a hand squeeze mine and looked down, Arlo's fingers were locked in mine under the tablecloth; he was obviously hoping I wouldn't retaliate. I took a deep breath and decided for the sake of everyone I would ignore him. Until he muttered under his breath;

'But then again; your scum, Mutts are scum, so I suppose you would want to be friends with something like that.' That was it,

I had, had enough.

'The only Scum I can see in this hall; is you.'

Before Charlie could answer back, the sounds of a crash filled the room, everyone turned towards the sound. Lori was standing with Adela and Harper; all three were laughing and looking down at the floor, I pushed my chair back to get a better look at what the bitch pack had done; Piper was on the floor holding her head. My whole body trembled; I had never felt anger like this before. My vision had turned to red.

Arlo met my gaze and gently grabbed my hand once more, squeezing my fingers and causing me to look at him. His expression was stern, and his eyes held a look of fear.

'Amelia don't.' he mumbled also pushing his chair backwards with his body weight. I yanked my hand away from his and glared at him; the muscles in my jaw tensed as I fought to do as I was told. *But that's not me!* I leapt across the table, knocking glasses and plates with my foot as I did so, and ran to my friend. Blood was dripping from the back of her head. It took all of my strength to not say anything to the girls who were still laughing amongst themselves, but I knew Arlo was standing behind me.

'Amelia; please take Piper to the medical room, I will have someone clean this all up.' He said, watching as I helped Piper off the floor. I leant into his ear and whispered,

'Please; this is not fair. Do something!' He nodded at me and then turned to Lori. Before Arlo had a chance to say another word Lori turned to her friends and glared at us; whispering in a voice so that only I could hear.

'Damn, a small cut on her head. I should have tried harder!' That was it. The rage erupted in my chest and I spun on my heel.

'*WHAT?*' I screamed. The windows behind the three girls exploded, causing a shower of glass to rain down upon them. Lori and the bitches squealed, throwing their arms over their heads. I watched in stunned silence as the shards sliced open their bare arms as it fell.

'Look at what she did!' Lori roared, throwing her arm forward and pointing at me. I blinked in awe and shook my head. *How the hell did I do that? I was all the way over here.*

'Amelia. Medic ward. Now!' Arlo's voice was stern, and his eyes blazed with anger. I narrowed my eyes and turned on my heel. *No way was he sticking up for that skank!*

Arlo;

I stood in shock looking around at the devastation that had just taken place. Lori was kicking off and making everything about her as per usual, as Amelia stood glaring at her. *What the fuck had just happened?* I turned my look from the three girls covered in scratches from the glass that had exploded around them back to Amelia who was hurrying from the room with Piper. This was all getting way out of hand now. I stepped forward about to follow Amelia and Piper when my father reached out and placed his hand on my arm.

'I think that we need to talk in your office!' He snapped quietly, making sure that no one else could hear what he was saying. I shrugged free from his hold and turned my stare to my mother's worried eyes. She nodded once and slowly made her way from the dining hall, my father motioned with his head that I should follow. I glanced around the room once more and noticed how the other Elites on my table had flocked around her, making sure that she was ok, but all the Mutts were sat staring at the windows that had shattered. All except one. Ethan. He just stared at the door where Amelia and Piper had gone through only moments before. The sound of my father clearing his throat impatiently had me turning back to face them and exiting the room.

We walked down the hall in silence, my father's anger apparent as he stomped towards my office. I don't know what the hell had just happened, and if he wanted me to explain it… then he was in for a shock. The moment I walked through the door, he slammed it shut behind me.

'Look… I don't know what happened then. You saw the same thing as me!' I barked, narrowing my eyes at him.

'This is not about what happened in the dining hall. This is about you and Amelia. Son… people have been talking. They have noticed how close the two of you have been getting and they are starting to doubt your allegiance to them.' My father said, his tone calmer than it was a few moments ago, but still assertive.

'That is ridiculous. What has my friendship with Amelia got to do with anything? She is an Elite. She is from this pack. It's not as though she is an outsider. And let's not forget; dad; you two were the ones that told me to get close to her; you were the ones that wanted me to keep an eye on her and now I am doing that, you are telling me that it's causing problems.' I responded, sounding bored.

'It's not about who or what she is. It is the fact that she has an overly friendly attitude towards the Mutts! I hear that she was standing out in the rain yesterday kissing one. In plain view, for anyone to see.'

'Tristan. What does that have to do with anyone other than Amelia and her lucky male friend?' My mother snapped, stepping forward and folding her arms across her chest.

'Who?' I growled, ignoring my mother's question and surprising myself with my own jealousy.

'The doctors son. Ethan. They were out there kissing like it was nothing!' He continued. My mother stepped in front of me once more, blocking me from sight.

'And? Like I said, what does that have to do with anyone other than Amelia and Ethan?' She said, this time sounding angrier than before.

'Because it is wrong. And now she is dragging our families name through the mud.'

'What is so wrong about a young woman kissing someone? Yes it was in the rain. Yes it was in daylight. But so what? Amelia is allowed to give her heart to anyone that she so desires!'

'It's wrong because he is a…'

'A Mutt?' My mother snapped, cutting my father off mid-sentence. He hesitated for a moment and growled angrily.

'Yes! That is my point exactly. He is a Mutt and she is still considered an outsider by most of this pack. They do not trust her. And now she is trying to take our son down with her!'

'So, it is wrong to love a Mutt, is it?'

'When you are involving the alpha then yes... yes, it is.'

'Well you have changed your tune since you decided to marry me!' My mother growled. *I had never seen her angry before, and I was beginning to see why the Luna was the one that people should truly fear.*

'This is not about us.'

'It is now Tristan. How dare you stand there and scold *our* son because he is interested in someone that is viewed as an outcast by others.' My father opened his mouth to reply, when my mother cut him off. 'If anything, that just goes to show that we as a pack are evolving beyond the primitive rules that had been forced upon us. I believed that you of all people would have understood that.'

'Marie! Will you just...'

'Ok... thanks for the talk guys. But I have a pack member in the hospital wing that needs checking on. I hope you... sort out... whatever this is soon. Catch you later.' I said, stepping around my mother and jogging out into the hall. I heard my father calling after me, but my mother was not going to let him off of this lightly. I needed to go and make sure that Amelia was ok. *And then question her about kissing that Mutt.*

Amelia;

'Okay Piper, all stitched up.' Benjamin; the doctor said holding a blood-filled antibacterial wipe in his gloved hand. I looked down at my friend who was still uncontrollably sobbing; my heart hurt for her. I just wanted to put Lori in her place, I know it was pack lore, but Elites treating *"Mutts"* like this was wrong and dated, we are in 2018 now, how can this still be okay.

I was seething with anger and really hoped Arlo would stop this from happening again. He says he loves his pack and wants to protect them, well now was the time to prove it. I knelt down next to the bed just as Piper had with me when I was hurt and spoke to her.

'I will do everything in my power to stop all of this, I prom-ise.' I paused for a moment and sighed deeply. 'And if I can't stop it, then I will do my best to protect you; okay?' Piper wiped her tear-soaked cheeks and weakly smiled.

'It will never stop, and you can't protect me without getting into trouble. I am not going to be the reason you get banished from the pack, look at what they did to you, we have no hope, neither of us do.' She sucked down a sob and twisted around to look at me. 'You are the only thing in this shit hole that makes life bearable. I don't want to lose you.'

Benjamin walked back into the room and coughed to get our attention; I hadn't even noticed that he had left.

'Amelia; our alpha would like to talk to you in my office.' I scrunched my face up in confusion. *Why didn't he just come and tell me himself?* I leant forward and planted a soft kiss on Piper's fore-head and glanced over to Benjamin. He smiled sweetly to me and gave a gentle nod. 'I will make sure that she is well looked after.' I pushed myself up from my best friend's bed side and made my way to the office.

I got to the door and pushed it open, walking inside. Arlo was sit-ting at Benjamin's desk with his elbows resting on the tabletop and his hands clasped together. No one else was in the room. I closed the door and sat down on one of the chairs. I assumed the pack meeting had been pro-longed or that Arlo's office was occupied.

'You summoned me?' I asked, jokingly. He sighed and looked at me, I could tell he was stressed.

'Thank you for not kicking off earlier at Lori. The three of them had their wounds looked at and it was nothing more than scratches. With their healing they should be good as new in a day or two.' He paused again and shifted in his chair uncomfortably, causing it to creak before continuing. 'I have spoken to her and the other two, but my hands are tied, there is nothing that I can do.' I looked at him confused.

'Tied? In what way, I don't understand what you mean?'

'Lia; I can't do anything about what Lori did, other than talk to her. Elites have been doing this for decades, if it was anyone else, I could punish them, but Lori's father is an important member of the Pack and we need him. He is the best tracker we have, he trains Mutts, so we have Trackers to protect our territory from outside threats.' He dropped his stare to the desk, no longer able to look me in the eye. 'If I punish Lori, then we will have an uproar. I do not like this either; Amelia, I hate it but there is nothing else I can do.' My heart sank at his words, he is the Alpha, he should be able to make his own Pack Lore surely? For me there was no excuse for what had happened, my disappointment turned to anger. My friend had to have her head stitched up because Lori tripped her over purposely. She hit her head so hard on the food table that it had split open, she had to have stitches because it would not heal fast enough to prevent infection. I put my head down and closed my eyes before standing up. *Breath; Amelia, breath.*

'There must be something more you can do. Maybe speak to her father and say you cannot have her hurting your pack members. Lori is the problem here; she is going out of her way to be spiteful for no reason at all. I know this is not your fault and I know it's the shitty pack lore, but my friend is in the medical centre with a stitched-up head! You say you want to protect your pack and you do an incredible job of protecting them from outside threats... but what about the inside threats? I am sorry but I need some air.' I turned and made my way to the door pausing. 'Oh, and Pipers not ok. I just thought you would want to know as you seemed so concerned!' I snapped.

'What is that supposed to mean?' He growled rising to his feet and leaning over the desk a little glowering at me.

'Well, you seemed to already know how the bitches were doing. I figured that you might like to know that Piper is ok. You know... considering that you never asked.' I turned on my heel and made my way towards the door when he called out to me again. This time stopping me dead in my tracks.

'Kissing a Mutt in the rain? Really Lia?' I slowly turned around to face him with wide, angry eyes.

'And what has that got to do with any of this?' I asked, looking him up and down. He hesitated for a moment, his mouth hanging open. *Did he even realise that he had said that out aloud?*

'Just… be more mindful of this pack while you are here. People are already beginning to talk. Just watch your back.' He snapped dropping back down into his chair and turning his face away from me. I let out a growl of anger and stormed through the door making sure to slam it hard behind me.

Arlo;

I watched as Amelia threw the door opening before she slammed it shut behind her. She was right, I knew she was right. I shouldn't be allowing this to happen and if I didn't need Jeffrey; Lori's father for the protection of my pack then I would happily banish Lori, Adela and Harper. But we did need him, and unfortunately, he came with some unwanted baggage. And why didn't I ask how Piper was getting on? *Sometimes I was my own worst enemy!* I rolled my eyes and rested my head against the back of the chair; thinking back to what Jeffrey had informed me about an intruder in the woods.

Jeffrey had been a Tracker for the pack since he had turned 18 and he was the one trying to track the scent of the wolf that kept coming back to the grounds. I chose not to tell Amelia this because I knew she would want to go and find him herself; she was nowhere near ready to face this threat that she was under, we all knew it was Amelia he wanted, though none of us knew why. I thought back to the windows that had shattered when she had lost her temper, was that her? Or was it a coincidence? Nothing else could have possibly caused the glass to shatter like that, but then how could she have done it? It frightened my pack and more whispers filled the hall as soon as she had left, I needed to get those windows replaced and I just hoped everyone would forget it ever happened.

Amelia;

I didn't walk very far before I spotted Matt, he was standing under the canopies of tree's punching the air, he must be warming up I thought. Matt was topless with only grey jogging bottoms on, he was wearing white hand wraps to protect his knuckles for when he started training, I never knew he was a fighter. I looked in awe at all of the fighting equipment that was neatly laid across black mats on the grass, the punching bag caught my eye more than anything though, oh how I would love to let out some of this anger, I could pretend it was Lori! I chuckled away at myself until I heard Matt call my name. I walked over to him and looked around 'This looks like so much fun!' I said grinning.

'I am just warming up before I start training my fighters, but what are you doing out here? Is everything okay' he asked looking concerned. I explained what had happened at breakfast this morning and about the injury Piper had sustained because of Lori.

'Are you fucking joking?' Matt cried angrily, 'I am so sick of this shit, what has Arlo said about it all?'

'There isn't much he can do; Lori's dad is the head Tracker and the pack need him.' I sighed leaning against a tree. Matt put his head down.

'I hate this, there are only a select few of us Elites that would never treat Mutt's the way Lori does, and even calling them Mutts; I hate it! But people are just stuck in the old traditions. To be honest, I think Arlo is the only Alpha that has treated the lower pack members with respect and even that is rare.' He paused for a second and then looked sad. 'How is Piper now?'
'Upset and sore. The doctor had to stitch her head up, he said she would heal within a couple of days but was concerned about infection getting in the wound... Do you think maybe you could speak to Arlo and see if he will give her some time off?' I asked. Matt nodded

'Yeah I reckon so, he is pretty good like that, you could probably ask lover boy yourself though, he seems to listen to you.' He grinned. I lightly punched his arm.

'He is not my lover boy.' I laughed.

'Hey; Lia, I have a bit more time before I start training the guys up, how about I teach you some basics? You did a good job at giving Lori two shiners, but if you really want to do some damage then maybe I can teach you to fight like the rest of us. Only thing is I want to keep it quiet. We need to practice in private, so no one knows, okay? That way when you do fight, no one will expect it.'

Arlo;

I watched Matt and Amelia from my office window. He had been trying to teach her the basics for about half an hour before they both stopped and had some water. It was clear that Amelia wasn't a fighter. Matt had managed to pin her down on her back every time and in the wild she would end up being killed. *There was a small part of me that envied him. I wanted to be the one that was pinning her down!* I shook my head. *Focus Arlo!*

She looked frustrated with herself, but she didn't give up. Matt must have said something to cheer her up, because she was now smiling. I loved the fact that she wants to learn to fight and defend herself, it was something that she needed to do. I noticed how much they were getting on, Matt will not talk to anyone but me and my parents, Amelia somehow broke down his walls.

It was so nice for me to see him laughing, he even tolerated Piper and we all knew how much she could talk for England. Matt's parents died when he was just four years old, his dad was killed whilst out fighting a pack of wolves from another pack, sadly he was on his own and overpowered.

Not long afterwards, Matts mum killed herself. She had become weak and unstable after losing her husband; losing a soul-mate can have drastic effects on the one that is left behind. It can even lead to insanity. It gripped my heart every time I thought of her leaving behind their little boy. My mum and dad decided to take Matt in and raise him themselves, I was nine years old at the time. He is more than my best friend; he was my brother. To see him become friends with Amelia, meant the world and more to me.

Amelia;

After training a little bit with Matt, I felt deflated. I was terrible at fighting, but I needed to learn. I mean, I could throw a couple of good punches here and there, but I think that was more luck than skill. I had to learn how to defend myself and thank fully Matt said he would teach me. He told me not to worry though, that even the most skilled fighters were once like me. I am not sure if he was trying to make me feel better or not, but it did and the fact that he was willing to invest his time in me meant a lot.

I went to visit Piper in the medical room again but just as I arrived her mother had turned up to take her back to their house, she seemed a lot better and Arlo had said she could have a few days off. Matt had definitely spoken to him. After dinner I went up to my room to have a bath and got into my pyjamas. I was ready to wind down and do some more reading.

Tap, Tap, Tap. I looked up from my book, startled by the knocking on my door, I only had one chapter left of my book and was desperate to know the ending.

'Who is it?' I called placing the book on the arm of my chair.

'It's Arlo, open up.' I smiled and walked over to the door; the chapter could wait.

'Yes?' I said playfully opening my door.

'Fancy coming to my room and watching some films with me?' He asked chuckling at my fluffy white Pyjamas.

'Ohhh, I don't know, see I have one last chapter of my book and I REALLY want to read it.' I said jokingly grabbing my key. Arlo smirked at me as I walked past, causing me to giggle. We entered his room and my eyes instantly locked on that painting. *Again!*

'So, what film do you have in mind?' I asked sitting on the end of his bed.

'Die Hard?' he asked walking over to his DVD selection,

'Die Hard?' I repeated screwing up my face, it really wasn't my sort of film. Arlo looked at my expression and then rolled his eyes,

'Okay, what do you want to watch then Miss Hunt?' I clapped my hands excitedly and picked a film I knew he wouldn't want to watch, I loved teasing him.

'How about Dirty Dancing?' I asked giggling as his face dropped.

'Oh, really?' he asked looking disappointed. I stared at his face and bit the inside of my lip. I had never seen anyone sulk in such a cute way.

'Hey what's wrong with Dirty Dancing?' I asked putting the disc in the DVD player.

'I have watched it so many times now, it's my mum's favourite and she killed it for me, I have to admit.' He said pulling me onto his bed. We both laid back, with pillows plumping our heads up and ended up not only watching Dirty Dancing, but Die Hard too, but I didn't mind, we cuddled the whole time but towards the end of the film I started getting too hot, these fluffy pyjamas were a bad idea.

'You okay?' he asked as I moved away.

'Yeah, I'm just so hot. I might go back to my room and change into something a little less fluffy.' I said fanning my face with my hands.

'Why don't you just put something of mine on? And I will go down to the kitchen and get us some snacks.' He said pulling a T-shirt out of his bedside drawers. I hesitated for a moment. *Why did the thought of wearing his clothes send a rush of excitement down my spine?*

'Okay, and then when you come back can you please tell me the legend of the two wolves?' I asked taking the T-shirt from his hands and fluttering my eye lashes at him. Arlo chuckled to himself and kissed me quick before hurrying from the room.

Arlo;

Just as I opened my bedroom door; Amelia came out of my bathroom wearing only the T-shirt I gave her and panties, it was miles too big and just about covered her backside, man she looked hot. I couldn't help but stop for a minute and stare at this beauty in front of me. Her hair was in a messy bun on top of her head and she had removed her make up; I rarely ever saw her without make up on and it was safe to say she didn't need it. She blushed when she saw me looking at her bare legs.

'What have you brought up to eat?' she asked walking over to inspect the snacks, her eyes lit up when she saw the big bar of chocolate. 'Yum' she grinned taking it from my hand. 'So, what should we do now?' She asked looking at my painted bedroom wall. I flicked my gaze over to the painting of the twin wolves and hurried over to her, holding out the bag of goodies that I had brought up from the kitchen. Amelia plucked the bag from my hands and I couldn't help but smile at the noises of excitement and happiness that were escaping her; she didn't even seem to realise she was doing it.

We sat back on my bed and made ourselves comfortable, starting to eat the snacks until Amelia asked me about the painting of our legend once again. *I had hoped that she would drop this subject. It was a silly folktale that had followed our kind for centuries!*

'Ok. I have to ask. What is with the picture of the wolves? It's beautiful and there is something about it that just keeps drawing me in.' she asked, raising her head up off my chest and staring at the picture some more. I chuckled nervously and brushed the back of my head with my hand.

'It's just some silly old legend about a set of werewolf twins that are destined to destroy the world.' I replied, shifting myself so that I was able to sit upright.

Amelia pushed herself up on my bed, curling her legs underneath herself.

'You mean, it ruins the fate of the werewolf world?'

'Um, no. Apparently these two wolves are destined to lead a war against one another. Just like day and night, destroying everything in their path. I guess that is why one is light and the other is dark.' I said looking up at the painting myself. 'And then that black circle is supposed to symbolise the Dark Moon. A rare and powerful time for werewolves. They only happen once every 500 years. Apparently, it is in this time that the twin wolves will take on their true power and destroy all that they touch.'

'That doesn't seem right. I mean, to me, one reminds me of the moon, and the other the night's sky. Surely that would mean that they are destined to work together. Wouldn't it? I mean, anger is not the feeling I get when I look at this picture. There is something about it that leaves me feeling… lonely.' She replied, tugging at the bottom of the T-shirt she was wearing. I watched as a sudden chill swept over her, goose bumps spread across her arms and legs. 'To me, it looks like they are howling in pain. Not in anger.' I thought for a second at what she had just said, really taking in the picture. *It had been so long since I last really looked at it and took it all in.*

'Huh. I have never thought of it that way before. Now you mention it, they do seem a little like the moon and sky.' I shrugged and turned back to look at her once more, before continuing. 'It's just some silly old legend that our kind have carried down through the generations.' Amelia smiled.

'It's really interesting. I love stuff to do with old legends. Especially one to do with our kind. I noticed this picture the first time I came in here. And honestly, it's been playing on my mind a little. That's why I had to ask. There is just something about it that seems to be drawing me in.'

'I can cover it up if it's really bothering you?' I asked, turning to look at her with a soft smile.

'No! No, I don't want you to do that. It's not a bad thing. I love this picture. I was just curious about it. Something about it seems… familiar, I guess. But this is the first time that I have ever heard that legend. Is there a book on this in the library I can read up on?' she whispered. The excitement in her voice was beyond adorable; it sent waves of goosebumps spreading across my body. I sighed looking at her face, it was full of curiosity.

'If I am honest, I don't know. I never have spent much time in there myself. I heard that many, many years ago, there was a tapestry on it. It was painted by one of our ancestors who had a close bond with our Goddess. It was said that back then, she would send messages to our kind while they slept. This is supposedly where this painting was copied from.'

'Where is it? The tapestry I mean?' Amelia asked. I shook my head and watched as her face fell a little.

'No one knows. Apparently not long after this was painted, the tapestry was stolen from the Temple of the Moon and no one has ever seen it since.' Amelia smiled and snuggled into me again once again, she took my hand and we linked our fingers through each other's.

Her hand was so small compared to mine and so much softer. I turned my head and smiled at her, *what are you doing to me Amelia?* I thought staring into her olive-green eyes. They say eyes are the windows to the soul, but for some reason I couldn't read hers, she was a mystery to me and could draw me in until I got lost. I had never allowed anyone to talk to me the way she did, no one would dream of arguing back with their Alpha, but this feisty young woman in front of me didn't care and it drove me crazy, what was this power she had over me?

Amelia:

I broke my fingers away from his and started running them down his naked chest, what was he thinking? Arlo was now lost in his own thoughts staring into my eyes. I turned my face away looking back over to the painting; the legends were just as much as a mystery to me as he was.

'I had better get to bed.' I said snapping him from his deep thoughts. He looked at me blankly for a moment, sort of as though he had forgotten that I was there. I smiled at him curiously before continuing. 'I am getting tired and will end up falling asleep here again.' I climbed off of the bed and smiled. 'Thanks for the T-shirt, I will give it back to you tomorrow.' Arlo eyed me up and down and then smirked.

'You can keep it, it suits you. It looks far better on you than it does on me anyway.' I laughed at what he said. 'Hmmm, I think you just like me wearing it.' I walked over to the door and then turned back to look at him. 'Goodnight.' I said opening the door. I unlocked my door and slipped into the room. It was cold and empty in here without Arlo by my side. I hurried over to my bed and slid under the covers; dropping my stupidly fluffy pyjamas on the floor at the side of me. My eyes were growing weary and I had to fight to keep them open. *How had I got this tired this quickly?* Just as my eyes were about to close, I heard it. The sirens call that had haunted my dreams. Except… I wasn't asleep when I heard it. I tried to force my eyes back open and the melodic tune rang out in my ears once more. The voice was high and angelic, and with every tune it sung I felt my eyes grow heavier. Darkness crept around the edges of my vision, and before I knew it; I was asleep.

When the Dark Moon meets its peak,
There's a brother who is your destiny
Hide, my child, safe and sound,
As in this brother, your destiny is found

In the Moonlight, she'll show you,
All the questions, that were kept from you,
Go in search until she's found,
Resist the evil all around.

When the Dark Moon meets its peak,
There's a sister who is your destiny
Hide, my child, safe and sound,
As in this sister, your fate is found.

In the Darkness, he'll show you,
All the answers, that were kept from you,
Go in search until he's found,
Resist the liars all around.

Yes, you will speak to those who'll hear
And in your words a sadness flows
But can you brave what you most fear?
Can you face what the Dark Moon shows?

When the Dark Moon meets its peak,
There are the siblings, and their destiny
Come, my children, homeward bound
When all is lost, then all will be found.

Strange white mist seeped into the darkest corners of my dreams. What was that? I watched as it swirled in the ghostly winds. It twisted and contorted until it began to make shapes. I could see a woman's face. Her lips were moving; she was trying to say some-thing to me, it was like a flickering image, but I could tell that she was young. I recognised her, but where from? Why did she look so familiar but yet unknown?

The woman was gone and in her place were a pair of blue eyes, they were shimmering and glowing in the darkness. The white mist merged into that of deep indigo and it sparkled as though it were stars shimmering in the midnight sky. A young man's face started coming out of the darkness. He stared at me. This image was a little clearer than the last. The two mists swirled and merged together, taking on the shapes of two wolves. One deep indigo like the nights sky, and the other pure white like the moon.

The unknown man and I slowly walked towards each other and yet we were getting further away. I stopped as his face and body morphed into the dark wolfs; his glittering fur was as blue as the midnight sky, he lunged forward getting closer and closer to me, he was snapping his jaws, was he going to kill me?

I woke up and sat bolt upright. I was out of breath and sweat was dripping from my forehead. It took me a while to snap out of the daze that I was in. It was just a dream and yet I couldn't shift the awful feeling that riddled my body. I shook my head and climbed from my bed. *What the fuck was that dream about?*

9

Amelia;

I woke up and sat bolt upright, I was out of breath and sweat was dripping from my head, it took me a while to snap out of the daze that I was in. *It was just a dream!* And yet, I couldn't shift the awful feeling that riddled my body. I shook my head and got out of bed. *I needed a cold shower.* I hurried into the bathroom and eagerly showered. *I knew that I was going to need another one after this, but I didn't mind.*

I stepped from the shower and threw on my clothes before hurrying down the halls unnoticed; *I had decided to go earlier than I needed, so that I could avoid the others.* Before I knew it, I was walking into the great hall that was at the back of the mansion; this was usually used as the ball room, but today it was my personal gym. We knew that no one really came in here, so it would be the safest place to train! The light brown glossed floors were gleaming like a mirror; *who ever had cleaned it did a spectacular job; and I certainly did not envy them.* The hall was incredibly big; you could have at least fit 500 people in here. I allowed myself to daydream; wondering what it could look like to attend one of the packs annual balls. I had never been to ball before, I could imagine myself wearing a stunning dress and dancing with my friends; *and him,* until the morning sun was beginning to peak up on the horizon, a girl could dream.

Today was the day that I would start learning to fight; properly. I wore a black spaghetti strap belly top and grey joggers; *so that it was easier to move about.* My dark long curls were put up in a messy bun on top of my head so that I wouldn't have to worry about getting tangled in it, and so that I wouldn't overheat. Now I just had to wait for Matt and Arlo. It was Saturday and pack meetings weren't held on the weekends; plus, Matt only trained the pack Monday to Friday; meaning that he was on his day off.

Matt had already set up for me. Two large training mats were placed on the floor, as well as the training weapons that he used to teach the others, I walked over to them; running the tips of my fingers over the thick wooden staffs, feeling the smooth grain of the wood before crossing my legs beneath me and dropping down onto the mat. Hopefully they wouldn't be much longer. I clasped my hands behind my head and laid back, staring at the ceiling. I thought back to my dream that I had, had the night before, *maybe I just dreamt about the blue wolf because of mine and Arlo's conversation?* It made sense though, everyone dreams about something that is playing on their mind, right? And perhaps I just felt such a deep connection to the wolves of the legends that they were all I could think about? Even while asleep. The sound of footsteps came from outside and I felt my whole-body tense in fear. *Please don't say that someone is going to catch me in here!* I held my breath as the footsteps grew closer before the double wooden doors flew open. I stared silently with wide eyes, my heart thumping in my ears; and the moment that I realised who it was the tension left me in a rush.

Finally, two of my favourite guys walked in who were about to start training me properly. I propped myself up on my elbows and watched as they both smiled as they saw me. I pushed up with my hands so that I was sitting up, and rubbed my hands together nervously taking in a deep breath. Arlo glanced up at me, he looked me up and down and smirked. I blushed and looked down at the floor. Every time he looked at me my heart skipped a beat, my face flushed, and I felt as though I couldn't breathe. No matter what he wore and no matter the situation, my attraction for my Alpha was growing alarmingly fast.

'Are you ready?' Arlo asked softly, grinning, standing in front of me. He was wearing a tight black T-shirt; *that showed off far too much of that mind blowing body*, and black jogging bottoms, his curls today were tied back into a short ponytail, I had only ever seen his hair down, I was surprised at how much I liked the "man bun" look on him. 'Matt is the packs best fighter; he will train you well.' He said walking over to the other side of the hall. I took another deep breath in and out.

'I'm ready.' I whispered.

'Of course, she's ready.' Matt shouted crossing his arms with a playful smile on his face. 'This girl has a fire in her, I am looking forward to the day she whoops your arse mate!' Matt teased, glancing over to his friend and smirking. Arlo narrowed his eyes and glared at the pair of us and shook his head gleefully.

'Sorry mate, that is never going to happen.' Arlo responded, folding his arms across his chest, causing his biceps and pecs to twitch and flex with the movement.

'Oh? And what is that supposed to mean?' I snapped playfully, placing my hands on my hips. Arlo waggled his eyebrows, clearly challenging me and I shook my head laughing. 'One day, I will kick your arse; Alpha. You have now set me a challenge, and I will gladly rise to the bait!' I said through giggles; *although I was trying to sound serious.*

'Guys! Focus!' Matt said, glaring at the pair of us. I bit my lip, trying my hardest to keep myself composed. But it was so hard to focus on anything when Arlo was sitting there, staring at me with those eyes that were beckoning me. 'Ok, Lia, just allow yourself to relax! I know that you are going to have to be someone to watch.' Matt said enthusiastically. *I am glad Matt had confidence in me, because I certainly didn't.* Matt gestured for me to follow him over to a stack of wooden shelves and pulled some items from it, before turning to wrap my hands up; protecting my knuckles and held up a black punching glove.

'The aim is to punch this as hard as you can, I know you can throw a punch so this shouldn't be too hard for you.' Matt smiled encouragingly. I did as he said and punched as hard as I could. The first punch I threw was weak and feeble. *Any other werewolf would have probably at least caused him to stagger. I barely even made him move is hand.* I turned my embarrassed stare to Matt, feeling the burn in my cheeks as my face flushed red.

'See, I told you that I was going to be useless at this!' I cried, dropping my head into my hands and growling in frustration.

'Hey, Lia.' Arlo called, raising himself up from the chair and slowly making his way towards me. I turned my eyes to meet his stare and waited for him to continue. 'I want you to focus all of your strength and anger into that punch. Every bad word that someone has said against you, every time that someone or something had left you hurt or heartbroken. Use that energy and push it into your punch.' He added, gently running his hands up and down my arms. It was in that moment that I lost concentration on everything else, and it was just me and him. Matt cleared his throat, snapping us both out of our own little worlds and causing us to look over to him.

'You, go and get warmed up again, we will continue with the punches in a moment.' He said, pointing at me. 'And you, get out of here and let the poor girl concentrate! How is she ever going to learn anything when her alpha is sat there staring at her!' he continued, turning his pointing finger from me to Arlo.

Arlo rolled his eyes and shook his head.

'Ok, ok. I am going' he said with a chuckle, holding his hands up defensively. I watched as he crossed the room and the moment that the doors closed with a bang, I squeezed my eyes tightly shut and mentally removed all thoughts of Arlo from my mind and turned back to Matt; who was now getting back into position with the punch pads. I rolled my neck on my shoulders, bouncing on the spot for a moment; reminding myself of a boxer waiting to get in the ring with his opponent. I exhaled through my nose and narrowed my eyes at the pad in front of me.

I raised my fists just in line with my chin and focused on all my anger. I held my breath and allowed all the hurt in my life to come rushing to the surface; *and goddess knows, that's a lot!* I shakily pulled my right arm back and pushed all my anger into my punch. The minute that my fist connected with the pad, a driving energy swirled inside me, bringing with it an anger that was alien to me. I punched the pad over and over again, not caring how I looked anymore. I kept on jabbing, left, right, left, right, and I could feel my rage rolling in the pit of my stomach. I lost all sight of everything other than my own anger. Maybe if I had been paying attention a little more closely, I would have noticed when Matt moved the pad down. But it was too late. The sound of my fist hitting skin made my stomach drop and I watched as Matt tumbled backwards, rubbing his jaw.

'Oh, my Goddess! Matt, I am so sorry!' I cried, rushing over to him and helping him back to his feet. 'Are you ok?' I asked. Matt turned his stare to look at me for a moment with a look in his eyes that I couldn't place; when he did the unexpected. He threw his head back and laughed. *A lot!*

'Excellent Amelia!' He chuckled, still rubbing his face; which was now turning red. *Woah, how hard did I hit the poor guy?* He cleared his throat and winked at me. 'Keeping going, imagine this is Lori's face.' He added, waving the paddle in the air. 'Not this.' He added; then pointing to his own face. My face flushed and I bit my lip, I wasn't sure if that was to stop me from laughing or crying; *or possibly both?* When he leapt back up to his feet and rolled his shoulders, holding the pads out for me once again.

'Are you sure that you want to do this again? What if I hurt you again?' I asked, feeling a little uneasy at the thought of hitting Matt again. He rolled his eyes and moved closer to me.

'Lia, I literally do this for a living. I am the one that teaches the younger pack members how to fight. So, please, stop worrying ok?' I nodded and drew in another deep breath. *Ok, here we go.* I closed my eyes and allowed my anger to build inside me once again. I threw my first punch and was filled with another rush, this time it felt as though every hit on the pad eased my pain a little. *No wonder people worked out when they were stressed!*

Although my hands were wrapped up, my knuckles hurt. I could already feel them burning from connecting to the leather pads and my skin was becoming red and slightly bruised; *but I didn't care!* I don't know how long I had been punching, but I could already feel the beads of sweat gathering on my forehead and others trickling down my spine. The temperature in the room had suddenly felt as though it had increased by 10 degrees and my lungs were beginning to burn from the over exertion. I stopped, bending over slightly and placed my hands on my knees, panting for breath when Matt jogged over offered me a bottle of water. I took it without hesitation and drained half of the contents in one gulp. The moment that cold refreshing liquid washed down my throat I began to feel my energy returning to me.

'Now for self-defence.' Matt said, dropping the punch pads to the ground beside us and snapping me from my thoughts. I stood up straight again and suddenly the world around me wobbled and the edges of my vision darkened. *I seriously needed a shit load of training!* Matt reached out and steadied me, keeping his hand on my shoulder for a moment, waiting for me to tell him that I was good to continue. He cleared his throat and I turned my eyes to meet his.

'So, let's try a little bit of combat now. I know that you really aren't that keen on this part, but trust me, this is going to be the part that benefits you the most.' Matt said smiling. I gulped down a deep breath and rolled my shoulders, hearing them crack and release their pressure. Matt stood in front of me and gestured for me to throw the first punch. And me being me, had to rise to the challenge!

I don't know why I expected any different but; Matt whooped my arse at self-defence. My back hurt from being pinned down so many times, but I didn't feel as defeated this time, I was being trained by the packs best fighter and he was my friend, I felt so lucky.

I had friends who cared about me, and my Alpha wasn't too much of an arsehole, so that was a plus. I suddenly realised that I had everything that I had ever wanted, right here within with walls. Matt and I continued to train, I don't know how long it was, but the morning sun moved into the afternoon, and then that faded into dusk. The only time we stopped was when Arlo came by with two large plates loaded up with so many different types of food. I never realised how hungry I was until I laid eyes on those plates and my stomach screamed out in protest. As soon as we had eaten; Matt was giving me another round of intense training. I had literally never worked so hard at anything in my life, and there was a feeling of satisfaction that it brought with it.

By the time that we did eventually stop, Matt was stood here in nothing but his shorts, his face was slightly flushed, and he had a few beads of sweat gathering on his forehead. I on the other hand; was as red as a beetroot, my lungs were burning as though I had just breathed in thick smoke from a camp fire, every bone, muscle and joint in my body were screaming out in pain and I had sweat truckling down my back and soaking into the material of my clothes. Matt locked eyes on me and looked me up and down.

'Well, I must say Lia, before we started this training today, I said that I thought you would be one to watch. Now, I take that back. You are definitely one to watch. Just after one day, look how far you have come.' Matt said, sounding pleasantly surprised. I offered an embarrassed smile and tucked one of my lose strands of dark hair behind my ear.

'I guess that's just because you are such a good teacher!' I replied, smiling with pure happiness. Matt nodded and turned back to face me.

'I wish that that was true, but trust me, I have seen a change in you that I don't see in most of my fighters for at least the first six weeks.' Matt paused for a second and rolled his shoulders once more. 'Why don't you got hit the showers. I think that this is enough training for one day. I don't know about you, but after today I feel like I could sleep for a week!' I nodded and slowly turned, dragging my feet towards the exit. He wasn't wrong. I had worked my arse off today, and every muscle was burning. *I was even feeling pain in muscles that I never knew that I had!* I fled from the great hall and made my way up to my room. For the first time in as long as I could remember, I was actually happy. *Genuinely happy!*

Arlo;

I dropped lunch off to Matt and Amelia before heading back to my office to sort through the agendas for the next pack meeting. I hadn't been there long when a knock at my door brought my attention away from work.

'Come in!' I called, without looking up from the pages before me. The door opened and my father walked in; this time alone.

'Arlo, we need to talk.' He barked, closing the door with a slam behind him. I let out a sigh and leant back in my chair.

'What is it now?' I asked, not in the mood for all the drama again. *I didn't need him to answer my question, I knew what was coming, but I braced myself anyway.*

'You need to call things off with Amelia. She is not good for the image of this pack! The rumours surrounding her are spreading through the pack like wildfire. Did you know that she was having sex with that Mutt in the stables?' He continued. I rolled my eyes and dropped my head onto the back of my desk chair.

'And who told you that?' I asked, sounding more than a little bored.

'Everyone! It is said that they were seen coming out of the stables looking extremely flustered, and that he ran out after her before they kissed in the rain. How do you think that is making you look? A girl that you are interested in is fraternising with Mutts? Do you not think that people are starting to question your authority with her? You are letting her get away with far too much… and your mother…'

'Speaking of mother, where is she?' I asked, raising an eyebrow.

'She is out shopping. That is why I thought that now was the perfect time to talk to you about this. Man to man.'

'So, you waited for mother to be out before bringing this up again?' I asked with a smirk. My father narrowed his eyes at me and let out a low growl; *his tell-tale warning that he was losing his temper.*

'This is not a game.'

'I know it's not. But as I said before; you and mother requested that I get close to her… because she is different and needs to be kept an eye on and now that I am and you do not like how she is with the Mutts, you want me to stop?! Well I won't stop, because she may be different from everyone else, but she is actually a really nice girl. Now I wish that you would stop interfering in my *affairs* and leave me to lead this pack. You may have been the alpha once, but now it is my turn. So maybe you can leave me to judge things for myself?'

'That night at the pub. You ordered that Mutt back into the building. What happened when you did that?'

'He did as he was told!' I snapped, starting to feel a little irritated. *What was my father's problem? Why was he acting this way?*

'Did he? You know that for sure?' He asked sarcastically. I opened my mouth and hesitated for a moment, allowing my thoughts to drift back to that night. *I ordered him back into the pub and he…* My eyes widened as realisation hit me. *I ordered him back inside and he… he stood in the doorway.* He never did what I ordered. And I used my alpha's influence. *What the fuck was going on here?* No one is resistant to the alpha influence. It is an ability that a werewolf gains the moment that they become the alpha. No one; especially Mutts, are able to resist the orders that are given to them. I turned my angry stare back up to my father's smirking face and growled. *He was right. Something wasn't right here. And it had to have something to do with Amelia!*

'See, something is not right here son!' My father said, his voice stern.

'How did you know that he resisted the alpha's influence?' I asked, my voice sounding hollow and drained.

'Like I said Arlo, rumours are spreading like wildfire.' He replied with a heavy sigh.

I glanced over to the clock on the wall and noticed that it was nearly time for dinner. I stormed past my father, and headed out into the hall, before storming up to my room. *Things needed to change.* I couldn't let the pack see that my authority was starting to be questioned by others!

Amelia;

By the time I was showered and changed, it was dinner 6 pm and dinner time and thank Selene because I was so hungry. *I know that we ate so much food at lunch, but us werewolves have a high metabolism, so that means that we get really hungry really fast.* As usual I was late, arriving just before Arlo and his parents and my father and Charlie gave me their usual disapproving looks. Although this time, I strolled into the room with my head held high. I was not letting anything bring me down this evening. I turned my stare to Lori who was glaring at me. *Not even she was getting to me today.* I stopped at my chair and sighed loudly.

'Late again; Amelia.' Charlie hissed as I stood behind my chair. I rolled my eyes and ignored him being a dick again. 'I am talking to you; Mutt.' He mumbled under his breath still glaring at me. Again, I ignored him, and it angered him even more, he slammed his hand down on the table and growled at me 'I said I am talking to you.' I turned my stare to him and smirked, sticking my middle finger up in the process. *One day I would hurt him so badly; that he would never disrespect me again. I would make sure of it.*

'Charlie! Amelia! What hell is going on?' Arlo roared, entering the room causing everyone in the hall fall silent. Arlo stared at his beta, who was too busy staring at me to notice.

'She was being disrespectful.' Charlie sneered. I looked at my brother in confusion.

'How was I being dis-respectful, I chose to ignore you because I do not want to argue again.' I said defensively. Charlie laughed at me mockingly,

'You are disrespectful, you are always late, you talk to your Alpha like he is one of your friendly Mutts and you gave an Elite member two black eyes and you stick your middle finger up at me! Know your place; Amelia.' I couldn't believe what was going on. In order to stop an argument breaking out I ignored Charlie, admittedly I swore at him but who wouldn't do that? But instead it made things worse and he had to cause a scene. I just couldn't win; *I would never win.* I looked up at Arlo trying to read his face, but his eyes were black, he was angry.

'Amelia; I would like to talk to you in my office.' He grumbled as Charlie started smirking. I looked at my father, *when will you ever defend me?* I thought sadly, I looked at Eddie who had his head down,

'Not either of you then, no?' I asked glancing at them both. 'He starts on me and not one of you will defend me?' I waited for them to respond and laughed. *Not one of them would ever protect me.* I pushed my chair into the table with force and stormed out of the dining hall. *I am done with this.*

'What?' I snapped as Arlo lent against his desk with his arms crossed. 'Why am I being called in here when I have done nothing wrong?'

'People are talking; Amelia… about us.' He replied.

'And?' I questioned; a bad feeling started building in the pit of my stomach.

'And, I can't be seen with you, like that. I can't defend you against my Beta and I can't let you get away with everything that I have been letting you get away with. I mean look at what just happened. You and Charlie arguing in the dinner hall, in front of everyone. That is my pack and my Elites are being disrespectful to one another. It's not fair to them and I cannot have anyone thinking something is going on between us.' My heart sank at his words. 'Not only that but rumours are spreading about you and Ethan. You slept with him, didn't you?' My jaw dropped and I stared at my Alpha, anger bubbling up through me.

'Are you joking? Are you actually being serious right now? No! No, I didn't fucking sleep with him! How dare you even ask me that!' Relief washed over Arlo's face and then his expression turned serious again.

'Wherever you go trouble follows, the Elites are questioning my authority insisting that I am showing too many signs of weakness. And that is because of you, with you I am weak, I don't know why, but I am. I am so sorry; Amelia. But I just can't do this with you.'

'Do what with me? We aren't doing anything Arlo; we are friends, are you not allowed to be friends with me? With anyone that isn't an Elite?' a tear fell down my cheek, this was hurting, more than I cared to admit.

'But we aren't just friends, are we? There is something more going on and I can't allow that to happen, especially when you are kissing Mutt's! Anyway, I have a pack to run. A job to do and you are a distraction.'

'That is a load of shit and you know it!' I cried walking over to him. 'Why are you really doing this? Is it because to everyone here I am scum? Because I have respect for people no matter what their status is? Or is this really because of Ethan?'

'No! Listen to me; Amelia! I can't be anything but your Alpha! I cannot imprint with you, it will never happen, and I do not want to fall for someone I can never be with, we can never be together and the sooner we both accept that the better.' He shouted.

'Tell the truth! It's nothing to do with that! You just don't want to be with me, you don't want to be with someone that your perfect Elites will never accept. This is not you talking Arlo, it's them! You call yourself an Alpha, but you are ruled by others. That is not an Alpha. That's pathetic!' I stormed out of the office slamming the door behind me, not bothering to wait for another answer that was an obvious lie. I couldn't believe what had just happened. It was only last night he was holding me, making me think that maybe there was a future for us somewhere; and now this.

I started walking to Piper's house, I had called ahead to ask her if I could stay at their house for a couple of days, I needed some time away from the mansion and from everyone in it. Matt had to stay with Arlo and eat dinner, he was the packs Delta, the next in line after the Beta wolf. I knew Matt wouldn't agree with this, he wouldn't agree with Arlo, but he had to stay loyal to his best friend and his pack. And I understood it.

'Hi, Hun.' Piper smiled opening her front door.

'Amelia, What a pleasant surprise. I would just like to say that it will be a pleasure having you stay with us, and if you need or want anything, anything at all, then please don't hesitate to ask.' Pipers mother said, appearing beside her daughter and gesturing for me to enter. I smiled at the woman and nodded.

'Thank you so much Mrs-'

'Please, call me Tanya.' She said, cutting in and smiling kindly. Tanya stepped aside and directed me up to Pipers bedroom, before quickly hurrying back down to the kitchen. Piper took my bag, hanging it on the end of the bed, before turning to face me.

'What happened?' She asked, with a look of concern in her eyes. I sighed and dropped down beside her; fighting the urge to cry.

'It is such a long story. Basically, Arlo is a prick!' I growled, clenching my teeth and shaking my head in frustration. Pipers eyes widened and her mouth fell open. *It suddenly dawned on me that people probably weren't used to pack members talking about their alpha this way.*

I sighed once more and smiled. 'Everything is just getting a little much for me. I am sick of all these rules. Charlie accused me of being disrespectful, Arlo agreed. So, I left... oh and apparently, I had sex with Ethan! Funny thing is; I don't recall that happening, but obviously they know more about my life than I do, everyone else said that it happened; so, that *must* make it true.' I said sarcastically.

'Oh, Lia. I am so sorry. You know that you can stay here as long as you like. My mum has already said so and if it is any con-solation; I didn't believe that awful rumour.'

'As long as I'm not imposing. I am sorry about putting you in this position. I just had to get away and you were the first person that I thought to call.'

'You have nothing to apologise for. I wouldn't have seen you stuck somewhere that you didn't want to be. And my mum has said that she is so happy that you thought of us as a place to escape to. As you know, us *Mutts* aren't really thought of by the Elites. The only time they do is when they are abusing us.' Piper said, gestur-ing to the extremely sore looking wound on her head.

'That is so wrong! I just don't understand how people could treat others in this way.'

'And that is what makes you so special sweetheart.' Tanya said, entering the room and smiling over to us. 'Now, I have just put the kettle on. So, how about we all go down and have a nice cup of tea? I put some cookies in the oven the moment that I heard you were on your way here. Triple chocolate chip.' She added smiling sweetly.

'That would be lovely, thank you so much Mrs- I mean, Tanya.' I watched as Pipers mother turned away and made her way back down to the kitchen as me and Piper both rose from the bed. I took a step towards the door when the distant sound of the lullaby filled my ears. I spun around on the spot and stared out of Pipers bedroom window and noticed that it overlooked the gates and stared out deep into the forest. The call continued, seemingly beckoning me to follow. I stepped closer to the window and placed my hand on the glass, refusing to blink, or tear my gaze away from the dark forest.

'Hey, Lia… what's up?' Piper asked, placing her hand on my shoulder causing me to flinch. 'Woah.' She said, taking a step back and holding her hands up defensively. 'Is everything ok? You look like you have seen a ghost.' I sighed and forced a smile.

'Of course, I just thought that…' I was cut off midsentence once more as the lullaby echoed around me once more. 'Did you hear that?' I asked, still refusing to take my stare away from her window. Piper stepped closer to me and followed my stare, standing in silence for a moment before shaking her head.

'No. I… I don't hear anything.' She replied, looking at me from the corner of her eyes. 'Lia… are you sure that everything is ok?' I sighed and pushed the calling to the back of my mind, trying my hardest to block it all out. *I trusted Piper with my life. But this secret, it was something that I had fought against my entire life, and now it was finally about to come out.* A single tear rolled down my cheek as the fear took over me.

'Pipes, I…' I paused and shook my head, sitting on the edge of her bed once more. 'All my life… I have heard this… calling… a lullaby. I hear it in my dreams. I hear it when I am awake. I heard it that day that I ran away from the cottage. And I hadn't heard it again until that morning that I woke in the medical ward, after Lori and her goons beat the crap out of me.'

'Lia, I don't mean for this to sound insensitive but… I don't think that that is normal. I mean, I have never heard anything like that… but then I am a Mutt. But I am pretty sure that it is something that we would have been taught about growing up.'

'That's what I was afraid of.' I whispered, sounding defeated. We sat in silence for a few moments, before she spoke again.

'Do you know what it is that this… calling is saying to you? I mean, you said that it was a lullaby, so does that mean that it has words?' I shook my head.

'It's more like someone singing the tune of a song. The only time that I hear the words are in my dreams. But… by the time that I wake up, I can't remember what the words are.' I hesitated. 'Piper… do you think… do you think that there is something wrong with me?' I asked, turning my saddened stare towards my best friend.

Piper hurried over to me and pulled me to my feet, staring at me intently. We stood in silence for a few seconds, her seemingly trying to figure me out.

'Do you know what. Yes. There is something wrong with you. You're a freak Amelia Hunt.' Piper said plainly. My eyes fell open in shock from her words, especially as they were matched with a serious look on her face. I held my breath as I tried to understand what was happening when a smile broke out across Pipers face. 'You… an Elite, are nice to all the Mutts you see. You stand up for yourself against the alpha. You treat everyone you meet with love and compassion. You are a major freak Amelia. And do you know what. That is why I love you. And I am so proud to call you my best friend.'

I felt as though my heart was about to explode as I narrowed my eyes playfully at my friend, grinning wildly.

'Piper… I may be a freak… but you… you are a bitch.' I giggled, bumping her with my hip. We both dropped back onto her bed laughing as she beat me playfully. She leapt back up to her feet and pulled me to mine.

'Come on. Let's go and get that tea before my mum thinks that we have run off into the sunset.' She said still giggling, pulling me in for a hug and kissing my cheek. *Through all the sadness that was happening with me currently, in this moment, I couldn't have been happier. Is this what it felt like to have a "true" friend?*

The two of us made our way down the stairs and I followed Piper into her cosy kitchen. I had never felt so comfortable in a house like this. Not even the one that I grew up in with my grandparents. I sat at the table as Piper made tea, her back was turned to me which gave me a chance to look at her head, the healing process had started but it was slow. *Why did I heal so quickly, and she and Lori didn't?* I guess that was just another thing to add to my list of things that I didn't understand.

I had been at Piper's house for a week now, even when she returned to work and went for the Pack meals, I didn't leave at all, hiding away was better than having to face everyone and that degrading rumour. She and her mum made me up a bed on the floor of Piper's bedroom although I ended up sleeping in Pipers bed with her and I would tidy their home when they were all at work, they said I didn't have to, but I wanted to, for me it was a way of saying thank you. Matt would come over and do some training with me in their back garden for an hour a day; Piper had even started joining in. We never discussed Arlo at all, I guess he didn't know what to say and I didn't want to talk about it, he was my Alpha; and nothing more.

I had just finished hoovering the bungalows main hallway when I heard the doorbell ring. In the whole week of me staying here; other than Matt, we hadn't had any visitors. I switched the hoover off and slowly made my way to the front door and sucked down a deep breath. I didn't know if anyone other than Piper, her mother and Matt knew where I was or not, I was hoping that I was going undetected. *But living with creatures that were some of the best scent followers in the world probably meant that everyone knew where I was.* I looked through the peep hold and gasped; Marie was waiting for me to answer the door. I sighed softly and cursed under my breath before hesitantly pulling the door open.

'Hey.' I smiled opening the front door, moving aside so she could come in.

'Hello, sweetheart. How are you?' she asked looking around.

'I am okay.' Pausing for a moment. I took a step back and gestured for her to enter the house. *I wonder if Marie had ever been to any of the houses of the "Mutts" before?* I waited for her to be in the hall before closing the door and leading her into the kitchen.

'We miss having you at the mansion.' She said sitting on one of the stools. I turned the kettle on to boil and lent against the kitchen side.

'You mean, you and Matt miss having me at the mansion.' Marie paused for a second and then weakly smiled.

'Not just me and Matt.' I sighed and got two cups out from the cupboard which was on the kitchen wall.

'He made his feelings perfectly clear to me last week at dinner.' I replied, feeling the burn of anger rush through me at the very memory. 'I know he's my alpha, and your son but he can be such a-' I stopped and pressed my lips into a thin line. *This was not the time or place to have this rant. Especially to his mother!* I decided it was best to change the subject. 'Arlo, told me that you are originally from another pack?' I poured us both a cup of tea and sat on a stool opposite Marie.

'Yes I am. I am originally from the Shadowfang pack, my mother at the time was the Alpha's daughter and she fell in love with a *Mutt...*; Marie paused and shook her head before continuing. 'Sorry sweetheart, I just hate using that word, let me rephrase, she fell in love with someone who wasn't an Elite and got pregnant with me. Once I was born, she abandoned me in the woods, just outside of our territory. I am not sure if she left me to die or if she hoped someone would find me but thankfully my adoptive father did whilst out hunting. They raised me; him and his wife, my adoptive mother, as if I were their own, always making sure that I had everything I ever could have wanted and more. I am extremely lucky; I know that not everyone who has had a life like mine could say the same.' She said, smiling sympathetically. I creased my brow in confusion and considered her words for a moment. *Was I supposed to understand what it was that she meant by that? Perhaps she was referring to my father and my brother?* Marie looked sad for a moment and then she smiled at me reassuringly.

'Have you ever been curious about possibly finding your biological parents?' I asked.

'That would be difficult darling, my biological parents were both murdered by the Alpha at the time… my mother's father, and he didn't stop there, he tried to have me killed when I was a child also. That is one of the reasons why we do not get on with that particular pack. It's only because I became Luna that he couldn't hurt me. Thankfully he is dead now, but my uncle took over and was just as bad as his father.' She paused for a moment, her gaze snapping from her distant memory back to my face and a slight blush crept across her cheeks. 'I am sorry sweetheart, you must think I am so horrible, thinking that way about my own biological family.' She added with a sad smile.

'Not at all! I can't believe that people would stoop that low. All because someone wasn't in a certain class? That is a vile way to live!' I retorted, balling my hands into fists under the table. *I have never met a woman as sweet and kind-hearted as Marie; other than Tanya and her daughter of course, and to think that there was someone in the world that wanted to take this beautiful woman's life for being "wrong" in their eyes!* In that moment I felt so bad for Marie. She must have lived in so much fear, maybe that was why she had always been so kind to me; because of the family that I came from. I am just glad she was found and got her happy ending. I looked down at the table.

'Marie; could you possibly tell me more about the legend, of the twins?' She shook of her and smiled

'Darling that is just a silly made up story, but I do have something to say.' She paused and then smiled, her blue eyes twinkling 'Amelia, just remember, it's not where you came from that defines you, lineage does not matter, status does not matter, parents do not matter. What matters is that you do not give up on yourself and keep being the good person that you are, fight for what is right no matter who tries to stand in your way.' Unshed tears shimmered in her eyes as she rose from her stool and turned back toward the front door.

'Thank you, Marie.' I said, my voice small. Marie turned and pulled me in for a tight warm embrace, kissing the top of my head and then holding me out and arm's length before looking me up and down.

'Remember Amelia, that beauty is found within. And not everyone could have as much beauty on the inside as they have on the outside. You are a rare one, Amelia Hunt.' With those final words, she gave me a wink and disappeared out the door.

After Marie left, I sat and thought about our conversation, why did she just change the subject after I brought up the legend? Why was she happier to talk about her sad past then that? I shook my head *You're just overthinking all of this; Amelia …but why?* I thought to myself.

Piper came home at half past 2 and sat with me in her bedroom.

'How are you feeling?' she asked, wondering if I was ready to go back to the pack mansion.

'Like I need to get my own house.' I replied, gazing out of the window. 'But I would have to ask Arlo for that, and I doubt he would allow me to have one.' Piper sighed and followed my gaze as I stared at the woods.

'You're not thinking of leaving, again are you?' she asked, sounding panicked.

'No, but I am thinking of biting the bullet and asking Arlo if I can move out of the pack mansion. I wonder if I can voluntarily become a… Mutt? I am not welcome to them and I can't keep putting myself through torture anymore.' I picked up my mobile and searched for Arlo's name and I started composing a message.

Amelia: I want to move out of the Mansion, so I was wondering if you would allow me to move in one of the empty houses, I could start working in the kitchen and do some jobs to earn my keep.

Arlo: No!!

Amelia: Why?!

Arlo: Because I said no!

Amelia: I am not staying at the Mansion; I am not welcome there by anyone one other than your mother and Matt. Your being selfish! And anyway, me moving out would help the rumours about 'us' stop spreading and then that way your life would be a lot easier. Wouldn't it? So just let me move into one of the houses...please

Arlo: My life would be easier if you stopped sulking and come back here! You are so stubborn!

Amelia: Sulking? What the fuck Arlo? I am not sulking... and my answer is NO! I do not want to go back to the shitty mansion, I hate being there, I would rather sleep in the stables with Pretty Girl! You are being so unreasonable now!

Arlo: Amelia I swear to Selene, you will come back to the mansion even if that means I have to bring you back myself! Get your stuff ready and come back... please, if you don't then I will come and get you myself.

I threw my phone on the floor and growled in frustration.

'I hate him!' I cried staring at Piper, a smile crept across her lips and she started giggling. 'What? What is so funny?' I grumbled. She shrugged.

'I think you have met your match in him, I have never known such a stubborn couple in my life, you were made for each other, I swear it.'

'We are not a couple! And we are not made for each other, he is an Elite and I am not; or I won't be once he agrees to revoking my status. We won't ever be able to imprint with each other so it's just a lost cause,' I said sulkily crossing my arms. We sat in silence for a few more seconds before Piper started shifting eagerly. *She clearly wanted to ask something but didn't know how...* I sighed and turned to face her. 'Just say it.' I said with a smile.

'Ok, I have been dying to know about this... you and Ethan? I mean. He is so hot. But... he's a Mu-' Piper paused as I narrowed my eyes at her before correcting herself. 'I mean, a Non-Elite. So, what is the truth about you and Ethan?' I paused for a second as I tried to process her questions. *What were my intentions with Ethan? I really did like him. A LOT. But he wasn't Arlo.*

'If I am honest, I really like him.'

'But, what about Arlo?'

'He infuriates me! He is stubborn, moody, sulky…' I paused as I took in the look on Pipers face. A cross between fighting the urge to laugh and confusion. 'What?' I snapped impatiently. She rolled her eyes.

'Hey, that sounds just like someone else that I know…' She said plainly with a slight shrug. I narrowed my eyes at her and hit her with one of the pillows from her bed.

'Now that's rude!' I said with a giggle.

'Rude… but true.' She cackled, throwing her head back and laughing hysterically.

'In all honesty, I do really, really like Arlo. But there are rules to follow. He told me that himself!'

'Hey, listen; stranger things have happened, like you always say to me, you have always been so different, and the normal rules definitely do not apply to you! Selene knows what hope the rest of us have, because I personally think you were made for each other. And if the Goddess hasn't made that official then I think she needs to have a stern word with herself!' She said rubbing my tense back. My phone buzzed again. Piper and I glanced down at it before looking at one another.

'Leave it!' I muttered, turning to look back out of her bedroom window. Piper sighed and reached for my phone glancing at the screen. I had a couple more texts from Arlo.

'Read them.' Piper said passing me my phone and placing it in my palm.

Arlo: Answer me.

Arlo: For fuck sake! Why are you being so stubborn?

Arlo: I am sorry for what I said… I was wrong, I shouldn't have listened to anyone, now will you please answer me.

Arlo: Fine! I am on my way to you now.

Arlo: I am nearly at Piper's house, stop ignoring my messages!

I growled angrily as I replied to his last text.

Amelia: Turn around! I am not coming back to the mansion, even if that means I live in the stables with Pretty Girl.

Arlo: Too late, I am outside.

I let out another growl of frustration. This man was seriously starting to piss me off! I rose from Pipers bed and stomped down the stairs; storming to the front door.

'What do you want; *Alpha*?' I grumbled closing the front door, so I was now standing outside with him. Arlo looked at me and then narrowed his eyes.

'What do you think you are playing at?'

'Excuse me? Arlo, What the fuck do you want? I have nothing to say to you!'

'I want you to come back to the mansion.' He replied, slowly starting to walk towards me.

'I don't want to come back though. It's horrible there, I hate it. Everyone thinks it's okay to talk to me like I am a piece of shit. I am so fed up of it all. I am not even allowed to defend myself without getting into trouble. I try to ignore the comments but somehow I am still in the wrong and to top it all off I am being accused of sleeping around with everyone.' I grumbled slowly backing away from him. He growled in frustration and grabbed my wrist before pulling me back towards the mansion. I tried to fight him. *Well, I sort of tried to fight him, it bugged the hell out of me that even just the feel of his hand on my skin was sending fireworks shooting across my arm.* We continued onwards, ignoring all the pack members that we passed. Arlo hadn't acknowledged any of them.

We went to his bedroom, both ignoring everyone's stares as I followed him up the stairs.

'So, I have another apology to make.' Arlo started as he sat on his settee. 'I should have never said all of that, you were right and before you say anything, you are part of this pack whether anyone else likes it or not. And that is why you are not moving into one of the houses. You are going to stay here and as your Alpha I will defend and protect you. Just like I should have done in the first place.' His face was serious, and he sounded sincere.

'What about them questioning your authority?' I asked

crossing my arms across my chest as I lowered myself down onto the deep purple rug which was next to the settee. *Note to self, I think that this rug was softer than most beds I had ever slept in! I needed one of these!*

'What about it? They can't question me; I am a good alpha and I look after my pack. I haven't let the power go to my head like most Alpha's do and I won't be told I am wrong for choosing who I want to be with. And I want to be with you.'

'But wherever I go trouble follows and I am a distraction' I said repeating the words he said a week before.

'Then let it follow, it's nothing I can't deal with and you are a good distraction. I am still working my arse off for this pack and in my spare time I spend it with my friends, just like I should do and plus I really like being around you.' He said a smile breaking out across his face. I couldn't help but smile back at him, *this man way driving me crazy! Literally!* He reached forward and took hold of my hands. 'Am I forgiven now?' he asked pulling me over to him.

'I don't know; *Alpha*. I need your word that you're going to let me have my own house, with one of those amazing rugs and then maybe I will consider forgiving you.' I smirked. A light in Arlo's eyes flashed and it was a cuteness that was almost too much to deal with. He reached down and helped me to my feet before leading me over to the sofa. He sat down and I mimicked his actions; all the while, climbing onto his lap, both of my legs were bent either side of him and I was sitting on his crotch.

'You think your funny huh?' he growled looking into my eyes. I smirked at him and nodded,

'Yup, and so do you.' I laid my head on his shoulder and closed my eyes as he wrapped his big arms around my waist.

'I have missed this.' He whispered.

'Me too' I admitted lifting my head to look at him. I stared into his golden eyes and allowed myself to get lost for a moment. Before I had a chance to process anything, I pushed my face forward and slowly locked my lips on his.

I pulled back from the kiss and stared deep into his golden eyes once more. I was scared to admit it, but I could slowly feel myself falling in love with him. *How could I be so stupid?* I knew that it wasn't a good thing. Nothing good would ever come from falling in love with an alpha. I had read all about it in one of the many ancient books of our kind in the library. The moment that he imprinted with someone else, I knew that it would be over for us. There was no guarantee that a werewolf would imprint. But the alpha always found their Luna. I guess that the Goddess made sure that that happened. I sighed softly and dropped my gaze down to our interlocked hands. I could feel every little movement that he made, it sent jolts of electricity rushing up my arm, seemingly directly into my heart.

'Why are you sad?' Arlo asked, snapping me out of my deep thoughts. I plastered a smile on my face and shook my head lightly.

'I'm not sad. Was just thinking I replied with a shrug. He ran his finger over my lips and smiled, a twinkling in his eyes. I leant forward and kissed him passionately, running my fingers down his chiselled abs. Before I knew it, I was playing with the waist band of his boxers; although he still hands jeans on, his boxers were poking out the top, and I could see the black elasticated waist band. I tugged at them, sliding the tip of my finger under the band and lightly stroked the soft skin just underneath. Arlo let out a short groan that sent me wild.

I pressed into our kiss a little harder, running one hand through his hair and the other stroking the prominent V of his abs. I glanced down at where my hand was stroking and watched as his jeans twitched as he slowly got hard. I pulled back from our kiss and bit my bottom lip. My hands were trembling. *Was it with fear? Or desire?* I leant in once more and softly kissed his neck. I felt his breathing turn ragged and knew in that moment that he wanted me. I dipped my fingers a little lower into his boxers and lightly stroked the trimmed hairs, causing him to drop his head bad over the arm of the couch and thrust his hips forward lightly. I had never done anything like this before, but there was a feeling in the pit of my stomach, a hunger that was new to me. I slowly kissed lower down his neck, across his collar bone, pulling his fitted t-shirt up to reveal his beautiful tanned torso. I flicked my tongue out between my lips and touched his nipple. He groaned once more and shifted, causing my hands to slip a little deeper into his underwear. My fingers grazed the base of his hardness causing him to gasp and sit upright.

'W-What is it? D-Did I do it wrong?' I stammered, my cheeks burning as they flushed bright red. Arlo laughed and dropped his head back on the arm of the chair? *He actually laughed! Prick!* He sat forward and met my eyes once more, pulling me onto his lap.

'Lia, why did you assume that it was you that had done something wrong?' He asked, tipping my head up with two fingers placed under my chin. I stared, almost hypnotised into his golden eyes and took in the multitude of colours; the hint of brown, a splash of yellow. I shook my head and shifted uncomfortably and shrugged.

'Well, you seemed into it, and then... then you stopped so quick. Did I hurt you?' Arlo let out a small growl of frustration before tilting his head back and closing his eyes.

'Lia! I am not letting your first time be on my couch. And...' He hesitated for a moment and I closed my eyes. *Shit! Here it comes. He's going to end it. AGAIN!* 'I don't want to hurt you. That's why I stopped.' He paused once more and bit his lip; an innocent action that turned my insides to lava. 'I really do like you; Amelia; a lot and it scares me because I don't want anyone else and what if we don't Impr-'

'Shhhhhh' I hushed putting my finger to his lips, feeling a smile tug at the corners of my lips. *That was it? He was scared of hurting me.* 'Don't. I don't want to think about that right now.' Arlo smiled at me and moved a strand of my hair and put it behind my ear.

'Stay with me tonight?' he asked looking into my eyes. I smiled and nodded yes. At that moment. *I wished I could stay with him forever.* I closed my eyes, drinking in this moment. I wanted to remember things just like this; how happy we both are in this moment. I drew in a deep shuddering breath, fighting the sobs that I could feel building in my chest.

'Is everything alright beautiful?' Arlo asked, tracing

the lining of my jaw with his thump. *Oh no! The tears were coming!* Without another thought, I pushed forward and gently placed my lips on his. He hesitated for the briefest of moments before he reached his hand up; tangling his fingers through my hair, pulling my face closer into his. A rush of heat exploded in my stomach and rushed through me, causing my inner wolf to rage on, giving me a sense of need unlike anything I had ever felt. A small groan escaped from me as he grazed his teeth across my bottom lip. I know that he said that we shouldn't have sex. I understand his reasoning. I understand that he is a gentleman. *But why the fuck did I have to find a gentleman as hot as him!*

10

Arlo;

BANG, BANG, BANG...

I sat up startled from the pounding on my bedroom door. I looked at my phone trying to get myself to wake up enough to focus; it was 6:30am. Why the hell was I being woken up on a weekend at this time? I looked at Amelia; she too had sat up, clutching her chest, clearly panicked from being woken this way.

'Stay there.' I whispered climbing from the bed. She nodded but the minute that I started walking across the room, I heard her follow me as I opened my bedroom door. Charlie was standing there as white as a sheet.

'Arlo, we have a big problem.' He panted, 'A tracker... a tracker in training has been killed.'

'What?!' I cried grabbing my hoodie that was hanging on the back of my door. I slipped on my trainers and kissed Amelia's cheek. 'Stay there.' I repeated widening my eyes, this time giving her a look that meant business. I did not want her a part of this. This was too much, even for me! But I was the alpha, this was all part of the job description.

Amelia;

I watched as Arlo left the room slamming the door behind him. A tracker had been killed. Charlies words repeated in my head over and over again. How could a tracker be killed? They all went out together for training, no one was ever separated. That is what everyone had been telling me about the non-Elites. I just didn't understand what was happening.

Maybe it was an accident? I thought as I unlocked the balcony door. It was just starting to get light, the horizon was shimmering a pink, golden bronze as the sun was beginning to rise. It was still freezing, I was only wearing Arlo's T-shirt and a pair of my PJ shorts, my feet stung and ached as I stepped out onto the ice-cold concrete balcony floor with my bare feet, but I pushed through it. I could hear shouting from below me, I looked down to see all of the Elite pack members running towards the woods, a bad feeling came over me. It was in that moment that I knew that this was no accident.

Arlo:

'How the fuck did this happen Jeff.' I roared as we finally got to the woods. 'Why was he on his own? And how the hell did all of you trackers not pick up the scent of this other wolf? Some unknown Mutt on our territory.' I was furious, I knew we had someone lurking in the woods every now and then because sometimes we could smell them; they were definitely male, but other than that, it was hard to define much about them. But somehow, after we started tracking him, the scent would just go; disappear as though he was never even there. It was like he had managed to mask his scent to stop us from following him. But that was impossible! There was no way a wolf could completely cover up their own scent from other wolves, especially not with the amazing trackers that we had in our pack. I had seen first-hand how amazing my pack truly were. I sniffed the air and that familiar scent hit me. It was the same wolf that tried to attack Amelia, and the same one who followed her through the woods, not only was she still in danger, but now my pack was too. I shook my head and supressed the urge to growl; I always knew when I was close to losing my shit, my animal instincts would try and take over. I clenched my teeth and stared ahead, following my pack to the spot that they claimed one of our own had fallen. I didn't need to look up to know that we had arrived. I would have smelt the blood a mile off. And from the smell of it, there was a lot. I looked up at the pale faces of my pack as they struggled to get a handle of their emotions. It was always hard losing one of our own.

I was led to the body of a young boy and I recognised him immediately; Jamie, his father was a retired tracker and his mother was one of the waitresses that tended to us most mornings. My heart sank. They were a genuinely nice couple; this news would devastate them. I turned my stare back to Jamie's corpse. He was only 18 years old and he was one of our Trackers in training; I remembered him signing up for this position. He was so excited to be following in his father's footsteps, all he wanted was to make his family proud. My mouth went dry as raw emotion hit me. I closed my eyes for a second before turning my stare back towards him; his throat had either been ripped out or bitten out, there was no way that this was a chance killing. This was done by someone that knew what they were doing!

How did this happen?' I asked, my voice quiet and as calm as it could be. We all stood in silence for a moment and I couldn't take it any longer. 'Answer me.' I shouted spinning around and staring at Jeffery.

'As far as I knew they were all behind me; Arlo, I was leading them all back to the pack mansion as we had finished training for the day. I don't know why but before we got back to the gates, I decided to do a head count; we were one man down and Jamie was gone. I got the boys back in the mansion grounds and took two of the more experienced trackers and went looking for him… that's when we found him… like this.' Jeffery paused for a minute, his voice quivering as he spoke. He closed his eyes and swallowed back his emotions before continuing. 'No one heard a thing; I don't know what happened I swear. Not one of us smelt someone else on the territory. I told them that there was a possibility that there was an outsider around, but nothing. I am so sorry.' Jeffery cried; his face paling slightly, clearly wracked with guilt. I felt the anger bubbling to the service once more and clenched my teeth.

'Then you have the job of telling his parents, he was killed on your watch.' I snapped, I turned towards Charlie and Matt. 'Matt; you carry him back, Charlie; you go and get a sheet, I need him covered. Take him straight to Benjamin. Jeffery; Once you have told his parents, we need to call an emergency pack meeting! Make sure that you get everyone gathered. Mutts and Elites alike!' At my orders I watched as Charlie turned to look at me after studying the body.

'I think…' He paused for a moment, his face contorting in an emotion that I struggled to place.

'What? Spit it out!' I snapped, glaring at him. I knew that this wasn't my packs fault. But I was furious with them. They should have been watching Jamie. Especially as this was his first-time out tracking. Charlie cleared his throat and turned his stare back to the bloodied sight and sighed.

'I think that Amelia and that Mutt did this.' He said, his voice barely above a whisper. I was stunned. I knew that I had to pay attention to what he was saying; especially as he was my beta, my second in command. But it infuriated me that he had such hatred for his sister, it disgusted me that he could easily put the blame on her. We all knew she hadn't even shifted yet, how the hell could she rip someone's throat out… but Ethan could shift, and he could rip someone's throat out… but then no one could shift on demand; *none of this was making any sense.*

'Don't be fucking stupid; Charlie.' I snapped, balling my fists tightly.

'I am not being stupid! I bet it was her and that thing, they probably sliced his throat and made it look like a bite.' He replied. Who was he trying to convince? Me or himself?

'I can guarantee you it was not Amelia! And I know that because she was with me all night.' Everyone stopped what they were doing and looked at me in surprise, Matt was the only one who carried on with the tasks that I have given him. I turned and glared at my pack once more, they knew better than to defy their alpha. 'Is there any more theories about the murderer? Or shall we wait for the pack meeting?'

Amelia;

I watched as the pack rushed back into the building, the younger ones looking a little more shaken than the others. I guess that they have never experienced anything like this before. I know that I have never even seen a dead body. I watched as Arlo, Charlie and a few of the others stormed back up the grass towards the mansion. Arlo looked up and locked eyes with me momentarily; I had never seen him look so worn down. This was clearly taking its toll on him. I watched until the last pack member disappeared below me; entering the mansion; and knew that it would only be a matter of minutes until Arlo was back up here. I hurried back into the warmth of the room and stood awkwardly, waiting for his return.

Arlo walked back into the bedroom and went straight into the bathroom, he looked angry and tense, I couldn't help but wonder what the hell had happened out there. It couldn't have been good no matter what it was. My heart went out to him. He was far too young to be going through all this stress. I know that it is all part of what comes with being alpha, but it wasn't fair. I knew deep down that this was affecting him more than he was letting on, but all I could do was be there for him. I closed my eyes and tried to think of any way that I could help him. But it was hard. How did you try to help someone run a pack that hated everything about you?

I walked over to the bathroom door and hesitated. Maybe it was best to leave him alone for a while. I had seen Charlie and Matt carry the body back with a sheet covering it, they both looked upset and for once it seemed that Charlie was showing real emotion.

I sat on Arlo's bed and looked around the room, wondering if I should knock on the bathroom door to see if he was okay, it was silent in there, I decided it was best that I leave him in peace.

'Arlo; I am going to go now okay? I said knocking on the bathroom door, I waited for a reply, but he didn't say a word to me. I sighed softly, and slowly crept from his room. I knew he was hurting; I just didn't know what I could do to help him. My stomach rumbled, so I decided to head down to the kitchen. Could I even eat yet? What if Arlo didn't come back down any time soon? We wouldn't still have to wait, would we? I got to the dining hall and glanced in at the open doors. The room was empty. There was an eerie stillness to the air that left shivers running across my skin. I glanced over my shoulder and followed the sound of pots and pans clanging around. I hesitated for a brief moment before placing my hand flat on the swinging doors and pushed. The minute they were open a friendly voice caught me off guard.

'Lia! What are you doing in here?' Piper asked, grinning as she pushed a trolley full of Pancakes, waffles and croissants towards the dining area. I could tell by her happy face, that she, and others still didn't know a thing.

'Fancy some help in the kitchen today?' I asked grinning. Piper stopped,

'You're not allowed to do that; you're an Elite. Kitchen work is the Mutts job' I bit my lip to stop myself from saying anything; but the more that I heard the non-Elites called Mutts it grated on me. I sighed and shrugged before turning into the kitchen.

'Who cares. I am not asking to get paid for it, I just want to do something to help.' I looked around, taking in the sight. The kitchen was just as big as I had imagined, it had a built-in freezer and four fridges, as well as four ovens. No one had noticed I was in there; they were all too busy working hard. The smell of freshly fried bacon filled my nose and my stomach rumbled; it was so loud that they all turned around; goddam werewolf hearing!

'Oh, my goodness! Amelia! What are you doing in here?' Pipers mother; Tanya asked. 'Shouldn't you be in the dining hall?' I opened my mouth to answer her when it suddenly dawned on me. I didn't know who it was who had been killed; and I certainly didn't know if their parents had been told yet. I drew in a deep breath and smiled.

'I should really, but I would rather help you guys out.' I smiled innocently.

'Oh, my dear girl, that's ever so kind, but I don't want you getting in trouble.' She replied, sounding a little panicked as she stood stacking a plate full of hot crispy bacon.

'Don't worry about me, honestly. I really do just want to help and if anyone has a problem then I promise I can deal with it.' I reassured her. 'And as for everyone in here, if they say anything then I will make sure that I tell them you asked me to leave but I didn't.' I paused and looked around the room at all the worried faces, before forcing a smile. 'So, what would you like me to do?' I looked around the large kitchen once more, it appeared that everyone had a designated area.

Some were cooking meat, some were cooking eggs, someone was cooking and buttering toast and some were making hot drinks. I spotted the overloaded sink full of used kitchen appliances. 'Can I wash up?' I asked rolling my sleeves up. This was nothing new to me, I always tidied my grandparents'

house out of sheer boredom, and I noticed that although considering there were many expensive kitchen appliances, that there wasn't a dishwasher! And this kitchen needed at least three of them! Tanya looked over to me; a little surprised, nodding.

'If you want to sweetie. But like I said, you don't have to help us at all. We are used to this busy workload.' Tanya replied, smiling sweetly. Wow. This woman truly was something special. After the way that she is treated by the Elites, she is still down here doing her best for them and is not complaining at all. I nodded in agreement then turned away from her. I wasn't quite sure what was getting me so emotional, but I needed to get stuck in with all this washing up to get my mind off of everything.

I got lost in my thoughts as I continuously washed up thinking of what had happened earlier that morning. Did the rest of the pack know or was it all a big secret? Who died? Arlo was so upset, and I didn't know what to do or say to him to make him feel better, maybe it was for the best that I kept out of the way.

'Oh my gosh!' Piper whispered not very quietly. 'There is not a single Elite sitting at the main table, it's just the rest of the pack in there this morning, something bad must have happened.' Play dumb Amelia. I thought to myself as I scrubbed a frying pan.

'Oh really? That is strange.' I replied still not turning around. Piper stood beside me holding a T-towel and picked up a freshly washed plate.

'Yeah, everyone is talking about why they think it is, but no one really knows. It is so odd, this never happens.'

'Piper; that is not our business dear; we must just carry on working and wait for everyone to eat. It is not our place to speculate or spread gossip!' Her mother cut in, taking the now dry plate from her daughter's hand. The phone on the wall rang and Tanya hurried over to it; plucked it from the dock and placed the receiver to her ear.

'Hell- Arlo? Oh, what a pleasant-' She was cut short by something he said, and her face fell slightly. She nodded and mumbled some uh-huh's and yes's but remained professional. She sighed deeply, nodded and placed the phone back in its cradle. 'Ok, ladies. Arlo has asked that we serve breakfast now. He said that he and the other Elites have an important issue to attend and doesn't want everyone else going hungry, so, let's get moving!' Tanya called sweetly. The rest of the ladies in the room sprang into action, each grabbing one of the many fully loaded trollies and hurrying out to the dining hall.

By the time we had eaten something ourselves and deep cleaned the whole kitchen, it was time to start preparing lunch. I was exhausted already, how the hell did these guys all mange to do this nearly every day? It was slave labour and I didn't think it was fair, if this was my pack, I would make the Elites work too.

'Amelia; you really do not need to help us, why don't you go and have a rest?' Tanya said looking concerned.

'Honestly I am fine. What would you like me to do?' I asked re tying my hair up as it had become loose.

'Why don't you cut up some sandwiches?' she said still unsure. I nodded and smiled.
'Sure thing.' Piper had left to serve some drinks with the other waitresses, so Tanya and I started talking.
'You know, my daughter is so lucky to have you as a friend.' I smiled at what Tanya had said, I felt lucky to have Piper as my friend too. 'And this pack is lucky to have you here. Us guys, the non-Elites really do like you. We have never had anyone stand up for any of us and for you to defend my daughter has not gone unnoticed.' The kitchen was silent for a minute, all of the staff listening in on what Tanya was saying. 'And you are perfect for our Alpha.' I paused for

a second as the blush swept across my face.

'There isn't anything going on between Arlo and me; we are just good friends.' I said, my mind wondering back to last night. There was something going on between us but not even I knew what it was, and I didn't think Arlo knew either. Tanya straightened a little and her face fell.

'I am sorry. There was me telling Piper not to gossip and speculate and there I was doing just that. Forgive me. I forget my place.'

'Your place?' I asked sounding confused. 'Please Tanya, don't feel that you can't be yourself around me. If I am honest, I feel like I fit in with all of you better than the Elites. So, your place, is being who you are and nothing else. No class lower than anyone else's and you don't have to treat me like one of them!' I said, jerking my chin towards the door. Before either of us had a chance to say another word Piper rushed burst into the kitchen; causing us both to flinch; pushing her empty trolley.

'The Elites are back; they are all ready for lunch. We need to hurry and get the food out quick.' She cried picking up silver trays full of sandwiches. I watched as all the other waitresses started stacking their trolleys full of food, all equally looking terrified. I can't believe that people in this pack were made to feel so small by those around them. Maybe that was why I sympathised with the non-Elites. Maybe it was the fact that I had been treated the same way by those that were supposed to love and care for me?

'Do you need me to help?' I asked picking up a tray full of cut up fruit.

'No, it's okay. They will have a fit if they see you in here. Arlo already looks irritated and on edge.' Piper answered swiftly plucking the tray out of my hand. I knew why he was so on edge and yet I couldn't say a word as to why, the pack obviously didn't know anything as Piper would have said if they had announced it. I glanced up at the clock it was now 1:30pm, I had been in the kitchen since 7:30 this morning and yet the kitchen staff had started at 6am. Did they even get a break? Piper hurried back into the kitchen and started loading her now empty tray up with more food to take out to the tables.

'Piper when do your shifts change?' I asked as she walked back into the kitchen, my poor friend looked exhausted, everyone did.

'We have to clean in here first, but then we should be finished by 2:30pm and then we all need to be back at 4:30pm to prepare dinner for 6. Tonight, it is a yummy roast.' I watched as everyone eagerly cleaned the kitchen desperately so that they could eat some lunch and then go home for a break. I was definitely going to be speaking to Arlo about this. The way that these people were treated was appalling. Something has to be done about it.

Arlo;

I glanced over at Amelia's empty chair and narrowed my eyes. Last, I had seen her she was stood in my bedroom waiting for me to come back from collecting Jamie's body. She must have thought that I was so rude. I strode into the room and didn't even look at her. If only she knew that was because of how disgusted I was that her own brother could accuse her of something like that! I turned my stare to Matt; I knew that the two of them had gotten close lately, maybe she told him that she was busy doing something else? I turned my stare to Matt and noticed the way that he picked at his food, seemingly uninterested, and he stared at Amelia's chair also. Ok, that made it perfectly obvious that he didn't know either. Me and Matt locked eyes and I nodded slightly towards Amelia's chair. But he just shook his head in answer. Me and that girl needed a serious talk! This was only going to fuel Charlie's vendetta against her. FUCK!

Amelia;

Tonight, was going to be the first full moon since missing the last one. Tonight, was the night that I was going to have my first shift. The thought of it caused my stomach to clench and I thought that I was going to throw up. I sighed heavily and shook my head. *As terrified as I was, I knew that I was finally ready.* The pack would be in for their dinner right about now, so it gave me the perfect opportunity to go and see Pretty Girl. *I was secretly hoping that she would calm me that much more. She always had that effect on me so... fingers crossed.*

I sat on the hay bale, brushing Pretty Girls mane, feeling the silky hairs beneath my fingertips, which sent rolling waves of calm over me.

'Hey, is everything ok? You weren't at dinner?' Piper asked, stepping into the stables and pulling an apple for pretty girl out of her pocket. I glanced over my shoulder to my best friend and forced a smile.

'I was hoping to see you before tonight.' I responded anxiously, turning back to face Pretty Girl as I placed my hand on the side of her neck, stroking gently.

'Piper, would you mind shifting with me tonight? I know that it's a little strange but, I just really need someone there that I can trust.' I hesitated for a moment before glancing back over to my best friend. 'I mean, if I am totally honest, I am completely freaking out.' Piper smiled kindly over to me and shook her head.

'Did you even need to ask? Of course, I will be there to help you through it. Although, it is unusual for an Elite to want to shift with Mutts; but I think that I am finally ready to accept that you are just a freak of nature, Amelia Hunt!' She retorted with a laugh. I smiled over to her and felt a little of the tension that I had previously felt fade. *Just knowing that I had someone there to watch my back was all I needed to ease my nerves a little; I was still terrified, but at least I knew that my best friend was there, and she had my back.*

I turned back to Piper and wandered over to the stable door. It wouldn't be long until the rest of the pack would be gathering for their shift. I felt as though my heart had turned to lead and I was suddenly feeling extremely sick. *Was this part of the transformation? Or was I just continuing to freak out?*

Piper and I stood just in the doorway of Pretty Girl's stable, staring up at the dark sky. I could feel the moon, preparing our bodies for the transformation, it was Selene's way of letting us know that the change was coming. It started like a pressure building up inside me; and it was about to be released any minute now. I hesitantly took my clothes off, folding them up and placing them neatly in a pile beside the closed stable door and folded my arms across my chest self-consciously.

I titled my head up to look at the sky above just as the dark clouds parted, revealing the beauty of the full moon. I felt the rays hit my bare skin and a tingling rush, washed over me. The sound of Piper sucking in a shard intake of breath had me looking over to her curiously. Her hazel eyes had turned from their normal green brown, to something else, something darker. They held the look of a cat's eye's reflected in a flashlight. The tell-tale sign that the change had started. I felt my heart hammering against my chest, and my throat felt as though it was lined with sandpaper. *This was it. I was finally preparing for my first shift.*

I closed my eyes and tilted my head back and bathed in the moonlight as the sound of the other werewolves panted and dropped to their knees. I knew that I didn't know much when it came to shifting, especially when it came to the first shift, but surely it wasn't supposed to take this long. I opened my eyes and looked around at the others out in the field and saw that they stood proudly in their wolf forms. That was when I heard the high pitch whining of a dog. I turned to look at Piper and took in the sight of her beautiful auburn hair in the dim moonlight. Her glowing hazel eyes looked up at me sadly before she hung her head. I dropped down to my knees and gently placed my hand on her muzzle.

'It's ok. Go. I'll be fine.' I whispered, biting back the tears that were threatening to fall. I forced a smile as Piper stood there staring at me hesitantly. I could tell that she was eager to run, but her duty to her best friend was clearly stronger. I smiled once more and stroked her head. 'Honestly, go and enjoy your run. I will be fine. I promise.' I added, climbing to my feet and pulling my t-shirt back over my head, swiftly followed by my jeans. Piper sighed and hesitantly stepped backwards, before I waved her away with a smile.

Without a second thought, she turned on her heel and bound

away after the others in the darkness. I stared from the stable door and watched as the wolves all darted between the trees, each one disappearing into the darkness. All except two. A black wolf that was darker than the darkness surrounding him, the only thing standing out were the glowing golden eyes that were full of pity and sadness. And a wolf with fur so blonde that he was almost like a ray of sunshine peering through the dark. His blue eyes shimmering dimly in the low moonlight *How ironic. The two guys that I have feelings for, and they couldn't be more opposite if they had tried.* I turned from the door and pressed myself up against the wall of the stables and felt as I lost all control of my emotions. I fell to the ground and allowed my tears to consume me.

I don't know how long I sat there in the stables, but by the time that I had gotten fully dressed and head back to the mansion, it was almost 1:30am. *What was wrong with me? Why couldn't I shift? Was it because I truly was a freak? Or was this something to do with the fact that I missed my first shift because of Lori?* I rose to my feet and dusted the dried hay from my jeans and pulled my hair up into a ponytail. *If there was once place that I would find the answers to all the questions running through my head, it would be the library.* I nodded to myself and exited the stable. All I needed to do was learn about why I couldn't shift. I could either sit here and feel sorry for myself, or I could actually try and figure a way out of all this. *But all I knew for certain was that I was done feeling sorry for myself. Now was a time to act!*

I entered the mansion doors and a chill swept over me. I never realised how creepy this place was when there was no one in it. I folded my arms across my chest once more and took another step into the building, when a loud growl caused me to jump. *What the fuck was that?* I glanced left and right, all kinds of thoughts filling my head. *Maybe it was demons? Or a monster under the stairs?* I took another step into the main hall and the growl happened again. This time louder. A sudden wave of sickness washed over me, and I thought that I was going to pass out. That was when it hit me. I knew that sound… *I was hungry!*

I rolled my eyes and laughed to myself, not believing how

incredibly stupid I could be at times and decided to make my way to the kitchen. Luckily with the amount of time that I had spent in there helping out, I knew where everything was supposed to go, as well as knowing where everything was kept. I hurried around grabbing the easiest thing that I could find, which just happened to be a few sandwiches wrapped in clingfilm on a plate, with my name on; *thank you Tanya!* And some chocolate. After eating, I poured myself a large glass of water and decided to make my way to the library. The longer that I spent alone in the mansion, the braver I was starting to feel. *Well, that's what I was telling myself anyway.* I pushed open the library door and hit the light switch, wandering inside and slowly scanning the shelves for anything that would help me figure out why I was so different than the rest.

I stepped back and took in the sight of all the books; there were literally hundreds, it was going to take forever for me to even find one that could be about werewolf genealogy; let alone find one that would explain why I was so broken! I took another step back just as the high-pitched singing of the lullaby filled the air around me. It was louder than I had ever heard it before, causing me to whirl around to see if there was someone behind me. I caught my foot on the leg of the coffee table, losing my balance and stumbling uneasily. I threw my hand out to catch myself and let the glass slip through my fingers. I tried to grab for it with my other hand, but it was too late; I had already lost my balance and was tumbling to the ground.

I hit the wooden floor with a thud and gasped for breath as the wind was knocked out of me and the sound of shattering glass filled my ears. I ignored the pain that was radiating through my ribs and pushed up to my feet, looking from side to side for something to mop the water up with, when a strange noise had me standing motionless. It sounded like... like... a waterfall. I shook my head, certain that I was hearing things when the lullaby rang out around me once more. I growled in frustration and clenched my fists into balls.

'What the hell do you want with me? Why won't you just leave me alone?' I cried, turning around in circles searching the room for the source of the song. In answer to my questions, the singing grew louder, almost to the point that it was deafening. It drifted around me as though the source of the voice was a ghost, circling me like a shark circling their prey, before turning my attention back to the trickling water that was coming from beneath my feet.

I dropped to my hands and knees, careful not to cut myself on any of the broken glass and placed my ear to the floorboards. The water was disappearing through the cracks and trickling through to what sounded like a cave. The sound of the dripping water was echoing up from below me, reminding me of the sound of a waterfall. That meant that there had to be something down there... but what? The library was located on the ground floor. Theoretically there wasn't anything else beneath us. *Or so we all thought.*

I ran my fingertips along the seal of the wood, trying to figure out a way into the underground passage that I had just discovered. This room was huge, there was no way that I was going to be able to search this entire place before dawn when the others all arrived home. *Come on Amelia, think... think... think...* I closed my eyes and shook my head; it was so hard to concentrate when all I could hear was that bloody lullaby. *That's it!* I opened my eyes and gulped down a deep breath, before mimicking the tune of the lullaby and letting it fill the room. With every verse the room filled with power unlike anything I had ever felt before. *Whoever was guiding me somewhere was clearly here now.* I continued singing and looked around the room, watching for any signs of help. That was when I noticed it. It was only the slightest of movements, but I knew that I had definitely seen it! The furthest bookcase from where I stood rattled ever so slightly against the wall.

I leapt to my feet and ran as fast as I could over to the furthest bookcase. By the time that I reached the case, the rocking had finished and was stood motionless once again. I ran my hand along the edge of the unit and tugged it lightly, noticing that it moved away from the wall a little. I wedged my fingers into the small gap that I had created and pulled with all my might. It was heavy and I was barely able to move it, but I knew that I was on the right track. I pulled once more, this time placing my foot against the wall and pushing with everything I had in me. The sound of the case scraping along the wooden floor was loud, but that meant that my hard work was paying off. My arms burned from all the straining, but I pushed on.

With one final tug, the shelf flew open and I stumbled backwards landing on my arse. I blinked rapidly and shook my head, staring at the blackened tunnel that was located behind it. *What. The. Fuck?* I climbed to my feet and hesitantly wandered over to the cavernous entrance and peered into the darkness.

'H-Hello?' I called, listening as the only sound that I heard in return was my own echo calling back to me. 'Seriously Amelia? If there was someone in there do you think they would just shout, "Hey, how are you doing?" Who even does that?' I muttered to myself. A sudden breeze whipped around me from the depths of the darkness and caused goosebumps to crawl across my bare arms. I placed my hand on the stone walls, feeling for a switch or something for the lights, but there wasn't one. I sighed to myself and shook my head once more.

I reached into my pocket and pulled my phone from within, turning on the flash to illuminate the darkness before me. It was so black that I could only see a few feet ahead of me, so I had to move carefully. I was about to turn back when I heard the sound of the siren calling me from the deep depths of the tunnel. A part of me wanted to turn and run. But the bigger part of me had the feeling that there were answers in this darkness that needed to come to light. Answers that would be brought from the shadows. I drew in a deep breath and stepped a little further into the tunnel… waited… then took another.

By the time that I had moved a few feet from the entrance, the bookcase swung shut behind me, sealing me in and shrouding me in darkness. *Thank Selene that I had my phone!* There was no going back now. I was so close to finding out something, I could feel it. I just hoped that it was all worth it in the end.

I exited the tunnel and felt as the closeness of the walls

disappeared, opening out into a huge cavernous area. I strained my eyes into the darkness. Wherever I was now must have been huge. I couldn't see anything other than the few feet that my phone lit up. I stepped back and placed my hand on the wall and followed it around until I found a large pillar candle that was stood on a wall holder. I patted my pockets, hoping to find a lighter within, but typically there wasn't one. *Where was Matt when I needed him?* I held my phone closer to the wall holder, praying that there were some matches or something similar standing beside it. *But who knew how long it had been since anyone else had been down here?* I shone the light down to the ground and then back up above the candle. *Nothing!* With a growl of frustration, I shook my head and turned away. When the sudden sound of a pop behind me had me whirling around. To my amazement, the candle that I had been staring at only seconds again had somehow sprung to life.

I watched in amazement as one by one, every candle on the wall popped alight, illuminating the darkness slightly. After the first ten candles I stopped counting, as my attention was caught by everything that was in this room. *Was it a dungeon?* There were shelves that held all sorts of books, mostly written in a language that I couldn't even begin to decipher; and that was just the spine! There was a cauldron, and shelves upon shelves of jars filled with all sorts of weird and wonderful things. I turned on the spot, not sure where to turn my stare to next. There was so much in here that I wouldn't have even known where to start. When I heard it again? The sound of the lullaby; the secret siren that had been calling me my entire life. She was down here with me. I could feel it. *What? What are you trying to show me?*

I looked around the room, searching for the source of the call. There was a reason that she had led me down here. So now it was time to find answers. That was when I noticed something unusual in the corner of the room. Something that seemed to stand out above everything else. A wooden pillar that held an extremely old, dusty cushion on top of it. I stepped up to the platform and looked down at the wooden box that was rested upon the cushion. With a shaking hand, I reached out and slowly lifted the lid of the box and stared down at two werewolf fangs. I placed my finger against one of them and ran it down the smooth tooth and felt a jolt of electricity rush up my arm. I jerked my hand back and clutched it to my chest, glancing over my shoulder anxiously. *What the fuck was going on here?*

I reached out once more and plucked the two teeth from the box and held them both in my hand. My arm vibrated with power as it radiated through me. It was unlike anything I had ever felt. I turned my attention to the leather cords that had been wrapped around each of the teeth and realised that they were fashioned into necklaces? That was when I realised that the sirens calling had stopped.

Was this it? Was this what she wanted me to find? What did any of this mean? I thought that I was coming down here to get answers. But all it has done is leave me with more questions. I placed the two necklaces over my head and tucked them into my top while closing the lid of the box. I looked up to see a ghostly white face staring back at me with black lifeless eyes, and a mouth twisted as though it was screaming in pain. I squealed and stumbled backwards hitting my head on the stone floor behind me. Then everything went black.

Matt;

I rolled over onto the grass and stared up at the morning sun. Last night was well needed. There was always something so satisfying about shifting. It made your whole body feel like you had, had a really good work out, stretching out every tense muscle in your body. I tilted my neck from side to side, hearing the satisfying crack and sat up and looked around. I was the one closest to the mansion. I didn't remember how I had gotten here, but all I could think about was Amelia. I had seen the heartbreak in her eyes last night once she realised that she was the only one that hadn't shifted. I walked back towards the mansion, deciding that it was probably best to put some clothes on before I went and found Amelia. *I don't think she would appreciate a naked guy searching for her.*

Once back in my room, I threw on my loose-fitting jogging bottoms and headed back out into the cool November air heading to the one place that I figured Amelia would be; no one had seen her since she had sadly watched us all shift. We were all so disappointed for her; Arlo and Ethan especially. That was the worst part about shifting. We all could sense what the other was feeling. It was a moment that was supposed to bring us all closer. *Until the alpha and a Mutt both had strong feelings for the same girl. Then shit got awkward.*

I had searched everywhere that I could think of but still couldn't find Amelia. *Where had she got to? I was beginning to worry. Would she have used that opportunity to run away again?* I closed my eyes and ran through a list of places that she would most likely to have gone. She had missed breakfast, and now lunch. People were seriously beginning to get suspicious. And I didn't know how much longer we could keep her name cleared. *I knew that she would never do anything to hurt anyone. But Charlie was getting everyone riled up!* And from the look on Arlo's face, he was seriously getting stressed out. He had dark circles under his eyes and looked as though he hadn't slept for a week. *I didn't know what it was that was wrong with him, but I was going to get to the bottom of it.*

I don't know why none of us had thought about it before, but she had to be with; Pretty Girl! I rounded the corner and there she was, sat under a tree reading a book as Pretty Girl pranced around the open field gleefully. I had to admit, there was something about that unicorn that seemed to call to me. She was super graceful and very beautiful. And I still didn't understand how Amelia thought that we were joking. I mean… Pretty Girl's crystal-like horn stood proudly on her forehead and her coat shimmered like freshly fallen snow under the moonlight. How did she think that that was normal for a horse? I turned my stare to Amelia and noticed that she looked pale and had dirt smudged on her cheek. And there was something about the way that she kept rubbing the back of her head that made me think that something was wrong. I jogged over to her and cleared my throat, doing my best not to startle her.

'You know, people are seriously starting to freak out that they can't find you.' I called, hopping over the fence and running over to her. Pretty Girl turned her head to the side and eyed me suspiciously for a moment before deciding that I gained her approval and continued to gallop. Amelia looked up from her book and smiled at me, tucking a stray strand of her dark hair behind her ear.

'By people, do you mean Arlo?' She asked, raising one eyebrow sceptically. I rolled my eyes and dropped down beside her.

'Actually, I was talking about myself. We missed you at Lunch, where were you?' I asked, bumping her shoulder gently with my own. She sighed heavily; a sound that made it seem as though she held the weight of the world on her shoulders.

'I was just in the kitchen. I was helping them out. I thought that I could keep my mind busy. Especially after hearing about that person that was killed.' She replied, staring off into the distance. *There was something that she wasn't telling me. I didn't know what, but I knew that she was hiding something.* Did she know that her own brother was accusing her? I turned to look at her once more and really took her in. I knew in my heart that she had nothing to do with this. This was Amelia for goddess's sake!

'You were in the kitchen? You mean, like working?' I asked, as I finally registered what it was that she was saying to me. She creased her brow and pulled away from me a little, looking at me in confusion.

'Matt. Why do you keep looking at me like that?' She asked, still looking very confused. I cleared my throat and shook my head.

'Looking at you like what?' I asked, playing dumb. I know that if she found out that Charlie was accusing her of the murder then it would destroy her. But at the same time, if I didn't tell her then she wouldn't know what's coming. I opened my mouth the tell her the truth when I smelt it. It hit me hard and strong; so much so that it took over all of my other senses. My eyes burned from the intensity of the stench and I sprang to my feet.

'M-Matt?' Amelia stammered, slowly rising so that she was stood next to me. 'What is it? What's wrong?' I ignored her question and sniffed the air. Even though there was a breeze blowing I was pretty certain that I could track this smell.

'Go back to the mansion where it is safe.' I ordered, turning to face her briefly and gently pushing her in the direction I wanted to go.

'What? No! Why?' she cried, fighting back and turning to face me. But I had already hopped the fence and started running out into the forest. I should have known better that she wasn't going to listen to me. I could hear the twigs snapping and the shuffling of the foliage on the ground rustling behind me as she tried to keep pace. The scent was getting stronger. I paused for a few seconds, sniffing the air once more; this time nearly gagging on the fumes.

I leapt around the other side of the large oak tree and con-tinued to run. I pushed harder, needing to see what I was about to lead Amelia. That was when I saw it. Victim number two. This one looked as though it had been cut from chin to groin and all its inter-nal organs were pulled from inside and draped around the body. I turned to warn Amelia not to come any closer, but it was too late. She tried forcing herself to stop at the slight drop but tumbled in. Landing face first in the remnants of our pack brother. She pulled back and glanced down at her arms; which were now coated in blood.

And screamed.

11

Amelia;

I tried to keep up with Matt, but he was going too fast, something had clearly spooked him, his face turned white as he leapt to his feet and ran. *I know he told me to stay here, but there was no way I was letting him go on his own.* I hesitated for a moment, knowing that I should have done as he had told but, stupidly, I followed him. When he told me to stop, there was a tone in his voice which made me know that I had to, but I had gone too fast, I had built up too much momentum so as I got to the ditch I slipped over the end and tumbled down. I fell through the air for a few seconds. I saw everything happening in slow motion, and there was nothing that I could do to stop me from falling into the dead body of another pack member. I hit the ground with a wet *smack* and squeezed my mouth shut as I fought through the strong scent of blood and tried to stop myself from throwing up. I laid there for a few seconds, my eyes tightly shut and unmoving.

I pulled back and looked down at my arms. There was blood everywhere. This killing was nothing like the first; *from what I had heard anyway*, I opened my mouth but was cut short by a high-pitched scream. It took me a few seconds to realise that the scream was coming from me. Matt leapt down into the ditch and grabbed my hands, yanking me towards him before pulling me into his arms, trying to calm my down. I buried my face into his chest and sobbed, this was by far the worst experience of my life.

The sound of running footsteps approaching us caused Me and Matt both looked up. Arlo and the other Elites were stood

175

there, staring down at us in shock. Arlo's face drained all colour as he looked down at the body and then at me. The other Elites; who were as equally pale and silent, were staring in horror at the naked, blood-soaked female, who's body parts were wrenched from her body and were out on display for all to see. I tried to focus on any-thing other than the fact that I was still sat in the ice-cold remnants of a deceased human. A familiar voice snapped me from my daze, causing me to focus on them.

'I fucking told you lot it was her and that Mutt, they killed Jaime! And because none of you listened, they have killed again.' Charlie cried; his face full of anger.

'What? No! This was not Amelia!' Matt shouted pulling my head closer to his chest and slightly covering my ears. 'I found her read-ing a book with Pretty Girl galloping about. She followed me when I smelt the blood, but she fell into the pit. She has nothing to do with this.' Matt continued, sounding angrier than I had ever heard him before. A sob escaped my mouth as Matt defended me. *What had I done to make these people hate me so much? What was it about me that made them think that I was capable of something like this? And worst of all, why was it my brother who was the one leading them all to this conclusion?*

'So, where the fuck has, she been all day? she wasn't with us at lunch. And I don't remember seeing her all morning!' Charlie sneered pointing his finger at me. I opened my mouth to answer but the look that passed over Charlie's face had me pausing in fear. *It didn't matter what I; or anyone else, said, he had clearly already made up his mind!*

'She was in the kitchen helping to prepare food and feed *our* pack!' Matt hissed; I could hear his heart beating faster. 'If you don't believe us, then go and ask Tanya!' Tears burned my eyes and there was nothing that I could do to stop them from rolling down my cheeks in warm waves. *Why would anyone believe I was capable of such a cruel and hideous thing? Me? Murder someone?* Anyone that truly knew me would know that. *I didn't have it in me.* I paused for a few long seconds, waiting for Arlo to just to my defence; but he never did. He stayed quiet, his wide eyes darting from the dead body to me. *Did he actually think that I did this?* I was distraught. The tears came faster, and I sucked in heavy sobs, allowing Matt to wrap his arms around me tighter. *Why was he the only one jumping to my defence?* I burst into tears again and tried to break away from Matt's comforting grip; which only caused him to hold on to me that little bit tighter. A feeling unlike anything I had ever felt before gripped my chest so tight that I thought it was Matt at first; I could hear my heart pounding in my ears, and I struggled to suck any breaths. I felt my chest heave and is struggled to breathe, my breaths coming in quick and shallow. *What was happening to me? I needed to get away from here.* With all my might, I wrenched myself free from Matts hold and ran. I ran as fast as I could, ignoring all the horrified looks and gasps as I ran though the gardens and people were taking in my bloodied appearance. I could see the mansion in the distance, getting closer with every step I took. My lungs were on fire and it was even harder to breathe, but I wouldn't stop until I was back I the safety of my room. I could hear my friend's footsteps behind me.

'Amelia please wait.' Matt called trying his hardest to catch up with me. I ignored his shouts as I ran past Piper. She turned to speak to me, but I didn't hesitate. I barged past her and took the stone steps to the mansion's entrance two at a time and continued to run. Before I knew it, I was stood staring at my bedroom door, my hands trembling so much that I couldn't even pull the key from my pocket; when a strong warm hand gripped my shoulder. I didn't need him to speak to know who it was. I stopped what I was doing, allowing my arms to fall limp and my sides, before spinning around and falling into Matts arms, letting go of all control I had on my emotions and stood there, uncontrollably sobbing.

I felt one of Matts arms loosen from around me and dip into the pocket of my jeans and pull the key from within. He slipped the key into the lock and threw the door open, ushering me inside before shutting; and locking, the door behind us.

'I am going to run you a bath, take these clothes off, I will take them downstairs and put them in the bin' Matt whispered, releasing me from his hold and walking me over to my bed. I slumped down onto my knees, shakily pulling off the blood-soaked T-shirt, and feeling the cold blood scrape over my face as I did so. Matt was already in the bathroom by the time all my clothes came off. I wrapped a blanket around my naked shivering body and sat on my bed staring into space.

'Come on Lia; the bath is running, and I have added some of those relaxing bath oils to the water. You're clearly still in shock so I am going to stay with you okay?' Matt smiled reassuringly as he sat on the floor next to me. I turned my blank stare to him and then down to my blanket wrapped body, blinking slowly. *Usually I would have protested about having a guy see me this vulnerable; but today I really didn't care.* I shook my head, feeling the clumps of hair stuck together with blood tap my face.

'W-w-why are you being so nice to me?' I stammered looking down at the floor.

'Are you kidding? Lia, you are one of my best friends. I know that we haven't know each other that long, but you have no idea how loved you are. You are an angel. You have so much love for this pack, I have never known an Elite to break every rule possible just so she can be kind to the *Non-Elites*. You have a heart of gold; and you do all this without expecting to gain anything in return.' He smiled rubbing my back. I was still shivering uncontrollably, but the fact that he used my term when speaking about the *Mutts* made me smile. *It may have only been a twitch at the corner of my mouth, but it was there.* I turned my blank stare towards him and sat for a few seconds, allowing my eyes to fully focus on him before speaking.

'You will make a woman really happy someday Matt, your so kind and caring, I have so much respect for you.' My voice came out sounding alien to me, it was hoarse and cracked. I sighed, while looking up at him and smiling. His face went pale and then he looked down at the floor. 'Hey, what is it?' I asked, sitting up a little straighter and twisting myself around to look at him properly. His face paled further, and he turned his face away from me, a look on his face that seemed as though he was fighting a mental battle in his head. *Had I said something to offend him?* I cleared my throat and reached forward, placing my ice-cold hand on his cheek; the warmth of his skin instantly thawing out the coldness that I felt. 'You know that you can tell me anything, right?' I asked, my voice softer, but no less panicked. *Whatever was happening right now was clearly very hard for him. He shouldn't have to face that alone.* Matt sighed heavily and closed his eyes once more.

'I...I'm gay.' He whispered, his shoulders sagging as though he had just dropped the weight of the world from then. I paused for a moment and creased my brow as I let everything sink in. *Everything made so much sense now; when he helped pick out my clothes. The way he is so closed off from the other pack members. The fact that I am so in love with him; but like a brother.* I smiled at him and rested my head on his shoulder snuggling into him that much more. He cleared his throat and turned his dark eyes towards me; 'I haven't actually told anyone else that. I mean, Arlo knows, but he is the only one. I am just worried that All the others would treat me differently if they knew. Do you know what I mean?' He asked. I nodded, still not looking up at him and rested his hand on his chest.

'Thank you for telling me, I know that must have been so hard for you.' And I was thankful. Matt trusted me with something he didn't feel he could tell anyone else, that was true friendship.

'Can I tell you a secret?' I asked, sitting up slightly and turning to face him. *If he could be honest with me, then I could finally open up to someone.* 'I keep having these really weird dreams. I mean, I have been having this same dream every night!' I paused for a moment and allowed myself to drift into the memory.

'So, you have been having *the same* dream, every night? Isn't that weird?' Matt asked, peering at me a little harder as though he was looking at me with new eyes. I sighed and shook my head.

'There's more. It gets weirder.' I paused again for a moment, not believing that I was actually about to tell someone my biggest secret, and the thing that scared me most in this world. 'For years, I have been hearing a woman. I don't know who she is, or what she wants. But I hear her voice. In the dead of night. In the quiet points in the day. Even when I am in the middle of washing up in the kitchens. I hear her. Singing her Lullaby.' Matt smiled at me and kissed my cheek.

'Does it scare you?' he asked, his voice soft and concerned, my fear of him thinking that I was going insane slowly began melting away. I nodded, then hesitated, actually thinking about the question.

'No, I mean, yeah… I mean… maybe. I don't know. With the dream, usually I just wake up with an awful feeling in the pit of my stomach and it doesn't go away. The singing. That scares me more. That happens when I am awake. It terrifies me.' I admitted, my voice barely above a whisper.

'Lia; you have been through so much shit in your life. And you have been living here, what? Over a month now? And life is still shit for you. I am not surprised you are having nightmares… have you told Arlo?' Matt asked pulling me up from the bed. I shook my head and walked towards the bathroom.

'No, I haven't. Please don't tell him.'

'What about the singing? Does anyone else know about that?' He asked. I shook my head and paused once I caught sight of myself in the bathroom mirror. My pale skin was a stark contrast with the dark, dried blood that was coating the entirety of my body. My knees trembled as I tried to calm myself down. But it was no use. Matt turned back to the bath water and swirled it with his hand, causing an array of scents to wash over me, calming me instantly.

'Get in the bath and try your best to relax okay?' Matt said walking to the bathroom door.

He paused and turned back to look at me once last time. 'I will be right out here waiting for you when you're done, ok?' He asked, smiling softly. I nodded and watched as he carefully closed the door behind him. And that was when I silently crumbled once more. Tears streaming down my face. I needed to get to the bottom of all these murders. And fast!

I climbed from the bath staring down at the red murky

water and shuddered; the images of the dead body scattered everywhere and me laying in the middle of it. I pulled the plug from the bath and watched as it quickly drained away. I tightened my towel around me and wandered out into my room. *How did my life end up this way? All I wanted was to be free, and now look at me. Apparently, the prime suspect in a series of murders.* I bit my lip in attempt to stop myself crying again and turned to the bay window and perched myself on the bench. There in the distance was the top peak of a mountain. *Maybe I could just run away and live there? Maybe that would make all my troubles disappear?* I sighed to myself and began to turn away when the sirens call echoed in my mind. I glanced back out the window and my eyes fell on the mountain once more. A sudden desire to go there filled the pit of my stomach and it took everything in me to not just up and run. I leaned into the call and allowed the full pull to consume me; the sound was beautiful and almost hypnotic. I reached my hand up and placed it on the cool glass when a loud knocking snapped me from my trance. I sat back and shook my head, feeling more than a little dazed and rose to my feet, rushing over to the door and pulling it open.

'What do you want?' I snapped, glaring angrily at Arlo as he stood sheepishly in my doorway. He creased his brow in confusion and shook his head slightly.

'What? What is that supposed to mean?'

'It means why are you standing here in my doorway Arlo. I have nothing to say to you.' I snapped angrily. He let out a low growl in his throat and stormed past me into my room. 'Why don't you come on in.' I muttered sarcastically, slamming the door behind him.

'Look, I'm not here to argue Lia. I really did just want to make sure that you are ok.'

'Make sure I am ok? Are you being serious? Where were you making sure that I was ok when my brother was fucking accusing me of murdering people. Do you honestly think that I would do that? Me... murder someone? You want to make sure that I am ok, how about you fucking defend me.'

'I wish that it was as simple as that. Do you not understand the position that I am in right now? Charlie is my Beta. Standing against him publicly is not how things are done in a pack! I can't just call him out in front of everyone!' He snapped, his anger clearly getting the better of him.

'Do you know what makes me laugh. Ethan is there by my side through all of this. And he actually tries to defend me. I know that he would stand up to you if he could. But *he can't*. You just chose not too in fear of disturbing the precious balance of this bull-shit pack!'

'For fuck sake Lia. You think that using him against me right now is the right thing to do? I am the *alpha*. I can banish him if needs be.' His words stunned me worse than if he had slapped my face. My eyes narrowed and I took a step closer to him, poking him in the chest.

'You do that, and you will lose more than just a member of the pack. You will also lose me, and any respect that I felt for you.' 'So, you would become a Deviant for this Mutt? Please, are you really that insecure that you would have to follow a Mutt into the darkness?' he asked with a humourless laugh. My blood boiled and I saw red. I reached down to the shelf beside me and grabbed large, leather-bound book that was resting there, and threw it at him.

'Who the *fuck* do you think you are?' I screamed, as he ducked under the projectile book and took a step closer towards me. He turned back to face me with a smirk, only to feel the sting of my palm across his face. My hand throbbed and I bit my tongue to stop myself crying out. *Damn, that was some slap!* 'If you are just here to insult me then get the fuck out of my room!' I shouted, clenching my teeth and trying my hardest to get my anger under control. *Why did he know all the things to say that caused my temper to ignite?* I closed my eyes and gulped down some deep breaths. I refused to let him get the better of me. I opened my eyes just as the lights above us flickered, and a small trickle of blood had escaped his lip from my slap.

Arlo dropped his stare down from the flickering lights to meet my eyes, flicking his tongue out and licking the blood away.

He swallowed and stared at me in shock; before breaking out into a fit of laughter.

'What the fuck are you laughing at? It's not funny Arlo!' I snapped, gritting my teeth and narrowing my eyes at him. He clutched his stomach as he continued to laugh, and I felt the anger melting from my face. 'I am serious! It's not funny!' I snapped again, this time a little less forcefully as a smile tugged at the corner of my lips.

'Get dressed!' Arlo panted breathlessly, trying his hardest to stop his laughter.

'Excuse me?' I snapped, still trying to be angry with him.

'Get dressed… we are going to the pub!'

Piper;

Today was the day that we were holding the funerals for our fallen pack members. I was terrified and had no idea what to expect. In all the years that my family had been a part of this pack we have never needed a funeral rite for someone who had died under these circumstances; except for Amelia's mother, but I was only a child when that happened, I don't remember it much.

I sucked in a deep breath and tried to calm my racing heart, but it was no use. I hadn't seen Amelia since before the second killing, no one except Matt and Arlo had seen her. *And I was so worried about her.* Everything seemed to be taking its toll on her, and I was terrified about what effect that would have on her.

I stood to the side and took in all the devastated faces of our pack; all looking equally as heartbroken as the next, watching as Arlo, Charlie, Matt and Eddie, piled more logs around the bodies wrapped in white sheets. Everyone watched on in silence for a few minutes before they all stepped back simultaneously, and Arlo crouched down to the side and struck a match. The smell of sulphur filled the air for a split second and then the logs were ablaze. The flames climbed up the dry logs, moving at a rapid speed. I watched until it was too bright for my eyes and then turned my gaze out across the crowd.

The smell was strong and unlike anything I had ever smelt, the mixture of charred flesh and burnt hair filled my nostrils and almost caused me to gag. The two bodies of our fallen were now fully ablaze and I wondered how long it would take before they were left as nothing but ash. I turned my gaze around the group once more, and then I noticed her, standing right at the back under the tree with a look on her face that finally broke me.

Amelia was so pale, paler than normal, she was thin and a shell of the person she used to be. I followed her gaze to our pack, the pain in her eyes was unbearable, she held back tears as she noticed members of our pack had started dividing. Some who believed she was the killer; mainly the Elites looked up and glared at her; baring their teeth in silent snarls, they stood away from all the ones who believed she was innocent; the Mutts. Arlo was standing in between everyone, with Jaime and Laura's parents either side of him. I felt as a warm tear rolled down my cheek and onto the end of my chin, I hurt for the parents of our young fallen members, but I also felt for my best friend. After the whole pack sung a song to help our fallen find their way to the Goddess Selene, everyone started departing and going back to their homes. Amelia left first, no one had even noticed that she had gone, my eyes met Matts with a look of worry upon his face. 'Amelia' he mouthed at me, I shrugged and nodded to the mansion. Matt looked like he wanted to go and find her, but he had duties and that was to stay with Arlo to support Jaime and Laura's parents. I tapped my mums' hand and smiled weakly at her.

'I need to be with Amelia.' I whispered. My mother looked down at me with sorrow filled eyes and nodded lightly. She too was just as worried about Amelia as I was. Before anyone had a chance to stop and talk to me, I ran.

Amelia;

I sat on the edge of my bed and stared at the wall, my gaze not breaking away as thoughts plagued my broken mind. I knew the Elites thought I killed Jaime and Laura, I could feel their hatred for me, and it broke my heart. My own father believed it was me and, in an instance, they would put me to death. Thank Selene I had

Marie on my side, she was my angel in disguise. Maybe I should just let them all kill me because as they all have said, people always died around me; my mother when I was born and now Jaime and Laura not even two months after I joined the pack. I was a bad omen and bad omens always affected the people around them, including the people they cared about. Piper, Matt and Arlo flashed through my mind, *what if something happened to them? Because of me.* I could run away, but no doubt I would be tracked down and that would show everyone I was guilty; guilty of something I didn't do. I dropped my face down into my hands and sobbed quietly. *Why did everything have to be so complicated?* The sound of a gentle tapping at my bedroom door had me turning my face around to stare at it. I didn't care who it was, I didn't want to see anyone. I needed to be alone. If I was alone then no one else was going to get hurt. I closed my eyes and held my breath, hoping that whoever it was, was going to just go away.

'Lia; it's me.' I opened my eyes as I heard Pipers soft voice. I remained where I was sat in silence, listening to my own heart pounding in my ears. I sighed and pushed up to my feet and walked over to my bedroom door and sat down, placing the side of my head against it.

'Please open up.' Piper cried softly, I heard as her voice went from above my head down to my level. She too was sitting on the floor and leaning against the door. 'You know none of this is your fault, right?' she asked. 'Ignore them all, the people that matter know you wouldn't hurt anyone and anyone who believes otherwise needs their head's testing.' Tears started falling down my face, soaking my cheeks. The people who mattered did believe me but the people with the power didn't, I had no hope.

'The pack have divided because of me. I croaked.

'No Lia; the pack have divided because of the real killer and because they are too fucking stupid and ignorant. Did you not notice how many were standing for you? Nearly all of us non-Elites, Marie, Tristan and Matt, we are all on your side here.' Piper cried, I could hear the frustration in her voice, she desperately wanted me to listen to her, but I had a feeling that I was beyond that now. My phone beeped causing me to glance down with my heart in my throat.

Ethan; Hey baby. I hope you are ok after the funeral rite. I noticed how you were stood aside and looked really out of place. But you have nothing to be ashamed of. Did you not see how many of us were gathered around you? We know that you are innocent in all this. Even if your dick of a brother doesn't.

I felt the corners of my mouth tilt up into a smile and all the fears and stress that I had been holding onto slowly melted away. How did he always manage to make me smile? It was almost as if he could just sense when I needed someone and there he was. *If only I wasn't so conflicted. Why did I have to really like two guys? And why did they both have to drive me wild in different ways?*

Arlo;

It had been two weeks since the murders, we had held both funerals on the same day a week after they had happened. No one knew who it was that killed them, we all had our suspicions; mine being that it was an outsider, but Charlie was still convinced it was someone in the pack; *Amelia to be precise.* He tried to persuade anyone and everyone he could into believing the same, *and much to my disgust that was a lot of the pack. Thank Selene for the Mutts.* Some had questioned if it was her as she was not far away from the second body; *laying on top when we found her.* I had spoken to Tanya the day that the second murder took place. She said Amelia was with them from 7:30 until 2:30, helping in the kitchen. *I just didn't understand why no one else could see that she was innocent especially since she had a fucking alibi.* Amelia wasn't the same though, ever since seeing that body, she had been becoming more and more withdrawn from everyone. *From me.* I knew that there was something she wasn't telling me. She wouldn't do anything on her own. If she was not sleeping in my room, then she was in her room with Matt or Piper. Or sometimes both. *I was so grateful to both of them for being there for her. I don't know what she would do without them.* Something was happening to her and it was destroying me seeing her go through this.

I would listen to her through my bedroom wall as she whimpered in her sleep. Sometimes, she would scream out sobbing. Most nights now, I had to let myself in her room just to wake her up just to calm her down, holding her trembling frame as close to me as possible and every time she would end up in my room; in bed with me.

Today was the first pack meeting of the new week and being that we are now in December; meant it was time to prepare for our Annual Yule Ball, our celebration of Winter Solstice. Maybe this was going to be the distraction that Amelia needed. Something to look forward to, but first I needed to get her to talk to me.

I climbed from the bed, before pulling on my jeans and a black t-shirt, before slowly making my way down to the meeting room. The moment I walked in the room fell silent as all eyes turned to me. *Wow. At least now I understand what Amelia feels walking into the dining hall.* I cleared my throat and smiled to my pack and the room fell back into their own general chatter. Matt, Charlie and Eddie were sat close together; *Matt looking as though he would rather be anywhere other than next to Charlie.* I dropped into my chair beside them and cleared my throat, trying my hardest to forget everything that had been happening the last few weeks and act as normal as possible.

'So, who are you all taking?' I asked looking at Matt, Charlie and Eddie. Matt shrugged; he didn't really like the yule Balls and would have rather had gone to the pub.

'Maybe Lori or Adela, or maybe Harper, I don't know. I haven't decided which one I want yet.' Charlie replied rubbing his chin. Eddie looked awkward

'I guess I'm taking whoever Charlie doesn't take.' He replied, 'And you?' he asked grinning. Matt smirked at Eddies question and Charlie rolled his eyes as he crossed his arms against his chest.

'Amelia.' I grinned sitting back on my chair.

'What the fuck? You're taking the murderer?' Charlie asked huffing, his eyes opening wider than I thought humanly possible; he was really starting to piss me off with this bullshit, but I had to remain calm and level minded but before I could say anything Matt spoke up.

'She isn't a fucking murder you moron.' He snarled through clenched teeth. Charlie narrowed his eyes and turned to face Matt, before laughing mockingly.

'Let me guess, your fucking her too? Wow, who knew that my *sister* was so lose and free.' I watched as Matt's face turned from red to purple with anger. I knew Matt, and he would only take so much, especially when it involved someone that he really cared about. I saw the muscles twitching in his arms as he fought to keep his emotions under control. He opened his mouth to shout back.

'Enough.' I roared, slamming my hand on my desk causing the room to fall silent. I turned and stared into my Beta's eyes; he knew he had overstepped the mark this time. he quickly looked away and put his head down, Matt had since walked out of my office slamming the door behind him.

Amelia;

I slowly made my way down the winding halls. I knew that I would be safe from the threats that I had been receiving lately as most of the Elites would be in the pack meeting. *Why was I letting all these bastards get into my head?* I hurried down the staircase and twisted myself around so that I was stood outside the main kitchen doors. I hesitated for a moment but knew that everyone behind this door was supporting me. With a heavy sigh, I placed my palm on the heavy door and shoved it, slipping in and smiling over to the friendly faces that greeted me.

'Amelia! What are you doing in here...again?' Tanya asked, hurrying forward and pulling me into her arms. I shrugged and looked down at the spotless floor, trying my hardest to fight through the fog in my mind. *What was I doing in here?*

'If I am honest, I just don't want to be alone.' I answered softly, I hated sounding so pathetic, but I knew that Tanya would understand. She planted a gentle kiss to the top of my head and squeezed a little harder.

'I thought you and Matt were out with Pretty Girl?' Piper

smiled wrapping her arms around me and her mother, cuddling me.

'We were planning to go after the pack meeting.' I replied, trying my hardest to not roll my eyes. I cleared my throat and turned my eyes around the busy room. 'Can I do anything?' Tanya smiled at me, her face full of sadness, I knew they all felt sorry for me. A lot of the Elites were questioning if I had killed Jaime and Laura; *which I didn't*, but I could say it until I was blue in the face, no one believed me. Arlo wouldn't even talk to me about it and I understood why, it was awful for him knowing that two of his own Pack members had been murdered right under his nose; and I was the prime suspect. *I just hoped that he didn't think that it was me also.* The only two people that did talk about it with me were Matt and Piper; my two biggest supports; my warriors! Tanya looked up at the kitchens clock and sighed.

'Okay, you can cut up some fruit, but you must go for lunch today; darling, you haven't gone for any meals since...since what had happened, you can't hide away for ever.' She whispered, untangling her arms from around me and walked over to one of the many huge fridges and pulling a massive tray of fresh fruit from within. I smiled weakly and hurried over to her.

'I don't want too; I can't sit with them all. The only people who talk to me are Arlo, Marie, Matt and Eddie.' I sniffled as a tear fell down my cheek. 'And even that is getting more difficult. I can literally feel the pack dividing around me. And it's all my fault.' I whispered.

'Hey, listen to me okay? No one else in that hall believes that you had anything at all to do with those killings. And the four people that matter the most on your table also know you didn't. Yes, the other Elites have questioned it, and yes it will be uncomfortable. But you hold your head up high; madam. You have done nothing wrong; you have nothing to be ashamed of. So, cut up this fruit, go and get showered, put a bit of make up on, put on some of those lovely clothes that you own and go for Lunch, you have 45 minutes. Go.' Tanya smiled motioning to Piper to join me. I chopped the fruit, allowing myself to get lost in my work with Piper at my side. And before I knew it Tanya was back at our table, ushering us from the kitchen.

'Come on, let's go and get you ready for lunch.' Piper said softly, linking her arm through mine.

I listened to Tanya and Piper, allowing their words to take over everything else. I had a shower and put some make up on, my lips were blood red and matched my tight-fitting long-sleeved top, I put some black leggings on and wore my red converse. Piper did my hair; two French plates fell down past each shoulder resting beside my breast. *Here goes nothing* I thought exiting my bedroom and making my way down to the food hall.

The moment that I entered the room, all the non-Elite pack members smiled at me and carried on talking amongst them-selves, but Charlie and the other Elite's turned their stone-cold glares on me; making me feel as though I didn't deserve to be there. I ignored all the hatred that was being pushed my way and locked eyes with Ethan. The minute that he met my stare he broke out into a goofy grin that melted my heart and caused butterflies to fill my stomach. I smiled back to him and looked away from him momentarily to meet the disgusted stares of my brother and father.

I turned my attention over towards where Matt usually sat; *and much to his disgust it was always next to Charlie*, he gave me a reassuring smile and nodded to the door. Arlo and his parents had just walked into the dining hall. I scurried over to my chair which was now between Arlo's and Marie's and stood waiting for them to take their seats. Matt was grinning at me and gave me a side glance towards Arlo, trying his best to be discrete, I looked up at Arlo, our eyes meeting each other's, he smirked and then looked me up and down as he walked closer to me. I felt his body brush against mine as soon as he walked past me before sitting at his chair. I bit my lip, every time he touched me, I just went weak. I never understood the expression weak at the knees until now.

'Nice to see you finally joining us.' He smiled rubbing my leg under the table, I smiled back and felt his hand running further up my leg. 'Stop.' I mouthed crossing my legs together, he chuckled quietly and pulled his hand away. *Not now Alpha!* I thought to myself.

Marie turned towards me and beamed. 'Arlo has given me permission to take you out shopping and we are going to get you a Ball gown, the only condition is, that Matt comes with us.' She excitedly clapped her hands. 'We need a dress that would match those beautiful eyes of yours.' She looked up at Arlo and he smiled. 'When are you going mother?' he asked. 'Well the ball is on Friday and we are on Monday, so ideally Thursday?' Marie said looking over at Matt. 'Yeah Thursday is good for me.' Matt smiled. 'It will be nice for Lia to get out as well.'

Arlo had told me that he was going to buy Matt's Tux this year because he knew he was saving up his money for a motor bike. Matt Loves Motor Bikes, especially Harley Davidsons! He always walked around in black jeans and leather jackets, girls and guys fell at his feet and yet he never showed any interest in any of them. He was a closed book to everyone but me and Arlo and I respected him for that, he had such a sad start in life and made the best out of it. Arlo adored him and he is the best friend a girl could ask for; I was so lucky to have him.

I noticed that Charlie didn't say a word, he didn't even look at me. I couldn't work out if that was through disgust because he hated how close me, and Arlo were or because he had been forbidden to say anything else to me, but I was thankful for it. I couldn't bear to listen to anymore of his nasty rumours. I knew Charlie hated me, but I didn't realise until two weeks ago how much he hated me. It broke my heart, what girl doesn't want to have a protective big brother? I had two big brothers and neither of them protected me, Charlie would rather me be dead and Eddie was too scared of him to defend me.

The rest of lunch wasn't as bad as I thought it would be. Me and Marie spoke about dress shopping, Arlo spoke to Matt about the training sessions with the Non-Elites and Eddie and Charlie spoke about their possible dates. No one mentioned anything about Jaime and Laura and if I am honest, that was a welcomed surprise, because I couldn't get that awful memory out of my head.

Arlo;

'You look beautiful today; Lia.' I said as we left the dining hall. 'It's so nice to see you back to your usual self, I have missed it.' I whispered, taking her hand in mine as we went outside; it had started to snow, and it looked beautiful, but Amelia still looked sad.

'I don't feel like I am back to my usual self.' She admitted wrapping her arms around herself, trying to keep warm.

'I know I let you down; Lia, but from now on you always have me and Matt.' I said putting my arm around her.

'Hell, yeah she has!' Matt grinned standing beside me. 'Pub?' he asked, his grin getting wider. Amelia started giggling.

'Pub!' she agreed.

Once we had got to the pub, I ordered a round for us and we all sat in Matt's favourite booth which was right next to the juke box.

'So, are you excited for the yule ball?' Matt asked Amelia, she smiled and nodded yes. 'I am so nervous though.' She admitted.

'Why?' I asked.

'Because I can't dance!' she replied.

'Shut up; Lia' Matt laughed shaking his head. 'I saw you dancing on that bar, you know how to dance!' Amelia blushed and put her head down.

'Yeah, maybe when I am drunk and pissed off.' She smirked looking up at me, Matt chuckled.

'So, that just means that we need to get you drunk beforehand?' Matt added with a wink. Amelia sighed and then bit her lip. Matt then turned a sideways glance to me; 'And I am sure that Arlo will piss you off soon so then we will be good to go.' He added with a chuckle.

'Seriously? Dude!' I said, sounding amused.

'I don't think my Alpha would appreciate that.' Her eyes still not moving from mine. *No, I wouldn't, well not until she was alone with me anyway.* Every time she looked at me or bit her lip it drove me crazy, I just couldn't get over how beautiful she was and she wanted to be with me of all people, a pang of sadness washed over me but I pushed it aside, I just wanted to be with her forever.

After a few glasses of Rose Amelia became tipsy and giggly, she jumped up in excitement when Piper walked into the pub.

'Dance with me?' she asked running over to her.

'Yes!' Piper laughed pulling Amelia over to the duke box. The girls chose a song I had never heard of and took their shoes off.

'Uh oh.' Matt laughed looking at me. 'She is going to dance on the bar again!' I shrugged and sat back smiling. This time I was here with her and with my best friend and today Amelia was going to enjoy herself, we all were, we needed it.

I watched as Amelia and Piper danced sexily with each other and put my head in my hands. Matt laughed at me,

'That bad, eh?' I looked up at him

'Man, you have no idea, she has literally got my head fucked. I haven't had sex in ages and her doing that is driving me crazy.' I admitted. Matt smirked and then looked over at Amelia.

'Yeah but when you do have sex with her, it's going to be special and worth the wait.' I nodded my head in agreement,

'We came really close to doing it a couple of weeks back and can you believe it was me that stopped it?' Matt looked shocked

'Really?' he asked raising his eyebrows.

'Yeah, I just want her to be truly ready you know? I don't want to hurt her, it's a big thing. I want her to be sure, but with the way she is going I don't think I could stop it next time.' Matt laughed at me. 'She is something special.' He smiled changing the subject.

'That she is.' I agreed. 'She idolises you, we both do.' I continued, looking at my best friend. Matt blushed and stood up taking a cigarette out from behind his ear. He could never take a compliment.

Amelia;

I looked up at Arlo who was now sitting by himself drinking another pint of beer.

'Dance with me?' I mouthed as we caught each other's eyes, he shook his head a chuckled. 'Pleaseeee' I begged playfully. I couldn't stop my mind from drifting back to the night that Ethan and I were drunk and dancing. Was this another way of showing me that I wasn't really destined to be with Arlo? *Maybe Ethan was the one that I was supposed to be with? Maybe this was Selene's way of answering my cries for help.*

'I don't dance.' He shouted over the music. I got off the bar and walked over to him.

'You okay?' I asked putting my hand on his broad shoulder.

'Yeah I am, I'm just glad seeing you have a good time.' He then looked down at his watch. 'You know we have missed dinner, right?' I looked at my phone, it was 9 pm already.

'Oooops, my Alpha is going to be so pissed off with me.' I joked sitting on his lap.

'I can never be angry with you; even when you slap me round the face… providing you don't puke down my back again.' He said wrapping his arms around me. 'But if you don't eat something soon, you will end up really sick.' I smiled lent my head back, so it was on his shoulder.

'We will go and get food soon and then come back here?' I said closing my eyes breathing in his scent.

'I will go and get you something to eat from the bar, they serve dinner here.' He said before kissing my cheek.

'Okay well I am going for a wee' I whispered getting up, I looked around, Matt had just walked back in the pub and Piper was gone.

'Have you seen Piper?' I asked concerned.

'No, she hasn't left so I presume she is on the toilet.' He replied holding my arm as my legs got wobbly. *I am so drunk* I thought trying not to fall over.

I locked the cubicle door and was about to undo my jeans when I heard two people panting, I recognised one of the voices and smirked.

'Piper, you dirty thing.' I shouted as I pulled my jeans down. The panting stopped and the toilets fell silent. 'Don't stop on my account.' I said leaning on the cubicle wall, trying my best not to fall over. 'I am just having a wee.' I announced, I heard giggling and then I recognised the second voice. 'Eddie?!' I cried realising my brother and best friend were having sex next to me. 'Oh, my goddess! You didn't tell me you two liked each other.' I said finally managing to pull my panties down. Piper and Eddie still didn't reply. 'Okay I get the hint.' I giggled finally managing to pee. I covered my ears and hummed away to myself; but I think I had probably already killed their moment. 'I am just washing my hands.' I slurred pulling my underwear and jeans up; unlocking the bathroom door and stumbled over, feeling as the cold tiled floor smashed against my face.

'Lia! Are you okay?' Piper called over Eddies hysterical laughter.

'Fuck sis! You really do know how to kill a moment; don't you?' He sniggered; clearly amused at the fact that I fell over.

I pushed myself back up and leant against the sink staring at the hot mess before me in the mirror. 'Yeah, I am good.' I said before throwing up in the sink.

I assumed that no one knew about them and I certainly wasn't going to tell a soul. Now I knew why Eddie wouldn't really talk about who he was going to take to the yule ball, because the girl he wanted to take was a Non-Elite. I stumbled back into the pub like nothing had happened, Arlo and Matt were sat with three plates of food in front of them, my stomach rumbled, and I sat down trying to not miss the chair on my way down. I glanced up as Piper walked back into the pubs from the toilets. Eddie wasn't with her; he must have secretly slipped out through the back doors. Matt moved over slightly so she could sit down, I shared my dinner with her, and we talked about the Yule Ball, her secret was safe with me. We all looked at Arlo as his phone started ringing loudly and vibrating against the table. He quickly answered it and his face softened.

'Hello mum. Yeah of course. Okay I will be there in 5 minutes and we can discuss it then. Yeah...Yeah...Okay bye!' He turned to look at me and smiled. 'My mum wants to talk about the yule ball and someone's shopping trip.' He winked, I smiled and took in his beauty. 'Meet me back in my room...when you are ready?' He asked rising from his seat.

'Okay.' I smiled standing up to face him, I stood on my tip toes and our lips met; gasps filled the pub as the Non-Elites watched their Alpha kiss the girl every other Elite hated.

Arlo;

I hurried back to my office, knowing that my mother said that she wanted to speak to me in private. *At least this way I knew that it wasn't going to be anything negative about Amelia. My mother seemed to be her biggest fan.* By the time I reached the door of my office, my mother rounded the corner and broke out into a beaming smile. I pushed open the door and held it open, pausing as she leaned in a planted a soft kiss on my cheek.

'How are you doing darling?' She asked, stepping past me and taking a seat on the sofa. I nodded, closing the door behind me and taking the seat across from her. *I knew that she hated small talk, but she was trying to be polite.* I forced a smile and shook my head.

'What is it that you wanted to talk to me about?' I asked politely, she sighed softly and glanced out the window for a moment before answering.

'This is about Amelia's dress for the Yule Ball. I wanted to buy it for her. I mean, I know that you wouldn't mind, but I always like to run things past you.' She answered sweetly. I hesitated for a moment, before shaking my head.

'No.' I watched as her face fell slightly and was replaced by a look of confusion. 'I mean. I wanted to buy it for her. I wanted it to be a treat from me.' I added quickly. My mother broke out into a huge grin and nodded excitedly.

'Brilliant! Then I shall take her out shopping as soon as she is available.' She said, clasping her hands together in front of her.

Amelia;

By the time that we all left the pub I was incredibly drunk. And I had the sudden need to go and see Pretty Girl. I stared up at the clear sky above me and stumbled onwards. Matt had insisted that he come with me, but I had told him that I was fine. *Why did everyone think that I need protecting?* It wasn't like the stables were far from the pub anyway, and since my little bust up with Lori, she had been keeping her distance, so I was certain that she wouldn't be an issue.

I continued walking onwards, allowing myself to get lost in the peaceful nights air, when a hand gripped my wrist and pulled me around to face them. It took me a second to keep up with the movement, which caused my stomach to lurch slightly, before I shook my head and forced my eyes to focus on my captor. The minute my vision came into focus I broke out into a beaming smile.

'Ethan!' I squealed excitedly, lunging forward and wrapping my arms around him. He chuckled lightly, and tightened his arms around me, kissing me lightly on the cheek.

'Hey baby girl, how are you doing?' He laughed, as I stumbled in his arms, causing him to tighten his grip on me.

'I'm grilliant!' I slurred, pausing for a second as I tried to make sense of what I was attempting to say.

'Grilliant yeah?' He asked laughing. 'So I take it that you have had a nice time at the pub with everyone?' He asked sweetly. I nodded enthusiastically and twirled in his arms.

'Yeah I did... but the boring old one wouldn't dance with me.' I pouted, looking up at Ethan through my eyelashes. He rolled his eyes and pulled me in close to him, holding his body against mine and dancing from side to side.

'Well, you know that I am always down for a good dance.' He whispered, resting the side of his head against mine and gently brushed a strand of hair away from my neck. I felt a rush of desire wash through me, as his fingertips brushed my neck and I leant back and stared up at Ethan once more.

'You're a really nice guy!' I whispered, staring at his beauty in the dim midnight light. He leant forward and gently placed his lips against mine. *He really was an amazing kisser. And so different from Arlo.* Arlo kissed like there was no tomorrow; like it was the last kiss that we were ever going to get. And Ethan's kisses were slow, passionate and full of feeling. *But... why couldn't I stop think-*

ing about Arlo? Ethan pulled back and cleared his throat and gently stroke the back of his fingers down my cheek.

'Hey, I wanted to ask you something.' He paused for a moment and shifted nervously. 'Would you… would you go to the Yule Ball with me?' My smile faltered and I dropped my stare to the ground between us.

'Ethan… I…' I sighed heavily and turned my stare back up to meet his. 'I am so, so sorry. But… Arlo already asked me… and I said yes.' I held his stare as he broke out into a smile.

'No, I mean… obviously… why wouldn't you be going with… him…' He sighed and looked to the side for a moment and stepped away from me. When his eyes met mine again, I could see the pain that I had caused, and it broke and little part of me.

'Ethan…'

'No, it's ok. Honestly.' He cut in, taking a step back from me and glancing over his shoulder. 'I better get going, I am working in the medical ward in the morning with my father… so… I better get some sleep.' He stepped back once again and began to turn away, before spinning back around and kissing me on the cheek. 'Sweet dreams Lia.' He whispered, before turning and disappearing into the darkness.

I shouldn't be doing this to him.

12

Amelia;

I heard a light knock on Arlo's bedroom door, I had practically moved in, I still had my own room but it was more used for me to keep my belongings and clothes in, I was still too nervous to stay by myself and Arlo always asked if I would stay with him. If anyone wanted to find me, they always came to Arlo's room first and today was no different. It was 10 am and Arlo was at one of his Pack meetings and it was also Thursday which meant Marie was ready for me to go shopping with her and Matt. I opened the door and Matt was leaning against the wall waiting for me. 'Ready?' he grinned taking my hand.

Marie was waiting for us in her car; it was a black Cadillac Escalade and looked brand new, Matt opened the front passenger door for me and smiled. 'Ma'am your lift awaits.' I laughed at him and lightly punched his arm. The snow had gotten heavier over the past couple of days so Marie drove as slow as she could to the nearest town centre. I stared out of the window and took in my surroundings, I had never been shopping before, I had never been anywhere other than at the cottage and Pack Mansion, this was a whole new world to me.

The dress shop was amazing, Ball gowns of all colours and styles were hung up on clothing rails and Tuxedos were hung up opposite them. Matt went straight over to the shop assistants and got himself measured up, I admired all of the beautiful ball gowns trying to pick out one I would love to wear. 'What one are you thinking of having?' Marie asked smiling at me. My eyes fell to a dark green satin and lace vintage Off-the-shoulder ball gown and I knew instantly that was the dress I wanted to wear. I pointed at it and grinned at her 'That one' I replied admiring it. Marie walked over to the dress and called over the shop assistant. 'Can we have this one to try on please?' she asked politely. She had chosen an emerald hair clip and a pair of stiletto glittery green shoes to match my dress as well as a silver necklace with an Emerald Heart encrusted into it, I had never been this spoilt in my life and it felt amazing; especially as it was Arlo that paid for the whole lot.

This was it. The night that we had been looking forward to. The Yule Ball may not have made miracles happen, but it was that small glimmer of light in the darkness that surrounded us. This ball wouldn't erase the pain that we are feeling, but it was that little bit of hope that kept us all going. I smoothed my hands down the front of my dress and smiled. This was one of the nicest looking dresses I had ever seen in my life. The emerald green satin material and the velvet swirl designs along the bodice were mesmerising. Add the fact that it was lines with tiny green gems that glistened under the dim lights and I felt magical. I sighed and glanced at myself once more in the large mirror in the hall, making sure that my emerald encrusted hair clip was holding my hair up in place. I turned to the side and admired the half bun half down look that Piper did for me. She was so talented when it came to hair and beauty. It reminded me of Belle's hairstyle from beauty and the beast. *I prayed to the goddess that this was going to be an uneventful evening.*

I walked into the ball room and smiled to myself. It seemed like so long ago that Matt and I were in here, him training me how to fight. So much had happened between now and then; it felt like a lifetime ago. I stood at the top of the stairs and took in the amazing way the hall had been decorated. Giant snowflakes hung from the ceiling of all sizes, and every time one of the strobe lights hit it, it cast a kaleidoscope of colours on the ceiling. Every table around the edges of the dance floor was dusted in a layer of fake snow, and giant ice sculptures were dotted around the room. I had honestly never seen anything look so beautiful. I looked around at the couples bobbing and dancing to the music and smiled to myself. Everyone seemed to be having a good time; that was always a positive.

I gulped down a deep breath suddenly feeling very self-conscious. I glanced around the room, again; taking in the sights of all the people dancing with their partners, until my focus stopped on one person. *Ethan.* He stood there while a girl I didn't know twiddled her hair and giggled about something that she had said, all the while he was staring at me. His mouth hanging open slightly in awe. The very sight of him caused my pulse to race and I felt a twinge of jealousy that he was here with someone else. *Not that I blamed him. He had asked me originally, but I was here with Arlo!*

I pulled my stare away from him and glanced down at the beautiful emerald green velvet and satin gown that Marie had helped me pick out and looked around the room. My heart was pounding hard against my breastplate, and I was certain that the others could hear it. It didn't help that I knew that there were people here that still believed that I was the killer. *What was I doing here?* I shook my head and began to turn away when his deep earthy scent washed over me, causing me to stop in my tracks.

'Going somewhere beautiful?' Arlo asked, stepping up beside me and wrapping his arm around my waist. I spun around to face him and was instantly lost in those golden eyes that always drew me in. I placed my hand on his chest and smiled up to him. His silky green tie looked as though it was made from the same material as my dress. *Did Marie play a part in that?*

'I was just looking for you.' I whispered, chewing nervously on my bottom lip. Arlo leant in closer so that only I could hear, flashing those perfectly white teeth as he smiled.

'Liar. Did you know that you always chew your bottom lip like that when you are lying?' He asked playfully. I opened my mouth to protest when I realised that he was right. I sighed and shook my head.

'I just... It's hard to relax when there is still a big group of people out there that believe that I am the one killing those pack members. But the thing is, have you not noticed that they were both Non-Elites?' I whispered back. Arlo pulled back slightly as a look of confusion washed over his face.

'Non-Elites? Are you talking about Mutts?'

'I seriously hate that word!' I grumbled, more to myself than him. Arlo reached up and placed two fingers under my chin and raised my face so that I could meet his gaze.

'Then Non-Elites it is. Oh. And Amelia. You look beautiful tonight.' He added, leaning in and planting a soft kiss on my cheek. He bowed slowly, reminding me of something from an old Disney movie and then held his hand out, ready to take mine. I placed my trembling hand in his and his fingers instantly closed around mine, making me feel ten times more confident than a moment before.

We made our way out into the centre of the dancefloor, where he stopped and spun me around to face him. The song was slow and romantic, and I suddenly felt extremely exposed out here in the open. Arlo pulled me closer to him so that our bodies were pressed tightly together and stared down at me with those hypnotic eyes.

'I have to say Lia, you look...' He stopped and blew out a breath. 'You look amazing.' I felt my face burn as the blush snuck across my cheeks and I dropped my eyes to the ground.

'You don't look so bad yourself.' I replied, running my eyes over every inch of him. The suit that he wore looked as though it had been tailored especially for him; *and specially to flaunt those rock-hard abs that were concealed beneath them.* I felt that familiar burn of desire, swirl from my chest and sink down low into my stomach. He was the first man that I had ever met that was able to drive me this wild over them. Everything about him just screamed sexy.

Matt;

I stepped through the large open doors and took in the sight of all the happy couples dancing. I forced a smile but inside it killed me. Don't get me wrong, I was not ashamed of what and who I was, but deep down, there was a part of me that longed for the normality of life. Things would have been so much easier if I could just find a girl and settle down; at least then I wouldn't have to attend this stupid ball alone. I would be one of those out there dancing together. I sighed and dropped my stare to the ground. *What the hell was I doing here?*

'Matty!' Came a familiar voice that instantly brought a smile to my lips. I looked back up to the dance floor just in time to see Lia throw herself into my arms. 'We have been waiting for you!' She chimed.

'Have you been drinking?' I asked, smirking playfully. Amelia narrowed her eyes at me and poked her tongue out. 'I take that as a yes then?' I added with a laugh. Arlo stepped closer to me and shook my hand, before pulling me into a brotherly hug. I seriously don't know where I would have been without this guy. *He was my rock. And now Lia was my diamond. They really did make the perfect pair. Even if they didn't want to admit it to themselves.*

'It's about time man. I thought that she was going to have me dancing all night!' Arlo laughed, patting me on the shoulder and gesturing to Amelia. I turned to look at her with confusion in my eyes and noticed the child-like excitement that flashed through her.

'Can we please dance Matty? Pretty please?' She whispered grinning like the Cheshire cat. I rolled my eyes and offered my hand out. As I did the music suddenly changed to that of the Tango. Amelia turned to look at me; her eyes wider than a moment ago; *I didn't even know that was possible and* dragged me out to the middle of the floor. I felt everyone's eyes on us as we stood there for a second. So, I closed my eyes, took in the rhythm of the music and we let our bodies do the rest.

I don't know where she learnt it, but damn! That girl could tango! The dancers on the floor slowly stopped their own dance and were soon gathered around the edges of the dancefloor, cheering us on. Before I knew it, the music had stopped, and a thunderous applause erupted out around us. Amelia blushed and dipped her head, causing one of her ringlets to fall loose from the clip and hand down her face. I glanced over to Arlo, and he stood clapping with a look of approval. I spun Amelia once more for good measure before we both dashed off back into the shadows where we could hide away with Arlo. As we walked over to him, he raised a single eyebrow and clapped.

'Wow… you two were… something.' He said with a huge grin. 'I can honestly say that, that dance is going to be the talk of the pack for weeks.' He laughed.

'Sorry about that man. I wasn't thinking. I just let the music take me!' I whispered, knowing that my face was now glowing the same shade of red as Amelia's.

'You have nothing to apologise for. I think you two were great.' Arlo added, wrapping his arm around Amelia and pulling her in close to him.

Arlo;

'Thank you, guys, for everything.' Matt said, as he pulled Amelia and I into a hug. I knew that it wasn't easy for him. He didn't want anyone to know that he was gay, I understood that. He was my best friend. My heart went out to him. *Would he ever find his one perfect mate? Could two guys imprint on one another?* Amelia pushed herself up on tip toes and kissed him on the cheek.

'Are you kidding. I have had the best night ever!' She said, fanning her face with her hand. I smiled to myself. I could seriously see myself falling in love with this girl. And I don't think that there is anything that could stop it; but then there was Ethan and although he was in the picture; more than I liked, I tried fighting the attraction with Amelia at first, but in the end; there was nothing to fight.

I knew that Amelia was dying to get back out on the floor and dance some more, so I allowed her to pull me forward. We got on the dancefloor and I pulled her close once again. There was something about the way that she just seemed to fit against me that made me feel complete. The song turned to a slow one and light dimmed down. I don't know how long we were dancing for, but in that moment, everyone else in the room seemed to just, disappear. I smiled softly to myself and lowered my face down to hers, gently meeting her lips with my own.

Lori;

I stood there and watched the pair of them together. It made me sick. I mean, what did she have that I didn't. She couldn't even shift yet. I was the best of the best. And he chose her. I let out a frustrated growl and stormed off out into the nights air. It was so damn hot in that room that I felt as though I was suffocating. Or maybe it was just their sickening display that was making me feel queasy!

'Hey, Lori. Is everything ok?' Adela asked running out into the gardens behind me. I rolled my eyes. *Seriously, this girl needed to get a life!* I spun back around to face her and glared at her.

'I'm sorry, I didn't know that I needed your permission to get some fresh air!' I snapped back at her. I knew that I shouldn't be treating my friends like this, but I really didn't care anymore. I was so done with pretending to care anymore. It was in that moment that I realised what I had to do. I needed to get rid of that vile creature that thought it was ok to try and steal my man. I closed my eyes and turned back to look at the ball room, catching sight of myself in the mirror. My ice blue gown shimmered like ice reflecting the moon light, and my blonde hair and pale skin complemented it perfectly. I narrowed my eyes at Amelia and chewed on my bottom lip. *Surely there was a way to get rid if her for good.* And then I laid eyes on him. The only other person in this place that was glaring daggers at her as much as I was. The only other person in this place that would help me get rid of that bitch! *Charlie.* I nodded to myself. I knew it was time for me and him to have a little chat. I guessed as he was second in command that he would have ideas and plots that I could only dream of. I held my head up head and made my way directly towards him.

If I wanted her gone then I knew that Charlie was the one to do it. This was going to be fun. I tucked my wrap under my arms and hoisted my dress up a little higher, so I was able to take bigger strides. I knew that there was one way to make Charlie be putty in my hands. I strolled back into the ball room and scanned across the crowds, searching for him in the darkness. The music was loud and pulsing in the air, while the disco lights glittered and bounced around the room. The heat from all the bodies dancing made it almost unbearable to be in the room. There in the corner was Charlie, propped up against the wall and staring at Adela and Harper as they swayed to the music. *I knew that they had always had a thing for Charlie, but I wasn't going to think about that now.* I charged forward, barging the dancing Mutts out of my way as I followed my plan. Charlie spotted me walking towards him and his eyes widened with pleasure. *I knew that he wanted me. It wasn't a secret. And tonight. He was going to get me.*

Without saying a word, I reached out and grabbed his arm, pulling him back in the direction of his bedroom, fluttering my eye lashes and smiled coyly at him every now and again. I could hear him chuckling to himself, clearly pleased with what was about to happen.

We entered his room and he slammed him up against the door, kissing him with my full force. He grabbed at my dress, pulling the zip and watching as it slid down my body, leaving me standing in nothing but my underwear. In one swift motion, he pulled his belt from his trousers and dropped them to the floor, kicking them to the side and pressing himself up against me, kissing me once more.

I kissed along his jaw and down his neck, undoing the buttons on his shirt revealing his toned body, and not stopping until I was at the waistband of his boxers. I glanced up at him once more through my eyelashes and watched as he stared down at me grinning. I ran my hands up his legs and watched as the bulge in his underwear throbbed excitedly. I allowed my fingers to brush over the front of the soft material before slipping them into the waist band and slowly peeling them down. I widened my eyes at the sight of him stood in all his glory. *He was bigger than I expected. Not as big as Arlo but… beggars can't be choosers.* I leant forward and slowly ran my tongue up the inside of his thigh, causing his body to tremble. *It was in that moment that I knew that I had him right where I wanted him.*

I took him in my mouth and allowed my tongue to travel

over his length, causing him to tilt his head back and groan slightly.

Charlie pulled me to my feet and bent me over, tugging my panties down and sliding himself in me. I reached forward and held on to the end of his bed firmly as he thrust himself deeper in with every movement. I slowly thrust my hips back, meeting his every movement with one of my own, causing him to groan loudly. *I knew that he wouldn't be able to last much longer.* I reached down further and grasped my ankles, using the buckles on my high heels as a grip allowing him to get deeper inside. I slowly rotated my hips, causing him to grip my hips tightly digging his fingers into me. With one final thrust, he released himself loudly. Slamming into me with every pulse, before flopping forward and laying on my back.

He lay there for a few seconds, before standing up straight and pulling out, rolling his shoulders, causing his muscles to flex. He turned and skulked into the bathroom, giving me a second to redress. By the time he emerged, I had already left. *I had given him the thing he had wanted more than anything. Now all I had to do was wait for him to come back for more.*

Amelia;

'I don't know how long Arlo and I had been dancing, but one thing I did know was how much my feet hurt. *And, I was also quite tipsy.* I lifted my foot and tugged at my shoes until they fell to the floor with a clunk. Arlo chuckled and shook his head. *It was nice to see him actually smiling for a change!* He scooped me up into his arms and grabbed my shoes from me.

'I think it's time that we went to bed.' He whispered, planting a soft kiss on my cheek. My face warmed and that hot desire course through me once more.

'I thought you would never ask.' I replied, refusing to break eye contact with him. He carried me all the way to his bedroom and placed me on the bed. 'Thank you for an amazing night.' I said taking off the beautiful necklace he had bought me. 'Thank you.' He smiling as I stood up from the bed. I studied his handsome face and I felt sad. We cared for each other so much and love makes you do crazy things. I knew I would never be the one he would imprint with;

he knew it too. We avoided the 'imprinting subject' at all costs. I couldn't bear to think about another woman being with him, he was mine and I was his. We couldn't give each other the future we both wanted; a future together, but I could give him something that once was lost, it could never be regained and the one thing only he could hold claim to; my virginity. The thought of having sex for the first time sent a wave of butterflies through my tummy, I knew it hurt the first time, Piper told me it did. But he was worth every ounce of pain I would go through.

I put my hands behind my back and fumbled with the zip of my dress, I couldn't get it off. 'Here, let me do it.' Arlo said after removing his blazer and tie. Chills went down my spine as I felt him undo my dress, all I was wearing underneath were black laced pantie's; I allowed the gown to fall to the floor and I put my arms over my breasts, my back was still turned to him. Butterflies filled my stomach and I started trembling, with nerves and with excitement. Arlo moved my hair to one side of my neck and started kissing the other side, I closed my eyes and a feeling of lust took over my body. I turned around to face him and removed my arm away allowing my bare breasts to be on show. Arlo's eyes fell straight down to them and then back at my face and within seconds our lips met, this time with a lot more passion than ever before. He started taking his clothes off our gazes not breaking away from each other. I sat on the bed and shuffled back so my head was on the pillows. I felt as he knelt on the bed and pulled down my underwear and a mixture of emotions flooded through my entire body, nervousness, excitement, lust and love for the man who was now hovering above my naked body. I ran my fingers down his abs, watching as they danced and twitched under my touch. My heart pounded so loud in my ears that it was deafening. I continued my descent further down his body, stopping only momentarily before I got to his erection. I watched as it twitched, begging me to feel it. I couldn't hold it off any longer, I allowed the warmth of his hardness to fill my hand. He gasped a desperate, ragged breath, silently urging me to continue. I didn't just want him, I needed him, I craved him. Arlo's eyes dropped from my face to my breasts and took my nipple in his mouth, I ran my hand through his hair and closed my eyes.

'Are you sure you want to do this? He asked. I nodded desperately wanting him to take me completely. I was ready for this, *I needed this.* He hovered above my body, his eyes studying my face as I took in his length, my eyes widened. *Oh, my goddess Selene.* He chuckled and put his finger on my chin, slowly raising my face to his.

'Are you ready? 'he asked before allowing one of his hands to spread open my legs. My eyes told him all he needed to know; I was so ready for this as scared as I was. He lowered himself onto me slowly, and my stomach flipped as I felt his hardness brush against my inner thigh. He slowly allowed himself to get closer and started kissing my breasts; working his way up to my lips, our eyes met again and he put his hand down to his crutch, I gasped as he gently started rubbing himself against me, his eyes stayed on me the whole time, watching my face as it revealed the pleasure that was building up within me, he carried on rubbing, his pace quickening as my thrusts met his.

And just before I met my peak he stopped before taking in a deep breath and looking into my eyes

'I will go as slow as you need me to.' He smiled before putting his weight on his elbows, his face was just above mine and he waited for me to be completely ready. I nodded nervously and put my hands on his hips, He put his beautiful lips to mine as he finally started entering me, I whimpered as I felt him, and he froze. *Fuck this hurt.*

'Want me to stop?' he whispered.

'N…no.' I stuttered. Arlo studied my face once more before pushing his whole self into me and he gasped as he felt all of me around him. Pain ripped through me and my eyes watered, *wow this really hurt.* He went slowly to begin with, his thrusts not hard, he was being so gentle with me and yet he probably just wanted to bang the hell out of me, but I appreciated it. Our eyes met and I pulled his face towards mine, looking at him made the pain slowly fade away, having him in me now felt amazing and those two feelings mysteriously entwined.

'You're so tight' he panted his thrusts becoming faster, I dug my nails into his shoulders and arched my back as I started climbing in arousal, it only seemed to turn him on more, his thrusts now becoming harder, my hips moved with his and his kisses became more passionate, his tongue filled my mouth as I fought the urge to cry out with pleasure. I wrapped my legs around his waist and finally allowed the orgasm to take over my body, it was a feeling of pure ecstasy, my whole body shook with pleasure and I let out a satisfied moan, Arlo looked down at my face, his breathing had become ragged, small gasps escaped his mouth each time he thrusted himself in deeper, before he came undone inside of me. We laid there for a short while, our bodies still entwined together as we panted, trying to get our breath back, I could feel our hearts banging against our chests and banging against each other. I loved this man more than anything. I had given him the one thing I could never give anyone else and I knew that it was the one thing I would never regret.

As Arlo rolled off my satisfied body, he pulled me close to him, my breasts pressed against his chest. I stroked my fingertips up and down his smooth neck and laid my head on his shoulder.

'I am sorry if I hurt you.' He whispered kissing the top of my head.

'Don't be sorry, it was worth it, I would do that again over and over if it meant always being with you.' I replied, my tone quiet.

Arlo smiled. 'Me too, thank you; Amelia.'

I sat up and gazed at his handsome face, admiring the man staring back up at me.

'For what?' I asked, an impish smile spreading across my face.

'For this, for being with me despite the risks it involves and for being...mine.' I smiled at his words and raised my eyebrows. 'Yours, huh?'

He pulled me back down to his warm body and wrapped his arms around my waist. 'Mine.' He growled playfully.

I looked up at him and bit my lip, his eyes met mine and he smirked.

'Again?' I whispered bringing my face back up to his, he kissed me on the lips; this time allowing his tongue to fill my mouth; my heart pounded as he climbed between my legs again before entering me.

13

Arlo;

I woke up and turned to the sleeping beauty next to me taking in her perfect features, when I told her that she meant so much to me, I meant it. It hurt that we could never be together, that we wouldn't imprint on each other and the thought of me falling in love with someone else just didn't seem possible, I could never love anyone else the way I did her. Amelia opened her eyes and groggily smiled

'Morning.' She croaked as she stretched her naked body, the duvet slid down revealing her breasts and I felt a rush come over me, it took me back to the night before, I remembered every detail, from when her gown fell to the floor to when I took her virginity and to when I made love to her into the early hours, the images in my head turned me on and I felt myself rise. Amelia looked down at the duvet which had now been raised slightly and she smirked.

'Really?' she whispered moving her hand down to my crutch. I took in a deep ruffled breath as her warm hand cupped me and started moving up and down, first slowly and then faster, I needed her. I got up on my knees and put my hands on her hips, flipping her over on to all fours, I run a finger down her and felt as the wetness rushed in, she needed me too. I grabbed a handful of her hair and wrapped it around my fingers, pulling the back of her head up to my face, she gasped as I bit into her neck, but being careful not to break the skin, I sucked on her warm flesh and then gently allowed her to lean back down on to bed; with her hands holding on to the wooden panel before her.

'Ready?' I breathed before putting all of myself into her.

Amelia let out a gasp and tightened her grip on my headboard, I felt as her whole body went weak and it only turned me on more, she was so tight and so wet, it made me throb as I thrusted faster and deeper. I listened as she moaned lost in a world of ecstasy, the whole mansion could probably hear her…they could probably all hear us, the bed slammed against the wall with every thrust I took, thank fully it was only Amelia's room that my bed backed on to but the room underneath us; that was Matts. Amelia's knuckles went white as she gripped the headboard tighter; her moans became louder and I felt a build-up of excitement and started throbbing, with every stroke, a sensation took over me and I pushed myself as deep into her as I could possibly go and got to a point of no return. I held onto her hips with a tighter grip and arched my back as the intensity built up and then I released myself into her, my legs were shaking and I was trying to catch my breath, Amelia's whole body shook with the orgasm she had just had and we collapsed into a heap, our bodies wrapping around each other.

Amelia;

'Wow' I sighed trying to calm my breathing, 'I did not expect that!' I looked at Arlo and he was pretty much falling asleep again. 'We have breakfast in an hour.' I laughed tapping his broad shoulder, 'Wake up.' I saw as a smile spread across his lips.

'I have an hour; you have 45 minutes. Time to get dressed and I shall sleep.' I crossed my arms against my chests and stared at him.

'How about you join me for a shower?' Arlo's eyes flicked opened as soon as he heard my proposal and he grinned.

'Deal.' He said sitting up.

'But no funny business Alpha, I am so sore right now.' I admitted walking over to the bathroom. 'You're a werewolf.' He replied, 'You will heal, I am sure you could go again.' He growled playfully gently pushing me into the bathroom before kissing me.

Not long after round four and after we had both showered Arlo's phone rang. I wrapped a black towel around my body and walked back into his bedroom, I watched as his whole face drained to white and then he put his head down, taking in a deep breath through his now and out of his mouth. I listened in on the conversation.

'Hello?'

'What has happened?'

'When was he found?'

'And when did it happen, do you know?'

'Why was he so far off the grounds? Did anyone see anything?'

'Do we know who the last person was to talk to him?' Arlo's jaw clenched and his eyes darted up to me as he hung the phone up.

'Another murder.' He mumbled grabbing his clothes. My heart sank and I pressed my body against the bedroom wall, this had to be some sort of sick joke.

'When?' I whimpered.

'Last night, body found this morning.' He replied pulling his jeans over his boxers.

'Who?' I whispered as I grabbed my underwear.

'One of the Elders.' Arlo admitted pulling a black T-shirt over his head. *Oh, my goddess; an Elder?* I thought as I started getting myself dressed.

'Who called you?' I asked; hoping it wasn't Matt. The poor thing always seemed to find the bodies; sadly, that was the shit part of his job. He trained fighters; but he also had to check around the perimeter of our territory every day.

'Matt; he found the body.' Arlo's face was still so pale, and his eyes were glazed over. I hurt for him, I hated seeing him this way, I wished I could tell him that I love him, but there was never a right time for us.

I hadn't even had the chance to put my shoes and socks on before I ran down the stairs following Arlo, I stopped on the bottom step, standing next to him, he put his hand out to mine and held onto me for dear life, he looked like he was going to break. Neither of us could go any further than the stairs because everyone was gathered in the hallway, their faces were full of confusion, anger, hurt and scared expressions. No one had noticed me or their Alpha, they were all either crying or talking panicked amongst themselves until a loud growl filled the whole hall, you could hear a pin drop afterwards.

'I would like everyone to make their way into the dining hall and to remain seated until the Elites come and join you. This is an emergency Pack meeting, every single member of this pack needs to be here, Elites will go and find the remainder of pack member's and the meeting will commence in 15 minutes.' Arlo said after the hall had finally silenced. He turned to me as everyone started standing in 3 single lines and squeezed my hand before pecking me on the cheek. 'I just need to speak to my parents okay?' I nodded and watched as the man I loved walked away from me with the whole world on his shoulders.

I sat in my usual chair and waited in silence for Arlo to finally enter the hall, Matt and I glanced up at each other now and then, we were both full of anxiety. *I could see that finding the Elders body had torn Matt up. I was there the last time and it traumatised me, so I couldn't imagine finding another one.* Poor Arlo had to now tell his frightened pack who it was that had been killed. Another soul ripped away from this world, I just hoped they were all at peace and somewhere better than here. It was obvious that this was all getting too much for everyone, no one said a word, all we could hear were quiet sobs, people sniffling and the off couple of coughs. Finally, Arlo stepped through the doors and into the hall with his parents both behind him. He walked over to his chair, he didn't look at me or anyone else, his eyes remained forward staring into nothingness. He stood behind his chair and finally looked at his pack.

'I have called every single one of you here today for this emergency pack meeting because something awful is happening. It seems as though our pack is under threat and under attack.' Arlo paused for a second and then cleared his throat. 'Another body was found this morning mutilated and dismembered; this time it was an Elder. Some that I know was loved by all of you. He meant the world to me and my parents and has always helped us in running our pack.' My stomach churned as those words left his mouth, gasps and cries filled the hall at the sheer horror of what had just been said; Arlo coughed and tried to clear his throat; his voice beginning to break.

'We think it happened last night because from what we can gather, he was still in his Tux. We do not know who is doing these killings, it could be another pack that are now targeting us, or it could be a rogue, either way we will find out who it is, and they will be put to death.' As Arlo said that, I could feel a pair of eyes burning into the head and I knew whose exactly they were; Charlie.

'Death' he mouthed staring straight into my eyes. I looked away from my hateful brother and glanced up at Matt, he was also looking at me, but this time with sadness. He put one finger to his lips discretely and I nodded. Now wasn't the time for me to bite back at Charlie even though at that moment in time I wanted to punch him in the face, all he ever did was accuse me of sinister and evil things and it was beginning to break me down.

Matt;

I took Amelia's hand and we went up to her bedroom to grab her a coat, she needed some fresh air and so did I. I still felt physically sick from what I had seen that morning, these deaths were getting worse every time and I do not know if it could get any-more sick than that. The Elder was one of Arlo's trusted advisors, the thought of him being murdered whilst everyone was having a great time at the ball made my skin crawl.

'Are you okay?' Amelia asked putting her hood over her head. Our wellies crunched as they sunk into the snow, which was beginning to now melt away, thanks to the rain we had started to have. She put her hands in her coat pockets and looked up at me, still waiting for an answer. I shook my head.

'Not really.' Amelia stopped and put her arms around me, she didn't have to say a word, just her being there helped me. 'Charlie is spreading rumours again.' I admitted as we both pulled away be-fore turning to walk again. Amelia rolled her eyes.

'I wouldn't expect anything less from him.' I rubbed her

back to comfort her. 'It's okay, we know you didn't do anything, and we know it wasn't Ethan; despite what Charlie is saying.'

'But it's not okay Matt; me and Ethan are being blamed for three murders that we haven't committed, Charlie will do everything in his power to have us killed because he is too scared to kill us himself and it will not be long before Arlo believes him too. I mean, I don't even know these people! I have no reason to harm them, I want to protect them.' Amelia started to get upset and tears rolled down her rosy red cheeks.

'Please don't cry; Lia. Arlo would never believe Charlie, he knows what he is like, we all do. And you nor; Ethan, will be killed, I would never let that happen and neither would Arlo.' I replied.

'But if you fought to protect me, then they would kill you too.' She whimpered rubbing her hands together as she began to get anxious. I watched in horror as she started shaking and then gasped for air. Her blood shot eyes darted around, and she put her hands on her chest. I then realised she was having a panic attack.

'Amelia; breath.' I said calmly, but she just knelt down on to the snowy ground, tears streaming down her face. I crouched down in front of her, thinking of what to do. 'Lia; I need you to take a deep breath in for 4 seconds and then breathe out for 4 seconds.' I looked around to see if Arlo was anywhere in sight. He would be able to calm her down; but unfortunately, he wasn't; he was probably in his office taking in the awful events that had happened this morning.

It took a while for her to come out of the panic attack and it was clear to see it had drained her, she looked terrified and confused. 'Have you had any before?' I asked as we walked back to the mansion. She shook her head using her coat sleeves to dry her cheeks.

'Neve and I don't ever want to go through that again. I thought I was going to die.'
I sighed and looked around making sure no one was in ear shot of us. 'I get them a lot... daily actually.' Amelia didn't seem surprised and she gave me a reassuring smile as she squeezed my ice-cold

hand.

'They are so scary; how do you cope?' she asked still taking in deep breathes.

'You get used to it if I am honest. I have been having panic attacks since I was four. After my parents died, I suffered with nightmares and anxiety… and then they started. Marie taught me how to cope with them.' I admitted. Amelia smiled when she heard Marie's name.

'She is such an amazing woman.' She whispered. I agreed; Marie was my light in the dark, she was never able to have any more children after Arlo, so she was more than happy to take me on as her own child and she always made sure that my parents were remembered, she and Tristan never tried to replace them and knowing Marie; she would have probably taken Amelia in if she had had half the chance, but Jake would have never allowed it, and neither would Tristan. I looked up at Amelia again before we walked back into the mansion doors, she looked drained and exhausted. It was obvious that the accusations were taking its toll on her mind and I knew it wouldn't be long before she cracked under the pressure.

Amelia;

A panic attack! That is what that was? I had never had one before and it was awful, I thought that I was dying, thank Selene for Matt. He said it was more than likely caused by stress and after hearing that I wondered why it had not happened sooner? My life was the definition of stress and Charlie seemed to always be at the centre of it.

I ran myself a hot bubble bath and added in some lavender oil. *This should help me sleep.* I thought as I stepped into the boiling hot water. I allowed myself to go under, my whole body warming like I was in a sauna and then I heard it again.

When the Dark Moon meets its peak,
There's a brother who is your destiny
Hide, my child, safe and sound,

As in this brother, your destiny is found

In the Moonlight, she'll show you,
All the questions, that were kept from you,
Go in search until she's found,
Resist the evil all around.

I sat up and heard as the water splashed all over the floor, I glanced around the bathroom looking for a towel and finally I spotted one; over the other side of the bathroom hanging on the door. *Just my luck.* I rolled my eyes and pulled the plug out of the bath before stepping on the soaking wet floor, and just as I went to walk over to the door, I slipped. I screamed as a sharp pain ripped through the side of head. I had hit it against the porcelain sink and was sure I had just cracked my head open. Blood started dripping down my face, the warmth of it quickly turning cold, it was a deep wound and I started to become dizzy. I crawled towards the door and reached for the towel, but the dizziness took hold of me and I felt myself becoming weak. I leant my head against the door; the blood was still pumping out, falling down my face onto my bear body, my eyes started feeling heavy and the lullaby continued.

When the Dark Moon meets its peak,
There's a sister who is your destiny
Hide, my child, safe and sound,
As in this sister, your fate is found.

In the Darkness, he'll show you,
All the answers, that were kept from you,
Go in search until he's found,
Resist the liars all around.

Yes, you will speak to those who'll hear
And in your words a sadness flows
But can you brave what you most fear?
Can you face what the Dark Moon shows?

When the Dark Moon meets its peak,

There are the siblings, and their destiny
Come, my children, homeward bound
When all is lost, then all will be found.

Arlo;

I sat in my office staring at the paperwork that was in front of me, the words all were just a black blur surrounded by white. I had so much to do and yet after this morning's awful turn of events, I just couldn't concentrate. My pack were frightened and looking to me to keep them safe and yet I couldn't even keep one of my Elder's safe, how could I protect over 100 people if I couldn't save the three that had been murdered right under my nose. A knock on my office door took me from my thoughts and I sighed; who wanted to talk to me now? It seems that is all I have this morning. I just wanted to go to bed and wake up when the day was over.

'Come in.' I called, watching as Charlie made his way through the doors. He grinned at me and held up a case of beers.

'Thought you could do with a few of these.' He said walking over to me, I looked up at the clock, it was only 10 in the morning. *Fuck it.* I thought, opening the can and gulping half of the beer down.

'Cheers.' I said before belching. Charlie sniggered and sat down on one of the settee's; he opened his own can of beer and sighed.

'You alright mate?' He asked looking as tired as me. I shook my head and placed the beer on my desk before running my hand through my hair.

'Nah, I am really not alright.' I admitted.

'Don't worry Arlo, we will find out who is doing this, I promise.' Charlie replied after taking another swig of his beer. I raised my eyebrows at him suspiciously and waited for him to again accuse Amelia.

'I hope so and I hope it is soon. I will kill whoever it is with my bare hands.' I growled allowing the anger I had been trying to conceal to arise. Charlie smirked and looked up at the photo of us on the wall. His eyes looked sad for a short while and he sighed.

'We were so happy back then.' He said still staring at the photo.

'What do you mean? That was only a year ago.' I laughed before finishing the rest of my beer.

'Exactly.' He said sulkily. I raised an eyebrow at him before rolling my eyes. *Here we go.* 'You were so fun before, we would go and get drunk nearly every night, fuck whatever Mutt or human we wanted, raced our ca-' I cut him off. 'That was before I became Alpha and you became Beta.' I grumbled struggling to find a reason why he was bringing this all up.

'Yeah and before Amelia got here.' He growled crossing his arms like a spoilt little child.

'Really Charlie?' I snapped; *I knew he couldn't control himself.* 'What do you have against her? I don't get it!' Charlie turned to look at me with pure hatred in his eyes.

'She is the reason my mum is dead.' He hissed. I shook my head.

'No, she isn't. She was a new-born baby! How is your mum dying in childbirth her fault? I don't understand.' I snapped.

'Exactly. She died in Childbirth bringing HER into the world, so it is Amelia's fault. Plus, she is a complete freak of nature. All she ever did at my grandparents was talk to herself and every time she got upset, she would make things shake. One time; she was so angry that my dad was leaving her again that every picture on the wall's fell and smashed…she is weird.' He shook his head and looked at me. 'She is not good for you; Arlo and she isn't good for this pack.'

'You know what Charlie; she isn't the problem. You are! You are cruel to that girl; both you and your father torment her and hurt her. I am sick of it. You may be my Beta but remember your fucking place. She is the best thing that happened to this pack and you know it.' I roared smashing my fists on my desk. Charlie rolled his eyes at me and shook his head.

'Seems like she has you wrapped round her finger already. There she is screwing that Mutt and screwing Matt and you don't bat an eyelid.' In that moment it took everything in my power not to snap his neck. His hatred for his sister would never falter and he would never change.

'Get out.' I growled staring into his eyes, he may have been my Beta, but my Alpha influence would still work on him. I watched as the colour drained from his face and he walked to my office door before sulkily leaving.

Amelia;

I opened my eyes and put my hand on my head, the wound was nearly gone, I rubbed my finger on where the gash was only 10 minutes before, it had started healing already. I shouldn't be healing this fast, no one else can heal the way I do. *Why am I so abnormal?*

'What is going on?' I screamed pulling my dressing gown onto my cold but now dry body. I slammed open my bathroom door and looked around my room, I was frustrated and angry, a rage took over my body and I grabbed the closest thing to me; a lamp. I threw it, the sound of it smashing against the wall was fulfilling, but only for a second, I screamed again and grabbed everything in sight, smashing it all up. After 5 minutes I breathlessly looked around my bedroom, glass was everywhere, my television was broken, and all of my belongings were destroyed.

A knock on my door startled me, but I stayed silent, I didn't want to see anyone.

'Open the door; Lia.' It was Arlo; of course, it was. I didn't answer him and tried to quietly walk towards my wardrobe. 'I can hear you breathing.' He said, he was getting annoyed with me, I could hear it by the tone of his voice. I walked over the glass allowing it to cut my feet open, it stung, but I didn't care. I jumped as Arlo slammed his arms onto my door. 'What are you doing?' he shouted. 'I can smell blood, what is going on? Are you hurt?' I could hear the panic in his voice, and he waited for me to answer. 'If you don't open the fucking door, I will break it down.'
I closed my eyes and took in a deep breath.

'I don't really want to talk right now.' I mumbled more to myself then at him, but I knew he could hear me, werewolf hearing and werewolf smell, made it hard for me to keep anything to myself.

'Why? What is wrong?' He asked, his voice calming a bit more, I knew he wouldn't leave until I let him in.

'I just can't cope with any of this.' I replied walking over to the other side of my room.

'I know; Lia, its shit, all of it, but let me help you, please just talk to me.' He pleaded. I opened my door and Arlo's jaw dropped. Dried blood was down my face, my eyes were red from all the crying I had done and as he looked past me, he could see my destroyed bedroom.

'What have you done?' he asked concerned as he put his hand on my face, looking for a wound that was now completely healed.

'I just hit my head, but its healed now.' I shrugged allowing him to enter the bedroom.

'What did you hit it on? That is a lot of blood, are you okay? Do you want to go and see Benjamin?' He asked before looking around and then straight at me. 'Why did you do this?' He asked.
I couldn't tell him; I couldn't tell him anything about what was going on; the lullaby, the dreams, the panic attack and the continuous accusations, everything was breaking me down. I was falling apart, and I didn't know what to do. How would I explain this to him?

'I slipped after my bath and hit my head on the sink... I think I might have passed out... I am not too sure but then I became really angry. I just can't cope with the accusations from Charlie and the hate that surrounds me, and it just got all too much... and I lost my temper.' I admitted looking around at the awful mess I had made. Arlo wasn't angry with me though; he didn't care that I had destroyed everything in my room, he was more concerned that I had knocked myself out and sympathetic of my emotional state. *This is my Arlo... right here. This is the man that I think I was falling in love with.*

'I am sorry; Lia. I know this is unfair, no one should be accusing you of anything. We will find out who is doing these killings and then it will all stop, I promise. Charlie is an idiot and if I am honest, I regret choosing him to be my Beta, it was a mistake. Please don't let him break you down, your stronger than that.' Arlo pulled me into his big arms and kissed the top of my head; he was my security blanket. With him I felt safe and he could instantly make me forget all the bad in my life. I just wished the bad would go forever. 'I think we should get you checked over by Benjamin; though baby. I know you don't want to, but it is really important that you do.' I shook my head and looked into his eyes. 'Look at me; I am fine… especially now that you are here.' Arlo sighed and then smiled before kissing me on the lips. 'Okay but if you start feeling ill, I will take you to be checked out.'

Arlo agreed for me to stay in his room for the rest of the day and excused me from going for dinner, he had Piper bring me up some food and allowed her to stay with me whilst he attended to some work. It was nice to spend some time with her, we watched films and talked about Pretty Girl.
'I think I will go and see her this evening.' I grinned as we stood on the balcony. I gazed at the stables and smiled even more, I adored my horse so much, she was light in the dark and the only thing who truly understood me.

'You are so lucky to have a Unicorn.' Piper sighed following my gaze.

'Why does everyone call her a Unicorn? She is a wild Horse.' I stated.

'No, she is a Unicorn and she loves you.' Piper smiled. I think deep down I knew something was different about Pretty Girl. At first, I thought everyone was joking. No one seemed to bat an eyelid at the fact I had her with me, was it normal for them to be around? I always thought they were an animal that hid away from the world.

'If she is a Unicorn then why doesn't she have a horn?' I wondered out loud.

'Huh?' Piper grunted confused, she studied my face and

then continued to talk. 'You can't see her horn?' I shook my head and sighed staring back towards the stables; *just another thing to add to my list of why I am such a freak.*

'Lia; can you really not see her horn?' Piper asked following my gaze. I shook my head and shrugged. 'I really am just a weird freak, aren't I?' I whispered feeling as a lump built in my throat.

'Listen to me; Lia!' Piper said turning me to face her. She looked me in the eyes and smiled.

'You are one of a kind. You are not a freak; you are not a weirdo; you are unique and special and that's why we all love you so much.'

I smiled weakly at her and allowed my gaze to go back to the stables. Piper followed my stare and grinned. 'You know, I think she is your guardian.'

'Do you?' I asked. I knew she was trying to change the subject to make me feel better and it worked. Piper nodded, 'Yeah, you found her in a time of need. If you weren't a werewolf, I would say she is your spirit animal. Unicorns are terrified of werewolves, but she isn't scared of you at all and when others are near her; as long as you are there, she is fine. It's almost like she was put here for you.'

The thought of Pretty Girl being my Guardian made me feel so special; Piper was right; I was Lucky.

'Right I had better go home.' Piper said looking at her phone, it was 8pm, Arlo would be back soon, and I was so excited to see him. Just as Piper left the room, he walked in, looking exhausted and stressed out.

'Hello, beautiful.' He smiled pecking me on the lips.

'Would you like me to run you a bath?' I asked noticing how tense he was. Arlo smirked.

'Only if you will join me?' I started giggling and walked into the bathroom, he had a really big bath, it could probably fit up to 4 people in it, I would most certainly be joining him. I lit some candles and spread them around the bathroom and added some bubbles into the bath. 'It's ready.' I called undressing. Arlo walked into the bathroom, he had already taken his clothes off, I bit my lip as I admired his perfectly sculptured body, my eyes fell to his manhood, even when he wasn't aroused, he was well endowed. Arlo looked smug when he noticed what I was looking at, I blushed and quickly turned away, but I couldn't help myself. Ever since I had lost my virginity, I just couldn't get enough of him, it was like I was a dog on heat. I stepped into the bath and sat down, the hot water soothed me, but having Arlo with me, soothed me more.

I smiled as he put his arms around my waist and pulled me towards him, I closed my eyes and lent my head on his shoulder, I just wanted to tell him that I love him; but I couldn't, I just could not bring myself to say it. And that was because I knew he wasn't mine, he would be someone else's.

'What are you thinking about?' Arlo whispered into my ear.

I smiled, 'Just, how lucky I am to have you.' Arlo kissed my neck and cupped his hands over my breasts.

'I am the lucky one.' I turned my self around, so I was facing him and kissed his soft lips, he pulled me onto his lap, and I placed my knees onto the bottom on the bath. I lowered myself onto him, so that he could enter me. He let out a growl, which was more like a purr and looked into my eyes as I built up a rhythm. The pleasure came over me in waves and this time I was in control. Arlo put his hands on my hips and pressed his mouth against mine and then my rhythm picked up. It was clear to see that he liked me being in control. He bit into my neck and I tilted my head back closing my eyes and moaning in pleasure as I reached my peak; the orgasm took over my whole body and I went weak, I slumped onto him and suck on his neck hard enough to leave him a slight bruise, he took over and controlled my hips with his hands as another orgasm started building, I sat up and watched his face as his eyes turned dark. 'I, I'm going to cum.' He panted making me move faster, his whole body jolted as he released himself into me and I collapsed onto his chest; *this man certainly knew how to please a woman.*

.

When the Dark Moon meets its peak,
There's a brother who is your destiny
Hide, my child, safe and sound,

As in this brother, your destiny is found

I opened my eyes and sat up, Arlo was asleep next to me, his gentle snores filling the room, he was peaceful and looked content in his dreams, I just wish that I could be too. I crawled out of the bed, careful not to wake him and quietly got dressed. I couldn't just sit in here and do nothing any longer. I was going into the woods and I was determined to get some answers. I glanced down at my phone; it was 6 am, hopefully I would be back before he woke up.

As I crossed the border and officially left our packs grounds, anxiety came over me, Arlo would be so angry with me, everyone would be, but I wouldn't get the answers I needed by doing nothing and no one at the mansion could give them to me, but maybe the brown wolf could.

'Hello; Amelia.' A deep husky voice growled, the brown wolf with Olive green eyes, appeared out from the trees and came towards to me, 'I knew you would come.' He chuckled. How could I hear him? He hadn't shifted and his mouth wasn't moving. 'You can hear me because you are special.' He answered, my face must have shown him my confusion.

'I need answers.' I croaked. 'I need to know why you are following me and killing people.'
The wolf sniggered. 'I am not killing anyone, I don't need to, nor do I want to.' He took another step towards me, but I didn't move.

'Who are you?' I gulped.

'They haven't told you anything about me at all have they. You don't know who you tru-'
The wolf stopped talking and his eyes went black, we both heard a break behind him and then an awful stench filled the air.

'Run' the wolf howled before being thrown into a tree, he yelped as his body hit the solid wood and I looked up, a shadowy creature with dead white glowing eyes turned his stare from the wolf to me and I ran.

14

Arlo;

I opened my eyes and stared up at the ceiling unmoving. *When had I fallen asleep?* The sound of rain tapping against the window caused me to pull my stare away from above me to glance out the window. It was really hammering it down. A streak of lightning flashed across the lightening blue sky, swiftly followed by the almighty crash of thunder. I looked at the spot on the bed beside me and noticed that Amelia was gone, I glanced at my watch 7:30 am, *maybe she had gone down to the kitchen again to help out?*

But no matter what I told myself, something was wrong; I could feel it! I sat up and the room spun around me, causing me to feel sick from the motion. I shook my head and felt my racing heart. *What was happening to me?* I climbed from my bed and grabbed my clothes; *Was I coming down with an illness?* I picked up my phone from my bedside table and unlocked the screen, I decided to call her. I rung her twice but both times she didn't answer; maybe I should just text her in hopes that she would call me back and let me know that she was okay.

Arlo; Morning! Where are you? I woke up and you aren't here. Can you call me when you get this message please? xx

I tossed my phone on to my bed and wiped the beads of sweat from my forehead, why was I feeling so ill? *Maybe the water would wash these feelings away.* I turned on the faucet and watched for a moment as the hot water gushed from the shower head, swiftly followed by hypnotic swirls of steam. I shook my head, tugging my boxers off and wandered into the hot water.

By the time I had got out from the shower, the sickly dizziness had faded; *but it was still there, lingering in the back of my subconscious.* I hurried back into my bedroom and threw on some clean lounge pants, my still damp hair sticking out in all directions. My heart was pounding in my chest and my muscles were twitching. It was as if my body had gone into autopilot and I was waiting for something drastic to happen. There was a fire racing through my veins unlike anything I had ever felt; it wasn't unpleasant, if anything it felt a little soothing.

I closed my eyes and gulped down another deep breath, turning around on the spot and catching my reflection in the window; the sky outside was dark, causing the window to act as a mirror. My skin was a little paler than usual, and there were bags under my eyes. *This didn't make sense. Alpha's never got sick...* That was when it dawned on me. I wasn't sick at all. I was beginning to imprint on someone. But, who?

Amelia;

I didn't understand what had just happened. Who was that wolf? And how was he able to speak to me through my mind? I pushed my legs harder, forcing myself to run as fast as possible. Whatever was back that had obviously spooked that wolf, and I was pretty certain that it was chasing me now. I could hear the gentle pop of twigs snapping under their feet. And from the sound of it, they were running faster than any one I had ever met. A strong smell of rotting flesh washed over me, so intense that it nearly caused me to retch. Tears stung my eyes and I didn't know if it was from the sickly-sweet smell of death, or from my own fear. The rain hit my skin so fast that each droplet felt like ice, burning wherever it touched. I shook my head, trying to get the rattails that was my hair out of my face; it was already hard to see, I didn't need my own hair making it worse.

An extremely tall dark shadow flew past me, causing me to glance out the corner of my eye. *Arlo was going to be so pissed that I snuck out alone especially to the woods!* I closed my eyes and pushed myself on harder, my thighs and calves were burning like hell, but I knew that this pain was nothing compared to what would happen if that thing finally got me. I fought through the uncomfortable burn in my lungs as I felt a stitch forming in my side. *Why was this happening to me? I was slowly beginning to doubt that I was even a werewolf. Animals loved me; I couldn't shift; I had been getting my period for years; I could disobey orders given to me directly from the alpha! Why was I such a freak?*

In the distance I could see the warm glow of the mansion flickering as the dark sky started turning light. I hadn't even realised that I had wandered so far.

The rotting smell overtook my senses once more and I felt myself becoming lightheaded. Then a flash of white shot passed me, with speeds that were matching the creature that had been chasing me. *Was this another one?* Something slammed into my back, causing me to fly forwards and hit the ground with a splat in the mud; I skidded across the floor feeling the cold wetness soak through my clothes. Another flash of lightning struck through the sky and I noticed the shadow creature a few feet away from me. It's glowing eyes boring into me like lasers. I rolled over and scrambled forward, trying my hardest to get my footing in the mud but it was no use; I just kept slipping and sliding until I was sprawled out, staring up at the dark canopy of the trees, getting soaked from the downpour. The smell grew stronger as the growls came closer. This was it. I was about to die. *At least that way everyone would be safe. They were all better off without me.*

The dark shadowy monster towered over me, white eyes boring into me, when something leapt into the air behind it, kicking its legs out aggressively. The minute I laid eyes on her I knew that I was safe. My one true saviour; Pretty Girl. The shadowy creature leapt back to its feet at lightning speeds and charged back towards us. I hopped up onto Pretty Girls back and wrapped my arms around her neck, as she lunged forward and ran as fast as she could. The snarling monster close on our tail.

We burst through the main gates and heard the low growling fade away; they clearly never entered the pack grounds. *Why was that?* Pretty Girl stopped at the stables, giving me chance to climb from her back and I took off; back towards the mansion. I needed to speak to Arlo, and I needed to speak to him now. I closed my eyes once more, this time fighting the tears that I could feel building within myself; when I ran into something with a smack. I stumbled backwards slightly and came face to face with Lori.

'For Selene sake! Watch where you're going to stupid little bitch.' She snapped staring at me angrily.

'Don't go out there.' I whispered looking back at the Iron gates. 'T... there is something in those woods.'

'You are cra-'Her words cut off as she took in the horrified expression on my face. 'A-are you ok?' She stammered, sounding more genuine than I had ever heard before. I stared at her face for a few seconds in silence, when she suddenly realised that she was stood with Adela and Harper. She shook her head slightly and narrowed her eyes before continuing.

'I mean, by the look on your face you saw something terrifying. I guess this means that Arlo finally allowed you to look in a mirror.' She sneered, causing her two groupies to throw their heads back and laugh. The anger in my chest tightened and I clenched my teeth together. The streetlamp above us exploded, causing a shower of glass and sparks to rain down around us. The three bitches squealed and huddled together, giving me a clear path to make my escape.

I jumped around the three drama queens, the sound of glass crunching beneath my feet as I continued running. Nothing else was going to stop me between here and Arlo's bedroom, I didn't care who or what it was that would try to stop me, but I didn't care. I needed to see him; *Now!*

I entered the mansion and ran up the spiral stairs, dodging everyone that I passed until eventually I was bursting into his room causing him to flinch. He spun around on the spot and turned his worried expression to me.

'L-Lia, what's wrong?' He stammered, crossing the room in two large steps and pulling me into his arms. His deep woody scent filled my senses and relaxed me a little. I was too shaken up to be able to speak. *And what the hell was I going to tell him? I didn't even know what that thing was that was chasing me.* 'Baby, you're trembling. What happened? Why are you covered in mud?' He whispered, walking backwards. He pulled my t-shirt from my head, dropping it to the ground with a splat, swiftly followed by my black skinny jeans that were now brown from the mud. I stood there in my underwear, still trembling; *I wasn't sure if it was from the cold, wetness or my own fear. But just being under Arlo's touch seemed to thaw out the ice that was coursing through me.*

He continued leading me backwards, guiding us to the bed before sitting down and pulling me onto his lap and draping one of his thick blankets around us. I turned my stare up to meet his golden eyes and finally stopped fighting the tears, allowing them to roll down my cheeks freely.

'I-It was horrible.' I whispered, dropping my face down and staring at my hands that were rested in my lap.

'What was? What has upset you so much?'

'T-There was something… in the woods. It was chasing me.'

'What do you mean in the woods? Why were you out there? Who was you with?' He asked, his voice taking on that of annoyance. I opened my mouth to speak but no words came out. Arlo slid me from his lap and leapt up from the bed. I watched as he paced up and down for a moment with both hands held tightly to his head; allowing all this muscles to dance a flex under the action.

'You went alone… didn't you?' He asked. He stared into my eyes and I felt as though he was looking directly into my soul. I opened my mouth, everything in my telling me to lie to him, to tell him that I was with others; but I couldn't lie to him. Fresh tears pooled in my eyes and I shook my head.

'I-I just…'

'Lia! How could you be s fucking irresponsible. You know that there is a killer out there in the forest, just lurking somewhere, waiting for the next victim to stumble upon it. How could you be so reckless? And why the hell didn't you answer my phone calls? I could have come and got you if you had!' He roared. I had never heard him sound so angry. He continued pacing back and forth, refusing to look at me. He turned his angry stare towards me once more and stormed over to me. He pulled me into his arms and held me tightly; *I understood that I had scared him. That's why he was so mad at me; but it didn't make me feel any better.* He placed two fingers under my chin and raised my face towards his.

'I'm sorry. Are you ok?' He asked, his eyes taking on a sadness that nearly broke me. I sighed softly and forced a half smile. He leant forward and lightly placed his lips on mine. A fire rushed through me, seemingly chasing away all my fears with its cleansing touch. I shuddered with pleasure and pushed into the kiss harder. *This is exactly the kind of distraction that I needed.* Arlo pulled back as he drew in a deep shuddering breath, and I felt him hardening underneath me.

'What? What is it?' I asked, feeling my cheeks burn red. Arlo chuckled and ran his thumb across my bottom lip.

'We can't. We have already missed breakfast and I have a pack meeting in five minutes. And I know for a fact that if we start now, we won't stop.' He answered, grinning at me with a new fire in his eyes. I leant forward once more and pulled his face back down to meet mine. Our lips crashed together, and I put everything into our kiss. All the hurt, all the pain, all the fear. Arlo chuckled and pulled back once more. 'Seriously Lia. I can't.' He laughed. I bit my lip before pulling him back down into our kiss, not caring about anything other than this moment.

I put my hands behind my back and undid my bra whilst I racked my teeth along Arlo's bottom lip, causing his whole body to tremble with desire. I threw the bra down on to the floor and watched as he licked his bottom lip. He flipped me over, so that I was lying on the bed facing him as he pressed himself back down on top of me. My breath caught in my throat as absolute pleasure and desire took over. Arlo kissed down my jaw line, down my neck, only hesitating to look me in the eyes. He kissed along my collar bone, and down between my breasts, while grabbing a handful at the same time.

He continued kissing lower until he got to my underwear. He pulled back and stared into my eyes mischievously for a moment. He pushed my legs open and kissed from my knee all the way to my inner thigh. I felt his fingers gently run down the inside of my leg causing my heart to pound in my ears. *Seriously, if he teased me anymore than this, then I think I would explode.*

He ran his hand over the elastic of my underwear before running the tips of his fingers down, pushing the material to the side and slipping his fingers inside me. The moment he did a wave of pleasure so intense washed over me, taking my breath away. He slowly circled his fingers, causing me to arch my back and thrust my hips in time with his movements. My breath became ragged and hard, and I gripped the blanket, trying my hardest to hold off the orgasmic wave of pleasure that was threatening to blow.

Far too soon he pulled his fingers out. I gasped loudly and turned my needing stare to him, silently pleading for him to not stop with my eyes. Arlo cocked an eyebrow and kissed up my knee once more, this time not stopping at my inner thigh. I felt the warmth of his tongue brushing over my centre before slipping his finger inside me. That was when I lost all control. I arched my back once more, causing him to go deeper with every thrust. My breath was coming in short waves and I was about to give in to my orgasmic rush… then his watched beeped.

Arlo stood from the bed and glanced down at himself. A huge hard lump showing through his tight-fitting formal trousers. I bit my lip and tried to hide the smile that I could feel forming but it was no use. This man drove me wild. He reached into his trousers and readjusted himself; tucking his hardness into the waistband of his boxers. He turned his hot stare to me and narrowed his eyes with a huge smile on his face.

'You think you're funny?' he asked, raising an eyebrow and smirking. I bit my lip a little harder, but it was no use. The giggle escaped my lips seemingly driving him wild. I saw his member throb with every laugh, and it caused me to want him even more. *I didn't even know that that was possible!*

'No, I don't think I am funny. I think I am hilarious.' I replied, laughing once more. Arlo slowly walked back over to the bed and leant forward, kissing me softly.

'You best still be here like that when I get back. We have

some unfinished business to attend to!' He growled, his eyes flaring with desire. He turned and slowly walked towards the door, looking back once and winking before exiting the room. I sighed in frustration and flopped back on the bed. *What was this man doing to me?*

Arlo;

I entered my office and all eyes turned to me. It was obvious that they had been here a while waiting, but I was the alpha. The meeting started when *I* said so. I crossed the room and dropped into the chair behind my desk; everyone's eyes following me as I moved.

'Arlo, what are you going to do about all this?' Jake asked, dipping his head at the memory of our fallen members. I cleared my throat and looked over to my father, who was holding my stare and looking at me expectantly.

'Clearly, there is something going on around here. I don't understand why all these Non-Elites and an Elder have been leaving the safety of our grounds. Our only saving grace is that whoever this is, is not coming in, beyond the gates. All the killings have taken place out there.' I said, gesturing towards the large woods that surrounded our village.

'Non-Elites? Don't you mean the Mutts?' Charlie snapped, narrowing his eyes at me. *He was seriously starting to piss me off.* I sighed once more and chose to ignore his comment before continuing.

'I believe that we must continue to patrol the perimeter of our village. Have people scout around the gates, ensuring that no one leaves without my say so. I don't know how many more losses this community can take.' I closed my eyes as the vision of Amelia sprawled out on my bed filled my mind. A red-hot wave of desire pulsed through me and I felt myself harden once more. *This was not the time, or place for this to happen!*

'Why is it only the Mutts and now an Elder that are being taken?' Matt asked, speaking for the first time since I had entered to room. I shook my head and stared down at my hands.

'I have no idea. But I think that that is why it should be us

Elites only that do the patrol runs. We are clearly safer than the others. I believe that it should be us that take charge.'

'So, what is it that you want us to do?' Eddie asked, turning to me with wide eyes. I sighed and shook my head. *I knew that I needed to focus, but all I could think about was being inside her again.* I cleared my throat and shook my head.

'I am saying that we need to be more vigilant! I think that we should set up twenty-four-hour patrols. We need to ensure the safety of our pack. As the leaders, that is our job!' I said, making sure that I looked at my Beta and Delta in the eye. Charlie rolled his eyes and glared at me.

'What? Are you saying that now we have to work? Just like the common Mutts?' Charlie growled, anger taking over him. 'How about why don't you speak to your "*girlfriend*" and her other boy-friend and just ask them to leave everyone alone?' Charlie sneered. My eyes flared and I gulped down a deep breath. I knew that he was trying to get a rise out of me, and I couldn't let that happen. But I also knew that there was nothing that I could say here that would get me out of this predicament. Luckily, Matt was to the rescue once again. He slammed his hand down onto the desk; so hard that everything upon it rattled violently.

'What the fuck is your problem with her? What was it that your sister did to make you hate her so much?'

'Don't call her that!' Charlie growled through clenched teeth. 'And like I said before, just because you are shagging her on the side, doesn't mean that you get to talk to me that way!' He continued.

'You know what. I am so sick of your medieval views of the world; your view of people that are different from you. Your view on your sister. You are just such a c-'

'Who do you think you are speaking to? I think you forget your place!' Charlie roared, leaping to his feet and squaring up to Matt. I rose from my chair with such force that it flew back into the wall with a loud crash. The others in the room rushed towards us, holding us back. *Everyone knew that I could have taken him. There was a reason that I am master of fighting. He was nothing com-*

pared to me.

'Really? This is pathetic! Our pack is in danger; real danger. What do you think is going to happen if we lose anymore members? When other packs find out that our numbers a dwindling. Currently we are the largest pack in England. But at this rate, we will be easily outnumbered by others. How are we supposed to keep everyone safe, if the leaders of this place are at each-other's throats constantly.' I roared, glaring at everyone in front of me. The room fell into silence as all eyes were back on me. 'This meeting is over! Everyone out of my sight.' I said, turning away from everyone and placing both hands on my desk for support.

'Arlo I-' Jake began, taking a step closer towards me.

'I said OUT!' I screamed, spinning around to face him allow my full power of alpha washed over him. Jake stiffened as though a heavy electric current was passing through him, the veins in his neck bulging. He pulled away from me and fled the room. As much as I hated using my power as alpha against them, sometimes they just needed to be reminded who was in charge. I waited until the last person left the room before I finally looked up again. I needed to get back to my room. *I needed her; now!*

Matt;

I threw open Arlo's office door and stormed forward, heading to the training area. I needed to release some of this tension; and fighting was the only way that I knew how. I hurried out into the cold nights air and rushed forward, pulling my t-shirt over my head and threw it to the ground before heading over to the life-sized mannequin and getting into my fighting stance. I closed my eyes and drew in a deep breath through my nose before opening my eyes and allowing my anger to come out. With every pinch, I felt my hits getting harder, and there was nothing that I could do to stop it; but it wasn't enough. *I could imagine that this is Charlie all I wanted, but until I got to beat the shit out of the real one, this would have to do.* I rolled my head on my shoulders, feeling the bones crack in protest. I needed to run!

I grabbed for my hoody and threw it on, not mothering to

find my t-shirt and jogged over to the main gates.

An awful smell filled the air, so strong that I almost gagged. It was a mix of sickly sweet, rotting flesh, and earthy mould. I covered my nose and mouth with my hand, hoping that it was enough to shield me from some of the stench. *It wasn't.* Suddenly, another scent hit me. One that was too familiar for my liking. I peered around in the darkness, using my werewolf vision to see if there was anything I could pick up.

'What the...' I muttered to myself, glancing down at the pool of blood under my feet and followed the scent until I found its source. *Something wasn't right about this blood. It smelt different than the others. It had a chemical smell to it.* There, hanging from the tree was Gabriel. This changed everything! Now whoever the killer was, was taking down Elites as well. I glanced around and noticed the struggle that had clearly taken place. This wasn't just as simple as someone being killed. There was a fight. I crouched down to the ground and felt the dirt. The blood was splattered in all directions. This just confirmed that it wasn't a clean kill. That sickly-sweet smell washed over me once more, this time stronger than before. I rushed to my feet and felt my head spin from the motion; the smell too strong for my heightened senses.

I turned on my heel and ran as fast as I could, back towards the mansion. Arlo needed to know about this.

Arlo;

I tugged at the top button of my shirt, feeling as though the air was getting too thick in here. There was so much going on with the pack right now, but all I could think of was Amelia. At the very mention of her name I felt myself throb with desire. Through the entire meeting, all I could think of was pounding her hard. Another wave of desire ripped through me. I pushed on harder, needing to be near her; in her, now. I reached the top of the stairs and spotted a barely dressed figure sneaking from my room. Using all my skill of sneaking, I slowly crept up behind her.

'Where do you think you're going?' I asked, raising an eye-brow as a growl of need slipped through my lips. Amelia spun on the spot, looking down the long hall behind me; her cheeks flushing that cute shade of pink she got when she was nervous.

'A-Arlo! You made me jump!' she squeaked, with a slight giggle.

'Your alpha has asked you a question miss hunt.' I whispered, taking another step closer to her so that we were only inches apart. I let my eye run up and down the length of her body, taking in every curve; and felt myself throb even harder. *I needed her. And I needed her now.* I slammed her into the wall; *a little harder than intended,* and she gasped. I went to apologise when she grabbed my face and pulled it down to meet her mouth. Our lips crashed together as she moved her hands up into my hair and tugged. A burn shot from my scalp down my spine, causing me to press myself harder against her. I felt her teeth scrape along my bottom lip once again and I shuddered. *I couldn't take this any longer.* I grabbed her hips and spun her around to face the wall. I yanked on my flies, freeing myself from the confines of my trousers and pulled her panties to the side. Amelia started to close her legs, glancing over her shoulder down the corridor once more, but I pressed my knee in between hers and pushed her legs open once more. She leant forward a little raising her backside in the air slightly and I shoved myself inside her. Her gasp of pleasure was all the encouragement that I needed. I thrust myself into her again, grabbing her hips and pulling her back onto me. Within no time, she had matched my rhythm and was groaning in pleasure. I pounded harder, causing her to groan a little louder. I wasn't sure how much longer I could go on. After everything that had happened, I needed that release!

I felt the familiar tightening sensation in my groin as the pressure built up rapidly. I felt Amelia tighten also, as she too was reaching completion. She thrust back into me harder and I couldn't hold it anymore. I thrust into her releasing everything I had, my throbbing hardness pulsing inside her. Amelia bit her lip, trying her hardest to contain her orgasmic groan but it was no use, she couldn't stop it. I felt her entire body tremble as she was overtaken by the ecstasy of the moment; her knees going weak. I pulled out of her and spun her around to face me, leaning forward and kissing her with ragged breathing.

'How about we take this inside?' Amelia whispered, running her hands through my hair once more. I flashed her a cheeky grin and pulled her up into my arms, getting her to wrap her legs around my waist, carrying her into my bedroom. I threw her on the bed and ripped my shirt over my head before kicking my jeans and boxers to the floor. Amelia ran her eyes up and down the length of my naked body and grinned. The thought of her liking what she saw caused me to harden once more.

'Round two?' I asked with another grin. Amelia's eyes flashed and she bit her lip once more.

'Bring it on, big boy.' She purred, flopping back onto the bed before pinging her underwear across the room. I felt my smile widen and strolled over to the bed, dropping down on top of her. I had never been the type of person to be this sex mad. But she was just driving me crazy. I slipped myself back inside her causing her to whimper with pleasure.

'Are you sure you're ready for this?' I asked, staring down into her eyes. 'I don't want to hurt you.'

'Don't you dare hold back!' She growled, dragging my face down to meet hers and biting my bottom lip. I slammed into her, this time not bothering to be gentle. With every trust I felt her become wetter, her warmness consuming all of me. *How was I going to tell her that this was nearly over? That I was imprinting on someone that wasn't her?*

We collapsed on my bed in a heap; our hearts were pounding, and we were both trying to catch our breath. I couldn't get enough of her but yet how could that be possible when she wasn't mine? How could I feel such a deep connection with a woman that wasn't my soul mate, the thought of it all made my stomach twist and my heart sank again. I needed to speak to her; was she imprinting too? Was I worrying for nothing? I opened my mouth, but before I could even say a word to her; my phone rang. I picked it up and Matt's name came flashing on the screen, I swiped up and put the phone on to my ear still trying to catch my breath.

'Hello? Fuck! Who? When? Okay I will be right there.' I hung the phone up and looked straight over to Amelia, she could already tell by the look on my face what had happened. But this time it was an Elite that had been killed; the one that was on patrol; the one that I had put on patrol.

Amelia;

I laid on the bed in shock, Arlo had already got himself dressed and ran from the room; his face drained of colour. The pack member that they found dead this morning was an Elite! *How could this be?* So far, the attacker had only been going after the Non-Elites, but now it looked as if their MO had changed! Ironically, the pack member that they had found today was the one in charge of surveillance. He was the one patrolling the outer perimeter of the grounds last night. *This changed everything.*

I thought back to when I ran to see the brown wolf; was the Elite dead before I left? There wasn't anyone around when I passed the Iron gates, guilt rushed over me. I should have known something was wrong; slipping away from the grounds was too easy. Why the hell didn't, I think? *As usual I was too wrapped up in my own problems to notice anything else.* I sat up from the bed still naked and looked across to the window; Who could do something like this? Who could possibly be evil enough to kill innocent members of the pack? The very thought of it broke my heart! All those innocent lives that were wasted, and for what?

The only logical thought that I could make sense of, was that it was a Deviant! I don't see why a member of another pack would do this to us. This would be an act of war against the packs and no one would be stupid enough to do that. The packs in England worked hard to keep up their strong alliances. *They agreed that it was better to work with one another than against them!* A Deviant wouldn't be thinking of the alliances between packs. I thought back to the brown wolf once more. Other than him, I hadn't seen any other outsiders; but I knew that he wasn't the killer. *I don't know how I knew; I just did.*

If it came to it, I would tell Arlo the truth about where I was last night. As much as I didn't want him to know, the thought of my new friend taking the blame for this was worse. There was no way that I was going to just stand back and let this happen! There was no way that I was going to allow him to be accused of anything!

I knew that I should have got up and faced the pack, but I just couldn't do it. I threw the covers over my head and pretended that the rest of the world had just disappeared. I should have been there when the others were told about the Elite being found, but I could already hear the accusations that were going to be thrown at me! I didn't have an alibi for where I was, and Lori and her bitch pack had seen me running from the woods; they would be the first to tell everyone about what it was that they had seen and would then go on to make sure that everyone believed that I was the murderer. And then there was Arlo, it was him that I ran to when I was frightened; he knew where I had been, and I was so scared that he would also be convinced that it was me behind this all. *The thought of that made me feel physically sick.*

A million thoughts were swirling through my mind and it was making me dizzy. *I was beginning to regret ever leaving that stupid cottage! Things would have been so much simpler had I stayed there.* I closed my eyes and tried to quiet the screaming fears that were bouncing around in my mind, but it was virtually impossible. It didn't matter what I tried to think of, it all led back to the same thing. *Everyone believing that I was guilty!*

By the time that Arlo had come back up to the room from his meeting, I had fallen asleep once more. It was the only way that I could get all the fears to quiet. I opened my eyes and watched as Arlo came in carrying a tray loaded with food. I dropped my stare to the tray and my stomach churned; *I didn't think that I could have eaten a thing!* I felt sick with anxiety and my head was pounding. I could feel the familiar sting of tears and threw the duvet over my head once more; I didn't want Arlo to see me cry, *again!*

'Lia… what is it? What's wrong?' He asked, placing the tray on the bedside table and sitting on the bed beside me. I pinned the covers down around me tighter refusing to let him break in. After the day that he had had, he did not need to see me crying now. I felt him tug at the covers a little harder and felt as they slipped away, all my strength had gone, and I was no longer able to resist. He wiped my tears away with his thumb and stared down at me with a sad smile. 'What is it baby?' He whispered.

'I am just sad for you.' I whispered, trying my hardest to get the tears under control. Arlo crawled into the bed and pulled me into his arms, tucking my head under his chin and holding me tightly.

'Don't be sad for me baby.' He whispered, kissing the top of my head and resting his chin there. I closed my eyes and listened to the rhythmic beating of his heart and felt the soothing motion of his breathing. His earthy scent enveloped my sense. I focused on nothing but him. I could feel all my worries and fears were melting away. And before I knew it, I was asleep.

15

Amelia;

I opened my eyes and noticed the empty spot beside me. Panic flooded through me for a moment as I sleepily reached out to Arlo's side of the bed. My eyes darted around the room until they landed on his hunched over silhouette. Something was wrong. I could feel it. *Don't ask me how, I just could, had someone else been killed again!?* I sat up and crawled to the end of the bed.

'Hey, is everything ok?' I asked softly. The sound of my voice causing him to flinch. He turned his sorrow filled golden eyes to me and hung his head a little lower. *My stomach dropped.* 'W-What? What is it? What's wrong?' My heart raced as dread took over all my senses. He cleared his throat and shifted his eyes to me.

'I-I...' He stammered and dropped his stare down to the ground once more.

'Ok, you are seriously starting to freak me out right now. Please, just tell me. What is happening?' I asked, my voice trembling as I spoke. He sighed loudly and closed his eyes.

'Lia... I am so sorry...' He paused once more, and I thought my throat was about to close up. *A familiar feeling of dread washed over me. He's breaking up with me! I knew it! But... why?* I closed my eyes and mentally prepared myself for the blow that was about to come. 'I don't know how to tell you this... but... I think... I think I am imprinting on someone.' He paused and looked to me hopefully.

'W-Why are you looking at me like that?' I stammered. He sighed once more and dropped his head low, causing his hair to fall in front of his face.

'That is all the answer that I needed.' He whispered. My heart felt as though it was about to break. 'I was hoping that it was to you, but, but I wouldn't need to ask.'

'Because I would have felt it too.' I answered. He nodded, but we both knew that it wasn't a question. 'So, what does that mean for us?'

'I don't know how to answer that. I am so confused. Imprinting on someone is supposed to be the happiest day of a werewolf's life! But… this is heart breaking. Why couldn't it be you?' He whispered, unshed tears shimmering in his eyes. There was something about the broken look of him that shattered my heart far worse than any words he could have said to me. I climbed from the bed and hurried over to him, pulling him into my arms and holding him there as he silently sobbed.

'Hey, it's ok. I…' I paused for a moment and held my breath, hoping that I could get through this sentence without breaking. 'I am actually really happy for you!' I whispered, tightening my arms around him. He glanced up at me with a broken stare and glared at me.

'Lia… Stop that! Stop being so nice about it. You have every right to hate me!' He snapped, balling his hands into fists and turning his face to stare out the window. I sighed once more and moved closer to him.

'I'm not being "nice" I love you.' I gasped, shocked that the words came out of my mouth. I blinked and shook my head. 'I do love you Arlo. And that is why I am not angry or hate you. I may not have been a part of this pack for very long, and I may not have grown up learning about the way of our kind like everyone else, but I do understand what it means to imprint on someone.' Arlo spun around to face me once more, this time a blank expression on his face.

'Lia I… I really appreciate you saying that.' He smiled weakly and turned his face back to stare at the horses running around the field. I forced myself to smile and slowly rose from the window seat.

'I am going to go and get myself ready for breakfast. A-Are

you going to be ok?' I asked, turning back to glance at him over my shoulder one last time. He sat there motionless for a moment before nodding once. I smiled once more and hurried towards the door. *I just needed some time to myself. I needed some time to breathe!* But before I could leave, he called out to me once more.

'Lia… I think that… I think that you should go and be with Ethan. You never know, he could be the one that you are destined to be with.' I shook my head, feeling as though his words had physically slapped me in the face.

'Arlo… what the hell are you talking about?' I mumbled, trying my hardest to keep my emotions in check. *Now was not the time for me to break down. I couldn't let him see how devastated I truly was.* He dropped his stare to the ground and shrugged. Before he had a chance to say another word I fled from the room, closing the door quietly behind me.

Arlo;

I waited for a moment in silence, holding my breath, too scared to move. *She loved me!* The sound of my bedroom door closing was the final straw. I broke. I felt all the tension in my body escape, and I crumpled to the floor. *Is this why it was called heart break?* How could I have been so fucking stupid! She told me she loved me, and I *"appreciated"* it and then I told her to be with Ethan. I shook my head angrily and stormed into my bathroom. I was about to turn the shower on when I heard something that was like a knife to my heart. I could hear her sobbing through the wall. I clenched my teeth and froze. Every muscle in my body locked and I just stood there listening to her cry. I had done this. This was all my fault. I had to make it up to her! I broke through my locked muscles and turned on the shower. *Anything to drown out the sound of her heartbreak; which was somehow making me feel worse. I just wish that I could have told her that I loved her too.*

I climbed out the shower and stood there for a moment, allowing the water to drip from me. I allowed the cold air to wrap itself around me hoping that the chill would take everything off of my mind. *It didn't work.* It was almost time for breakfast, and I knew that I would have to face her. *How were things going to be now? Would she still be sitting with me? Would she act normal in front of the rest of the pack? Would she even be there at all?*

I dried myself off and threw on my clothes. *I thought that imprinting on someone would make me want to dress to impress them, but I literally just threw on the first things that I pulled from my wardrobe.* I closed my bedroom door as quietly as I could, I didn't want to disturb her if she was still in there. After all that crying, she may be trying to hide it. *Even that thought killed me!* I jogged down the stairs, practicing my *"happy smile"* for when I was in front of the rest of the pack. As I approached the dining room my mother and father were stood together; looking as happy as they always did, but those smiles were forced; how could we be happy when one of our Elites had been murdered? My mum turned to face me first and her face fell.

'W-What? What is it?' I asked, clearing my throat trying my hardest to act normal. My mother's eyes ran up and down my boy and it was only then that I realised how mismatched I actually looked. *A tracksuit! I never wore this in front of the pack unless it was during training!* I turned to look at my reflection in the mirror and noticed that my hair was still shaggy from the simple towel drying. *How the fuck did I forget to brush it?*

'Sweetheart, is… is everything ok?' My mother asked, taking a hesitant step towards me. I hung my head for a moment before pulling it back up with a beaming smile.

'Of course! Why wouldn't it be?' I asked, pulling a face of confusion before striding over to the doors. I heard her take a few more steps towards me, and before she had a chance to say anything else, I threw the doors open.

The room fell into an instant silence as all eyes turned toward me; and all smiles dropped when they took in my appearance. *I was the alpha, and there was no way that I was going to let them know how shitty I was feeling.* I smiled, and nodded at Matt, acting as though everything was fine when suddenly I felt as though I had been hit in the chest with a sledgehammer. *She was there. In her seat… beside mine… and she was… smiling.* Her green eyes turned to meet mine and she smiled sweetly. *What the fuck was going on here?* I blinked rapidly a few times and returned her smile; walking over to her acting as natural as I could. As soon as I was stood beside her and everyone else had sat down and continued their own conversations, I leaned in close to her.

'Are you ok?' I whispered. She turned to look at me with a slightly confused look and nodded.

'Of course I am?' She replied. *Did this morning actually happen? I was so confused.*

We made our way over to the breakfast trollies and loaded our plates. *Although for the first time in my life I actually wasn't hungry.* I glanced around the room and tried to take in all the faces looking over to us. *Did it mean that one of these people were my soulmate?* No one looked as though they were desperate to come over and speak to me. I blinked a few times and turned back to the goddess of a woman in front of me. She was piling her plate with the plain croissants. *Her favourite.* I closed my eyes and inhaled the scent before me. Her sweet, flowery scent filled my senses and drove my insides wild. *I thought that once someone had imprinted that they no longer cared for anyone other than the one they were destined to be with. So, how did she still have this effect on me?*

Amelia;

Breakfast was finally over, and I was out in the cold. The cold air was refreshing, and it always calmed me, but I think that that was a werewolf thing. Matt had promised me that we could get some more combat training in. I think after the morning that I had, had this was a perfect idea. I slowly walked out towards the training area and saw that Matt was already there waiting for me. He was topless; *as usual. Damn, why was he gay? That man was fiiine.* I allowed my eyes to travel over his rippling muscles and smiled to myself. One day he was going to make some man extremely happy. *I couldn't help but wonder how well packaged he was.*

'Lia! You were here quickly!' He said, bringing my eyes from his bulge back up to his face. My cheeks burned as a flush crossed my face. *Oh, my god! Please Selene, say that he never caught on to where my eyes had travelled.* I forced myself to smile and pulled my hair up into a bun.

'You know me. Always eager to learn.' I chimed with a grin. Matt cocked an eyebrow and shook his head laughing.

'Yea. I know you. Always in the mood to try and kick my arse. And I am sorry to tell you; today is not the day.' He laughed. I narrowed my eyes and pulled my baggy jumper over my head and threw it to the side.

'Oh, you're on twinkle toes!' I said taunting him. His smile faded and a serious expression crossed his face.

'I love it when you try to fight dirty.' He said grinning. He raised his already wrapped fists up to his eye level and motioned for me to step forward. I took up his challenge and hurried over to the fighting arena. I wrapped my knuckles; the way he had taught me and stood before him. I watched as he bounced on his feet, preparing himself for our fight. I locked eyes with him and focused on my breathing. Matt flung his fist forward; no longer holding back, and I stepped to the side his punch narrowly missing my face. He threw me a crooked smile and nodded.

'Nice. I see you have been practicing.' I opened my mouth to respond when he threw two more punches at me and a low, sweeping kick. I bobbed and weaved under his punches and hopped over his leg. His eyes widened and a massive grin broke out over his face. 'Ok. Now I am impressed.' He added, nodding. But I didn't hesitate. I threw a punch directly at his jaw, taking him by surprise. He tried to duck but was too slow. My fist connected with his chin causing him to stagger.

'How do you like that?' I smiled, bobbing and weaving the same way that he had. His eyes flared with excitement and he got back into the fighting stance.

'I see how we are playing this today.' He leapt towards me, kicking me square in my stomach causing me to fall backwards. I turned my stumble into a backwards cartwheel and landed back on my feet. *There was no way I was going to let him beat me. Not today!* I tensed my stomach and worked through the pain and rolled my neck on my shoulders. I dove towards him, dropping down into a roll as he swung his fist. I jumped back up to my feet and kicked him in the back of his knee, causing him to drop to the ground. I didn't waste a second. I was on him once again. Matt rolled backwards, narrowly missing my foot and swung his leg around knocking me off balance. He rushed forward, slamming his fist down at me, but I managed to evade it; causing him to punch the ground. I swung my leg around once more, which he blocked. But I had another move in mind. I swung my elbow around, hitting him in the back causing him to lose focus and drop to the ground once more. This time I was on him too quickly. I pinned him to the ground and placed my hands on his head ready to break his neck.

I froze and stared down at him helplessly in my grasp and leapt to my feet. Matt rolled over and flipped back up to his feet and just stared at me in amazement.

'Y-You actually did it! You beat me? But... how?' He asked, looking more than a little bemused. I shrugged as he hurried over and pulled me in to a hug.

'I guess that you are just a brilliant teacher!" I squealed, still bouncing up and down. He shook his head and rolled his eyes.

'I still can't believe it. Lia, we have only been training for a few weeks. Every fighter in my squad has never been able to take me down. But you... you did. How the fuck did you do it?' He asked, still sounding dumbfounded. I leant in and kissed his cheek gently.

'Thank you... Matthew.' I whispered. He pulled back and glared at me.

'You may have beaten me this time... but you ever call me Matthew again, and I will kill you.' He said all humour leaving his voice. I smirked at him and laughed shaking my head.

'You wouldn't do that. You would miss me too much!' I laughed. He rolled his eyes laughing and gestured for me to go back to my room. *I couldn't believe that we had been out here for four hours already!* I slowly started to walk away and glanced back over to Matt once more. 'Oh, and one more thing...' I called out, causing him to look at me. 'I love you... Matthew.' His eyes widen and he dashed forward, lunging towards me and laughing; it was so nice to see him smiling especially after yesterday's awful events. I took off and ran back to the mansion laughing as I went.

'Lia. Hey…' Ethan called out to me, jogging over to me from the direction of the stables. I turned and smiled over to him, opening my arms and pulled him in for a hug.

'Hey, how have you been?' I asked, tucking my hair behind my ear and smiling up to my friend. He offered a slight shrug in reply and ran his hand through his hair. His blue eyes sparkled in the evening light, and drew me in.

'Things have been alright with me. You know, still buy in the infirmary, but I guess the busier that we are, then the healthier the pack is right?' He asked with a chuckle. I glanced over his shoulder and noticed the girl that was stood waiting for him, staring at him with love-struck eyes.

'How are things going with you and…'

'Hannah. Yea, things are ok. I guess.' He hesitated for a moment and cleared his throat taking a step closer to me. 'I miss you.' He whispered, dropping his stare to the ground at our feet, while shoving his hands in his jean pockets. I turned my eyes back to the girl watching us and shifted uncomfortably.

'I seriously need to get back to my room. But… can we arrange a night to hang out? Maybe watch a movie? I am in a serious need for a horror marathon!' I asked with a smile. I paused and glanced back over to Hannah. Me and the girl locked eyes for a moment and I smiled and waved over to her. Her eyes widened and she waved back, a little shocked by my gesture.

'That would be great! I would really like that.'

'Bring Hannah too? We can make a proper night of it. Junk food. Popcorn. Horror films… what more could you want?' I added with a laugh. I perched myself up onto tip toes and kissed Ethan on the cheek and waved to Hannah once more.

'That sounds great. Catch you later Lia!' He called after me. *I was glad that he had found someone that could make him happy. He deserved that.*

Arlo;

I stood out in the shadows under the tree. The light had

already began to fade. They had been at it for hours! It was nice to see her smile. I was glad that she was happy; *even though it killed me inside.* I stood in silence feeling anger bubble within me. He wasn't even bothering to hold back. When I saw him kick him in the stomach I wanted to fly over there and kill him. But it wasn't right for me to act like that anymore. I belonged to someone else. Someone that wasn't her. *Was I really angry that he wasn't holding back? Or was I angry that it was him that was making her smile like that. I knew that he was gay, but he was still doing something that I couldn't do for her. Not anymore.* I continued to watch in silence, making sure that neither of them knew that I was there. I was actually really impressed that she was holding her own. I never knew that she had such potential. I was proud of her. At least I knew that she was going to be safe once I was finally with my intended.

I was about to turn away when I saw something that I had never seen before. She pinned Matt to the ground and had him in a deadly headlock. *She won!* My best fighters in this pack couldn't even do that. She was something special! It took everything in me to not run over there and pull her into my arms.

I was so lost in thought that I never even saw her run straight towards me. Luckily my training allowed me to sidestep just in time, so she ran past and never even knew I was there. The sound of her laughter filled my ears and pain radiated through my chest. I watched as Ethan jogged over to Amelia and the pair were chatting. *At first, I thought that she was going to take my advice and get with him, and then I heard the conversation between them. I broke her heart and all she is worried about is how he is getting on in his own relationship?* I watched as she waved to the young Mutt girl and kissed Ethan on the cheek before continuing on with towards the mansion.

I held my breath and waited for her to jog up the main stairs towards the entrance of the mansion, and just stared after her.

'Ok, seriously mate, what the fuck is going on?' I spun around, coming face to face with Matt. A concerned look on his face. I opened my mouth to answer but no words came out. *How had he managed to catch me off guard?* He stepped closer and placed a hand on my shoulder. 'Arlo. You're scaring me.' I couldn't contain it any longer. The tears erupted from me, taking me by surprise. Matt pulled me into his arms and held me as I cried silently in the shadows.

'I-I've imprinted.' I whispered, trying my hardest to get my sobbing under control. *This was not me. I didn't cry. No one had seen this side of me other than Amelia.*

'Aww man, that's brilliant. I am made up for you and Lia. No wonder she was so perky today!' he said smiling. I turned my tear streaked face towards him and watched as everything slowly fell into place for him. His smile dropped and he took a step back and swallowed. 'Mate I...' I held my hand up cutting him off; shaking my head. He lunged forward and pulled me into a hug. 'I am so sorry.' He whispered, sounding just as heartbroken as me. *Selene... fuck you. Why couldn't you have let it be her!*

Amelia;

I walked back to my room after a long day of training with Matt. He had said how impressed he was with me. *Apparently, my skills had trebled since I had first started and that was only within a few weeks.* I had smiled, laughed and joked with my friends. Hung out with Piper. Glared at Lori and acted natural. None of them knew that inside my heart had turned to ice. I had always known that I was good at hiding my true emotions, but I didn't know that I was that good. I strolled into my bathroom and turned on my shower; this would be my second one of the days, but there was just something about the way a shower always lifted my spirits. Something about the way that water could wash my "*sins*" away. I pulled off my sweaty clothes and tossed them in the laundry hamper by the sink before jumping under the water. It was freezing; but I liked it. It was refreshing and uplifting. I washed my hair before climbing from the shower and throwing on my pyjamas. I had hoped that, that would have been enough to change my mind; to change the way that I was feeling. But it wasn't. Another pack member was dead; bringing the head count to four and the man I loved was Imprinting with someone that wasn't me. I slowly walked back into the bathroom and stood in front of my mirror and looked at myself. *When was the last time that I stood here and just looked at me?* Something was different. I finally felt at peace. This was definitely the right decision.

I placed my hand on the large knife that sat beside the sink and stared down at it for a moment; raising my wrist so that it was illuminated under the light. *Finally, my nightmares would end.* The annoying sirens call filled my mind once more; this time sounding desperate. *I didn't know if it was trying to stop me or lure me. Either way, that call would be over forever.* I placed the sharp edge of the blade against my skin and dragged it, feeling the burn as my skin tore open. Without a moment's hesitation, I gripped the knife in my other hand; *it was a lot harder this time, clearly the cut was deep enough to do some nerve damage.* And did the same to the other wrist. The blood welled to the surface and flowed onto the floor; pumping like a river. It was a deep red and I could literally feel it leaving my body. The edges of my vision started to darken, and I lowered myself to the floor and just watched. I felt my eyes growing heavy and I allowed the darkness to consume me. I wasn't scared. This was the first time in my life that I had ever felt certain about anything. I was about to die. And that thought made me extremely happy. I finally gave into the darkness and all went black.

Lori;

I knew that something wasn't right here. Something was definitely off with Arlo. And Amelia now that I come to think of it. They looked as smiley and irritating as always, but I could sense it. Something was... *wrong!* She had been in the woods when that Elite was killed; but for some reason I knew it wasn't her; she was too small and petite to take on a well-built Elite, but she *was* hiding something, and I wanted to know what. I slowly climbed the stairs, just trying to get close enough to their rooms so that I could try and hear something. *Obviously not close enough so that they could sense me. Just enough to listen in.* That was when it hit me. The strong metallic smell that I would recognise anywhere. Blood! I dashed forward and placed my hand on Arlo's door, but it wasn't coming from there. I hesitated a moment longer and glanced to the wooden door beside his that was slightly cracked open. *Her room.* The smell was coming from there. I placed my hand on the wood and pushed lightly; and I was not prepared for the sight that I saw. Everything was completely destroyed and thrown around the room. *What the fuck was going on?* I hesitantly stepped into her room; realising that I had never been in here before.

'H-Hello?' I called out quietly, taking another step into the room. The smell was so strong now that it almost made me heave. *All this time that I thought that she was the murder… had she been killed by the same person? I know that I always went on about how much I hated her, but that didn't mean that I wanted her dead!* My stomach twisted into knots as I slowly approached her bathroom. The door was closed but not locked. I reached out with a trembling hand and twisted the handle and pushed gently. The door swung open and that was when I saw the blood. It was everywhere, staining the white tile floor red. I covered my mouth, trying my hardest not to scream. Then I moved my eyes over to the corner by the sink and noticed her laying there… unconscious. She was pale. Paler than anything I had ever seen, she almost looked transparent. I hurried over to her, making sure that I avoided all the blood, and stared down at her wrists. There were two long gashes that were oozing blood. *Had she done this to herself?* I turned and ran from the room; I knew that I needed to get help; but what the fuck was I going to say? I was always the bitch that hated everyone. I was the one that was queen of mean. I burst through the main doors and found Matt and Piper sat together under a tree laughing. That was when I knew what I had to do. I plastered my famed scowl upon my face and folded my arms across my chest before storming over to them. They each looked up to me simultaneously and narrowed their eyes at me.

'What do you want Lori?' Matt snapped, glaring at me. I flipped my long blond hair over my shoulder and sneered at them.

'I just went up to speak to Arlo and noticed a strong smell of blood. I think your skank of a friend is seriously on the blob! You need to go and tell her to control that shit. I don't want to be smelling that sort of thing every time I go up to the alpha's room!' I snapped, turning and storming away from them as fast as I could. I held my breath and listened in to the pair of friends bitching about me. *Seriously! How stupid were they? Everyone knows that our menstrual blood doesn't smell like normal blood!* A white blur shot past me, causing me to flinch. I spun around to follow the direction that it went in when I realised that it was Amelia's horse. He galloped straight over to the friends and danced on the spot erratically. I watched as the two friends leapt to their feet and tried their hardest to calm the creature down. I was too far away to hear their words, but I was still able to pick up their heartbeats. *Finally! They had got the message!* I made my way around one of the buildings before peaking back around the corner; just in time to see Matt and Piper dash through the main doors, leaving the frantic beast pacing on the spot. *At least know I knew she was getting help. But… why would she do something like that to herself?*

16

Matt;

'Matt, what the hell is going on here?' Piper called, taking the steps two at a time a little behind me. I pressed my lips into a thin line, not wanting to think about what the hell could be happening behind the closed doors. I knew that the moment that Pretty Girl appeared in front of us, rearing back onto her hind legs and nearly kicking each of us in the face that something was wrong. I leapt up the last three steps and was finally on the landing that was Arlo and Amelia's. I hadn't had chance to tell Piper about what had happened with Arlo, I was about to when Lori appeared and then Pretty Girl… and…

'Oh, my Goddess. Do you smell it?' I asked, glancing over my shoulder and taking in the horrified look on Pipers face. She barged past me and threw open Amelia's bedroom door. The smell of blood was so strong now that it almost took my breath away. The last time I had smelt it this strong was that day in the woods with Amelia when we found… 'Piper get back!' I shouted, hurrying over to her and grabbing her arm.

'What are you doing? Our best friend is in there!' She snapped, spinning around to face me. A mutt had never spoken to an Elite in this way; especially as it was forbidden. But in that moment, I knew that Piper was a fighter at heart. I sighed softly and nodded.

'I totally agree. But we just need to be cautious! We don't even know if there is anyone else in here. Just… let me go first, ok?' I whispered, pushing the door open wider and looking around at the destruction site before me. 'What the…'

'D-Do you think that someone broke in here?' Piper asked, taking a step closer to me and holding on to my arm with trembling fingers. The longer that we stood in the room the stronger the scent of blood became. Her blood. I shook my head and closed the bedroom door behind us. If anyone was still in this room, then there was no way that I was going to let them get away!

We hurried into her bathroom and was locked in place from the sight of the blood. There was so much of it. Surely no one could have survived losing this much. My eyes travelled over to the sink and locked onto the one thing that stood out in the darkness of the blood all around. A hand so pale that it almost looked blue. I ran into the room, no longer caring if I was disrupting a crime scene, and dropped down onto the ground cradling Amelia's head in my lap. I looked her over and noticed two faint pink gashes across either of her wrists. And that was when it hit me.

'Matt, what is it? What's wrong?' Piper whispered, reaching out with a trembling and brushing a blood-soaked clump of Amelia's hair out of her face.

'I think that she… that she did this to herself.' I whispered in reply. I refused to take my eyes from the horrifying sight before me, but I already knew that Piper was shaking her head in disbelief. I understood why. It was only a matter of hours ago that we were laughing and joking while she kicked my arse. Other than Piper and Arlo, I didn't think that anyone could read her as good as I could. How did I not see this? I heard Piper snivelling as she wiped her blood covered hands on her jeans, staining them red.

'B-But, why? Why would she do this? I thought that things were staring to look up? I mean… look at her today. I haven't seen her look that relaxed since… well… since she arrived here.'

'It'd because she was too far gone. T-That is how it starts. I have seen this before.' I whispered in reply, still refusing to look away from my bloodied friend. Before Piper had a chance to ask anything more, I turned my face back towards her and sighed heavily. I cleared my throat and looked around the room.

'Ok, here is what we need to do. Go and shut her door. We

need to get this place fixed up and try and get rid of as much of this blood as possible. We can't let Arlo know that this has happened!' I said, my tone coming out strong and confident; basically, every emotion that was opposite to what I was feeling in this moment.

'What? Matt that is… ridiculous. We have to get her to the medical ward!' She snapped whirling around to face me.

'Look, Pipes… her wrists are already healed. Yes, she has lost a lot of blood but how the fuck are we going to be able to explain this to anyone?'

'And Arlo? He has a right to know! They are practically boyfriend and girlfriend.' I remained silent and dropped my face to the ground. 'Oh, right.' Piper whispered, fleeing from the room and closing Amelia's door as quietly as possible. We didn't have long before dinner was going to be ready, and when I didn't show up; and neither did Amelia and Piper, then people were going to know that something was wrong. If we can at least get this room looking at least semi normal and get rid of this blood, then we can just say that she wasn't feeling too good after the training session that me and her had. *Shit! What about Lori?*

'Matt, I understand that you want to get this covered up, but what if she has done damage that we can't see? What if it is more than what she is able to heal from?' Piper whispered, appearing in the doorway tears running down her cheeks freely. I pulled Amelia up into my arms and placed her in the bathtub. *Not conventional; especially as she was still fully clothed in her pyjama's, but I figured that at least her being here I could keep an eye on her.* I turned back to Piper and pulled her into my arms, sighing softly.

'Look… there are many questions that both of us have. And right now, the best thing that we could do is get this room and bathroom cleared up. And how about, as we get it all sorted, I will fill you in on everything I know?' I asked, gesturing her out into the bedroom as we both began scooping up all the broken furniture that littered the room.

Piper;

Two hours later we had tidied the entire bedroom, repaired what we could, mopped the blood from the bathroom; including washing it thoroughly over with bleach, the only substance that I could think of that was strong enough to mask the smell from even the most trained werewolf. I had washed Amelia, getting all the blood off of her and carefully removing the dried clumps from her hair as gently as I could. I just couldn't wrap my head around everything. Matt had explained everything that had happened after his training session with Lia, and what Arlo had told him. But I still can't believe that she would do something like this. I knew that she had always hated life, and that she hated life just as much in here, but I thought that she wanted to live? I thought that she wanted to run away and start a fresh, somewhere that no one knew her. It broke my heart to realise that things had gotten this bad. Bad enough to try and end her own life.

'What are you thinking?' Matt's voice called out from across the room. I flinched and turned to face him trying my hardest to put together the broken pieces of my mind.

'S-She can't stay here! I mean, how do we know that she is going to be safe here. Perhaps she should come and stay with me and my mum for a while?' I paused for a moment and sighed. 'I hate to say this but, thank the goddess that Lori smelt this.'

'I have been thinking about that. Something just doesn't add up to me. I mean, Lori of all people would know the different between blood and menstrual blood. So, why did she taker her time coming down to us? I mean, if she was that worried her then… why did she take so long coming down to us?' He paused and shook his head before continuing. 'But, if she really wanted her dead, then why did she come down at get us at all?' His eyes clouded over as he seemed to drift off deep into thought. There was so much left unanswered here, and I knew in that moment that I was not going to rest until I had gathered all the answers. For Amelia. *And for us!*

Amelia;

I opened my eyes and stared up at the ceiling. Whatever I was laying on was seriously uncomfortable! And there was a strong smell burnt my nose. *Kind of reminding me of the time that I ate too much horseradish in one go. That burn in my nose scarred me for life!* I raised my hand to my hair and realised that it was slightly damp. *Had I passed out in the bathroom?* I sat up and looked around at everything. *What had happened?* I glanced down at my skin that was so pale that I was almost transparent as the memories flooded into my mind. *I had done this. I tried to end it all. And I failed. Fuck! I couldn't even do this right!* I sighed and glanced down at my pain-free wrists and noticed that there wasn't a mark on them. *What the fuck was going on? Had I dreamt all of this?* I climbed from the tub; weakly, and held myself steady for a moment, trying to maintain my balance. And that was when I noticed the hushed voices coming from my bedroom.

I slowly walked forward, keeping one hand on the wall to steady me at all times and gasped at the sight. Matt and Piper were stood in the centre of my room; now fully restored back to the way that it had been; *before my tantrum.* And were now stood close to one another whispering.

'W-What are you guys doing here?' I asked. My voice so weak that it was alien to my own ears. Piper gasped and whirled around on the spot so that we were face to face. She crossed the room so quickly that I almost didn't register her moving until her arms were around me, squeezing me tightly. I could feel the warmth of her tears soaking into my clean pyjama top as she buried her face in the crook of my neck. I glanced over to Matt weakly who rolled his eyes and shook his head. *Typical Matt, even in the direst of situations, he still made me smile.*

Oh, Lia. Why didn't you speak to me? To Matt? Why did you think that this was your only option?' She continued breathlessly. I didn't know what to say, I couldn't tell them that I meant to do it, even though we all knew that I did. I had to lie.

'It, was an accident.' I croaked, trying my best not to look at Matt, I knew neither of them believed me, they aren't stupid, but I wasn't ready to talk about it... not yet anyway. 'Just one thing, please do not tell Arlo about this.' Matt and Piper looked at each other and then at me.

Okay.' Matt nodded. 'We won't say a word.'

The next day to take my mind off things, me, Piper and Matt went Christmas shopping. It would be Christmas in two days and I still hadn't bought anyone anything, I felt like such a bad person, a bad friend. Matt drove us into town, and it was packed with people who too had left everything last minute. Piper had done my hair, it was put into a high ponytail and I had finally put some make up on, anything to make myself look less like a zombie and more like me; Amelia-May. I wore a pair of light blue skinny jeans and brown ankle boots as well as a baggy pink jumper, it was still so cold outside and since losing a lot of blood, I felt the cold more than I ever had done before. It would take some time for my body to replace what I lost.

'Where do you want to go first?' Matt asked as we stepped foot in the large indoor shopping mall. I looked around and took in everything, it was beautifully decorated and had a large glittery Christmas tree standing in the middle of the floor, white and silver decorations and baubles glistened and shimmered as the large lights reflected off them.

'I want to look in the jewellery shop.' I smiled; I already knew what I wanted to buy everyone except for; Arlo... With him I didn't have a clue. Do I buy him something? We had practically broken up, but I still loved him so much. I feared rejection, what if I bought him something and he didn't want it? My mind was so messed up still, why did my suicide attempt have to fail? Everything was so fucked up, for everyone and I was to blame.

Finally, after hours of shopping Matt agreed to us going for some food, mine and Piper's stomachs had started rumbling after the first shop we had been in and all we talked about since then was food! Matt could shop for England; I had never known anyone to love shopping so much, this was my second time of going; in my life and I had already decided I hated it, it was too busy for me and so overwhelming.

'Okay, okay, you hangry ladies, what do you want to eat?' Matt laughed as we stood in the food court. Me and Piper both looked around at all the restaurants and squealed excitedly.

'A hotdog' we both replied in unison.

'The American Diner it is then.' Matt laughed.

We sat in a red booth at the back of the Restaurant and looked through the menu. I had never been so hungry in my life, my weak body craved energy and carbs! I ordered a hot dog with a side of chips, as well as a chicken burger and a large peanut butter flavoured milkshake and I devoured the lot. Matt and Piper looked so happy to see me eat, smiles spread across their faces and they looked at each other. These crazy pair loved and cared for me so much, I was lucky but and they meant the world to me, but after everything, I didn't know if it would be enough.

'So, have we got everything?' Matt asked as we walked to his car.

'I think so.' I concluded staring at all the bags that he was carrying. He insisted that me and Piper were not to carry anything, especially me. I felt like they were treating me as though I was a little china doll, that I was Fragile. I never wanted anyone to feel like they had to walk on eggshells around me and that they had to be careful with what they would say. No one brought up Arlo and no one had brought up the suicide attempt, but I wanted to talk about him, he was mine once and he still had my heart, but we acted like he didn't even exist.

'Lia; how do you feel about staying with me for a while?' Piper asked as we pulled up to the pack mansion. I looked through the windshield in front of me, staring at the large grey building in sadness. A feeling of dread panged in my tummy and I bit back tears, all that it represented to me now, was darkness. Memories flooded my head, talking to him for the first time, laughing with him, being held by him, the ball and making love to him. It all ran through my mind like a tape, I just wanted to be in his arms, snuggling into his chest, but he wasn't my man, he was another woman's and the thought of anyone else being intimate with him made my skin crawl.

I looked up at my friends they were both staring at me as I was lost in thought. 'I think that, it would be for the best for now.' I admitted sadly, undoing my seatbelt.

I agree.' Matt smiled, looking relieved, he placed his hand on mine and squeezed it reassuringly, although he was smiling, his face told a different story. I knew exactly why they wanted me to stay at Piper's house and that was because they wanted to keep an eye on me, neither of them trusted me to be on my own, and I didn't blame them. I wouldn't trust me either.

It was Christmas Eve, and I was helping Piper make Gingerbread men for the children of the pack, we played Christmas music and did anything possible to distract ourselves from the last two days. I was trying to mentally prepare myself for Christmas day, I should have been excited because Christmas for me as I grew up, was just like a normal day. My grandparents never decorated or put a Tree up and I never got any presents. But this year was supposed to be different, I was meant to spend it with my new family… with Arlo and now it would be as lonely as ever. The sooner it was over with, the better and to make things worse, everyone had to attend Christmas dinner at the mansion. 'It will be okay, you know.' Piper said looking up at me. I took another swig of wine and rolled my eyes.

'I don't want to see anyone.'

My friend weakly smiled and sat on the stool opposite me, she poured herself another glass of Rose' and refilled my now empty glass. 'You mean you don't want to see Arlo?'

The sound of his name made my stomach fill with unwanted butterflies and a lump built in my throat. 'I do want to see him.' I croaked, desperately biting back the tears. 'But I can't, it will hurt too much.'

Tears started to fill Piper's big brown eyes and she rubbed my hand. 'I know and I am so angry. I'm so fucking annoyed that this is happening to you both. Hand on heart; Amelia I believe you and Arlo are meant to be together and even if it's not in this life, it will be in the next.'

I know she was trying to make me feel better and I appreciated it, but being dead, was much more appealing than feeling like this. I felt like a lost soul, nothing in my life made sense and I was not destined happiness. I do not know what Selene had planned for me, but I was sure It wouldn't get any better. She could have my life, I never asked to be born and I didn't want it.

Piper and Tanya had gone to bed at around midnight, I did go to bed as well, but I couldn't sleep. I wrapped a blanket around myself and sat on the front porch gazing up at the stars. My mind wondered to the Elder and Elite that had been killed, their funerals were being held the day after boxing day and everyone was expected to attend; but after the last two I don't think I would be able to do it. I shook my head, *stop it Amelia; it's Christmas! Think of something that makes you happy.* But the next person that filled my thoughts was; Arlo, what was he doing right now? Was he okay? Did he miss me as much as I missed him? I took the box of cigarette's out of my pyjama bottom pockets and lit myself one. I only ever smoked when I was drinking or when I was upset and Arlo hated me doing it, but it helped me relax a little, even if it was for only a couple of minutes. My stare went from the stars, to the moon and I decided to talk to Selene. I don't know if she was listening to me, but there was a small bit of hope, that she was. 'Why?' I asked, 'Why this life? What is my purpose? Do I even have one? Why does the only person I have ever truly loved have to belong to another? He made me so happy, I made him happy and you have destroyed it.'

Arlo;

I stood on the balcony and looked up at the clear night sky. I hadn't been able to sleep in my bed since I told Amelia I was imprinting with someone else. My whole room smelt of her and my bed was now cold. I had been sleeping on my sofa ever since she had left, I just wanted to hold her. I leant over the balcony railings to see if I could see Piper's bungalow, but it was too far away, as I pulled back, I looked down at the balcony underneath me and spotted Matt. He was standing in his training clothes, his knuckles still wrapped, and he was having a cigarette, I wondered what he was thinking. He and Piper were the only two people that Amelia would open up to and I knew that he had taken them shopping. I just wished it was me that went with her. Since the day I watched Matt and Amelia train together and I told him what was going on, he hadn't been the same. It was almost like he was hiding something from me, either that or he just didn't know what to say. I looked back up at the moon and stared at it intently, I knew Selene could hear my thoughts. I turned away and walked back into my room, I wanted to see Amelia so desperately. From the very first moment I saw her in the woods and looked into her eyes, I knew she would be special to me, her beautiful pale face instantly drew me in. My mind wandered back to that the day we first saw each other.

I was sat in my office and my phone rang, I remember looking up at my clock, it was 7:57 am. I answered it only to hear the panicky voice of Amelia's; grandmother. '*She has gone! Tell Jake she has gone*!' she shrieked.

I shot out of my office and found my parents and Jake. 'Amelia has gone.' I said pulling my car keys out of my pocket, I gave them to my parents and headed for the woods. The cottage was about a 90-minute walk from the mansion and I had a gut feeling that she would be there. If I am honest, I don't know why I had the feeling. I have never met Amelia, I knew of her and listened to Charlie spit hatred, but my gut was telling me she was there. Once I got into the woods I started walking and got a familiar scent, it was the brown wolf and then I got another scent, it was sweet and flowery, there was a hint of lavender; *Amelia?* A familiar pain shot through my spine and into my head, my bones started cracking, I was shifting? *But how? We can only shift during a full moon, no one could shift spontaneously!* Once I shifted into a wolf, I started running, following the two scent's, Amelia was in danger! My ears twitched as I heard the galloping of a horse and then I heard a heartbeat, it was racing out of fear, I crept forward from behind a tree and saw Amelia on the floor, the brown wolf was walking towards her, but she tried her best to stand, I realised she was hurt and then I pounced.

I heard her cry and I looked straight over to her but as I did I felt the brown wolves teeth bite into my neck, he threw me over his shoulder and I smacked into a tree, I was hurt, but I needed to get to her before he did. Before I could get up the brown wolf pounced, he was going to hurt her and then a flash of white ran over to him, it was a Unicorn!

'Oh my gosh!' Amelia squealed. 'You came back?' *She knew this Unicorn. How?* Unicorn's are terrified of us werewolves and yet this one was saving Amelia? The Brilliant creature kicked her back legs into the wolf, the sound of cracking bones rang through my ears and the brown wolf was skidded into a large tree.

I watched in amazement as the Unicorn ran away with Amelia on her back, this girl was special, very special. I got up and followed them, they were going very fast and I struggled to keep up with them, my neck and back were still in so much pain but I needed to get to Amelia and get her out of these woods, we were not in our packs territory, we wasn't in anyone's for that matter, so if anyone wanted to attack here, they could.

Amelia turned to look at me and shouted 'shift.' She wanted me to shift back to my human form, but I couldn't something wouldn't let me. I saw the desperation in her eyes, she thought I was going to hurt them. I watched as Amelia leant into the Unicorns neck and listened to what she said, *'Pretty Girl, slow down.'* But she wouldn't instead she got faster. Amelia sat back up and as she did a thick branch smacked her in the head forcing her to be sent flying off of the Unicorn. She landed on her back and her hid hit the dry soil, the sound of her skull smacking into the earth made me wince. She screamed in pain and the smell of her blood overpowered my nose, she started to quietly cry. I inched myself closer to her and started smelling her blood, I was trying to find where she was hurt.

'Please no' she whimpered. I looked at her beautiful face and took in the beauty of her Olive-green eyes, I could have got lost in them, but she started to slowly close her eye lids. I nudged her face lightly, trying to stop her fall into a state of unconsciousness, but it was too late.

It was then I was able to shift back into my human form, I was completely naked, my brand-new suit had been ripped to shreds when the shift happened. I picked her up and carried her back to the mansion in my arms, her Unicorn walked beside me the whole time. I wasn't sure why she was not uneasy around me I expected her to kick me the way she did the brown-wolf, but instead she stayed walking by my side occasionally nudging her face into Amelia's neck, it was obvious they had a connection, but the question was, why?

17

Amelia;

I was woken up by Piper bouncing on her double bed, I be-grudgingly opened my eyes and looked at her beaming face.

'Merry Christmas; Amelia!' she squealed. I sat up and looked at my watch through one squinting eye. It was 8am, I had, had 5 hours sleep. After sitting on the porch for 3 hours cursing at Selene and smoking a whole box of cigarettes, I finally dragged myself to bed. 'Come on. My mum leaves for work in an hour, it's present time.' Piper jumped off her bed and ran out of her room, I groggily followed her yawning. When I walked into the living room, the smell of spiced apples and cinnamon filled my nose, I was in awe of their lit up Christmas tree, so much effort had gone into it, red and gold foiled garlands hung from their ceiling, the fire was lit and candles were neatly spread around the room, it looked like Santa's Grotto.

I couldn't help the fact that my whole face lit up, I loved it, it was beautiful. I sat down on the blue sofa whilst Piper and Tanya sat down at the Christmas tree pulling out the beautifully wrapped presents, they had bought for each other. I leant down the side of the settee and pulled out a gift bag that was full of the presents I had bought for them but before I could give mine out, Piper handed me a little square box which had a red ribbon around it.

'This is from me and mum.' She grinned proudly. I opened the box and smiled. They had bought me a charm, it had two dan-gly hearts on it, one said Best and the other Friend.

'Thank you.' I whispered gently closing the box. *Although I didn't own a charm bracelet for them to go on; I would definitely be buying myself one now.*

'I have some gifts for you guys too.' I passed them both all their presents and sat back. This is what Christmas was truly about, giving gifts and watching the happiness spread across their faces.... And being with family.

'I love them.' Piper cried happily, she stared down at her presents fighting back tears. I had bought her a bottle of perfume, a framed photo of me, her and Matt and two pairs of diamond earrings. I had bought Tanya a Candle gift set; *as I had recently discovered her love for them,* and a gold necklace, they both seemed absolutely thrilled with their gifts and for the first time, I felt genuinely happy. Tanya left for work at 9 so I helped Piper clean up the house, from top to bottom; *another Christmas gift for Tanya. What woman doesn't want to come home to a tidy house after a long day of work?*

Whilst I washed up, Piper disappeared into her room, I assumed she was getting changed but when she came back into the kitchen, she was holding up a glittery red dress.

'This is for you.' She smiled proudly. I quickly dried my hands and looked at the dress; it was stunning.

'Oh my gosh; Piper!' I gasped, 'You didn't need to get me another gift! You didn't need to get me anything at all.' I threw my arms around her and pecked her on the cheek.

'You can wear it today at dinner.' She grinned. I bit my lip and then sighed.

'Oh yeah, dinner.' I did not want to go to that stupid meal, I didn't want to face anyone, and I was sure that my dad, Charlie and Lori would be thrilled that me and Arlo had broken off, whatever we had. Piper looked deflated and weakly smiled.

'Matt told me about...Arlo. But he hasn't found his mate yet; Amelia, you can still be with him, nothing says you can't. I mean look at me and Eddie, he is an Elite and I am a Mutt, we are not allowed to be together...ever, but we are and yes it's in secret and I just wish I could kiss him in front of everyone, proudly show off my man. But I can't and I can't let him go, so until he Imprints on someone and until I do, we will be together, and you and Arlo can too.' I appreciated what she was saying and I understood it all, it devastated me that my best friend and my brother were so in-love with each other but couldn't be together, they were strong, they had accepted that they could never truly be together, but it was different with me and Arlo. He is the Alpha and I don't know who I am. I am an abnormal werewolf, one that is so different to everyone else; *one that can't even shift yet!* He deserved better than me, and one day he would get better than me. I just wanted so desperately to have one more night with him, I needed closure, but I knew if I did that then it would be so much harder to let him go. *Just one more night; Amelia.*

I looked up at Piper and smiled 'What time is Christmas dinner?' She smiled at me and then bit her lip.

'Well, it's actually Christmas Lunch and we have to be there at 12:30pm, it's now 11:30, so let's get ready.' I had a shower and washed my hair, allowing it to dry by itself, it brought out my curls more and I decided to wear it down. I did my make-up, making sure to wear black eye liner with a pin-up flick's, the eyeliner brought out the colour of my eyes and the blood red lipstick suited my new dress, which; *may I add was my new favourite item of clothing.* The dress was fairly short, revealing the bottom part of my thighs, *my father would definitely have a fit.* It was strapless with a scallop sweetheart neckline and glistened every time I moved. I pulled on a pair of platform black stilettos and looked in the mirror. Piper came up behind me and looked at me in amazement.

'You look fucking hot.' She grinned taking in the beautiful dress she had bought me. I blushed and turned to look at her.

'As do you.' I gasped. Piper was wearing a green mini dress with laced off the shoulder sleeves, her silver stilettos complimented the dress nicely, her red hair had been straightened and she was wearing her diamond earrings.

'Wow!' we both turned around after hearing a familiar male voice. Matt was standing at Piper's bedroom door with his jaw practically hitting the floor.

'You, girls look incredible.' He looked us up and down and then smirked. 'Who are you ladies trying to impress.' I smirked at him and then fluttered my eyelashes.

'Obviously you! You're the only man I will ever need.' I giggled. Matt flashed his famous grin and winked at me.

'And you ladies are the only… well *ladies* I will ever need.' We all started laughing and then left the house. It was quiet outside; everyone had probably already gathered in the dining hall; waiting for their Christmas feast. I looked over to the stables and smiled admiring my handy work. I had decorated them the day before with silver and white tinsel to match my beautiful Unicorn and made sure I filled her bowl up with oats and apples and also gave her a salt block to snack on. It was Christmas for my girl too.

As we got closer to the mansion, I heard footsteps behind us. I turned around and smiled when I saw Ethan and Hannah; they were holding hands and dressed formally, his tie matching her Black dress. 'Hi guys!' I smiled given them wave.

'Hey; Lia can I talk to you for a minute?' Ethan asked holding back.

'Of course, you can.' I replied stopping where I was so he could catch up to me. Piper and Matt both turned to see what was going on and nodded to Hannah.

'Come and walk with us.' Piper smiled linking her arm through Hannah's.

Ethan looked up at me and smiled. 'You look gorgeous.' I blushed and looked down to the ground linking my arms through his.

'Thank you. And I must say; you and Hannah make such a beautiful couple. It is so nice to see you happy.' I grinned staring at his beautiful blue eyes.

'It means a lot to hear you say that; Lia; thank you. I just wished that you were happy.' He admitted studying my face. I frowned at him in confusion.

'I am happy.' I lied reading his unconvinced expression. He sighed and raised one of his eyebrows at me. 'No, you are not; I can see it. What is wrong and don't tell me you are fine because I know you aren't.'

I closed my eyes and looked anywhere but at his face. 'I guess it is just the usual; Charlie is being a prick and accusing me of being a killer. My dad doesn't defend me, he never has, and I just feel let down by my own family.' I bit back the tears and stared straight ahead; we were now at the mansion doors.

'You know if I could protect you from them... I would. But all I can do is promise to be here for you whenever you need me. Don't shut me out okay? You mean so much to me; Lia, don't ever forget that.'

I watched as Ethan caught up with Hannah and I smiled, but it was short lived because being in the mansion brought me back down to reality. Now it was time for me to face everyone and although I looked ready, I wasn't.

The smell of roast turkey filled my nostrils and my stomach rumbled, neither me or Piper had eaten today and is still felt weak from my blood loss, the sound of clattering plates echoed in the hall as the kitchen door opened, the servers were bringing out roasted vegetables and potatoes and the sight of them made my mouth water, it was definitely time to eat something. I nervously walked towards the dining hall with Matt and Piper either side of me, I started to feel sick, I still was not ready to see anyone, especially; Arlo. I took a deep breath in and squeezed Matt's hand as I tried to steady my breathing. Piper went into the hall first and me and Matt waited for a couple of minutes before going in ourselves.

The doors swung open and I felt my mouth fall open. Whoever had been in charge of decorating the food hall had seriously outdone themselves. This place looked amazing. I hadn't been in here since the morning that I tried to end it all; *so, this could have been like this for weeks for all I knew.* The moment I appeared in the doorway all eyes turned to me. I cleared my throat and held my head up high. I wasn't going to let these people know that I was on the verge of cracking. That was none of their business. To them, I had been away hanging with my best friend having the time of my life. I locked eyes with Lori and held my stare for a moment. There was something odd about her. There was a certain glimmer in her eye that almost looked concerned. But I knew better. There was not a genuine caring bone in that girl's body.

I paused at the table for a moment, unsure where to sit. After spending so long sitting by Arlo's side, I didn't think that I was able to sit back with my father and brothers. That was when I noticed the little red place markers in front of each chair. Names were scrawled across them in elegant metallic script; each letter curling around neatly. I slowly walked the length of the table, looking for my name. The red card was placed next to Arlo's and a mixture of emotions came over me, I was scared to see him but excited too, I longed to be close to him and see his face, but it would be a bittersweet moment.

I stood behind my chair, my eyes focusing on the red card in front of me, I didn't want to look up at anyone, they would easily be able to see that I was a nervous wreck. I held on to the back of my chair tightly; so tight that my knuckles were white, when the sound of the doors opening caused me to flinch. The whole hall was no longer filled with hushed whispers and excited chatter as all eyes turned to our Alpha. I held my breath waiting for him to pass me; still not strong enough to make myself look at him. *Would I be able to keep my secret hidden from him? He had always been so good at reading me. I wondered if anything like that had changed since the imprinting.* The sound of shuffling came from my left, as people moved aside to let Arlo pass, and I felt the heat from his body roll over my bare shoulders as he passed me. I focused all my energy on not trembling in his presence. My desire for him was stronger than it had ever been. *Maybe I was just one of those girls that wanted the one thing that they couldn't have?*

The sound of scraping chairs filled me ears and I looked up to see the rest of the pack sitting down. I hurried to catch up with the others so that I wasn't the last person standing. I suddenly felt extremely self-conscious. As I fell into my seat, the hem of my dress rode up higher than I thought. I grabbed for it and tugged it down, only to make the cleavage line plummet. *Who thought that this dress was a good idea for a Christmas lunch? Oh yeah... Piper!* I closed my eyes tightly and tried to fight through the blush that I knew was about to rush across my cheeks when a deep low voice snapped me from my nightmare.

'You look… amazing.' Arlo whispered. I turned to look into his golden eyes and instantly all the fear that I had been holding melted away. *How was it that we weren't meant to be? How could someone that wasn't destined to be mine have this effect on me?* I cleared my throat and smiled up to him.

'Thank you. You look good too.' *And boy I was not lying.* He wore skinny fit suit trousers that shimmered a strange blue in the light, with a pale blue dress shirt tucked into them. Both items of clothing showed off every one of his perfectly sculpted muscles in a way that made my mind go blank. *Well, not blank. There was only one thing on my mind, and it wasn't his suit. It was what was underneath it.* I stared up into his eyes and noticed them running up and down the length of my body. He licked his lips and that was almost enough to send me over the edge. Arlo opened his mouth to say something when the main doors burst open and servers entered the room, each pushing trolleys loaded to the brim with food. They weaved in and out of the other pack members, placing plates in front of them smiling the entire time. *It amazed me how people could look so happy around people that clearly thought so little of them. That was one reason I loved the non-Elites so much. They were the ones with the true power around here!* Arlo and I received our plates and the smell of the food consumed me. It was like heaven. The sound of someone behind me caused me to glance over my shoulder. One of the servers smiled down at me and offered a glass of rose that was practically overflowing. *It was scary how well they knew me.*

'Merry Christmas Lia.' The server said with a beaming smile, before straightening up and glancing at Arlo nervously. 'Oh, um. I mean.' I placed my hand on the servers and smiled sweetly.

'Merry Christmas Lu.' I smiled, causing the worry to fall from her face once more. Arlo looked at me out the corner of his eye and tried his hardest to hide the smile. But I knew it was there. We ate in silence; *the food was so good that it left me speechless, I doubt I would have had the patience to talk, even if I wanted to.* By the time we had cleared our plates and eaten our puddings. *All three of them!* Arlo offered me his hand and helped me to my feet.

'Would you mind escorting me to my office?' He asked, his voice a little louder than needed causing a few of the other wolves to glance at me nervously. 'I think that we need to talk.' He added, dipping his head lightly. I pulled my fingers free from his hand and held my head high once more.

'Of course, alpha.' Arlo turned his stare to glare at me and I fought the smile tugging at my lips. 'After you,' I continued. A few of the other pack members gasped at my *"audacity"* but that only added fuel to my fire. We slowly walked back to his office; him throwing the door open and storming inside angrily. I stepped into the room and turned to close the door softly behind me. *I wasn't sure what was about to happen, but either way, I was not going to let it be bad!*

Before the door had closed fully, I turned only to be slammed into the wood causing it to slam shut. Before I could say a word, his lips were on my consuming me. I ran my hands up his arms, feeling his muscles flex under my touch. He pushed me against the door once more and ran his hands over the curves of my body, only stopping when his hand touched my bare skin. He pushed my dress up over my hips and pushed his fingers into the waistband of my knickers, ripping them from me with one swift motion. *Selene! They were new. AND LACE!* But I was too lost in the moment to care. I ran my hands down his chest, tugging open the fly on his trousers and feeling his hardness throb within the material. I slipped my hand inside pulling him free.

He slid me up the door, causing me to wrap my legs around him. He thrust forward and entered me, and I was overcome with an orgasmic rush. He thrust his hips into me deeper, nearly causing me to cry out. This was unlike any time we had done it before. This was raw, and desperate. I placed my face into the crook of his neck as his thrusting grew faster. Another wave of pleasure rocketed through me and I clamped my teeth down onto his shoulder; so hard that I drew blood. He fisted my hair and pulled it, wrenching my teeth from his skin, only to crash his lips back down onto mine. I couldn't control myself any longer and a cry of pleasure escaped my lips. *Now was not the time to be loud but... hello?*

He pulled his tie from around his neck with one hand and placed it around my mouth gagging me. A look in his eye that I had never seen before. *That only made it worse.* I didn't know how much longer I could fight off this ecstasy. I felt myself grow wetter with every thrust, and I could feel him throbbing inside me. Our eyes locked on to another once more and he pulled the tie from my mouth, before kissing me passionately. His breathing grew ragged and I felt the familiar tightening in my stomach that only meant one thing. We finished together at the same time, him thrusting into me with every pulse. In that moment, we were one. I placed my arms around his head and pulled him in close to me. We stayed there like that for what could have been an eternity. Him still inside me; and me not wanting him to be free. He kissed me once more, before lowering me to my feet and tucking himself back into his trousers. While I shimmied my dress back into place. He glanced around the office and noticed my tattered underwear lying on the ground.

'I'm uh, sorry about that.' He said, sounding more than a little embarrassed. I bit my lip to hide my smile and slowly wandered over to him.

'It's ok. It just means that you owe me a new pair.' I whispered with a giggle. Arlo smirked and wandered over to his desk before dropping into his chair. I hesitated for a moment, before he turned to look at me once more.

'Please, take a seat. There really was a reason I wanted you to come in here.' He said, running his eyes over my body. Arlo cleared his throat and look back up to my eyes. 'I am sorry about that by the way. I know that we shouldn't... but you know. When you arrive at the food hall looking like that, I am afraid that I was a little overcome with...' He stopped and turned his stare away from me; his cheeks flushing. I slowly made my way over to the chair opposite his and lowered myself into it. *My bones had already started aching from the roughness of us. But it only made me smile.* He leant forward and pulled a small bag from beneath his desk.

'T-This is for you.' He whispered, placing it on the tabletop and smiling at me. The bag was white, with a red ribbon tying the two thin handles together. I loosened the red material and put my hand into it, I could feel a small box inside it. I pulled it out and opened the black velvet box gasping at what I saw. He had bought me a Charm bracelet, something that I had always wanted, four charms had already been clipped into place, one was a wolf's face, one was my birth stone; an opal, one was a moon charm, with a moon stone encrusted into it and the other was a Love heart charm, it was beautiful and such a thoughtful gift. I bit my lips and swallowed back the lump that had built in my throat, trying my hardest to contain my tears. His smile fell as a look worried concern crossed his face.

'If you don't like it, I can take it back.' He said quickly, swallowing nervously. I shook my head and laughed softly.

'No! I...I love it; Arlo...Thank you.' My voice started out normal but ended in a whisper, I looked up at him, I loved him so much that it hurt. A weak smile spread across his face.

'You are more than welcome; Amelia.' He said before standing up. I too stood up, so we were facing each other, he looked down at me and put his strong arms around my waist. I just wanted to tell him how much I loved him and that I couldn't bare him being with anyone else but me. I wanted to tell him I could never love another man the way I did him. But he would forever, be the one who got away. Arlo allowed his face fall to mine, our foreheads touching, I placed my arms tightly around him, this was where I should have belonged. *But Selene clearly had other plans.* We closed our eyes, and just like magnets drawn to each other, our lips met again, this time although it was a passionate kiss, it was one full of love instead of Lust.

Our embrace was interrupted by a knock on the office door, we slowly pulled away from each other and I put one finger up to Arlo.

'Wait.' I whispered scurrying over to my black laced underwear which were still on the floor. Arlo started chuckling and held his hand out, I passed my now scrunched up underwear to him and he threw them in his little bin which was neatly tucked under his desk. 'You really do owe me a new pair.' I giggled blushing.

Arlo cleared his throat and called for whoever was at the door to come in. Matt and Piper both sheepishly entered the office, checking to see if they had interrupted anything. 'Hey, guys.' Arlo smiled sitting back down in his seat. Piper turned to me and grinned.

'Amelia, you left this with me; it's the gift you got Arlo.' I looked at her puzzled and then realised what my legend of a friend had done. I didn't end up buying Arlo anything, because I didn't think he would want anything from me, so Piper had picked something up for him instead. *Thank you.* I mouthed reaching forward and taking the bag from my friend; *which strangely enough matched the bag that he had given me only moments before.* I turned back to face Arlo and dropped my stare down to the bag as my heart pounded in my chest. *Why was I so nervous?* A confused look crossed over his face as his cheeks turned a slight pink.

'Y-You didn't have to get me anything Lia!' He said, trying his hardest to hide the appreciation from his voice. I placed the bag on his desk and stepped backwards crossing my arms over my chest nervously. He gently tugged the red ribbon and I watched as the bag fell open and he pulled a square white box from within. The box popped open and his eyes widened slightly, before flicking from the gift in his hands back to me. He pulled a thin leather bracelet from inside it and held it up to the light. It was a bracelet from the same place that he had bought mine from; and hanging from it was one charm. A wolf with mismatched gemstone eyes. One opal and the other an emerald. I gasped as realisation set in. *It was our birthstones.* He rose from the desk and offered it out to me with one hand while holding out the other.

'Would you?' He asked softly. I nodded and eagerly loosened the catch before fastening it around his wrist. He glanced down at the black leather and stared at it with an emotion crossing his face that I couldn't place.

'I'm glad you like it.' I whispered, still conscious that my friends were still standing behind me. He reached forward and pulled me into his arms. *This was the first time that he had ever displayed that sort of affection in front of anyone other than when we were at the pub together, and I thought that I was about to cry.*

Arlo;

I cleared my throat and pulled back from Amelia, taking in the tear-filled stares of our two friends, who were stood behind her. I thought that I had done well to hide my emotions from them in that moment, but it was clear to me then that I hadn't. I smiled down at Amelia and kissed her softly on the cheek.

'Thank you so much for this. I really do love it.' I paused and looked over to Piper and Matt once more. 'Would you mind if I spoke to them alone for a moment? I was going to call them in after speaking with you this morning anyway, but as they are here, I may as well get right to it.' Amelia glanced over to them anxiously as they nodded in unison, before stepping back and walking over to the door.

'I will speak to you all a bit later?' She asked smiling softly.

'Sure thing. I'll look forward to it.' Matt answered, glancing back at her once more before she slipped through the door. The moment the door had closed I turned back to them, claiming my seat once more and gesturing for them both to sit in the chairs opposite my own. I waited as they did.

'I-Is everything ok?' Piper asked, her tone was soft, but I could feel the waves of anxiety rolling from her. Matt looked calm as ever, but that was only because he was and always would be my best friend.

'I know that you both know everything. And... and I just wanted you to hear from me that if I had my way, none of this would be happening.' I paused and glanced over to Piper and sighed. 'I know that it is uncommon for an Elite to ask this of a Mu- a non-Elite, but she trusts you more than anyone in here. Both of you. And for that, so do I.' I hesitated once more, trying my hardest to find the right words.

'Arlo. You can trust me. And yes, I know that it is unusual for Mutts to speak to Elites this way, but I can sense that there is something different about you. Ever since Amelia arrived her you have been... changing.' Piper whispered. I gasped slightly, shocked at the confidence in her words; *but I also realised that I was not the only one that she had changed.* Amelia was having a good impact on everyone here in the mansion, and she never even realised it. It was almost as though she was a warrior queen that was sent to save us all.

'I want you both to promise me something.'

'Anything' Matt and Piper said at the same time.

'I want you to protect her. She may seem strong to the rest of the world, but I know that deep inside her, there is a frightened girl trying her hardest to stay afloat in a never-ending sea of misery.' Matt and Piper glanced at one another, a strange look upon their faces, before turning back to look at me.

'I am flattered that you are asking this of me Arlo. But you never needed to ask me. I would fight to the death to protect her.' Piper said, rising from her seat and smiling down to me. Matt smiled proudly as he looked to his friend in awe.

'For someone so quiet you have a fire in you. I like it. And I want you to keep that fire alight. Stay vigilant and keep your guard up. If you haven't noticed, only one Elite and one Elder have been attacked, but the rest have been... Non-Elites' I replied, rising to my feet also and walking over to Piper, who nodded with a sad smile. I pulled her into my arms and held her there for a moment, her body going ridged from shock before hugging back.

'I know about you and Eddie. So, I know that you understand how I feel.' Piper gasped and pulled away from me.

'H-How did you know?' She whispered, her eyes shimmering with unshed tears.

'Because I have eyes.' I replied softly. 'I see the glances that you give one another when you think that no one else is looking. The way that his hand lingers on yours for a second longer than necessary when you hand him his drink.' I paused and looked down to Matt. 'And, I also had a suspicion that Matt and Lia also knew, and I am so happy to know that you have good friends like them to keep your secret.'

'We should have known that the alpha would suss this out.' Matt said, speaking for the first time in what felt like forever. 'So, why are you bringing this up now?' He added. I smiled.

'Because I want to warn you. You need to be more discreet. Just because I am ok with this, doesn't mean that Charlie would be. We all know his feelings against those that aren't Elites, and I fear what he would do to you and his brother if he were to find out.'

'Thank you, Arlo.' Piper whispered, stepping forward and kissing my cheek lightly. 'Promise me one thing. Whenever you find your soulmate, please don't ever change.' With that, she turned back towards the door and left my office. Matt rose to his feet and wrapped me into a bear hug, before turning and flocking after Piper. I stood there for a moment, staring after them smiling.

Amelia;

I left Arlo's office, still lost in a daze from what had just happened. I wasn't sure if that was a good thing or not. Were we both still too fragile for this? Who knew? But I was glad that it happened. I wandered aimlessly down the corridor, heading towards the main doors. It was Christmas after-all and I hadn't spent some quality time with Pretty Girl for far too long.

A strong hand flew out of the open doorway, latching onto my arm and dragging me into one of the empty rooms. I gasped as I was caught off guard and turned to face my attackers, and my heart sunk. *Charlie and my father.* I stared at them both taking in the angry glares plastered upon their faces.

'What the fuck do you think you are doing?' Charlie hissed through clenched teeth. I blinked in surprise as I tried my hardest to figure out what he was talking about.

'Do you not understand the danger that you are putting this pack in?' My father said, his voice full of sorrow and hurt. 'Just own up to the murders. We all know that it was you.'

'W-What?' I shrieked, anger swelling within me. 'Fuck you! Fuck you both! Who do you think you are to accuse someone of that-' I was cut short as the back of Charlie's hand slapped across my cheek, so hard that it knocked me to the ground?

I clutched at my face and waited for the burn to die down and looked to my father for support. But all he did was turn his face away from me.

'Tell everyone that it was you. Or we *will* make sure that you are caught.' He looked down at me in disgust and shook his head. 'I always said that it should have been you. You should have been the one to die that day and not our mother.' He paused for a moment, as a realisation washed over his face. 'Is that how it all started? On the way out you killed our mother. So, now you need to continue your killing spree?' He sneered. The anger within me had reached a point that it was almost too much to bear. *How fucking dare, he. How dare he mention our mother in the same sentence as the murders that had happened. And how dare he blame them all on me!* I pushed myself up to my feet, knocking Charlie off balance as I did, and leant over him.

'You know what. If I was the murderer, don't you think that I would have started with *you?*' I shrieked. He scuttled back a little and I couldn't contain myself. I kicked out with my foot and caught him straight in the groin, causing him to crumple up in pain. My father leapt forward, pinning me up against the wall by my throat. I turned my cold, angry stare to him and tensed all my muscles. In one swift movement I threw my elbow forward and caught him in the stomach causing his grip to loosen on me. I threw my head forward, headbutting him and causing a sickening crunch to fill the silence. It was then that I threw all my weight in front of me and made my escape.

I ran out into the hall and hurried past Matt and Piper, who both held shocked looks upon their faces. *Had they heard?* I never stopped. I just kept running. Just when I thought that my life might be getting back on track something like that had to happen. Why did I need to be constantly reminded that my life was one big fuck up? This was it; I may not have been able to kill myself by slitting my wrists, but I knew one way that even I wouldn't be able to survive.

I stopped at Pipers house and just stood in her room for a moment. I wrote a small note and tucked it beneath her pillow with tears streaming down my face. I hurried back out into the cold afternoon air and ran towards the wrought iron gates. I hurried past the stables, only glancing at them fleetingly but I kept on running; watching as Pretty Girl leapt over the gate containing her and chasing after me. She dipped her head and flipped me up onto her back and we both disappeared off into the forest.

Piper;

I paced back and forth in my room, it had been hours since any of us had seen or heard from Amelia. Not since she was cornered by those sick people that claimed to be her family. *How could those that were supposed to love and protect you be the ones to throw you to the wolves?* I glanced out the window and took in the darkening sky. Soon it would be night and that would mean that Amelia would have been missing for eight hours. A knocking at my bedroom door had me whirling around on the spot. *It was Matt.*

'Any news?' he asked, stepping into my room and closing the distance between us in three large strides. I opened my mouth to answer but no words came out. I shook my head and fell into his arms. That was when a second voice had me looking over to the doorway. There behind Matt was Eddie.

'Babe, I have been out there looking, but I can't find her. She doesn't even have a scent for me to track.' He said, crossing the room and pulling me into his arms. The minute that his arms were locked around me I felt as though his warmth was chasing all my darkness away. I sank into his scent, allowing it to overcome all my senses for a moment.

'What made you come back here?' I asked, pulling my head back and looking up into his eyes.

'I-I could sense that you needed me. I don't know how. It was weird, like I could hear you calling to me in my head.' He answered, a confused look upon his face. I snuggled myself into his embrace once more and sobbed silently. 'What caused this? What made her run?' He added, placing his cheek against the top of my head.

'It was-' Matt started, but I cut him off.

'It was your prick of a brother, and that spiteful man that

you call father. They are *vile* creatures!' I snapped. Matt and Eddie both paused and stared at me in shock. *It was only then that I realised that I never usually cursed. Or spoke so angrily about others. What was happening to me?* I pulled myself from Eddie's grip and sat on the edge of my bed when something small and white fell from beneath my pillow landing beside my foot. I reached down and plucked the square of paper from the ground and unfolded it. I leapt to my feet once more as I realised what was happening. I knew where she was. Without a word I ran forward, barging past Matt and Eddie, not bothering to tell them where I was going. The white piece of paper fluttered from my hand landing on the ground. As I turned to go down the stairs, I noticed that Matt had scooped it up.

It was those two words that had made everything fall into place. The two words that I you never wanted to see from your best friend.

I'm Sorry!

Amelia;

I had been gone for hours. Just riding around on Pretty Girl, getting lost in my surroundings. I had been silently battling myself in my head. But I had made my decision. I took a deep breath and tied my beautiful horse to a nearby tree. 'I love you so much; Pretty Girl. You have been my Guardian Angel since the day I left the cottage. Piper was right; you came to me in a time of need but now you can help Arlo. Look after him.' I whispered before kissing her on the nose.

I stood on the edge of the cliff that Arlo had found me at once before, looking down at the twinkling lights from the buildings below. My heart pounded in my chest and my stomach churned. I thought back to all the times my father had left me when I was a child. The horrible insults from him and Charlie rang in my ears and I allowed the tears to flow. I remembered when I first saw Arlo; his beautiful eyes drawing me in. Images of when I first met Piper, Matt and Ethan flooded through my mind, but it was no longer enough for me to stop what I was about to do.

I closed my eyes, feeling the wind whip around me. It was soothing, but at the same time reminding me of all my pain. In the back of my mind that stupid lullaby played, taunting me, teasing me, urging me on. Without another seconds thought I leant forward, feeling the ground disappear beneath my feet. This was it. This was finally the end.

18

Matt:

I paused and looked over to Piper, my heart thundering in my chest. Something was wrong, I could feel it in my gut! Piper's eyes widened as she suddenly had the same thoughts as me. She opened her mouth to say something, but her expression was all I needed. I took off at a run, not bothering to check if Eddie was following us. Seeing Piper take off like that was all I needed. When I noticed the paper falling from her grip, I picked it up and read the two words scrawled across the page in Lia's handwriting. I'm Sorry! We all ran as fast as our leg's would allow us too, this was when we needed to be able to shift at will. I could feel a pounding in my ears as my pulse rang through them, my heart was thundering but the adrenaline kicked in for us all.

We passed through the iron gates, out into the darkness of the forest; we were now officially out of our territory, so we had to keep our wits about us, rain heavier than anything that I had ever seen pelted against my skin as thunder rumbled overhead. Eddie grabbed hold of Piper's hand as she struggled to keep up with us. I was so scared that we had run out of time, would we be able to save her? There was no certainty that we were heading in the right direction, her scent was still masked beneath the aromas of the forest, but that didn't make sense, I know that I wasn't the best tracker, but even I knew that you would always be able to pick up on another person's scent! That question ran through my head consistently until we all saw Pretty Girl, she was tied to a tree and was standing on her back legs, a noise coming from her that was inhuman; it was almost sounded like a scream. I looked up at the cliff top and saw her; Amelia! And she was about to jump! Panic took over me, and I lost all senses of everything else around me.

I pushed on harder, putting myself to my full capacity, ignoring as my muscles protested from the exertion, my feet slipping and losing traction in the mud. The world seemed to slow around me as she leant forward and allowed herself to fall from the cliff. My pulse thundered so loud in my ears that all other noises faded. I jumped forward and managed to grab the top of her arm as she began to fall to her death. I could hear Piper's and Eddie's screams behind me and then Amelia shrieked, her screams sounding like that of a banshee. I pulled her back up to safety and we both tumbled to the ground with a crash, her sobs filled the night sky as I pulled her into my arms tightly, holding her against my chest.

'Noooo' she screamed, 'No, no, no... I just want to die, why won't you just let me die.'

Amelia;

My heart dropped as both of my feet left the soiled ground and for a second, I was free and would be for eternity, but a warm hand grabbed hold of my arm pulling me straight back up. I shrieked in frustration and tumbled onto the ground with them, sobbing like I had never cried before. I just wanted it to all be over, I didn't want this life, why could no one understand that?

'No, no, no... I just want to die, why won't you just let me die?' I cried, in between sobs. Matt, Eddie and Piper all dropped down on the ground next to me, I felt my Matt scoop me into his arms and rock me back and forth, the rhythm would have soothed anyone else but the devastation of my second failed attempt took over everything else. Eddie and Piper both started crying each placing an arm around me. For the first time in my life I heard Eddie cry, it shocked me because he was always the joker, he was always laughing and was the life and soul of any group that he was a part of, but today he too was hurting. And that was all because of me.

'Why? Why would you do something like this Lia? Why didn't you just speak to me? Please, please don't do that again. I love you' He whispered through tears. 'I can't lose you baby sis.'

'We love you so much, they are not worth this heartache.' Matt said rubbing my back, his voice gentle and full of raw emotion. I felt him kiss me on my cheek.

I don't know how long we sat there, but the four of us just huddled together in silence, the only sound that could be heard was me crying. Thunder cracked overhead, with a flash of lightning briefly illuminating the darkness. I glanced over to Pretty Girl, who had now calmed slightly, and was glaring out into the darkness protectively. I was suddenly overcome with exhaustion, and I sagged in Matt arms. Eddie scooped me up and carried me over to Pretty Girl and placed me on her back. Another flash of lightning illuminated the darkness surrounding us and I tried my hardest to fight through the haze of my own fatigue. Something caught my eye in the lining, something that didn't seem right. I strained my eyes into the darkness, and I could have sworn that I could see dozens of pairs of glowing white eyes reflected from the flash. I shook my head and collapsed onto Pretty girl, no longer able to keep my eyes open. I was exhausted and could sleep for hours at that point, I was just emotionally and physically drained. I finally gave in to my exhaustion and slipped into the darkness.

Matt;
I turned back to Eddie and Piper who both looked equally as distraught as I felt. How was it that we never noticed her slipping this far into the darkness? Some friends we were! Eddie glanced over my shoulder back to his sister, who was now sound asleep on the back of her unicorn and shook his head. I untied Pretty Girl from the tree and gently placed my hand on her neck and we all slowly started making our way back to the mansion in silence.

'Would someone please tell me what the fuck is going on?' Eddie asked, storming in front of us, causing us all to stop, looking from me to Piper. We glanced at one another and his eyes narrowed at us both. 'What is it that you both aren't telling me?' Piper sighed and turned to face him.

'A few days ago, Matt and I...' She paused as her voice caught in her throat, causing it to wobble.

'A few days ago, what?' He snapped. Piper sighed and turned her stare to the muddy earth beneath her feet before answering.

'A few days ago, Matt and I found her in her bathroom unconscious. And there was a lot of blood on the floor. Her blood and we think... we think that she tried to slit her wrists.'

'What?' Eddie roared, anger taking over him causing us both to flinch. 'And no one thought to tell me? Does Arlo know about this?' He continued shouting, hurrying over to his sister and looking at each of her wrists.

'She told us that it was an accident. And although we knew that it wasn't, we didn't know what to do. We didn't want to break her trust.' I answered, knowing how stupid that, that sounded now.

'And she asked us not to tell anyone. Especially Arlo.' Piper replied, her voice so quiet that it was almost inaudible over the sound of the torrential rain.

'And neither of you thought that something was a bit off with that? The fact that she didn't want anyone to know?' he continued, his tone cold and angry. Piper closed her eyes as tears rolled down her cheeks.

'We were keeping an eye on her.' I replied. Eddie whirled back around to glare at me.

'And well done to both of you. I am so glad that you managed to keep her safe!' he snarled. Anger washed over me, and I couldn't control myself any longer.

'Do you know what Eddie... why don't you speak to your brother and father? I have seen how often you defend her in front of them. And if you really want to know, the reason that we lost track of her today, was because they pulled her into a room, hidden out of the way so that no one could find them. They practically told her to confess to all the murders. They don't give a fuck if she was the one to do them or not. They just want her to own up.'

'Wait... but...'

'I'm not finished!' I shouted, cutting Eddie off midsentence. 'When your sister tried to stand up for herself, Charlie hit her!'

'What?' Eddie replied, his voice flat and emotionless.

'Yea. So, next time that you want to start blaming Piper and myself for not keeping an eye on her, maybe you should go to the source!' I stormed passed Eddie, patting Pretty Girl's neck gently, urging her forward. That was when I smelt it. A wolf!

'Get behind me!' Eddie urged, pushing Piper tightly against his back. 'You smell it?' He asked, looking to me. I nodded, refusing to take my eyes from the line of the trees. The sound of bushes rustling had me looking over to my left, just in time to see a brown wolf emerge from the foliage. How long had it been there? What did it hear? And what did it want?

'You have no business here!' I said, keeping my tone calm but assertive. 'You are seriously outnumbered!' I continued, gesturing to the others around me. The wolf watched me with green eyes that looked familiar. Where had I seen those eyes before? The wolf stepped forward slowly, not in a threatening manor, but more in a curious manor. I homed in on my senses, trying to pick up whether there were more hidden in the shadows. But we were alone. The wolfs stare switched from me to Amelia his head hanging slightly. I summoned my wolf senses once more and realised that there was no threat. The only feelings that I could pick up on from him were fear and concern. He looked to me once more before taking a hesitant step towards her. Our eyes locked for a moment, and it was as though I could feel his question burned into my brain. He wanted to see her. I nodded once and we all watched with wide eyes and he wandered over to Amelia and gently pushed his face against her limp hand. He closed his eyes and allowed her hand to rest against his head for a minute, before throwing his head back and letting out a heartbroken howl.

A putrid stench washed over the clearing. A smell unlike anything I had ever smelt before; a mixture of rotting flesh, wet dogs and vomit. It was so strong that it stung my eyes. The brown wolfs head whipped around to look at the three of us before growling. Even though we couldn't communicate, I knew what it was telling us. He was telling us to run. So, we ran!

Pretty Girl took off at speeds that were almost impossible for any horse, while Eddie, Piper and I did our best to keep up. The sound of the brown wolf's growls and snarls could be heard, growing further into the darkness as we grew closer to the mansion.

Eddie;

I wasn't sure how much we could trust the brown wolf, but the heartbreak that was put into the howl was enough to tell me that he wasn't a threat. I gripped on tightly to Pipers' hand, practically dragging her along behind me. The awful stench was closing in around us. I didn't know what it was, but all I knew for certain was that I didn't want to find whatever it was that the smell belonged to.

We could see the glow of the mansion in the distance, so we pushed on. The sound of rustling was gaining on us, and I knew that if we didn't do something soon then we were all in danger.

Amelia;

I sat up and looked around the room. I was back in Pipers house. A sudden sadness crashed down on me. I thought that it had all been a terrible nightmare. But no, I was still alive. Still here to suffer for another day. I sighed and flopped back on the bed and glanced out the window and allowed myself to drift off into a daydream, when a gentle knocking brought my attention back to the reality of everything.

'Come in.' I whispered; my voice hoarse from all the screaming I had done the night before. Eddie walked into the room, a tray in his hands loaded with all types of foods. The minute that I laid eyes on the food my stomach growled loudly, causing my brother to chuckle.

'Well, I am glad to see that your appetite hasn't changed. Here, I thought that you could do with something to eat.' He said, placing the tray on the side table before taking a seat at the end of the bed. He sighed loudly and kept his stare focused out the window.

'I-Is everything ok?' I asked, already knowing the answer. He turned to look at me and the grief in his eyes almost broke me all over again.

'Why, Lia? Why did you do it?' He asked, his face was full of sadness and confusion. I thought for a minute, how much did he already know? Had Matt and Piper told him anything?

'Have you ever felt trapped?' I asked, staring into my brother's eyes. I continued. 'Well, I have felt trapped my whole life. I have lived in the shadow of mum's death and I do not know who I am, I only know how I am perceived. To everyone I am the child who killed her mother, I am a freak of nature and the person committing these heinous murders. How can I expect anyone else to see the real me, to know the real me when I don't even know myself? To answer your question, I did it because I am a burden, not only to everyone else but myself. I don't want to live anymore; anywhere is better than here even if that means I fall into a darkness for all of an eternity.' I looked out of the window and stared at the half moon; I heard my brother sigh sadly.

'But you are not a burden to everyone; Amelia. You have Arlo, me, Piper, Matt and Marie and all the mutts. We all love you and adore you and whether you think it or not, we know you, the real you.' I nodded, considering his words for a moment. It was true, they were the only people who truly cared for me and so did my beautiful Pretty Girl. But was that enough. I closed my eyes and shook my head.

'Eddie, I-'

'I love you; Lia and I am so sorry that I haven't defended the way I should have, against dad and Charlie. I am ashamed of myself and I have let you down. But I won't ever let you down again, I swear it, on my heart. I will protect you and defend you to my death.' Eddie said, interrupting me. Tears were now falling down his cheeks, I could see that he meant everything he said, I could feel it.

'I love you too big bro.' I whispered crawling over to him and leaning my head against his shoulder. We sat in silence for a few minutes before my brother asked me something I never expected.

'What is going on between you and Arlo? He hasn't been right for a few days, he has become, more... aggressive, he is impatient, angry and just not himself.' He asked, his eyes glazing over as though he were drifting into a distant memory. I closed my eyes and nervously licked my lips.

'W-we… broke up, if you can call it that, whatever we had is over.' I admitted nodding my head, still trying to come to terms with it all myself. I smiled weakly and looked at my brother. 'I love him.' My lips started to tremble as a lump built in my throat. 'I am in love with him, but we cannot be together… ever and yet I can't let go of him.' Eddie nodded, I knew that he understood how I felt, he was in love with Piper and if anyone ever found out, uproar would fill the mansion.

'If only things were easier for the both of us.' He answered, his voice coming out no more than a whisper. Anger swelled within me. Arlo was the alpha, why wasn't he doing anything about this? He may not have been able to be with me, but why did others have to suffer? I cleared my throat and slowly rose from the bed; my bones cracked from the movement and my muscles were tense. How long had I been asleep?

'Who knows, one day you and Piper might have the chance to be happy together. No one knows what the future holds. But then, I know that the non-Elites and Elites never imprint.' I answered softly. Eddie nodded and forced a smile.

'Is that what happened between you and Arlo? He imprinted on someone?' I paused for a minute, considering his question. I never was one to talk about others, but in a way, this involved me also. I nodded, not wanting to trust my voice. Eddie rose from the bed and crossed the room to stand beside me. 'Well, at least things never got too far with you both.' He replied sweetly. I closed my eyes and fought back the tears that were threatening to fall. Eddie paused as he caught my reflection in the window, before turning me back around to face him.

'Well… we actually… um…' I blinked rapidly as my cheeks flushed. I couldn't believe that I was about to talk about this with my brother. 'He took my… vir-'

'You what?' Eddie cut in, his voice low and deadly. His eyes blazed with a fire that I had never seen before and he balled his fists as though he was about to punch something. 'I'm going to kill him! I'm actually going to fucking kill him!' He roared, so loud that it caused me to flinch. I stood there frozen to the spot for a few seconds, my brain not registering what was happening. This was all new to me. I wasn't used to someone being this protective over me. Especially not a member of my family. I lunged forward and latched on to Eddie's wrist, just as he started towards the door.

'Wait. It's not like that. I wanted to do it too.' I said, my cheeks now burning hotter than a furnace. I cleared my throat before I continued. 'And, I know that he did truly love me. It isn't his fault that he imprinted. I bet if that hadn't had happened, we would still be together today.' Eddie screwed up his face for a moment as he tried to accept my words. His muscles were still tense, and I knew that he was still resisting the urge to kill our alpha.

'I don't like it. I don't like it at all. And I am not happy!' He mumbled, a scowl on his face that reminded me of a sulking child. I pulled him in to my arms and hugged him tightly.

'Thank you. No one has ever defended me this way before. It's… strange, but also super sweet.' I said, kissing him on the cheek. Eddie turned his glare to me and stared into my eyes, and I watched as his they softened slightly. He rolled his eyes and rested my head on his shoulder.

'I told you. Things are going to be different from now on. I'm no longer going to stand by and let others hurt you.'

'Even if it's our alpha, and you know that you are rushing into sudden death?' I asked, raising an eyebrow questioningly. He clenched his teeth and nodded, all joking aside.

'Especially if it's an alpha that wants to take advantage of my little sister.' He replied. I couldn't contain it any longer and a giggle escaped my lips. 'Seriously? You're laughing at me?' He said, now smiling along with me. I cleared my throat and shook my head.

'Not at you. Just at your logic.' Eddie kissed my cheek softly and smiled before clearing his throat once again.

'Lia; I have to ask you this because of the rumours that are swirling around about you… which may I add I don't believe. But I am curious to know about this Ethan guy.' I froze and looked up at his serious face before shaking my head.

SAM KETTLE & NATASHA SLEE

'There is nothing going on between me and Ethan. I care for him and I do really like him, but I love Arlo and before you ask; No, I haven't slept with Ethan and no I haven't slept with Matt.'

Eddie smiled down at me and pulled the hair away from my face. 'I don't care who you are with, just as long as they are treating you with the respect you deserve and not taking advantage of you. I just want you to be happy.'

Piper walked into the room and smiled over to me and Eddie. I glanced at the clock on the wall and turned my confused stare back to my best friend.

'Pipes, why aren't you at work?' I asked, worry settling in my voice. Piper rolled her eyes at me and shrugged, dropping down onto the bed beside me and resting her head on my shoulder.

'I spoke to Arlo earlier and told him that I was having a few personal problems, and he said that I could take a few weeks off to deal with it.'

'But… Pipes, what about your money? You have been working like crazy to save up to do that intense beauty course! What about your dreams to own your own salon?' I asked, my eyes wide. Please don't tell me that my own selfishness has cost my best friend her dreams? She wouldn't even let me pay for it. She was too independent that way.

'Arlo said that I should have a few weeks off with full pay.' I pulled my head to the side so that I could look down at her.

'Wow. That was really nice of him! Didn't he ask what the personal problems were?' Piper shook her head and sighed.

'Nope. I know this isn't exactly what you want to hear right now, but he is a truly amazing alpha. We are extremely lucky.'

'Pipes, I never said he wasn't a great guy. I am heartbroken, I don't hate him. Like I said to Eddie, it's not Arlo's fault that he has imprinted on someone else. It's just the way that it is supposed to be. And I am so glad that he is going to make an amazing leader for you all in the years to come.' I smiled weakly to myself. As much as I hated to admit it, I knew that what I was saying was right. Arlo really was an amazing guy, and whoever it was that he was imprinting on was one seriously luckily girl.

'What do you mean by that? The way that you worded that sounded like you aren't planning on being around here much longer?' She asked, her voice quivering from worry. I shook my head and smiled. Eddie stared at me with a worried expression on his face.

'Don't panic guys. I realise now how that came across that is not the way I intended.' I paused for a moment and sighed once more. 'Hey is Matt still here? I think that the four of us need a talk.' Piper looked to me with a concerned expression and then glanced at my brother before nodding slowly and leaping from the bed. She disappeared out into the hall and down the stairs, giving me the chance to wander over to the window and look out across the horizon. I listened as hers and Matt's footsteps climbed the stairs once more, faster than I had hoped they would, and someone rushed back into the room.

'Ok, we are all here, so what was it that you wanted to talk to us about?' Piper asked, taking one of my hands in hers and squeezing it gently. I turned my stare from the darkness outside the window and locked eyes with her. I noticed that Matt was hanging around in the doorway and I waved him in. I waited for a few seconds, telling myself that I needed to be brave. I exhaled loudly and closed my eyes.

'I know this is not something that you are not going to want to hear, any of you. But I think there is only one way that I can promise you that I will not try to do anything else to cause myself harm.' I paused and took in their puzzled expressions and sighed. The room fell into an eerie silence and I turned away from them once more, pulling my hand free from Piper's.

'You are seriously starting to freak me out!' Piper said, stepping forward and forcing me to look at her. I admired how much she had grown since me arriving here. She never would have had the courage to stand up to an Elite this way before. I looked into her eyes and smiled as best I could.

'I want the three of you to promise me, that you will help me find a way to run away from this place.'

'What? No!' Eddie snapped, turning away from me and placing both hands on his head. 'Lia, what the fuck is going on? Why did you even think that we would agree to this?'

'Because it's living here that is making her feel so shitty.' Piper said in reply. Eddie turned to look at Piper and sighed heavily.

'Look… Lia… I understand what you are feeling right now. I understand what it is like to love someone that you can't have.' He paused and glanced at Piper from the corner of his eye. He thought that no one noticed it, but I did. And it broke my heart.

'I know that you are in a similar situation to me. And it completely sucks! But, watching Arlo fall in love with someone else is not going to help. It was bad enough when Arlo was by my side. But now that he is destined to be with someone else, what do you think is going to happen with me?'

'Lia, nothing is going to change.' Eddie whispered, rising from the bed and stepping forward, placing his hands on each of my shoulders.

'That's the problem though, nothing is going to change. Dad and Charlie will continue to make my life a living hell, and there is nothing that anyone can do about it. Arlo was the only one that had the power to stop them. But now that's over. Do you really think that all the other Elites are going to just sit back and accept the girl that they all blame for these sick murders?' The room fell into silence for a moment, as they allowed my words to sink in.

'I promise.' Matt said, speaking first and taking a step closer to me and holding his hand out. I took it in one of mine and glanced over to Eddie and Piper. Both of them looked torn. Piper nodded and placed her hand over mine and Matts and the three of us turned to look at my brother. He stared at us in silence for a moment, his eyes flickering back and forth as he thought everything through. He sighed and held his hand out, not touching ours but still holding my stare.

'I'm not happy about this, and I have conditions. But I agree. I will help you.' For the first time in what felt like forever I had a genuine smile.

'And what are these conditions?' I asked, pulling the three of them into a tight hug. Eddie wriggled free and stared at me.

'Firstly, you have to wait until you have your first shift!'

'Wait! That's not fair-' Eddie held his hand up, cutting me off midsentence before continuing.

'Secondly, you need to wait to find out who is the culprit behind all these killings. And that is for two reasons, one, so that I know that you are safe while you are out there. And two, if you run now, that is only going to spur the others on, making them think that you ran away out of guilt. I know that you have nothing to do with these murders. But there are plenty of others that disagree with me.' I paced back and forth for a moment, thinking over his conditions. I could see that he had a point, and that was what was so frustrating. If I left now, that would only give Charlie more ammunition to come after me. And now that there have been so many murders, they won't even hold a trial. It will be an automatic execution.

'You have a deal!' I said, turning back to face them. They all glanced at one another anxiously. I knew that none of them wanted me to leave, but at the same time they all loved me too much to want me to die. And I swore it. If I didn't get to leave here, then I would die. I would have to end it all and this time I would succeed.

19

Arlo;

I opened my eyes and shielded them from the stream of light that was blasting through a crack in the curtains. I sat up and rolled my neck on my shoulders, loosening up my muscles and preparing myself to face the day ahead. _What the fuck happened yesterday? Where did everyone go?_ I closed my eyes once more and tried to ignore the dull ache that had formed behind them.

I hadn't slept very well at all, not only was all the usual alpha duties playing on my mind and I had an Elder's and Elite's funeral to take care of but so was the fact that there were four members of my pack missing at both mealtimes, and that _never_ happened. What the fuck had happened after I asked Amelia if I could speak to Matt and Piper in private? She had seemed absolutely fine with it and after I spoke to them, they went to find her. I expected to spend the whole of Christmas day with them all, but they all disappeared, including Eddie and to make things worse; I couldn't go to find them as I had to stay with the Elders and Elites.

This Christmas was certainly not what I expected it to be and that disappointed me. _This was going to be the last time that I had to spend a Christmas with her, with Amelia._ I just couldn't shake that feeling that there was something wrong, like a niggling at the base of my spine. Everything would be fine and then out of nowhere, there was an awful feeling that came over me which I couldn't get rid of, no matter what I did. _Was this all a part of the imprinting process? As much as that was all new to me, I thought that I had learnt most of what I needed to know prior to it happening._ I felt sick and clammy; I imagined that, that was one of the feelings that a human suffered, when they caught a common cold, but us werewolves do not get ill like humans do, we are immune to most diseases and this feeling disappeared after an hour. It was so strange, I had never felt like this before, I thought that it was just in my head, but even my mother noticed something was wrong. She commented on the beads of sweat that had formed on my forehead and was concerned at my sudden pale complexion. Although I told her that I was fine, I still noticed her worried stares, not only on me but out of the window, what was she thinking?

I was abruptly broken out of my thoughts by the high trill of my phone ringing, making the dull ache in my head hurt even more and a sharp pain shoot through my ears. I looked at the bright screen; it was Charlie. I let out a deflated sigh, *what now?* I touched the green phone symbol and swiped up.

'Hello?' I said sitting on my bed, rubbing the stiffness of my neck.

'Arlo, we need you now. It's happened again!' Charlie cried, fear in this voice.

I hung up the phone and jumped up, diving over the bed to grab some clothes out of my bedside table. Another killing. Will this ever end? We let our guard down for one day and it happened again.

I arrived in my office with panicked force, slamming the door wide open, I felt sick. Three, three more dead, this time it looked as though they were all poisoned. Their faces were purple and white foam had built up around their mouths. Deep red blood had trickled from their eyes, noses and ears. Staring down at those bodies this time made me shake, it wasn't just two adults that were dead, it was two adults and one child. I slumped back on my chair and stared at the ceiling, wondering how I would find the words to tell my pack that the killer had changed his/hers normal MO and that he/she had murdered an innocent child. The bodies had been there; in the same place as the others since yesterday, murdered on Christmas day.

I had requested the bodies to be taken to Benjamin and for their autopsies be performed immediately, I needed to know what was used to kill them, although it would take at least 24 hours before the toxicity results would come back. I walked to the library deciding I needed to do some research on the poisons that could kill a werewolf, the only two things I could think of were; Belladonna and wolfsbane, two plants that were not easy to come across. Just the slight touch of both these plants could burn a werewolf's skin and could cause extreme pain, I shook my head sadly, the weight of the world was on my shoulders, I was supposed to protect my pack and now the body count was up to 8.

I opened the library door, the large room looked empty, but I could smell her; Amelia, she was in here somewhere, but I had work to do, I had to find these books. I gazed around at the large wooden bookshelves which went from the floor to the ceiling and wondered where the hell I should start looking. I closed the door behind me and cracked my knuckles, taking in a large breath before breathing out. I walked over to the lines of books, looking for the letter *'B'.*

After finding the two books I needed I noticed Amelia walking towards the library door, *she hadn't even acknowledged me*, had I done something wrong? Before she put her hand on the door handle, she glanced around jumping at the sight of me. I watched amused as she pulled the earphones out of her ears, *that explained why she didn't know I was in here.* She blushed and started to walk towards me.

'I am so sorry, I had no idea you were in here, I feel so rude.' I smiled and tilted my head to the side, as usual she looked stunning, wearing her usual skinny jeans and converses with an off-shoulder baggy jumper. Her hair was in one big plait and rested over one of her shoulders.

'Where did you go yesterday?' I asked placing the books down on the table I was leaning against.

'Just for a walk, I wanted to see Pretty Girl.' She smiled sweetly. 'I am sorry I never came back, I got really tired and went to bed.' She bit her lip nervously and turned her music off.

'It's okay I understand.' I said running my hands through my loose curls, Amelia's eyes fell to my arms and I noticed her eyes widen and a familiar feeling washed over her face, I felt it too.

'I guess I had better go.' She blushed obviously trying to fight the sexual chemistry we had between us. We were like magnets to each other, we both knew we couldn't be together the way we truly wanted to be, but this was the next best thing and we both eagerly accepted it, I would take anything if it meant I could be with her, showing her my feelings through intimacy. I grabbed her hands and pulled her up against me, feeling her breasts against my chest caused a heat to spread over my body. We locked eyes and she dropped her phone and book on the floor, she too couldn't fight this any longer. I pulled her jumper over her head and allowed my eyes to fall to her pink lacey bra, I pulled down the straps and watched as her breasts fell out of the laced material that had covered them.

Amelia undid the button and zip to her jeans and took a step back as I put my hands on her hips, gripping each side and gently pulling the down. I picked her up and gently placed her on the carpeted floor, being sure to hold the back of her head as I did. She wriggled nervously as I slowly pulled down her underwear, admiring the view that was right in front of me, I gently opened her legs and kissed her thighs, leading myself up, she shook as my tongue touched her and she desperately tried to grab hold of something opening her legs a little more for me to completely divulge her. I placed two fingers inside her, moving in rhythm with her hips, the sounds of her pleasure turning me on even more. 'Please.' She panted, wrapping her legs around my neck. 'Please.' I pulled my fingers out and slowly worked my way up her body before pulling myself free from my jogging bottoms.

Listening to her beg me to make love to her drove me insane, but I fought the urge, watching her desperately trying to grab my hard shaft. I grabbed hold of her legs and pulled her towards me before leaning down to her beautiful face, she leant hers up to mine and closed her eyes; our lips met, and I couldn't hold back any longer. I gently eased myself into her; a lot slower than usual, I wanted to make love to her; connect with her on an emotional level and show her through intimacy how much I loved her because I just couldn't say it; as much as I wanted to. I lifted her arms and placed them either side of her beautiful naked body; wrapping my fingers through hers; my thrusts although slow gave me a chance to look into her eyes and take in the moment completely; I didn't want this to ever end. The sounds of her moaning in pleasure were like none that I had ever heard before; this was different. We had, had sex so many times before but had only ever made love once and this time I wanted it to be like the night I took her innocence.

Amelia;

He looked me in the eyes and continued to keep the slow and gentle motions as he thrust himself towards me, all of the hurt and stress that I could see in his eyes faded away and he became lost inside me; not just physically but mentally, I could feel the deep connection that we had built and it was bittersweet. I buried my face into his neck and turned towards his ear.

'I love you; Arlo.' I whispered. He closed his eyes and turned towards my face and kissed me; the passion in his kiss was just as deep as his love making, he had never kissed me this way before and I wanted him to keep doing it. The images of when we first met flashed through my mind; the day he first smiled at me and the day we first spoke. The memories of our heartbreak faded away and I could feel the familiar feeling of pure ecstasy start at the pit of my stomach and work its way all over my body; my toes curled and I gripped his hands, he continued to passionately kiss me and our breathing became in sync, I pulled away from his mouth slightly and gasped as the orgasm took over, we looked into each other's eyes and I felt as his movements became fast but still as gentle as they were before, 'You are so beautiful.' He panted as he throbbed and went into me deeper; his breathing became heavier and he let out a gasp releasing himself completely. His grip on my hands softened and his perfect body collapsed onto mine; our hearts were still beating in rhythm and in that moment, we became one.

Matt;

It was the day of the funerals and the atmosphere was incredibly dark and depressing; hardly anyone spoke to one another and no one made any eye contact. We all watched in sadness as two respected members of our pack were sent to eternal paradise with Selene. The Non-Elites stood one side of the burning bodies as Arlo stood in between his parents whilst every Elite stood the opposite side; every Elite except Amelia. Again, she stood in the shadows of a towering tree; hidden away from her accusers. I noticed Arlo occasionally looking up at her with heartbreak in his eyes. I wished that I could go and stand next to the shell of the broken person she had become but I had to stay where I was. Just as the final prayer had been said; Amelia turned away and quietly starting walking towards Piper's and Tanya's house. I was so relieved that she had turned up; it would have only given Charlie more ammunition to use against her; but then in a way I wished that she hadn't, I was so frightened that she would attempt to end her life again and although she promised she wouldn't do that again, it was still in the back of my mind.

Everyone started to depart and go back to their homes and jobs whilst me and Piper followed; Amelia's direction. Arlo went off for a walk by himself and saying to us all he needed to clear his head, and no one was to disturb him. It was such a blessing in disguise that the annual pack meetings were coming up, it meant that Arlo had to go to Ireland; he needed the break from everything and it would give him time to clear his head and although I usually went with him he asked for me to stay behind and keep watch on the pack and Amelia, which I gladly agreed to.

Arlo;

I stood by the glowing embers from the funeral pyres and watched as my fellow pack members slowly started walking away. *How could this be happening? What did all of this mean?* With a heavy sigh, I turned my gaze to the broken families of our fallen. The heartbreak and devastation on their faces was enough to break me. I fought back the lump in my throat and turned away from them. *I needed to clear my head.*

I slowly walked away from the remnants of the pyres and make my way towards the main gates. *So much had happened in such a short amount of time.* I just needed to be out in nature for a minute. Being surrounded by the forest always seemed to have a calming effect on me. *I guess that is just where us werewolves feel more at home.* The moment that I left the threshold of the gates I instantly felt a little better. It was as though the pressure that was building inside me was easing ever so slightly. I closed my eyes and tilted my head back, fighting through the emotions that were clouding my mind, when the sound heavy breathing could be heard from a few feet away.

I glanced over my shoulder and strained my eyes into the darkness; *but even with my wolf visions it was impossible to see anything other than the wood surrounding me.*

'Hey, who's out there?' I called out, stepping closer to the shadowy figure that was peering out from behind the trees. At the sound of my voice the person stepped back, disappearing from view once more causing me to go after them. *If this was the person that was responsible for the deaths, then I would kill them myself!*

I darted around the large tree trunk and to my surprise there was nothing there. Not even a scent trail that I could follow. *This was impossible.* Everything had a scent. And me being the alpha meant that my senses were heightened above all the others. There is no way that I would be able to miss something like that. The sound of snapping twigs behind me had me whirling around, letting out a warning growl from low in my throat.

'I mean it. Whoever is out there, show yourself? Right now!' I barked, clenching my teeth and looking around the area. *I didn't like the fact that these killings were gradually getting closer to the mansion grounds. How long until the intruder made their way into our homes?* I spun around to look behind me once more when a strange feeling washed over me. Red sparks flickered around my head momentarily and then all the concerns that I once held were gone. All emotions were overtaken by that of anger. *I needed to check her room! My instincts were telling me that she was behind this. I just needed to prove it!*

Amelia;

I made my way up the stairs, heading back to my room for the first time in what had felt like forever. It was strange being back here. So much had happened since that night. In some way, I felt as though I was a changed person, grown into something new and stronger. I smiled weakly to myself. *I knew that there was no way that I would be here without my friends, and my brother; Eddie.* They had been my rock through all my tough times. But now, it felt as though everything was starting to fall into place. I jumped up the last two steps and rounded the corner. Something was wrong. I could sense it. I strained my eyes and looked into the darkened hall and noticed that my bedroom door was opened slightly. I could just about make out shadows dancing across the walls as whoever the intruder was passed by my light. Anger boiled in the pit of my stomach. *How dare someone break into my private space. It shouldn't have mattered if I was staying there or not.*

I put all my practicing with Matt to the front of my mind, and moved silently down the hall, getting closer to my room. I slowed my breathing and tried to make as little noise as possible. *With all these murders happening, I didn't know who it was that I was about to bust in on.* I clenched my fists in attempt to quell there trembling and carried on.

The strong scent of bleach stung my nose, and I could still faintly smell an undernote of blood. My blood. My heart pounded in my chest as I continued forward, until I paused outside my bedroom door. I paused and wrinkled my nose, trying my hardest to pick up any other scent, but the bleach was too strong. I closed my eyes, gulped down a deep breath and threw the door open, my fists raised to my eyes just as Matt had taught me. *But I was not expecting what I saw.*

'A-Arlo. What are you doing in here?' I asked, glancing around the room in confusion. He never moved, just stared down at something in his hands. 'Seriously, you are starting to freak me out, what the hell is going on?'

'Amelia… what the fuck are you doing with this?' he asked, turning his golden eyes to me with a look in them that I couldn't quite place. *Was that disappointment?* I turned my stare from his golden eyes, down to the glass vial that was pinched between his thumb and forefinger. I tilted my head to the side slightly as I tried to figure out what the hell it was. But I had never seen it before.

'I-I don't-'

'Don't fucking lie to me Amelia!' Arlo roared, so loud that it caused me to flinch. I stepped back, surprised by his tone and shook my head. *As much as I didn't understand what was going on, there was no way that I was just going to stand back and let him speak to me this way.*

'Excuse me? Just because you are my alpha does not give you the right to speak to me this way.' I snapped, narrowing my eyes and focusing all my attention on controlling my anger.

'This isn't a fucking joke Lia. Why do you have this in your fucking bedside table?' He turned to me once more, this time with a fire in his eyes that sent a shiver of fear racing over my skin. *I had never seen him look so... alpha-like.* I drew in a deep breath through my nose and took a step closer to him, causing him to take a hesitant step away from me.

'How the hell am I supposed to tell you what it is if you keep moving away?' I snapped, reaching out with lightning speed and snatching the vial from him. Arlo paused for a moment, staring at his now empty hand, almost as if he was still trying to figure out how I had managed to take it, before stepping towards me and balling his fists.

I held the little jar up to the light and looked inside. A strange powdered herb shimmered a deep purple under the light. I had never seen anything quite like it. It was almost hypnotic. I brought the vial back down to my level and prepared to pull the cork from the top of the bottle, when Arlo snatched it back from me. 'What are you doing?' he snapped.

'I am trying to see what it is!' I cried angrily. 'What is going on with you; Arlo?'

'What is going on with you; Amelia. What happened to you?' he grumbled, his eyes darkening.

'What the hell are you talking about? I don't understand what is going on with you right now?' It was only this morning that he held me in his arms, and I felt so safe and so cared about and now he is snooping through my room and I did not feel safe, he was frightening me.

'Where were you yesterday; Amelia.' His voice was low, and he refused to look me in the eyes.

'I..I... went for a walk.' I lied knowing full well that he didn't believe me, somehow, he always knew when I was lying.

'Don't fucking lie to me.' He said through clenched teeth as he took a menacing step towards me. I nervously lipped my lips and gulped as I took a step back.

'I needed to get away from everyone, I am not lying.' I whispered as tears built in my eyes.

'Why? Why could you possibly need to get away? It was fucking Christmas day; Amelia.' Arlo took another step towards me, getting angrier and angrier. My heart slammed against my chest as an awful feeling came over me, I had never seen him like this before.

'Arlo what is going on? What have I done that's angered you so much?' Tears started to stream down my cheeks as I looked into his black eyes, this wasn't my Arlo, my Arlo would never be like this towards me, he would never accuse me of lying and he would never hurt me, but this one was going to hurt me. I stepped back, hitting myself against the wall, whilst the man I loved was standing right in front of me, he looked furious, sad and hurt and I could not work out why. He slammed his hand into the wall next to my head and held it there, his other one balled into a fist by his leg.

'Do not act like you don't know what you have done. I was so fucking blind not to see it before, they were all telling me, and I refused to listen. You have had us all fooled.' he roared slamming his fist into the wall next to my head, at that moment I was scared for my life but fear had me frozen on the spot and then it clicked and rage took over from the anxiety that riddled me.

'What are you accusing me of; Alpha.' I said slowly looking up at his face. Our eyes locked and I refused to be intimidated. 'Spit it out.' I mumbled.

'You did it. You killed them all.' He said and my heart sank to the floor with a crash. I closed my eyes as he said those words. Charlie had succeeded, he had finally persuaded the man I loved that I was capable of killing my fellow pack members. I opened my eyes once more.

'How fucking dare, you.' A rage like nothing I felt before shot through my body and I exploded, barging into him with a force I didn't know was possible. Arlo staggered back, shocked at what I had just done. 'You seriously think it was me?' I shook my head in utter disbelief. 'I thought you knew me; Arlo.'

'I thought I knew you too, but you are a murderous, calculated bitch.' He bellowed slamming my bedroom door closed so I had no escape route. His words stung me to the core, I had been called a lot of things in my life, but this was by far the worst.

'I did not kill anyone; you fucking idiot.' I screamed, 'How could you even think that?'

'Then what the hell is that?!' Arlo roared pointing to the vial that he had placed on my bed moments before he punched my bedroom wall.

I don't know. How many times do I need to tell you that?!' I pushed my hands against his chest in frustration. ''If I was going to kill any members of this pack, it would not have been the Mutts, it would have been the Elites.' I started sobbing and fell to the floor, the anger seized to exist and the pain and heartbreak of the whole situation that I had found myself in, swept over my body like a disease. My sobs filled the silent bedroom, I had never cried like this in my life but Arlo thinking that I was a monster did that to me, he didn't know me at all.

Arlo;

I stood frozen on the spot realising what I had just done, I had broken the one thing that meant the most to me in this world, I was just like them; Charlie and Jake. The realisation of what I had actually accused Amelia of hit me like a tonne of bricks, she was right, she would never hurt the Mutt's, she defended them day in and day out, no matter the consequences she had to face in doing so. And she certainly would never hurt an innocent child. I thought back to blank and confused expression on her face when she looked at the vial of Wolfsbane, she did not know what it was, but if she didn't know what it was, then why was it in her drawers? Did that mean someone had placed them there so I would think it was her?

I dropped down onto my knees in front of her heaped over body, she was still uncontrollably crying, trying to catch her breath every now and then and it was me that had done this to her.

'Amelia...I am so sor-'

'Do... not... touch... me' she said in between breaths as she sat up and backed away from me, I could see the pain in her beautiful green eyes, something had snapped in her, she looked almost different.

'I... am really sor-' I tried to apologise but she cut me off again, this time with a pained scream, but it wasn't the shrill of physical pain. She stood up and slammed the door open and then stopped, turning ever so slightly towards me. 'Do not ever talk to me again.' I watched helplessly as she walked out of the room, disappearing into the darkness of the hallway.

Amelia;

I fled from the room needing to get out of this place. I felt as though the walls were closing in around me, crushing the breath from my lungs. Complete panic had taken over me and I was done! I couldn't be here anymore. Every time that I thought that I could start to fit in here, something happened to make me question that. The tears in my eyes turned my surroundings into a blur and I could just about make out the concerned looks of pack members as I ran past them.

The moment that I was through the main doors the cold night air stung my face, burning my lungs as I gulped down deep breaths. I pushed on and continued running towards the iron gate; *I needed to be out of here.* I didn't know where I was planning on going. I just needed to be gone. The panicked sound of people hurrying towards me filled my ears, but I didn't attempt to stop to find out who it was. *Would Arlo have sent people after me to have me locked up?*

'Lia?' I heard Piper's familiar voice call, my legs gave out under me at the sound of my best friends voice, causing me to trip and stumble. I felt myself fall forwards only to land in Matt's strong arms. The sound of footsteps came rushing over to us and Matt glanced from me to Piper.

'What the fuck is going on?' He asked, the need to protect me evident in his tone.

'He… found… something in… my room.' I sobbed, struggling to catch my breath. 'He said that… it's me.' I continued.

'What? What are you talking about?' Matt asked, twisting me around to face him and wiping the tears from my face with his thumbs.

'A-Arlo. He was searching my room. He found something in a glass vial and said that he knew that it was me. I am the one that has been killing everyone.' I paused and I struggled to gulp down a breath. 'I can't be here. I need to be out of this place. I am sorry but I need to get out of here.'

'Wait, what? Why would he think that it was you? Did you say that he was searching your room?' Piper asked, creasing her brow in confusion. I filled them in on the events that had just taken place, telling them every detail as best as I could remember. By the time I had finished Piper and Matt were furious.

'I don't even know what it was that he found. It was purple and shimmering and in a glass vial.' I whispered, shaking my head, trying my hardest to make sense of everything.

'Wolfsbane? But… where would anyone have gotten that from? It's not like it grows much around here. But… he still accused you? How dare he!' Piper growled, balling her hands into fists and clenching her teeth. Matt shook his head as the pair slowly led me back to Pipers house.

'That doesn't sound right. That's not Arlo. I have grown up with him. He is family to me! That's not a way that he would act.' He whispered, more to himself that either of us. 'It almost sounds like he was hypnotised. Who the hell would have put him up to this?'

'More to the point… who would have framed Lia by putting

the wolfsbane in her room?' Eddie asked, appearing beside us with anger flowing from his eyes.

'I don't know, but I swear that after this, I will never speak to Arlo again. This was the final straw!' I growled; my panic being replaced of that with anger. *He wanted to blame me, he wanted me gone... fine. He wins!*

20

Matt;

It had been a long 3 weeks since the last murders had happened and the atmosphere in the pack was dark and cold. Amelia still wouldn't talk to Arlo after his accusation and in all honesty, I didn't blame her, but he was a much happier person when she was around. During this time that they haven't been speaking, he had changed; his moods were dark and his temper short, he wouldn't confide in me about his private life refusing to reveal what had happened between him and Amelia. But she told me everything, including that he punched the wall right next to her face. In my entire life I never thought that I could love anyone as much as I loved Arlo and my adoptive parents, but since meeting Amelia, my outlook on everything had changed. Amelia was a sister to me, and it was hard to listen to everything that had happened between the two of them because that wasn't Arlo, my best friend; my brother, would have never done anything like that, ever! It was almost as if he had been possessed.

Thank fully he was still preparing to go on his annual trip to Ireland, maybe time apart was what they both needed. He was hoping to speak to some of the Alpha's and see if they could help our pack solve these murders. He desperately needed a break, so I was sure that this trip would do him good, Tristan, Charlie and Jake were all going to go with him, and Amelia was extremely excited. The thought of not having to be around her father and brother thrilled her, she could be herself without treading on eggshells. And maybe now she could finally be herself.

I stood on my balcony and stared out to the woods, wondering who was out there looking back at me; wondering what they wanted; wondering why they were killing off our pack? I jumped when my phone started ringing and without looking at the screen, I knew it was Arlo, he wanted to know everything.

'*I need to speak to you. My office, now.*' He mumbled before hanging up the phone. I slide it back into my pocket and slowly wandered back into the mansion, he sounded more emotionless than I had heard him yet, it seemed that all this time apart was seriously messing with him. I hurried through the corridors until I was stood outside his office door. I drew in a deep breath through my nose and shoved the door open, plastering a smile on my face.

'Hey bro, you wanted to talk to me?' I asked, walking into his office. He was sat in his chair looking up at his portrait; a look of disappointment was written all over his face and then he turned to look at me, he was hurt mentally. There were dark circles under his eyes, his cheeks were slightly drawn, and he just looked deflated. I sat down and stared at my best friend; my brother, my Alpha and anxiety ripped through me, I knew the questions were coming. The questions that I didn't want to answer. But I had no choice.

'I need you to tell me about Amelia; and I need to know why you didn't tell me anything.' He said staring straight into my eyes. Damn you Lori! I cleared my throat and pressed my lips into a thin line, shaking my head slightly.

'What is it that you want to know?' I wasn't stupid enough to just blurt out everything, I wasn't going to be the one to tell him anything that he didn't already know. I blinked a few times and smiled at him. Arlo narrowed his eyes and stared at me. My heart began to race, and I knew that he could hear it. Arlo tilted his head forward and waited for me to answer. Fuck! He knew it all! I sighed and dipped my head forward.

'Arlo... I... I didn't say anything to you because Amelia asked me not to, she wanted to tell you herself; but when she was ready. You know me bro, if I give someone my word, I stick to it. And yes, I know it was stupid of me, maybe if I said something then none of this would have happened... what has Lori told you? How much do you know?'

Arlo;

I stared at my best friend; he was panicking. I could hear his heartbeat picking up the moment I asked him the question. Why did everyone keep secrets from me? Why did they insist I be the last to know everything? I was their Alpha for fuck sake, and she was my girl and yet no one would tell me a fucking thing.

'I know about the blood in Amelia's room; I know that Lori is certain it was Amelia's and no one else's, but what I don't know is what happened, but I know that you do. So, what happened Matt?' I asked, my tone a little harsher than necessary, but I was getting answers, and I was getting them now.

Matt sighed and shook his head; and I could almost hear the battle he was having with himself in his head. This was one of the reasons that he was my best friends. Aside from growing up together as brothers, he was actually the most genuinely nicest person I had ever met. Once you were in his circle of trust then he would fight to the death for you, and when it came to them asking him to keep his mouth shut, he did. But we had never been in this position before. He rarely let anyone in, it has always just been me and my parents. But since she came, everything has begun to change.

'Look… Arlo…'

'Please Matt, just tell me. I am so tired of the secrets. How am I supposed to keep this pack safe if I don't know what is happening in it? I think I am ready to hear and handle whatever it is.' I said, cutting him off mid-sentence. Matt closed his eyes and exhaled defeatedly.

'She tried to kill herself.' He whispered. 'She slit both of her wrists and tried to bleed out. Lori knew because she was the one who found her and believe it or not instead of just leaving Amelia to bleed to death, she came and got me and Piper. When we got to her room, she was in the bathroom on the floor unconscious, but her wrists…they were already healed by the time we got to her, all we could see were scar like marks and a bloodied knife.'

I sat staring at him, stunned by what he had just told me. I most definitely was not ready for the answer he gave me. She had tried to kill herself. When? Why? I needed these questions to be answered and I knew Matt had the answers I was seeking.

'When was this?' I asked, what could have sent her over the edge? Matt raised his dark eyes to meet mine and stared at me in silence for a moment with wide eyes. I knew I wasn't going to like what was about to come out of his mouth. And I knew that it was probably going to break my heart.

'Do you remember the day that you told Amelia you were imprinting on someone and she acted absolutely fine about everything?' Matt asked trying to read my expressions. I nodded slowly and tried to swallow down my pain and anxiety.

'The day she told me she loved me for the first time...and I never said it back. I couldn't say it back to her and yet she accepted it all...' I paused and closed my eyes as the realisation of everything came crashing down on me. 'At least I thought she did.' I whispered as the memories of that morning came flooding back. Why didn't I say it back? Why in that moment could I not bring myself to tell her how much I loved her? Deep down I knew it was because I didn't want to tell her something that I couldn't mean. But I did. I loved her. But Selene had other ideas. I closed my eyes once more and sighed, trying my hardest to quell the voices that were arguing in my head. It was only when Matt spoke again that I remembered that he was there.

'Arlo you couldn't have known, heck I didn't even know anything was wrong. She was laughing and joking with me one minute, then she literally kicked my arse in training and then the next... she...' he couldn't finish his sentence he just put his head in his hands and sighed.

'Is there anything else I need to know? I want to know everything; I am sick of these fucking secrets.' I growled, taking the anger that I had for myself out on my closest friend.

'After we found her, Tanya move her in with them for a few weeks over Christmas.'

'So, that was why she was staying there? I just thought that she was mad at me.' I paused for a moment and took in the look on his face as he nodded hesitantly. I just knew that there was more heartbreak to come.

'She tried to kill herself again.' Matt admitted and I then was speechless. She had tried to do it twice. What? She was going through so much pain and I didn't even know it. Some fucking alpha I was turning out to be. Not only could I not protect the pack from these murders, but I didn't even know when the one person that I was closest to was slipping into a darkness that I feared that she would never recover from. Matt nodded as though he had read my mind.

'Christmas day.' He mumbled. I leant my head back and ran my hand over my chin. I had fucked up royally. That is why she didn't come back that day, and why she lied about where she was when I had questioned her! And that is why she refused to talk to me. The only person Lia was guilty of hurting was herself. A tear rolled down my cheek and I looked straight at Matt.

'Tell me everything. I don't understand, why Christmas day? We had such an incredible afternoon, everyone had dinner, she slept with me and we exchanged gifts and I held her. We were all going to spend the rest of the day together, what went wrong?' I was so confused that it was beginning to fuck with my head.

'Wait… she slept with you? When?' I paused for a moment and realised that I had spoken that one out loud. I opened my mouth to reply Matt spoke again. 'After Piper and I left your office we heard people shouting at her.' He paused and closed his eyes, but he didn't need to tell me the names, I already know. 'Charlie and Jake is what went wrong.' Matt said, anger now in his voice.

'What happened?' I asked sitting forward with my voice low and dangerous. Of course, it was them dickheads. Matt hesitated further. 'Look, I know that Charlie is our Beta, but that still puts me above him. And I am not asking you this as your alpha, I am asking as your brother.' Matt creased his brow and dropped his eyes down to his hands that were folded in his lap.

'They threatened her. Told her to confess to the murders and then Charlie.'

'Charlie did what?' I asked, my voice raising.

'Charlie hit her.' That's all Matt had to say, I was seething, he fucking hit her, that runt, hit my girl. He was supposed to be someone that protected the pack in my absence. Now I knew that he could lay his hands on a woman, I was having seconds thoughts. There was nothing I could do about him being my beta. But if he ever touched Amelia again, I would see to it personally that he is exiled.

'I'm going to kill that bastard.' I roared leaping from my chair and slamming my palms down onto the desk. I balled my fists and stormed to the office door, kicking it open as I went, but Matt jumped in front of me.

'Arlo stop, don't do anything, not yet. Think of the pack, they can't see you like this. They are scared enough as it is.' Matt pleaded. He was right, but Charlie had no idea what was coming for him.

'You know she kicked him in the balls, right?' Matt grinned trying to lighten the mood a bit. 'And she headbutted Jake.' A proud smile crept across my face, that's my girl, never one to back down from anything, even if it did get her into trouble. I paused for a moment, thinking back to her trying to harm herself again.

'How did she try to do it the second time?' I asked, leaning up against the door. I needed to know it all and I needed to talk to Amelia.

'She threw herself off the cliff. You know the one deep in the-'

'I know it.' I said cutting in. It was the place that I had seen her before. Standing there looking out at the twinkling lights of the houses below. 'There is no way that she could have survived that. How is she still...' I stopped before I finished my question. I couldn't bear to speak the words aloud.

'I caught her just in time, and I mean literally caught her. I grabbed her arm just as she jumped. She was so out of it that she didn't even know that we were there.'

'We?' I asked, raising my eyebrow and looking at him sternly. Matt hesitated for a moment, his mouth hanging open. He cleared his throat and looked away from me for a moment.

'I caught her, but, if I had been a second later… she… she…' Matt couldn't finish what he was trying to say but looked straight into my eyes. 'I am sorry I didn't tell; Arlo, she begged us not to, she said she would tell you when she felt mentally ready, but everything just went wrong.' Matt sighed trying not to look at me again. I noticed his swift change of subject, I didn't need him to tell me who the others were, I already knew. They were the only four missing at the meals. But I admired his loyalty. That is what a true defender of the pack was all about. Not even backing down in the face of the alpha. I cleared my throat and looked to my brother.

'Matt, I need to talk to her, please try and get her to talk to me.' I whispered, first I would talk to her and then I was to pay Charlie a little visit.

Matt;

After my conversation with Arlo, I met up with Piper and we had decided that we were going up to Lia's room to hang out, but I had already thought to myself that I was going to persuade her to come down and meet up with everyone; including Arlo. She hadn't been down there or spoken to him since they argued. Piper and I opened the door; with the matching keys that Lia had given us, and were now sitting on her bed, where we had been for the past hour and a half.

'What are you thinking; Matt?' Amelia asked, me, her and Piper were all sat on her bed, both girls were wearing mud masks on their faces and drinking wine, Piper insisted they were good for the skin, but I decided to give that a miss. Although now secretly regretted that decision. I looked up at Amelia and sighed. I hadn't realised that I had been quiet for so long.

'I was just thinking about you and Arlo.' I responded, turning my face to look at her. Amelia's face dropped and she shook her head. 'Don't you think that it's time that you guys had a talk? I know he has hurt you Lia but, he is so different, I think he regrets everything he said, and I really do think maybe you two having a talk before he goes away is the best thing to do.' I continued looking at Piper, hoping she would agree with me. She met my eyes but shrugged, she didn't agree at all.

'I think if he wants to talk then it is him that needs to approach Lia.' She grumbled before pausing. 'Lia has he said anything to you at all?' she turned, looking from me to Amelia who had tucked her knees up close to her chest and was now resting her chin on them, she looked so sad.

'No, he hasn't, but then again even if he did, I probably would have told him to fuck off.' She mumbled resting her cheek against her knees. 'But I agree, we do need to talk. I just don't know if I am ready for that yet. And I wouldn't even know what to say.' I sighed and rubbed her shoulder.

'He wants to talk to you. I spoke to him earlier on and I... I told him everything.' I admitted waiting for her to get angry with me, but she didn't, her eyes widened, and a look of panic crossed her face, and then she just nodded and smiled weakly.

'I am so sorry, to both of you. I should never have put you guys in this situation, and I should never have asked you to keep my secret from Arlo. I am sorry Matt, I know that he is your brother, and I put you in the worst position possible.' Amelia apologised reaching her arms out to me. I was taken back, I thought she would be upset but she wasn't, she seemed more relieved than anything. I cuddled her back and smiled at Piper. 'I love you Matt.' Amelia whispered, as a single tear rolled down her cheek and dripped onto my shoulder.

My entire body froze for a second, no one had ever told me that they loved me before. Was this what loving someone felt like? I lump of emotion formed in my throat and I coughed quietly to try and clear it.

'I love you too, Lia.' I whispered, kissing the top of her head lightly. 'You too bitch bag.' I added, pulling Piper in for a group hug. After a few seconds, I pulled back and looked Lia up and down. 'Right, go and wash that crap off your face and make yourself look pretty. I think you need to go speak with him.' Piper and Lia paused, looked back at each other and then back to me with a mischievous smile on their faces.

'What? Why are you both looking at me like that?' I asked

cautiously, slowly starting to back away from them. In unison they leapt forward, pulling the mud facemask tube from the pocket of their dressing gowns and pinned me to the bed. I struggled against them, but it was no use. I laughed so hard that I couldn't breathe and lost all my fight. They pulled back giggling to one another and ran into the bathroom shutting the door behind them. I walked over to the full-length mirror and took in my reflection. I rolled my eyes just as they opened the door and peered out, giggling.

'Love you.' They sang together before falling into a fit of laughter once more.

Amelia;

Piper, Matt and I all washed the mud face masks off our faces, Matt playfully glaring at us the entire time, before heading back into the bedroom, where they made me sit on the bed while Matt rummaged through my wardrobe and Piper grabbed my makeup from the vanity table. Matt pulled out a red dress that was extremely well fitted. I mean, it looked like a second skin it was so tight. My black heels that would go perfect with it. But was now the right time to be wearing something like that in front of him? I closed my eyes and drew in a deep breath. I needed to just go with it. I trusted the pair of them with my life. So, I nodded.

I was surprised at how good my makeup looked, especially as it all happened so quickly, Seriously, Piper was magic with her makeup skills. And now, I nervously walked into Arlo's office avoiding his big golden eyes, I couldn't look at him. There was a part of me that was still so angry with him, angry and disappointed, but then, there was the other part of me that loved him unconditionally. And now those two parts of myself were raging war in my head. I looked up at Matt, who was leaning against a wall with his arms crossed, he gave me a reassuring smile as I walked over to one of the settee's and sat down. He was determined to get me and Arlo to talk, and I had no idea why.

Maybe it was time? It had been a long 3 weeks after all, but I still wasn't ready for this, it was over between me and Arlo. And us talking now would just confirm it. I looked up at my Alpha and studied his face, he looked uncomfortable and nervous, just as I did. I took in a deep breath and closed my eyes momentarily here we go.

'So, Matt thinks we need to talk and although I don't want to, I think he is right.' I blurted, turning my eyes from Arlo back to Matt then back to Arlo, watching as he stood up from his chair. He nodded in agreement and walked over to the settee opposite, nodding at Matt before he sat down. Matt cleared his throat and pushed off from the wall.

'And, this is where I leave.' Her said playfully, with a cheeky smile on his face. He thought he was cute. I thought he was sneaky! He knew what he was doing the moment he picked this dress out for me. At the thought of my dress I glanced down at myself, suddenly feeling extremely self-conscious and noticed that Arlo's eyes were drawn to how low cut it was. There was that twinkle in his eyes that only meant one thing... I listened as our friend walked to the office door and quietly slipped out of the room carefully closing the door behind him. Arlo cleared his throat and forced his eyes up to meet mine.

'I think he is right too, and I would like to start by apologising.' Arlo said, nervously rubbing his hands together. I was still so furious with him, but with the feelings I had towards my Alpha I knew this conversation wasn't going to be as straightforward as I had planned it to. Damn you Arlo.

'Arlo, I...'

'Can you ever forgive me for what I said and what I did?' He asked, the sincerity in his voice made it hard for me not to.

'I think that maybe I can forgive in time, but I will never ever forget.' And oh boy did the words start flooding the air, I had so much to say. 'I never for one moment thought you would question me, I honestly believed that you knew me well enough to know I would never harm anyone, let alone kill them; and I would like to think, if anyone would be dead at my hands... it would be Charlie. But that is beside the point. I let you in; Arlo, I let my guard down and allowed you to break down the walls that I had put up to protect myself for the past eighteen years of my life, I feel betrayed. I gave you everything I could possibly give you, my heart, my trust, my virginity and now I have nothing left, it's gone…it's broken.' Tears had started forming in my eyes and that familiar pain had built up in my throat. Do not let one tear fall; Amelia, you promised no more tears.

'But you didn't completely let me in; Lia. You didn't tell me how shitty you were feeling, you lied to me when I asked where you were Christmas day, you tried to kill yourself twice for fuck sake and I had no idea… because you wouldn't tell me.' Arlo cried holding back his own tears.

'Don't you dare!' I snapped, jumping to my feet. 'What the fuck would you have done? Come rushing to my rescue like a knight in shining armour? Took away the shit that I have had to deal with in my life. Stop all the pain that has been caused to me by the people that were supposed to love and protect me?' I shouted, glaring at him angrily. He stared up at me with unshed tears glistening in his golden eyes. 'That's what I thought. There is nothing that you could have done. There isn't anything that anyone could have done. So, don't you fucking dare say that I never let you in.' My heart was pounding so hard that I could hear every beat in my ears and my hands were trembling. I no longer felt as though I was going to cry, but I did feel the need to punch someone.

'I am so sorry Lia.' He whispered, hanging his head in shame. He was right I didn't completely let him in, but I was trying to protect him, he had a pack to protect without me bringing my shitty feelings to him. I turned back to face him and lowered myself down onto the sofa once more.

'You have so much on your plate; Arlo, everything that was going on with me was far from important, people are dying for Selene's sake!' I tried my best to argue my point, but he wouldn't have any of it, refusing to accept any excuse I came up with, but I was just trying to protect him and that was the truth.

'Oh, so I could just add you to the body count then? Another one I couldn't save? Another one who should be able to come to their Alpha about anything, but my own… gi-' I paused and growled to myself before continuing. 'But you couldn't.' this time there were no tears, he was frustrated and disappointed. I didn't want to argue with him over this, so for once in my life I backed down to my Alpha.

'You are right, I should never have kept any of it from you and it was not fair of me to make Piper, Matt and Eddie to do the same. I am sorry.' But he knew what I was doing, this would have to be an agree to disagree argument.

'Amelia, no more secrets okay? Promise me.' Arlo looked me in the eyes, he was desperate for me to agree and I would promise him, even if that meant he didn't like what I was going to say.

'Okay, I promise, so here is my next secret.' I whispered. His face dropped, a mixture of anger and sadness filled his beautiful eyes. 'I am leaving... once we find out who is doing these killings and the threat is over, I am going, and I am not coming back.' I said as my heart ached. I wanted to leave, and I would leave, but the thought of walking away from him tore me apart. 'I am leaving for a number of reasons. The first is; I can't watch you fall in love and be happy with someone that isn't me. I think that would destroy the one bit of sanity that I have left. The second; I cannot live with my father and Charlie, after years of their abuse, I need to break free and learn who I truly am. There is a part of me out there in the world, and I feel it calling to me, every second of every day. I need to find out who I am. And the third reason is... ever since I have come here 8 members of your pack have been killed by someone who, I honestly believe wants me dead too.' I thought about what I said, whoever it was wants me dead, he/she was killing people to get to me, so why am I still here? 'I think I should go now and then maybe the threat will follow, that way, you will all be safe and then you can all get on with your lives.'

'No' was all he said, the word coming out more as a growl than a word, a fire burned in his eyes. 'No, you aren't going any-where Amelia, not now, not later. You belong here.'

'Arlo, you need to think of your pack, if I go then the threat goes with me and everyone will be okay.' I snapped angrily. 'Plus,

I do not belong here. I never have, and I never will. I feel it deep in my bones that I am destined to be a deviant! I cannot live my life being controlled by others.'

'And what if it isn't you that they are after and they still kill people? Then what? Please; Lia let me find out who it is, whether you go or not, I need to know who is killing my pack and they need to be put to death.' He pleaded. I knew I wouldn't win this argument and I knew only too well that if I left now, he would track me down and bring me straight back here.

'Fine, I will stay, but only until you catch the killer and then I am gone.' I answered in a matter of fact tone. 'And that is only because I don't want these people thinking that I am the killer. I have already been accused of it once, I will not be accused of it again!'

'Please don't go, I can't live knowing you're out there, not knowing if you are okay, if you are safe, I just can't.' He begged.

'Just as I cannot live here and watch you fall in love with someone else; Arlo. It breaks my heart already, knowing that we are not meant to be together. Seeing another woman touch you, love you, hold you and do everything I want to do with you… I just can't. And even the thought of it makes my skin crawl, it makes me feel physically sick.' I stared at his face… his beautiful face… waiting for him to argue back…Again!

'I understand.' He whispered. I closed my eyes and let out a sigh of relief.

'One more thing.' I mumbled looking up at him nervously. 'I don't want to live in the mansion anymore.' Arlo looked shocked and shook his head,

'Why?' He asked.

'Because I don't trust myself with you and I don't trust you with me. Living in this mansion with you, let alone having a room next to you is not working for us.' I admitted. 'We are over Arlo, there is not any going back from this, you need to move on, and I need to move on.'

My stomach twisted as those words came out of my mouth, I didn't want it to be over, I wanted him so much and I wasn't sure if I could ever truly fall out of love with him.

'Okay.' He grumbled sulkily. 'Where are you going to live?' he asked crossing his arms against his chest.

'In a house, in one of the empty houses and then when everything is done, I will leave.' I said standing up from the settee, waiting for him to say no.

'Fine, you can have a house, but If I give you the house, then you stay.' He said refusing to meet my eyes. If I stayed, I would need someone to live with me; *I didn't want to be alone; the very thought of that filled me with dread.* If only; Arlo could live with me. I couldn't ask Piper because she wouldn't leave her mum and Eddie and Matt had to stay at the Mansion. Then a person's face appeared in my head; Ethan! Maybe I could ask him. I froze for a second and gathered my thoughts; *this is ridiculous. I can't ask him even* though he is my friend; more rumours would just spread around about us and that's the last thing we both needed.

I nodded at Arlo; before leaving his office, try as he might, I was still going to leave. He leapt to his feet and grabbed my wrist, pulling me back around to face him, our faces were inches apart. We stared into one another's eyes and he leant in and kissed me. I gasped in surprise and began to lean into the kiss also, when I suddenly jumped back.

'No, Arlo. I just said that this is over. That is the exact reason that I am moving out of that room. We are dangerous for each other!' I whispered, turning away from him. I slowly started walking towards the door, when I paused and stared at the wood. The memories of Christmas day flooding through my mind. I heard him take a hesitant step towards me and paused. I closed my eyes and clenched my teeth. I was so going to regret this!

I turned back to face him and bit my lip. I stared at him for a few seconds just stood there in silence before grabbing the collar of his shirt and pulling his face down onto mine. Our lips met and I was suddenly filled with that familiar fire that burned through my entire body. The familiar fire of desire. I spun him around and slammed his back against his office door, forcing a low growl to escape his lips. I pulled back and smiled up at him as I pressed my body to his. I could already feel his hardness throbbing against my thigh. I glanced down as he smiled at me and I slowly began kissing down his cheek and along his jaw line.

I touched his pecks and ran my hand over them, feeling him flex them beneath my palms. I gripped his shirt and ripped it open, the buttons scattering around the room, as I slowly lowered my kisses down his neck and run my tongue over one of his nipples. A small groan of pleasure escaped his lips as he tilted his head back against the door and ran his fingers through my hair.

I grazed my teeth against his nipple and felt a tremor rock through him, before lowering myself down further. I dropped onto my knees and slowly ran my hands up his legs and thighs, grasping his hardness through the material. He thrust hip hips forward lightly, moving in time with my hand as small gasps of pleasure escaped him. I reached up and unclasped the button, holding his suit trousers closed, and slowly pulled on the zipper, releasing him from within.

I leant forward and slowly licked from the base, all the way up the shaft causing it to twitch and dance, before placing the tip in my mouth and running my tongue over the end. Arlo reached out and grabbed my head and wrapped his fingers in my hair. I took more of him in my mouth and began to suck. He slowly started moving his hips in time with my motions and I felt him stiffen even more.

'L-Lia… if you don't stop that soon I think I am gonna…' I pulled my head back, so far that I nearly released him from my mouth, but instead of stopping grasped the base with both hands and slowly moved them back and forth, while still moving my head. 'Lia… I-I mean it… I think I'm gonna…' I tightened my grasp around him and sucked harder. His whole body jerked as I felt him release in my mouth. I climbed back to my feet and swallowed, leaning in and kissing him on the lips once more. His mouth fell open as I winked at him. I kissed him once more on the cheek and slowly began to open the door when he grabbed my wrist and pulled me back again.

'What are you doing?' I asked, looking up at him through my eyelashes; his cheeks were flushed, and he panted breathlessly.

'We're not done here.' He growled with a smile crossing his face. He slammed his palm on the door, closing it loudly, before grabbing for the hem of my dress and pulling it up over my waist. I glanced down and noticed that he was still throbbing and bit my lip seductively. He gripped my hips and turned me round so I was facing the door. As he slowly stood up, he kicked at my feet, causing my legs to part as he pushed me forward slowly. He ran his fingers up my thighs and felt the how wet I was already. He chuckled lightly and dropped down to his knees.

He slowly slipped his fingers inside me before following with his tongue, sending rockets of pleasure rippling through my entire body. I bit my lip harder, trying to stop the cries that were begging to escape my lips. He was just far too good at this! He pulled his fingers back and slowly climbed to his feet, leaving my body begging for more. He placed his hands on my hip and thrust himself into me; hard.

This time there was nothing that I could do to stop the groans. The faster he moved the more I felt my legs turning to jelly. He gripped me tightly and slammed into me. All the anger and aggression that we had felt for one another these past few weeks were manifesting… now. And I liked it. He pounded me harder, until I felt the tightening in my stomach. I knew what was coming and I didn't want it to end.

'A-Arlo… I think I am going to…' He pulled out of me and spun me around to face him before sliding himself back inside, holding both of my hands above my head with one of his while the other ran over the hardness of my nipple. I lunged forward and sunk my teeth into his shoulder, biting down so hard that I could taste blood; and this only seemed to spur him on more. I threw my head back as I was overcome with waves of orgasmic pleasure that I had never felt before. Swiftly followed by him pulsing within me. He dropped his head forward and sank his teeth into my neck; matching the bite that I had just given him. I gasped and struggled against his hands, but he was just too strong; and that only aroused me further. He slowly pulled back and stared into my eyes, with a cheeky grin on his face before placing his forehead against mine. I still felt his pulsing within me, and my body cried for more.

'You're mine.' He whispered, as he slowly pulled back and stepped away from me. He noticed the way my eyes travelled up his body, taking in every single one of his features and raised an eyebrow.

'W-What?' I asked innocently. He chuckled and shook his head. Grabbing me and throwing me over his shoulder. I squealed as a laugh erupted out of my chest. 'Arlo! Where are you taking me?' I giggled. His voice was low and gruff and still full of desire.

'Oh, this isn't over. We are going to my bedroom.' He chuckled, carrying me up the stairs as we went. I looked around at all the amused faces and could feel my cheeks burn from the flush that was spreading across them. But all I could do was giggle.

21

Amelia;

I couldn't believe he said yes, he finally gave me the house I wanted, a beautiful 3-bedroom house and one of the biggest here. I know he only let me have my own place because he didn't want me to leave, but I was so thankful to be out of that damn mansion and if I am honest away from him as much as it broke my heart. We had sex again after our chat, the talk was meant to be us clearing the air and for us to both agree we were over, but again we couldn't fight the attraction between us and it ended up being a very wild night and everyone heard us, every single person in that bloody mansion heard…me.

'Where do you want this?' Piper asked holding up a crystal lamp that Marie had given me as a gift. She broke me out of the thoughts that filled my head and thank goodness she did because I had to stop thinking about him.

'I think that can go into my bedroom.' I smiled sitting down on the charcoal velvet crush sofa that came with the house. Piper nodded and went upstairs; I sat back and rubbed my stomach wincing as a cramp came across it. *How could I possibly be still on this period?* 'Typical' I muttered rummaging through my handbag trying to find a pad. Only my period could last longer than a week and get heavier the day I move into my house.

'Are you okay?' Piper asked walking towards me with concerned look on her face. Another pain came across my belly and I winced; it was getting more painful each time I got a cramp.

'Yeah, I am still on my period, it's already been a week, but it's a bit more painful than usual.' I shrugged trying to ignore the pain. 'I just need to keep myself busy.' I smiled standing up, I looked around at the carboard boxes in front of me, there were only six, I didn't have many belongings. Piper read the expression on my face.

'We can go shopping tomorrow and buy loads of new stuff, don't worry.' She smiled cuddling me. My body froze as another cramp hit me and I felt a gush between my legs.

'Oh crap.' I panicked and rushed over to my handbag, grabbing the sanitary pad before looking down at my grey jogging bottoms, the blood had filled the crutch of my trousers.

'Oh my gosh; Amelia. Are you normally that heavy?' Piper asked staring down at me in disbelief.

I shook my head, 'No not normally but I was a week late so maybe that's why I am bleeding so much and maybe that's why it's still going on?'

'Hmmm, I don't think you should be bleeding that bad, I have been a couple of days late before and it's never been like that and it's definitely not lasted any longer than a week' She concluded leading me up the stairs to my bathroom. 'Let me run you a bath.' I took my trousers and knickers off and threw them into my bathroom sink. I wrapped a towel around my waist and leant against the black and white tiled wall, the pains were getting worse and the blood wouldn't let up, I could feel it running down my legs. *This was like no period I had ever had before.* Piper looked back at me and then down at my legs.

'I…I think we need to get you to Benjamin.' She whispered turning the bath taps off.
I shook my head.

'No, it's fine, it's just a heavy period.' I said still leaning against the wall.

'Amelia, when was your last period before this one?'
I thought for a minute. 'Erm, I think it was a couple of weeks before Christmas.' I said trying to work out the dates.

'And today is the 26th of January? Which means your period was…like…6 weeks ago. W… when did this actually start; Lia?' Piper asked as she sat on the edge of the bathtub.

'Last week.' I replied, grimacing as another pain shot through me.

'Come on, we are going to the medical room now, this isn't right.' Piper said running into my bedroom to find me some clean underwear.

Arlo;

I watched as Matt stepped outside to take a phone call before carrying on the meeting, it was so unusual for his phone to ring at this time, everyone knew he would be here, so I assumed it was important. Everyone looked up at him as he walked back into the office, colour had drained from his face and his eyes full of worry.

'Arlo, it's an emergency, I need to talk to you. *Now*' He said, his tone serious before walking back out of my office.

'Excuse me a moment.' I said, rising to my feet and following him from the room, panic beginning to set in. I stepped out into the hall and closed the door softly behind me. 'What is it?' I asked, wondering If another body had been found, the thought made my skin crawl, I didn't know if my pack could take any more of this.

'It's Amelia; something is wrong. Piper got her to the medical room, b… but I think you need to be there… she is asking for you.' He whispered, his gaze travelling to the room across the hall. My heart sank. *Not again; Lia.* Matt's words filled my head again, *did that mean that Amelia had tried killing herself?* I shook my head, please not again. I stood motionless for a moment when Matt reached out, grabbed my hand and dragged me to the infirmary.

We stepped into the medical centre and both looked around, neither of us could see Amelia or Piper, but Doctor Benjamin was waiting for us. He nodded to me sadly and led us to a private room. Amelia was laying on a bed, only a white sheet was covering her bottom half, her white vest top was rolled up to her breasts and she was staring out of the window, with tears rolling down her cheeks. Piper got up from the chair which was situated next to the bed and weakly smiled.

'Matt and I will wait outside.' she said, nodding for me to sit down while taking Matts hand and leading him from the room. I was so confused, what the fuck was going on? I scanned my eyes over her bare arms, searching for any signs that she had self-harmed again, but there was nothing.

I sat on the chair and looked at Amelia, her eyes wouldn't meet mine, every now and then she winced in pain and grabbed hold on the bed sheets, she was deathly pale, and her eyes were red and puffy, she looked exhausted. I looked up at Benjamin who had a bottle of gel in his hands, he squirted it below Amelia's belly button and turned to look at the machine next to him. A black and white image appeared, and I stared trying to work out what he was looking for, Amelia's face was still turned away from the screen, *away from me!* But I could see she was trying to hold back the tears. I so desperately wanted to hold her, but I still did not know what was going on.

Benjamin closed his eyes and sadly turned to us before opening them again, he gently wiped away the gel from Amelia's belly and sat on the end of the bed.

'Amelia, you are suffering a miscarriage.' He mumbled looking down at his hands. 'I am so sorry to you both.'

My skipped a beat, *miscarriage? What did he mean miscarriage?* I looked down at Amelia, whose face was now covered by her hands, she let out a sob before allowing herself to cry out, my heart sank and at that moment broke into a thousand pieces. 5 minutes ago, I had no idea that she was even pregnant and now we had lost our baby. It doesn't matter that we aren't destined to be together; it was still a life that we both created that we have now been robbed of. I sat next to her on the bed and pulled her into my arms, her hands slowly flapped helplessly as everything hit her all at once, she took in a deep breath and let out a cry, a cry of a person who just lost a baby.

'Shhhh' I soothed holding on to her tighter. I should have been here for her these past couple of weeks, but I had to go to Ireland, I had to have these meetings.

Amelia was still bleeding so much that the nurses rushed in to change the large pad that protected the sheets, I stepped outside and looked at Matt and Piper.

'Did you guys know?' I asked leaning against the door, I needed a stiff drink. They both shook their heads.

'Amelia didn't know until we got here, Benjamin did a blood test on her and it showed that she was pregnant, but the levels were low and with how much she is bleeding he warned her she was more than likely going to lose the baby.' Piper said, her voice nearly a whisper as a tear escaped from the corner of her eye.

'How long has she been bleeding for?' I asked feeling guilty, If I hadn't been such a dick, she would have said something and maybe we could have found out sooner and possibly saved our baby.

'She was a week late but then she thought her period had come last week, she hasn't stopped bleeding since and it was getting painful and she started passing clots, Benjamin said that she would have started losing the baby when she first started bleeding. Going by her last period, he said she was around 4-5 weeks.'

Thank Selene for Piper! Matt said nothing, he just looked helplessly to the door of Amelia's hospital room.

'Thank you for getting her here Piper.' I smiled weakly. She shook her head, as her bottom lip trembled.

'Thank Matt, he carried her here, I just called him.' She said rubbing Matt's arm. I turned my stare to my best friend; *my brother;* and noticed the pained look on his face. I had never seen him so heartbroken before.

'I wish you would have called me.' I said feeling deflated.

'I wanted to, but Amelia told me I couldn't, she knew you would be in a meeting and to be fair, she thought it was just a really heavy period. I told her that this wasn't normal, I could just tell that something was off. I had a feeling that it was a miscarriage, and when I told her that she said that she wasn't sure if she could look you in the eye. She thinks she was the one who caused this, and she is convinced you would think the same.' Piper said tears filling her eyes once more.

I was devastated, she didn't want to bother me because of a bloody meeting. Or was the real reason because she felt like I would blame her again? This wasn't her fault, this was mine, I did this to her, all of the stress and accusations put too much stress on her body and now she is sobbing in a hospital bed grieving the child she didn't know she would have let alone lose. Piper burst into tears and looked at Amelia through the glass.

'She said she would have wanted this baby because she would always have a part of you and this baby would have loved her unconditionally.' I felt myself crumbling at Amelia's words, I would have wanted that baby too and as he or she would, I loved his/her mother unconditionally, no matter what she thought.

We all turned around when we heard the door of the entrance to the medical word open. In walked Ethan as white as a sheet looking worried and on edge.

'Is she okay?' He asked looking straight to Piper. 'I-I saw Matt carrying her and all of the blood. What happened?' Piper sighed and looked at Matt hoping he would do the talking. We all stood in silence for a moment, overcome with emotion. 'Guys? Seriously, what is happening? Is she ok?' Ethan asked, his voice desperate.

'She… she has had a miscarriage.' Matt stated looking from me to Ethan. I watched as the Mutts eyes fell to the ground. Why the hell was he so upset? *It wasn't his baby… was it?* Anger filled the pit of my stomach and I balled my hands into fists, turning and glaring at him.

'Did you sleep with her?' I growled my eyes turning dark. I watched as his face turned from shock to anger.

'What? No, I didn't! The only thing we ever did was kiss! Who the fuck are you to even ask me that?! You have made it pretty clear to her that you don't want to be with her; you're always fucking with her head! So, I don't even know why it matters whether we have or not.' I growled at his words; *how dare he, he knows nothing of mine and Amelia's situation, and he had no right to speculate.* Piper and Matt both stared at each other with wide eyes and then shifted uncomfortably.

'Watch your mouth!' I snapped walking towards him balling my fists in anger.

'Why don't you watch yours?' He shouted, taking a step

towards me, his blue eyes shimmering angrily. 'Who the fuck do you think you are?'

'I am your Alpha! Don't you ever speak to me like that again. What is going on between me and Amelia is between us; no one else, do you hear me? I needed to know if the baby she just lost is mine! I care for that girl more than anyone will ever know or understand. If you ever raise your voice to me in anger like that, ever again I will snap your neck.' I pushed him into a nearby wall and stared into his eyes and all he did was look back into mine just as angrily. He pushed forward and made his way forwards, his face turning red, when Matt stepped forward and wrapped his arms around the Mutt.

'Enough! Both of you.' Piper cried putting her hand in between us. 'Amelia is in that room in bits! And here you two are, selfishly arguing over her. Do you think Amelia would stand for this? Allowing you two to tear each other apart?' She looked from me to Ethan; her face a shade of red I had never seen before. *She was right. What the hell was I doing?* I stepped back leant my head against a wall and sighed; I was deflated. *I had never seen this side of Piper before, and in all honesty. It scared the hell out of me! She was not someone to mess with.*

'Ethan; leave. As soon as Amelia can have visitors, I will call you, but right now she is in no condition to deal with this… any of this.' Piper said her face turning back to a normal colour. I watched stunned, as Ethan nodded at Piper and turned away walking back towards the entrance and slamming the door behind him. *Why didn't my Alpha influence work?*

'Arlo; that baby was yours. Amelia has only ever been with you. She may care for Ethan, but she loves you.' Matt said turning his face to mine. He put his arm around me and led me out of the medical centre, leaving Piper to go and sit with Amelia whilst I calmed down.

I walked into the office and noticed everyone staring at me. *How was I supposed to get through this meeting? All I could think about was her; and the baby that we almost had.* I sighed to myself and concealed all the emotions that were whirling around in my head, but just as I sat down, I heard Charlie mumble something.

'What did you just say?' Matt asked, his voice so cold that it brought a shiver across the back of my neck. Charlie sneered and moved a little closer to our delta and chuckled before repeating.

'I said... that we should think ourselves lucky. Who wants another one of her running around?' My world fell into slow motion as the reality of his words sunk in. My body moved as though it was on autopilot. I lunged forward, grabbing Charlie's wrist in one hand and the back of his head in the other, before slamming his face down onto my desk with a sickening crunch. *I know that I should have stopped there but it was too late, the gate to all my anger and hurt had now been opened.* I flung him across the room; *as easily as a rag doll* and leapt from my seat and landed on top of him. I brought my fists down onto his face over and over again.

I could feel hands on me, trying to pull me off of him but all I saw was red. I held my breath as I continued slamming my fists into his face, not even stopping when I felt the warm sticky blood coating my knuckles. I rose to my feet once more, dragging him with me and slammed him against the wall.

'Next time you want to talk shit about someone losing a baby, maybe think that it could be hurting more than one of them!' I snarled, my voice ferocious and full of anger. Charlie flicked his bloodied, swollen eyes in Matt's direction, and I laughed, it was humourless and full of malice, but I couldn't stop myself. I let go of him and watched as he slid down the wall and crumpled on the floor before turning back to face the shocked faces in the room.

'Sweetheart, it's ok.' My mother whispered, placing her hands on both of my shoulders. I shook my head and cleared my throat, hoping to keep my voice strong around the lump of raw emotion that had formed there.

'It was mine.' I roared, the gasps filled the room and I turned my eyes to my mother's shocked expression and noticed as the heartbreak set in. She held her head up high and turned around to the other pack members in the room.

'This meeting is over.' She said, making sure to hold eye contact with everyone in the room.

'But… we still have issues to discuss…' Jake said, helping his son to his feet and holding him up as he swayed back and forth. My mother turned to look at him with a hard stare, a look of anger blazing in her eyes that I had never seen on her before.

'I don't give a fuck. I said that this meeting is over. Now out.' Everyone stood stunned. *My mother never swore, she always stood aside while my father ruled as she should have done. Something had changed within her. And I couldn't help feeling that that was down to Amelia too.* No one moved. 'I said get out!' She screamed, causing everyone to flinch and scramble to the door; *Jake literally carrying Charlie out of the room.* The moment that everyone had left, my mother and father rushed over to me and pulled me into their arms. *It wasn't until that moment that I realised that I was crying.*

Amelia;

'I want to go home.' I whispered as Piper laid on the bed next to me wrapping her arms around mine.

'Benjamin said he wants to keep you in overnight just to keep an eye on the bleeding, if it slows down, then you can come home first thing tomorrow.' She whispered back, stroking my hair, her voice hoarse from all the crying.

'Where is Arlo?' I asked realizing he hadn't come back into the room.

'I think he needs some time to absorb what has happened.' I nodded at her words; I felt so guilty. 'He is coming back though, he said he wants to stay with you tonight.' She whispered rubbing my hand with her soft, warm fingers.

'Thank you so much for being here with me. I love you.' I whispered around a yawn, I suddenly felt exhausted and I couldn't fight the heaviness of my eyes any longer, the pain medication was clearly taking effect. I stopped trying to fight it and gave in to the darkness and slept.

Piper;

`

I waited for her to fall asleep before leaving, I need to go for a walk to clear my head. Watching her go through that was one of the hardest things to see, I now understood why she attempted to take her own life, there was no let up for that girl. At the tender age of 18 she had been through hell, abusive father, a brother that wanted her dead and accused her of murder. She had been through the ringer and it seemed Selene hadn't finished throwing shit her way. I finally got it and it tore me apart. Amelia leaving was for the best; for her. I don't want her to go, Matt doesn't want her to go and neither does Eddie but watching the man you love imprint with someone else, I couldn't do it, in fact I won't do it. Maybe I could go with her? Me, Amelia and Pretty girl on our own adventure, starting a new life as deviant's. I toyed with that thought, but I had already made up my mind, I was going to go too.

I hurried from the room, trying my hardest to hold back the tears. Amelia was my best friend, and she was hurting more than anything I had ever known. I just wished there was something more that I could have done for her. My chest constricted as I felt the panic crawling up my spine. I stepped out into the cold January air and slowly walked over the gravel path, Eddie would be so mad at me for this, but I needed some time to myself too. I dropped into a crouch and pulled my palms up to my face, holding them there as I tried to compose myself. My cheeks flushed as heat washed over my skin. I gulped down a shaky breath and climbed back to my feet and turned to look up at the crescent moon sitting prominently in the sky above me. '*Why? Why would you let this happen? All she has ever done is try her best to make this pack a better place, and this is how you reward her?*' I screamed in my head. *Selene was supposed to protect us, watch over us. And look. So much death surrounding this pack. How was that fair?* I pulled myself together climbed back up to my feet. I needed to see Pretty Girl; *she must have been going out of her mind. I knew how close the two of them were, and she always seemed to know when something was wrong with Amelia.*

I checked in on Pretty Girl who was standing in a corner of the stables, she looked sad almost like she knew what was happening; *just as I thought she would.*

'She will get better soon girl.' I smiled unlocking the stable door. Pretty girl nodded her head up and down and started moving her legs in excitement. 'You know she has her own house now, which means she will probably be with you every day. She misses you; she calls you her guardian angel. And I can believe that you are.' I said filling her bowl with some oats and a couple of apples. I looked at the Unicorn in front of me, she understood everything I said, what an incredible creature. 'Hey Pretty girl, do you reckon you could find me one of your Unicorn friends?' I joked stroking her silver mane. 'I have a secret, not even Lia knows yet, but I am coming with you guys when you leave.' I grinned walking towards the stable doors.

The sound of people coming towards me snapped me from my angry thoughts and had me recoiling into the shadows. As a Mutt that was one thing that I had mastered; keeping hidden from sight. I pressed myself as flat against the wall as I could and held my breath, focusing on my racing heart and getting it under control. I strained my eyes out into the distance and noticed the long blonde hair shimmering in the moonlight. *Lori!* Her and the twins were looking suspicious as hell, all dressed from head to toe in black; *and I am pretty sure that Lori was wearing leather?*

'I mean, do you really think that it could be her? The one that has been killing everyone?' Harper asked, leaning in closer to Lori and lowering her voice. Lori rolled her eyes and shook her head.

'How many times does she have to tell you? Of course, it isn't! Think about it. Where are we going now?' Adela snapped back at her sister. Harper scowled and turned her face back to the path in front of them and continued in silence. *Where the hell were the three of them going at this time of night? And what did that mean? Think about where they are going now? Something was seriously wrong here.* I slowly inched forward and ducked down, making sure that I kept to the shadows.

'Why are we doing this again?' Adela asked, chewing her thumb nail nervously. Lori turned to her preparing to reply when she tilted her head to the side and paused. She narrowed her eyes, before shaking her head and continuing onwards.

'Look, I have already told you both, if you are too much of a pussy to come with me, then stay here! I am not forcing you to come with me!' Lori snapped, keeping her voice low. Adela and Harper paused for a second to glance at one another, their eyes wide and their mouths twisted in uncertainty. Adela shook her head and Harper rolled her eyes, before the twins spun back to face their "leader" and ran silently to catch up with her.

'You're right.' They both said in unison.

'This is for the good of the pack! It has to be done!' Lori said, cryptically. I narrowed my eyes as a million thoughts whirled around in my head. *Could she be the one that has been killing the Mutts? She would have the means, and the desire to do so. Lori always made it clear about how much she despised us.* I grit my teeth and slowly wandered forward, keeping myself as silent as possible.

I watched as they snuck out the gate and made their way towards the darkness of the forest. Lori paused and glanced over her shoulder one last time, her eyes scanning around the mansion grounds, seemingly checking that they were unnoticed. Her stare washed over the shadowed area that I was crouched in but moved on quickly. *She hadn't noticed me!* She pulled her long blonde hair up into a ponytail and flipped it over her shoulder before striding out into the darkness, with the twins hesitantly following behind her. I waited for a few more seconds, straining my hearing and making sure that they were far enough out of sight for me to make my break for it.

I pressed myself up against the wall and peered around the corner, scanning the darkness for any sign of the ghastly trio, but they were long gone. I sighed in relief and jogged out through the huge gates and wandered out into the darkness of the forest; paying attention to keep a track on my surroundings in case I ran into the three Elites once more; this walk started off as a need to clear my head, but now I had a mission. I needed to find out if it really was these three that were destroying our pack!

I knew that it wasn't safe out here, especially for a Mutt, but I needed to clear my head. So much had happened in such a short amount of time that I felt as though I was suffocating in all the misery. Just being out here was already seeming to take a little of the pressure off and my breathing seemed to ease a little. It was strange being out here at this time of night; *strange and stupid!* I was officially off of our territory, I knew it was stupid of me to do, especially with what was going on, but I swore to myself I wouldn't go too far.

I dropped down onto the grass, laid back and folded my arms behind my head. I stared up at the moon just allowing every-thing to run through my head. There was so much to try and process that it was hard to keep up and I felt that all the time I kept my eyes on the moon, that Selene would hear the shit that we had going on. I sighed softly and closed my eyes. It was so peaceful out here in these woods, the sounds of the wildlife scuttling about their business, the little squeaks and chirps of the life surrounding me. It was blissful! I drew in a deep breath and allowed myself to begin to relax when the sound of a twigs cracking underfoot had me snap-ping out of my daydreams.

I sat upright and looked around, straining my eyes into the darkness, trying my hardest see through the velvety blackness; although I had been listening to the wildlife a moment ago, these footsteps were louder, it was obvious that whoever, or whatever was coming towards me, was big!

The rustling of leaves had me spinning around to look in the other direction, whoever it was out there, there was more than one of them. I slowly climbed to my feet, cautiously turning around in a circle, trying my hardest to locate the source of the noise. Then a smell unlike anything I had ever smelt before washed over the clearing. It was so strong that it took my breath away. It was a mix-ture of mould, singed hair, wet dog and… rotting flesh! I raised my hand to cover my nose and mouth, attempting to shield my senses from the horrendous odour as it seemed to take over all my senses.

The sound of someone running, had me spinning around, preparing myself to fight, when something blew into my face, entering my eyes and leaving a bitter taste dancing across my tongue. A few seconds passed as I blinked, trying to get the sand-like grit from my eyes, when a pain unlike anything I had ever seen before swirled through me. My face felt as though it was on fire and every breath that I took in seemed to be getting more strained. *Shit! This is it. The killer has got me!* I grabbed at my throat with both hands, trying my hardest to gulp down oxygen. My eyes stung as though someone was jabbing needles in them and my vision was becoming darker. I dropped down onto my knees, fighting with everything I had in me to stay conscious. There was no way that I was going to give up without a fight. *But with each passing second it looked as though I had no choice.*

A shadow blacker than anything I had ever seen before flew past me, causing me to flinch. I strained my eyes, fighting my way through the pain to get a better look at my attacker; but it was useless. Whatever they had thrown at me was slowly causing my entire body to shut down. I felt as my limbs all started to numb, and I fell, landing on my back and staring up at the sky above me. The stars the only thing that I could make out through the increasing darkness.

A shadow caught my eye as it hovered over me. It must have been at least eight-foot-tall, and there were no distinctive features. It was almost as if this thing was a void in time. Something that existed but didn't. My eyes flickered from side to side as I tried my hardest to understand what it was that was happening. And that was when I noticed them. Eyes that were glowing white hot. Nothing but two spheres of white, slowly inching closer to my face. *This was it. I was a goner.*

Lori;

I stepped out through the gates of the mansion grounds and paused, glancing over my shoulder one last time, scanning our surroundings ensuring that we were alone. *If anyone caught us right now then we would be in so much trouble, but sometimes there were risks that you just had to take. And this was one of them.*

'You're right.' The twins mumbled as they ran to catch up with me. *Of course, I was right.* As much as it pained me to say, Adela and Harper didn't have a braincell between them. They were so used to following people around that they gave up on trying to think for themselves years ago.

'This is for the good of the pack! It has to be done!' I answered, shaking my head lightly. *I had been over this with them both countless times, and yet they still questioned me! When were they going to learn?* The three of us snuck out of the gate and I paused once more, scanning my eyes over the mansion grounds once more, making sure that we had not been seen. Lingering on the spot where that Mutt Piper was hiding; *I mean, did she really think that I hadn't noticed her? I could scent her the moment she pressed herself into the shadows when she first heard us.* I pulled my hair into a ponytail and flicked it over my shoulder. I wandered out further through the gates and ushered the twins along with me. *We needed to lose Piper. She couldn't see what we were up to.* I motioned for the two other girls to hide behind the trees and watched from the shadows as Piper hesitantly stepped through the gate and scanned her surroundings. I waited for her to go back inside. *But she didn't.* She glanced left and right once more before taking off and disappearing into the woods. I tightened my pony-tail; once more and rolled my neck on my shoulders. This meant business, and there was no way that I was coming back here tonight until I had done what needed doing. *Tonight, was going to be a success. I just knew it!*

I sniffed the air every now and again, hoping to catch her scent. But it was useless. Wherever she had gone, she didn't want to be found.

'Are you sure that this is the right way?' Adela asked, her voice a hushed whisper. I rolled my eyes and glanced over my shoulder to glare at them both. *How could they be so stupid? I blamed their parents. What Elite would raise two daughters to end up like… well, like these two.*

'Of course, why wouldn't it be this way?' Harper snapped back, her eyes wide and full of fear. I whirled around on the spot and crossed my arms over my chest, continuing to glare at the pair of them.

'What is wrong with you two? Do you not understand how important this is?' I growled. The two girls squeaked and straightened up, and I knew that my eyes were glowing from my anger.

'Sorry Lori. It's just-' I held my hand up to cut them off while shushing them. 'No, please, I just want to apologise for-' I leapt forward and clasped my hand over both of their mouths and scanned the line of the trees surrounding us. I sniffed the ait once more. *Gotcha!* I pushed up onto my tip toes and looked through to a clearing. *There was Piper, laid on the grass with her hands folded behind her head.* I slowly uncovered the twin's mouths and slowly made my way towards the unsuspecting mutt. *How stupid could a girl be? Just lying there like that, exposed in the open. And a perfect distance from the mansion that no one would hear her scream!* I inched closer to her, trying my hardest to keep as quiet as possible, when a stench unlike anything I had ever smelt washed over me. I clasped my palm over my mouth and tried my hardest not to throw up. *But the scent was relentless.*

From the corner of my eyes I could make out shadows that appeared to be make a black smoke. The edges of their form were wispy, and it was hard telling where they ended and the darkness surrounding them began. The only thing about them that stood out where the glowing white eyes; that reminded me of animal eyes caught in a night vision camera. Whatever these things were there were loads of them, and they all seemed to be focusing in on Piper.

I turned my attention back to her and noticed that she was now standing, looking around herself with fear in her eyes, when a blast of purple shimmering powder blew into her face. *Wolfsbane!* She flinched for a moment and blinked rapidly. She opened her mouth and gasped, stumble slightly backwards, clutching at her neck as though she were struggling to breathe.

I watched in horrified silence as she fell to the floor and burn-like blisters began to form over her bare skin. The shadow creatures moved forward; *at speeds that were fast, even for us werewolves,* and hovered around her for a moment. I wasn't sure what was about to happen, but all I knew was that it couldn't be good. The sound of ragged breathing came from behind us and I whirled around just in time to see one of the eight-foot shadow creatures' swipe at the twins. Both girls dropped to the dirt and scrambled as fast as they could, running back in the direction of the mansion. *I was not going to let fear control me.* I glanced down at the ground around me and grabbed for a large branch that held some weight and swung it in the direction of the creature's face. Its glowing eyes blinked rapidly before it disappeared in a swirl of mist to reappear on the other side. *What the fuck were these things?*

It swiped at me once more, but I swung the It swiped at me once more, but I swung the branch at it once more, throwing it off balance. Its limbs were far too long, which I noticed as it dropped down into a crouch and threw its head back and howled towards the sky. The howl was unlike anything I had ever heard. It sounded as though it were able to shatter glass.

I swung my foot forward, catching one of its long thing gangly legs and throwing it off balance as it snarled at me and ran away, disappearing into the darkness. I turned back to face Piper and she was surrounded. The creatures were slowly lowering themselves down towards her. I had seen the pictures of the other bodies. I knew that this was only going to end one way.

I leapt out into the clearing, swinging the branch back and forth, feeling it hit nothing but air as I did. The other creatures leapt back and mimicked the actions of the other, throwing their head back and squealing. I threw the log towards them before dropping to the ground and scooping up Piper into my arms and running as fast as I could.

I didn't stop for a second, I pushed on until I was racing through the gates of the mansion grounds. It was late, and there was no one else around. I leapt up the steps to the main entrance and whirled around to the right, heading towards Benjamin's quarters. I carefully lowered Piper to the ground before slamming my palm against the hard wood five times. I waited for a moment until I heard noise coming from the room on the other side of the door when I turned and ran, hiding around the corner and waiting until Piper was taking inside by our best medic.

The moment his door closed I exhaled in relief, glad that she was finally getting the treatment that she needed. I just hoped that it wasn't too late.

Arlo;

I sat in my office chair thinking about everything that had happened, Eddie and Matt were both sitting on one of the sofa's talking about Amelia. They had waited for my parents to leave and come back to me. I couldn't express how much I loved these two guys. No one knew what to say to me, I knew most of them were disgusted that I had been sleeping with Amelia, but it angered me so much. They acted like she wasn't part of this pack and that I had betrayed them, but she was part of this pack and she was an Elite. The more I thought about it, the more it angered me. Her own father didn't go to check on her to make sure she was okay, his daughter nearly haemorrhaged to death and he didn't care. I clenched my teeth and balled my hands into fists as I tried to get my anger under control.

We were all startled when we heard rapid banging out in the hall, Matt and I jumped up and looked at each other.

'What the hell was that?' I snapped, running towards my office door. Matt and Eddie followed me out into the hall. Benjamin had just opened the medical centres door and stared down at the floor, a purple coloured girl with blisters forming over her body was having a fit, I watched in shocked horror as her body convulsed violently where she lay, thick foam bubbling from her mouth and pooling on the ground beside her. I noticed the shocking auburn coloured hair. The pretty features that were distorted from the burns.

'Piper.' Eddie cried running over to her and dropping down to her side. I dashed forward, closing my hands-on Eddie's shoulders, feeling as he tried his hardest to fight against me.

'Don't touch her.' I said, my voice cold and hard. He turned tear filled eyes to stare at me before looking back down to her.

'Wolfsbane.' Matt growled angrily, appearing beside us.

Amelia;

A woman's voice singing the tune to the lullaby that haunted my dreams filled my head. I thought that I was free from this, but it was now clear that I wasn't. I opened my eyes, Piper was no longer in the bed with me and I had since been hooked up to an IV, I must have slept through it all. I looked up at the clock, it was 3:47 am, the last time I checked the time it was nearly 6pm, I had slept for nearly 12 hours. I lifted my hand and studied the canula, deep red blood was being pumped into me. I must have lost more blood then I thought and then I realised another canula was in my other hand, this time a clear liquid was entering my blood stream. 'It's morphine.' I looked up, sitting on the chair next to my bed was Arlo and he looked like he hadn't slept a wink. I sat up and looked at him, I didn't know what to say except.

'I am so sorry.' Arlo looked confused.

'What are you sorry for? This wasn't your fault; Lia, none of it was, if anyone is to blame, it was me.' He put his soft had out to mine and I allowed our index fingers to hook around each other, trying to hold his hand would have been too difficult.

'You're not to blame.' I whispered feeling a lump build in my throat, he looked broken, but I honestly thought he wouldn't care. 'Hold me?' I never thought I would ask him to do that again, but I needed him, *and I think that he needed me too.* Arlo stood up and walked around the bed, gently laying on it as though he was scared, I would break. I snuggled into his chest and took in his scent, it soothed and consoled me, why did I have to feel the safest when I was in his arms.

'You know; Lia, despite everything I would have been so happy to have this baby... I am so sorry for how everything turned out; I will never ever hurt you again.' I looked up at his face, stubble had formed, and his curls were pulled up into a messy ponytail, he looked drained.

'You will have babies one day; And your soul mate will be an incredible mummy, I can feel it.' I replied rubbing my fingers on his forming beard. It suited him.

'But I don't want anyone else, I want you, I want you to give birth to my children.' He mumbled looking down at me. And I wanted that too, but I had to be strong and this time I had to mean it and not give in to my desires.

'I know, but Selene has other things planned for us. I would do anything to be with you, I want marriage and I want loads of children, I want to be your wife and I want to grow old with you, but I can't and I can't stay and watch you have that with someone else, once this is all over, I am leaving and I won't ever be coming back, we can't do this anymore, me and you. It's not fair to either of us, we are just torturing each other.'

Arlo met my eyes, I knew he understood, it just pained him as much as it did me. He smiled, trying to change the subject slightly. 'How many kids do you want?'
I grinned at him 'About 6.' He started chuckling.

'Woah; Lia, that's a lot of babies! Are you sure you really want that many?'

'Yeah, I am sure. I have always wanted a big family and 3 months ago I thought I would never have the freedom to even make friends, so I am going to make the most of it. Six or seven will suit me fine.' He started laughing.

'7?! This number is getting higher!' It was so nice to hear him laugh and it made me smile.

'I think I will give birth to one first and see how painful that is.' I reasoned jokingly.

'You will handle labour like a champ, you are a strong girl and you have balls of steel and by the way, I don't believe you when you say seven babies, I think you will have about 8.'

'How many do you think you will have?' I asked fighting the urge to touch him.

'With you 10, with someone else… probably none.' He said looking down at my hand, I knew he was fighting it too. This was going to be so hard. After today it was over, no more touching, no more kisses, no more sex, the whole lot would be done. *Who was I trying to convince? Selene or me?*

'Ahh I don't believe that, you have to have one at least, you need to make this pack a new Alpha.' I smiled imagining him running around with a toddler, it was a beautiful image. Thinking of him having a child with someone else made me feel sick but I would do anything to try and make him feel better. Arlo turned his head to me a more serious expression on his face.

'I am so sorry you are going through this, if I could take it away... I would.' He whispered before kissing my forehead.

'Go and get some sleep; Arlo, you look shattered' He ran his hand through his hair and nodded in agreement.

Arlo;

I walked into Pipers hospital room and listened to the low rhythmic beating of her heart monitor. I gulped down a deep breath and tried to shift the lump that was forming in my throat and slowly made my way over to the chair that was situated beside her bed, and hesitantly reached out and placed my hand over hers. It was ice cold and so pale that it was almost see through; and then there were the burns. Dark red and lumpy legions dotted over her bare skin. I couldn't believe that it was only a few hours ago that she was found outside the medical ward on the brink of death.

I glanced over to Benjamin who was frantically reading over her charts and searching his cupboards for anything that could make this easier on her, before hurrying back over to us and shifting the pillows behind Pipers head in attempt to make her more comfortable. There wasn't an antidote to Wolfsbane poisoning, and it was only a matter of time before Piper would pass away. Benjamin assured Tanya that he would heavily sedate her daughter; so, she didn't feel anything.

I sadly watched as Tanya sat beside her daughter and took hold of her limp hand; the tears of a mother losing her child was something I never wanted to see again. Eddie was sitting on the end of the bed rubbing Piper's legs begging her to somehow pull through and it took me back to Amelia. I honestly did not know what I would do if I lost her.

22

Matt;

I had been sat here for hours, staring at my friend. How could someone do this to someone like her? She was one of the sweetest girls that I had ever met, and when she loved, she loved hard. Who, or what, would have done this to her? I dropped my head back onto the backrest of the chair and closed my eyes. It was late, and I was exhausted. But I needed to be here for her especially as she was going to pass away at any given moment. I looked over at Arlo who nodded for me to go and get Amelia. *I was dreading this.* Before I left the room, I listened to the steady beeping of the heart monitor when suddenly it grew faster. A terrible chattering sound filled my ears and I threw my head forward just in time to see Piper's body begin to convulse. The beeping increased further as she violently shook.

I let go of the door handle and rushed over to her bedside just as an army of nurses hurried in, Arlo jumped up and stared down at the shaking body of Piper, Eddie and Tanya were both crying and were ushered to stand away from the dying girl.

'P-Piper?' Me and Arlo both spun around on the spot and took in the ghostly pale sight of Amelia, tears falling from her face.

Amelia;

I opened my eyes and stared up at the blinding lights above me. I knew that I was still in the medical ward, but something was wrong. There was no one around and I could hear a strange screeching from down the hall. I climbed from the bed and slowly wandered over to the door of my room, trailing the IV's along with me. *What the hell is happening?* I watched in silence as a group of nurses made their way down to another of the rooms and followed them as quietly as I could. I entered another of the rooms and my eyes instantly landed on the convulsing girl on the table.

'P-Piper?' I stammered, my eyes wide and full of tears. Matt and Arlo both turned around; their eyes landed on me. I turned my horrified stare back over to my best friend and noticed the blood that seemed to be trickling from her eyes, nose and ears. *She was dying.*

I went to say something to them, but I couldn't, I just turned back to Piper and watched as the heart monitor flatlined and hurried over to the side of the bed.

'Arlo please get everyone out of here; just Tanya can stay.' Benjamin shouted rushing over to my best friend who was about to die. Arlo and Matt took hold of Eddie who was uncontrollably screaming and escorted him from the room. Nurses grabbed me, and tried their hardest to pull me away, but there was no way that I am leaving my best friend here alone to die. A sharp pain shot through the back of my hand as my cannula was ripped from me, causing me to throw my head back and scream. The nurses and Benjamin were thrown backwards, tumbling to the ground in horror. Blood sprayed from my hand, coating Piper's bare, blistered skin.

We all fell into silence as the burn blistered seemed to shrink and vanish under the touch of my blood. *What the fuck? Am I doing that?* I glanced down at the back of my hand and noticed that the blood had stopped, and the wound had healed almost instantly. I glanced around the room and grabbed a scalpel, bringing it down on my palm and watching as blood swelled from the open wound. I cupped my hand for a moment, allowing the blood to gather there before throwing it over piper. The sound of sizzling echoed around the room as the blistered faded away to nothing. That was when an idea hit me.

I pressed my palm to her mouth and watched as the blood trickled in. Her convulsing body fell still almost instantly, and the erratic beeping of the machine fell back into a steady rhythm. Tanya stood motionless, her mouth hanging open in awe.

'Amelia... how did you... how did you do that?' She stammered. I pulled my hand away from Pipers mouth and watched as the deep cut closed in front of my eyes.

'I-I don't know.' I mumbled quietly, just as shocked as everyone else. I felt the room around me sway and knew that I was about to pass out. My legs gave out under me and I felt Benjamin's strong arms wrap around me.

Arlo;

We stood in the main hall trying to call Jake; no matter what sort of father he was to Amelia; he was a better one to his sons. Finally, I had contacted him; just as Matt was trying to comfort Eddie. As I hung up the phone; the medical ward fell in silence; *was she dead?* The only sound we could hear was Eddie curled in a ball in front of us sobbing. I froze as I realised Amelia was still in the room with Tanya and Piper, everything was in such chaos that we literally just removed Eddie from the ward as his cries got louder and he begged Piper to wake up. 'I need to get Amelia.' I said to Matt before we all heard a scream. *Her scream.* I threw open the double doors and ran down the corridor, Matt and Eddie were not far behind me both eager to get back into the ward. I entered the room and came face to face with Piper, sitting on the edge of the bed and giggling lightly. *What the fuck is happening?*

'Piper?' I asked, frowning at the sight before me. At the sound of my voice everyone turned to look at me. Amelia was sitting there on Pipers bed, smiling over to her best friend. 'What the hell is going on here?' I asked, taking another step into the room.

Eddie barged past me, pulling Piper from the bed and pulling her into his arms. He held her at arm's length for a second before grabbing the back of her head and pulling her face up to his and kissed her with such passion that it took my breath away. I had never seen anyone act on love this way and it was beautiful. I glanced down at Amelia and noticed the smile that tugged at her lips. Her brother and her best friend, a dangerous combination, but neither of them would ever find someone as loyal as each other.

'What the fuck is this?' Came an angry voice from the doorway behind us. I turned just in time to see Charlie, glaring at them both kissing. Eddie broke from the kiss and turned to look at his brother. The look of rage on Charlie's face said it all. 'How could you taint yourself by being with this… this… Mutt!' he snapped. At the mention of the word Mutt, Eddie stiffened and narrowed his eyes, glaring at his brother.

'Do not speak about her that way.' Eddie said, his voice low and deadly. Charlie stepped closer to his brother and squared up to him.

'Why not? It's the truth!' Charlie said, his voice low and serious. Piper jumped down from the bed and shuffled over to the brothers.

'Please. It's not worth fighting.' She whispered, placing a hand on each of the boy's arms. Charlie growled and swung his elbow upwards away from her and hitting her in the face. Piper toppled backwards, with Amelia jumping from the bed and catching her friend before she had a chance to hit the ground. In the blink of an eye, Eddie had gone from the bed to standing in front of his brother; pinning him up against the wall, baring his teeth and growling at him. I ran forward, about to pull the brothers apart, at the same time as Jake. We collided with a crash, knocking each other backwards, just in time to see Eddie's fist slam into Charlie's face repeatedly. There was another sickening crunch as Charlie's nose broke under the force; even though he had not healed from the beating he received from me the day before. Charlie moved his head to the side, causing Eddie to punch the wall with such force that it cracked under his touch.

Charlie swung his arm up and caught Eddie off guard, knocking him backwards, before punching him repeatedly in the face. I leapt forward and jumped between them both.

'Enough!' I roared, throwing them apart, I used the full force of my alpha powers and told them not to go near one another. They both stood glaring at each other, but neither of them moved. I turned my stare back to Jake and looked him up and down. 'Get him out of here!' I ordered, jerking my chin in Charlie's direction before turning back to Eddie.

'You're dead to me!' Eddie snarled, as Jake placed his hand

on Charlie' shoulder and dragged him from the room.

'Ahem.' A voice coughed to get every one's attention and it worked, we all looked over at Benjamin who was standing glaring at Eddie with his hands on his hips. He looked over at Piper, his expression softening. 'Piper, I need to take a quick blood test and then you may be discharged, but any problems at all today, then please do not hesitate to call me and come back in, although it's not a full moon tonight I would say when it is; you can shift, but please make sure someone is with you.' Benjamin smiled. Eddie took hold of Pipers hand and kissed it.

'I am not leaving her side.'

Then Benjamin turned to Amelia, his smile turned into a big grin and the mischievous look in his eyes made the hairs on my back stand up. 'Amelia; you too may be discharged, but I must say your bodies way of healing itself…and others fascinates me. You are an extraordinary werewolf; I was wondering if maybe I could take a blood test from you as well as Piper? It would be incredible if we could have our very own wolfsbane cure here…in you.'

'No.' I growled angry that our own doctor would suggest putting Amelia under some tests like she was a freak of nature. She would not be used for others, no fucking way. I watched in horror as she put her hand up to me and smiled at Benjamin.

'One sample and that is all I will allow, if you can find out why I am so abnormal and different from other's then that would be great.' She smiled sitting on the bed next to Piper. I sighed and rolled my eyes; she will always do what she wants and although she frustrated me, I also admired her.

Piper;

I snuggled under the covers on my bed and peaked over the duvet, my mum and Eddie both were sat on the end looking at me in amazement. 'I just can't believe how much better you are already!' Eddie said still getting over the shock of what had happened in the medical ward. 'One minute your flatlining and then the next your sitting up laughing like nothing happened, I am amazed.' I nodded in agreement and looked over to my mother.

'Your extremely lucky to be alive, we are all so lucky you are still here, thank Selene for Amelia and her...blood...' she said her voice turning into a whisper.

'She really is a mystery.' I said agreeing. *What was it about her? Why was she so different?* She couldn't shift, her blood had healing properties and a Unicorn was her pet, we may not have known why she was so special but the best thing about Amelia, is that she is my best friend, and none of us cared that she was different.

'Piper what happened out there? What did you see?' Eddie asked a look of concern spreading across his face. I shook my head and looked towards my window before answering.

'I went for a walk to clear my head and found a spot in the woods that I could just sit at and process everything that had happened. And whilst I was laying down just looking up at the stars, I heard a rustling and then a stench like no other filled my nose. I stood up and covered my nose and mouth to try and block out the smell before hearing someone running towards me, I turned around to see who it was but something was blown in my face... wolfsbane and to be honest although I could make out what was happening around me I couldn't process it and the next thing I remember is being in the hospital with you and Amelia.' I said turning to my mum.

'I am in total shock that this is still happening. Who could it be that is doing this? I just don't understand and why would they want to attack you? You haven't done anything to anyone.' She turned her face towards me and smiled. 'I am so happy you are okay, I thought I had lost you.' A tear rolled down her cheek and I sighed.

'Can we talk about something other than this?' I asked tiring of the whole situation.

'I need to ring Arlo.' Eddie said his face paling, my mum smiled at me lightly and then put her hand put to Eddie.

'We need to talk about you two first.' She said stopping him in his tracks. Eddie and I looked at each other and then back at my mother. 'I have absolutely no problem with you two being together.' She turned to Eddie. 'You make my daughter so happy and it is clear to see how in love with each other you are, but you both need to remember…she is Mutt and you are an Elite, this *will* cause many problems for you both, as you both already know. But Charlie and Jake are just the start of the things you are both yet to face. Remember, Elites cannot imprint with Mutts.' She cautioned, now looking over to me. I nodded my head and bit back the tears, she was right, but I felt like Eddie was the one I was imprinting with, or was that just me loving him so much

'Um, Mrs. Quinn, firstly, please don't use that term in front of me, Piper is not, and never will be a Mutt, at least not to me. I am willing to fight tooth and nail for what me and Piper have, I love her and would die for her, today I thought I lost my girl… my soulmate. You see things have been different lately, I knew I loved Piper; and I didn't think I could love her any more than I already did, and yet every day the love and bond that we share grows stronger. These past couple of months have been a whirlwind of emotions and I am pretty sure Piper feels it too? I know this is going to sound… odd to you. But when Piper was attacked, I could have sworn that I felt her pain… her need for help and-.' The sound of my mother gasping stopped Eddie midsentence. 'M-Mrs. Quinn, is everything ok?' Eddie asked taking a hesitant step closer to her.

'T-This can't be…' My mother whispered, so softly that we almost never heard it.

'Mum? What? What is it?' I asked, sitting up a little straighter in my bed and reaching out to her. She turned away from us for a moment and started pacing back and forth in front of the bed.

'By the sounds of this, the both of you are… are…' She closed her eyes and pinched the bridge of her nose as if deep in thought, before sighing. 'It sounds as if the pair of you are imprinting.' We all fell into silence for a moment as Eddie and I turned our stares to one another.

'But… that's impossible. Elites and Mutts aren't able to imprint. It keeps the balance in pack life.' I whispered, closing my eyes as I fought back tears. Eddie turned away from my mother and slowly walked over to the bed, refusing to take his eyes from me. 'It's not possible! Tell her Eddie!' I continued. He reached out and took my hand.

'I…I think…we are imprinting' Eddie said looking over to my mother who was still nodded with unshed tears shimmering in her eyes. *So much was not making sense to me, and there were still so many questions that I needed the answers to.* I closed my eyes and focused on the warm sensation that was slowly spreading from under where Eddie's skin touched mine. *Was this what it felt like when you imprinted?* Oh boy, I was so relieved he was feeling this too, but we couldn't imprint, that was impossible!

'I know this feeling only too well guys, I loved a man before I imprinted with your father; Piper, but you cannot be imprinting… that's not… possible.' My mum sighed sadly looking down at the floor, she looked so sad for us and the tears fell from her eyes and rolled down her cheeks.

'Mum, we didn't think that blood could have healing properties and yet here we are, Amelia's blood can heal, after today, I am so sure that anything is possible.' I said trying to argue mine and Eddies case. My mum took in a deep breath and then sighed.

'I hope for you two, that this is an imprint.' She whispered, giving me half a smile.
I decided to change the subject, it was hurting us all and right now after nearly dying, I did not want to talk about having to live without the love of my life.

'So, who did you love before you imprinted with dad?' I asked looking up at my mother sheepishly, I wasn't sure if she lying to make us feel better or if she genuinely knew how we felt. I couldn't imagine my mother loving anyone else, she and my dad were smitten with each other, my memories that involved them together were always happy ones, they inspired me to find a marriage that would be just like theirs. When he died, I remember my mum being so heartbroken, crying in her room when she thought I was asleep. It a well-known fact that if your mate dies, you normally follow, but she didn't, she was strong enough to stay with me and raise me by herself, my mother was my inspiration.

'Oh, it was a long time ago, it doesn't matter.' She blurted, her cheeks flushing crimson.

'Mother…come on…tell me.' I smirked winking at her cheekily.

'Piper; it was many years ago; darling and in the end, he didn't matter because I fell in love with your father.' She said standing up from my bed.

'Pleaseeeeeee mum.' I begged playfully fluttering my eyelashes.

'Fine…Eddie; cover your ears.' She said eyeing him up and down. We both watched as Eddie put his hands over his ears and then I smiled.

She said the name and I nearly fell off of my bed and by the look on Eddie's face he was clearly not covering his ears properly.

'Jake?!' I gasped wide eyes, looking at my mother and then to Eddie.

'Yes, Piper. Jake was my first love and then he imprinted with Molly and I imprinted with your father… the end.' She clarified before walking out of my room. Me and Eddie just stared at each other in disbelief, was she being serious? Oh, my goddess Selene! I needed to know more. I leapt from my bed and chased after my mother; as strange as it was, I was moving much faster than I had before, I caught up to my mother in seconds, leaving Eddie scrambling behind me. We followed my mother in silence for a moment, until I reached out and placed a hand on her shoulder, causing her to flinch.

'Mum tell us more, please? I assume he wasn't always like this… a…' I tried to find the right word, but Eddie beat me to it.

'A knob?' he said also as curious as me. My mother sighed and lead us over to one of the seats that lined to corridor and we all sat, waiting for the explanation.

'No, he wasn't. There was a time when he was a gentle soul and a very loving person. When Tristan imprinted with Marie everyone was in shock, how could an Elite imprint with a mutt? But for a while we all thought it was possible. Jake and I were together in secret for 2 and a half years and madly in love, when Tristan and Marie became mates, we thought we had hope but then it was confirmed she was of Elite blood. It broke our hearts and we agreed to end our relationship. It was pure hell for me... I don't know about him. But then he and Molly became mates, watching them devastated me, but she was such a sweet girl, she was always so polite and kind. And as much as I hated to say it, I had never seen him so happy. It was in that time that I knew I had to truly let go.'

'Mum, how comes you have never told me any of this before?' I asked, my heart breaking for my mother all over again. She kissed the top of my head before continuing.

'Then a new family joined out pack, they were once deviants, they had fled from their pack many years before hand and had been on the run ever since. We were the first pack that had welcomed them, and they requested to stay. They had a son, a young man who was my age and he joined the kitchen, your father Piper, and I fell deeply in love with him, a love I had never felt before and I knew we had imprinted. Jake and I were both so happy for one another, from that moment on there was no feeling left between us, all of that had gone. The day that your father died it nearly killed me, but I survived the turmoil for my little girl.' My mother paused and sniffled as she tried her hardest to get her tears under control.

'Oh, mum.' I whispered, sliding closer to her and placing my head on her shoulder. I glanced up to Eddie who was looking just as heart broken. My mother straightened up a little and twisted around so that she could see Eddie and I clearly before continuing.

'Jake and Molly moved away from the pack, Jake still came to meetings but they wanted to live separately and their lives were kept a secret, we knew they had little boys but that was it, Molly never brought them to the pack mansion, we aren't too sure why exactly but we all respected that. Tristan and Marie would take Arlo and Matt there and the boys would all play. And then one day we were all hit with some awful news. I remember it like it was yesterday, November the 1st, we all discovered that Molly have given birth to a baby girl, but she died shortly afterwards. No one knew how she died but it was heart wrenching. Jake came back to the pack mansion with his little boys, but he left the baby with her grandparents, he never spoke about it or her, nor did anyone else but we all knew he couldn't look at the child after that and that's why... we think... he is so horrid to Amelia... which isn't the Jake I knew, he would never have been like that before. But the death of your soul mate changes you, you just have to be strong enough to fight that change. I just don't think that he was strong enough to beat it.'

I looked at my mum, she was such an incredibly strong woman, I was so proud to be her daughter. I took hold of Eddie's hand a squeezed it, I knew it would have been hard for him to hear that all, but maybe it would have helped him understand his dad more... *or maybe not.*

Amelia;

I took the golden key out of my jogging bottoms pocket and turned it in the lock. Arlo had insisted he walk me back to my house, determined he wouldn't leave my side. I allowed Benjamin to take my blood and so did Piper, he wanted to see if my blood was any different to anyone else's and was curious to see how it had had that effect on Piper.

'So, this is my new home... thanks to you.' I smiled as I pushed the white front door open. I spun on the spot, so I was facing Arlo and bit the inside of my cheek. I knew he wanted to come in, but I wasn't sure it would be a good idea. Him actually being in the house he gave me just because he didn't want me to leave would be adding salt into the wounds and I didn't want to hurt him anymore, we had all had a shit couple of days, I didn't want to make it worse. And then there was the fact that I wasn't sure that I was strong enough to be alone with him without wanting him. I bit my bottom lip as the memories of his touch flooded my mind. The sound of Arlo's voice snapped me from my thoughts.

'Can I come in?' He asked curiously. I bit my lip and paused before nodding.

'Okay but excuse the mess.' I mumbled stepping to the side and allowing him to walk past me. After giving Arlo a tour of my new abode, I laid on my settee and rested my feet onto his lap wondering who cleaned my house and unpacked my belongings. The blood that was all over the floors had been cleaned, the dirty clothes in the sink had been washed, there was food in my cupboards and fridge and new furniture had been neatly placed around the house.

'Did you arrange for someone to do that?' I asked knowing he would know what I was talking about.

'No, my mother did it... it was my mum's idea.' He admitted looking down at me.

I closed my eyes and listened to sound of his breathing, allowing myself to imagine what it would be like to be normal. Me and Arlo living together as a human couple in our own home, not having to worry about the imprinting with someone else, just us together until we were old and grey, why couldn't we just be normal?

'What are you thinking about; beautiful?' Arlo asked rubbing my legs. I opened my eyes and looked at him sadly. I hesitated for a moment, unsure whether I should actually tell him what I was thinking or not. But I knew that he would have known instantly if I was lying to him or not. With a heavy sigh I dropped my head back onto the arm of the sofa and threw my arm over my face.

'Us... living as humans, oblivious to the supernatural world around us, living together as a couple not having to deal with the crap that comes with pack life.' I confessed. He nodded and ran one of his hands through his messy curls.

'I wish I could give you that.' before I could reply back to him, my phone rang, I looked at the caller ID; it was Benjamin, *does he have the results already?* I started to feel sick, what if he discovered I was abnormal; or what if he discovered everything was as it should be, and I was just a freak? Butterflies filled my stomach as I swiped the green button. *Here goes nothing.* I accepted the called and raised the phone to my ear.

Amelia; 'Hello?'

Benjamin; 'Hello miss Hunt, I hope you are feeling better. I have just received yours and miss Quinn's blood results back.'

Amelia; 'Is everything okay? Is there something wrong?'
Benjamin; 'Would you mind coming in to see me, just you?'
Amelia; 'Erm...okay, I will be there in 10 minutes.'

I ended the call and twisted in my seat to face Arlo.

'Is everything ok beautiful?' Arlo asked, eyeing me with a worried expression on his face. I nodded and tucked a stray strand of hair behind my ear.

'I just need to go see Benjamin.'

'I'll come with you.' Arlo cut in, leaping to his feet and holding his hand out to take mine. I allowed him to help me to my feet shaking my head.

'Actually, he asked me to go alone. And, I am starving. So, do you think that you could hang back and make me something?' Arlo nodded looking more than a little confused as I scurried from the room before he had a chance to say anything else.

I wandered into the medical ward and one of the nurses; Aleah, smiled over to me.

'Amelia! What a pleasant surprise!' She chimed, hurrying over to me and pulling me in for a quick hug. 'Are you feeling ok?' She asked, taking a step back, holding me at arms-length, and looking me up and down. I smiled and tucked a stray strand of hair behind my ear.

'Yeah, I am ok. Benjamin called, he said that he wanted to see me. Before Aleah had a chance to respond, Benjamin poked his head around one of the office doors and waved me over to him. Aleah stepped aside and gestured for me to go to him and waved before hurrying off down one of the corridors and disappeared into another room.

I entered the office and was surprised to see Piper already in there, and Marie stood behind the desk with her arms folded across her chest. Piper turned and smiled uneasily at me as I entered and shifted over, patting the seat beside her motioning for me to sit beside her.

'Do you have any idea why we're here?' Piper whispered, eyeing me nervously. I shook my head lightly and offered a sad smile. We turned to look at our doctor in unison and watched as he crossed the room and sat behind his desk across from us nervously; not breaking his stare from Marie the entire time. I glanced over to our Elder and she smiled that famously motherly smile that only she could do and nodded encouragingly.

'So, you are both probably wondering why I have called you here.' Benjamin said, finally tearing his eyes away from Marie and staring at us quizzically. *Well... staring at ME quizzically. What the fuck was going?* He cleared his throat anxiously and nodded, seemingly answering an unasked question.

'Oh, for Selene's sake, tell the girls already. You are probably scaring them to death Benjamin!' Marie scolded, crossing the room and standing between Piper and I and placing a hand on each of our shoulders, giving them an encouraging squeeze. Benjamin nodded nervously and cleared his throat.

'So, before we go into anything, Amelia, did you know that you have an extremely rare blood type.' He paused for a moment and cleared his throat as I stared at him in silence. Marie narrowed her eyes at the doctor, seeming to make him stutter that little bit more.

'Oh, for Goddess sake.' Marie hurried out from behind us and sat on the edge of Benjamin's desk. 'If you need something done then its best to do it yourself.' She muttered to herself shaking her head before turning her smile to us. 'Look girls, we found an anomaly in both of your blood works.' She hesitated for a moment and turned her kind eyes to me. 'Amelia, we never had your bloods on record, so we had to have check it to begin with to make sure that everything was ok. So, I'm not sure if you are aware but all werewolves share the same blood group. We have some of the world's best haematologists in the world. They study blood from around the world and see how blood is affected by diseases and how to prevent them. Many years ago, it was discovered that the werewolf gene was only carried by those with the O blood group.' She paused once more and folded her arms across her chest.

'Wait, so are you saying that Amelia has another blood group? But how is that possible?' Piper asked, sliding forward in her seat a little and placing her elbows on her knees. She looked over to me for a moment and looked as though she wanted to say something else.

'What? What is it?' I asked, my heart thundering in my chest.

'Does that mean that she is not a werewolf?' Piper asked, refusing to look away from me. The thought had been going around in my head, but the reality of the question never sank in until I heard it allowed. *That made so much sense.*

'Well, I think that that would be the easiest answer for us all, however, that is not the case. You definitely have the werewolf gene in your bloods. We have had it tested and checked multiple times. However, your actual blood group is AB positive. The two genes that do not have the ability to possess it.'

'So then, what is wrong with me?' I asked, pulling my hair over my shoulder and twiddling it in my fingers.

'Nothing. That's the other part that is extraordinary to us. There was absolutely nothing wrong. In most of us werewolves, there is some sort of deficiency in some form, something that we lack which is made up for by the wolf gene that we harness. You have nothing. If anything, you have one too many.

Humans all have twenty-three chromosomes. Werewolves have twenty-four. You, Amelia, have twenty-five.' We all sat in silence for a moment, not moving. *I wasn't even breathing.* Piper reached out and placed her hand on my arm causing me to flinch as she spoke.

'So, what does that mean?' She asked, squeezing my wrist gently in support.

'If we are honest, we don't really know. I mean, you are practically a super-'

'And Piper...' Marie cut in, eyeing Benjamin angrily from the corner of her eye, before turning back to look at us and smiling sweetly. 'We already had your bloods on file, and, we had to check it again after you were poisoned with the wolfsbane and...' she sighed and frowned. 'Well, we wanted to make sure that there wasn't any permanent damage done. The good news is that it seems that you have healed completely and there was no damage done. However, there has been some…' Marie paused once more and glanced to Benjamin seemingly for support.

'Well, we noticed that there have been some changes to your genetic make-up.' Pipers eyes widened and her bottom lip trembled slightly.

'What does that mean?' She asked, her voice weak.

'According to our records, your blood type was…'

'O negative' Piper cut in, answering the question before our doctor had a chance to ask it. Benjamin nodded and then shrugged slightly.

'Yes, that's correct. However, this time… your bloods have come back as being…' Benjamin paused and stared down at the file that he had clutched in his hands. *Had he been holding that the entire time?* 'It appears that you are now… ABO negative.' Piper gasped and shook her head.

'I'm sorry if this sounds rude but, there's no such blood group. I mean, biology was one of my favourite subjects. I literally got the highest marks possible for all my sciences. ABO isn't real.'

'We know.' Marie answered. 'We also had your bloods tested five times in total. At first, we thought that there was a malfunction with the testing, but we had the same results every time.' Marie paused and held out a plastic bag in her hands and turned towards me. There was a large lump of something within that held the most mesmerising shade of purple, and it even seemed to shimmer under the dim lighting. She slowly walked over to me and took one of my hands.

'W-What are you doing?' Piper squeaked, jumping to her feet. Benjamin hurried over to my best friend and pulled her away from me for a moment gently shushing her.

'Sweetheart. I need you to hold this. If it hurts at any time or causes you any discomfort, then please drop it. This is purely a test for all of us.' Marie whispered, tugging open the bag and turning it upside down as it handed in my palm. We all stood there in silence, staring at the unknown rock-like substance. *It really was beautiful.*

'H-How?' Piper stammered, breaking free from Benjamin's

grasp and walking over to me. In the blink of an eye, Marie knocked my hand causing the object to fly towards Piper. With lightning reflexes; *much faster than even she should have been able;* Piper threw her hand up and caught the thing mid-air. I watched as Marie and Benjamin's mouths fell open and their eyes widen.

'T... th... that's impossible.' Benjamin gasped looking from Marie to Piper and then back to Marie.

'What is this?' Piper asked staring at the purple glittering rock in her hand.'

'It's wolfbane.' I replied walking over to Piper. 'It doesn't affect you anymore.' I looked up at Benjamin 'Did I do that to her too?'

23

Amelia;

I walked into my kitchen and groggily looked around at my surroundings, I was still half asleep and did not want to be out of bed; for the first time in weeks I had slept like a baby, I don't know if it was because the exhaustion had finally caught up with me or it was the fact that I was in my own home with no one else to pretend for; it was just me in my own space. I sighed and glanced out the window, fully allowing the reality of everything that had taken place over the last few days. There was still so much that I didn't understand. And deep down I felt that the only way that I could get the answers I desired was to leave this place.

The quiet was so refreshing, I hadn't even watched any television and hardly looked at my mobile I just read books and got lost in my own little world. I had withdrawn myself from the pack, I didn't want to be part of it anymore and I didn't know how to escape, I couldn't run as I made a promise to Arlo, so distancing myself seemed to be the best thing for me to do. I sat at the kitchen table and thought about how I would let the non-elites down if I went, *I was damned if I did and I was damned if I didn't*. Why did I even care about the non-elites so much? It wasn't like they had done anything for me. It wasn't like I had grown up watching them be treated badly by the elites. And yet, here I was, torn about what to do. It was strange, there was a part of me that just didn't want to care anymore. But I couldn't just do that to them. They needed their warrior to fight for them. And if I was gone then who would do that? I was beginning to think I was cursed; It didn't matter what I chose, someone was going to end up getting hurt. *And I just knew that that person was going to be me.*

Today is Valentine's day and it had been five days since I had been released from the medical ward, swiftly followed by Piper. We still didn't understand how everything had happened. Whose blood can heal someone? Isn't that what vampires were meant to be able to do? Did that mean that I was part vampire? Is that why I was so different? I mean, I know that vampires exist, but they are an extremely reclusive race. They tend to keep themselves to themselves and only do what suits them. *Not that that is a bad thing.* But taking that into consideration, how the hell would I be part vampire? I mean, both of my parents were werewolves. *Unless there is something that my father isn't telling me?* I never did hear the story of how my mother died. It had always been such a secret. So, did that mean that there was more to it than they had been letting on?

Since moving into my own house, Pretty Girl had practically moved into my garden, Arlo had given me a house closest to the stables, so that I could be as close to her as possible, *as well as be as far away from the others as possible.* In this time, I had spent every day with my Pretty Girl as I grieved the little life I very nearly had and tried to come to terms with the fact my blood was now running through Piper's veins. *Did this mean that I finally had a sister that I had always wanted?*

I hadn't planned on becoming pregnant, it was the thing furthest from my mind and now it was the only thing that I could think about. *How could I miss something so much when I never even knew I wanted that?* In a way, I wanted that baby, a part of me and a part of him. But I knew that it would be a bad idea. I was about to become homeless and on the run. *How could I expect to bring a baby along for that?* I guess that's why Selene had others plans for me. But, still... how did I overcome this emptiness that I was left feeling? How was I supposed to carry on with my life as normal when there was a permanent void within myself?

I looked up at the clock as I sat on the sofa with my cup of tea and sighed, it was 7:00am and I was still expected to go to breakfast at the pack mansion, something that I was dreading. I had avoided meals and gatherings with everyone since my last hospital visit, everyone knew the Alpha had got me pregnant. The Elites all thought I was sleeping with Matt and Arlo; and news about Eddie and Piper being together had spread around like wildfire; and I was being blamed... again. I had been here for four months and apparently in that time I had influenced my brother and best friend to become a couple. *I mean, seriously, how the hell was it my fault that they had imprinted? It wasn't like I had that power!* Everyone ignored the fact that they had been together in secret for two years; before I had even come to live in this mansion... but I guess that, that was just another thing that I was to blame for. The sooner I could leave, the better. I wanted to leave. I was ready to leave. I *needed* to leave. My phone vibrated on the coffee table in front of me, and I didn't need to read it to know who it was from. I rolled my eyes and reached forward, plucking it from the smooth glass table-top and swiped at the screen. *Arlo!*

Arlo; I expect to see you at breakfast this morning!

Amelia; Are you kidding me?

Arlo; No! I am completely serious.

Amelia; Goddess forbid that you would have grown a sense of humour in the last few days!

Arlo; What is that supposed to mean?

Amelia; Nothing, *alpha!* I will be there. Much to my own disappointment!

Arlo; What the fuck is that supposed to mean? Seriously Amelia, what the fuck have I done now?

Amelia; See you soon... *alpha.*

I know that I was being rude to him, but, what did he expect? He was forcing me to this stupid breakfast with the rest of the Elites; *who, all hated me as much as I hated them!* And then ordered me to be there? Seriously, who did he think he was? Another part of me knew that the only way to make my leaving easier, was to push away everyone as much as I could. *The thought of leaving Matt and Piper was almost enough to kill me.* But it needed to be done! I know that Piper was going to come with me; *but now that she had imprinted on my brother, I couldn't expect her to just leave.*

With a heavy sigh, I pulled myself from the sofa and began getting myself ready to go to breakfast. I had put make up on to hide the bags under my eyes and had made an effort with my appearance; wearing a pair of ripped light blue skinny jeans, a pink off the shoulder jumped and pink pumps. My hair was tied up in a high ponytail and wrapped into a neat bun, revealing my gold earrings and my gold necklace both with matching glistening Amethyst stones secured into them. I rushed out into the grounds of the mansion and made my way towards the building that stood before me.

I opened the large doors to the entrance of the mansion and took in a deep breath as I momentarily closed my eyes, it was time for everyone to meet for breakfast and I was dreading it, I hadn't seen Arlo in five days purposely and had ignored all his phone calls and text messages, I needed space not only from the pack but from him too. I loved him so much and we were good together when life was treating us good, but we were also toxic together, toxic for the pack and it was becoming unhealthy. I caught my reflection in one of the large mirrors that were built into the walls in the main hall and stared at myself.

I looked up and caught sight of Arlo and his parents coming out of his office, they were all bickering about something and I was sure I heard Marie say my name, Arlo's face was like thunder and although I wanted to know what was going on, I quickly ran to the dining hall doors trying my best to avoid any eye contact with him. *But that didn't stop me wondering what was going on between the three of them.* I pushed open the dining room doors and braced myself or the stares and whispers, but the greeting got was much warmer, the non-elites all smiled at me and nodded their heads as in to say hello, Matt and Eddie both beamed when they had realised that I had finally come to breakfast. I noticed that Eddie was no longer seated next to my father but with Matt instead, clearly Charlie and my dad hadn't accepted his imprint with Piper and were now shunning him just like they were me. I stood behind my chair and waited for the sound of the doors to open, it was now inevitable, I had to see Arlo face to face and talk to him whether I liked it or not. *But all of this was going to be over soon.* It seemed as though time had slowed as I watched him walk down the room towards his seat, *did it always take this long?* I felt as his warm body slowly brushed past mine sending waves of desire rolling through me. *How was I ever going to be able to fight this attraction and my feelings for him?*

I glanced up at him studying his beautiful face and noticed he didn't look at me once his golden eyes looking straight ahead. I listened to sounds around me; chatters of the pack and chairs being pulled out ready for everyone to be seated for their breakfast. I sat down and stared at the plate on the table in front of me and sighed; *it wouldn't be long before I left and didn't have to do this for much longer.* As much as I love my friends here... I needed to leave. And I think the only way to do that was distance myself from them be-forehand. No goodbyes. I'll just disappear into the night.

I rose from my chair and stormed out into the main hall. *How dare he!* Who orders someone to be somewhere and then ignores them the entire time! *Arlo, that's who!* I let out a growl of frustration and made my way to the front doors. There was only one thing in this world that would calm me, and I needed her now. *Pretty Girl!* I felt a strong hand grip my wrist and pull me back around to face them.

'What do you want Arlo?' I asked, I didn't need to look to see who it was. And I kept my eyes looking everywhere except at him.

'What do you think you are doing?' He snapped, his eyes blazing with anger.

'Excuse me? What the hell is that supposed to mean?'

'Have you forgotten the pack lore? The alpha always leaves the dining hall first.' I glared at him angrily and folded my arms across my chest before answering.

'Your point?' His stare turned deadly for a split second, and it took everything in me not to laugh. *Did he think that this alpha crap was actually going to work on me?* I knew that he was trying to use his alpha's influence on me, I had seen him give that look to many others. But it never worked on me, so why did he think that it would now? 'You can stop that too.' I muttered, rolling my eyes and turning away from him. He let out a deep guttural growl, something that almost made him sound feral and terrifying. *But all it did to me was turn me on.*

'My office! Now!' He barked, storming past me and heading down the hall to his office. I sighed and rolled my eyes once more before glancing over my shoulder back towards the dining hall. Matt and Piper were peering around the corner, both looking equally curious and terrified. I flashed them a smile and a small wave before skipping down the hall to catch up with *my alpha.*

The moment I entered the room he slammed the door shut behind me and closed the distance between us in one swift motion. He got in my face and began to shout.

'Do you have *no* respect for me as your alpha? How dare you act this way in front of the pack. I have been letting you get away with far too much. That leniency is over! Do you hear me!' He screamed, his face flushing red with anger. I stepped back slightly and cocked my eyebrow.

'Dude. You have some serious anger management issues. Did you know that?' I asked sarcastically.

'And you have an attitude problem. And I am sick of it. This has gone too far now Amelia!'

'*I* have the attitude problem? Wow. That's rich. At least I know what it is that I want in life. Whereas you on the other hand, you are worse than a menopausal woman with bipolar!' He paused for a moment, speechless and staring at me.

'You have no right to speak to me like that' He whispered, his voice low and dangerous.

'And you have no right to order me to breakfast and not say a word to me the entire time. You never even looked at me once. You know how much I hate being there with everyone, yet you made it that much more unbearable.'

'Amelia, you have ignored me for the past five days! I have been trying to make sure that everything was alright with you. You left to go and speak to Benjamin, and that was the last that I had heard. I even asked him to tell me what it was that happened. But he said that it wasn't for him to discuss. I even asked Piper. Actually... if I am honest, I tried to use the alpha influence on her, but it didn't work. So now, I am asking you. Please... what the hell is going on around here?'

'What is it that you want me to say to you Arlo?'

'The truth.'

'The truth about?'

'Are you just trying to wind me up? I just want to know that you are ok?'

'Well, I am stood here, talking to you, aren't I? Doesn't that answer your question?'

'You know what I meant. I mean, how are you after...'

'Oh, you mean after losing our child? Yea. I am great. Thanks for asking.' I snapped, no longer able to hold my irritation in.

'Yes. That is what I meant. So... was everything ok when Benjamin called you in? Was there a problem with the blood results?' He asked, stepping closer to me once more and placing his hands on my hips.

'Look, Arlo... I really don't want to talk about this right now. If you really want to know then why don't you just ask your mother?'

'My mother? What has she got to do with any of this?' he snapped, the anger crossing his face once more.

'S-She was there...' I replied hesitantly. *The last thing that I wanted to do was get Marie in trouble. But at the same time, I knew that she was one of the only other people around here that could put him in his place.* 'Look Arlo. I really want to just go and see Pretty Girl. I have a few things that I need to sort out at home too. So, if it's ok with you...' I stopped mid-sentence and turned away from him, heading towards the door of his office.

'This is not a game Amelia. *I* am *your* alpha. Does that

mean nothing to you?' He continued. I sighed and shrugged lightly, before slowly turning back around to face him.

'If I am honest. No. It doesn't. And you being alpha means nothing to me. It never has done. I fell-' I paused and bit my lip. *This was not the time to talk about this.*

'What?' He asked, his anger fading slightly as he stepped closer to me once more.

'It doesn't matter. Just forget it. Consider me told. So, can I go now?'

'Amelia, what were you going to say?' He asked again, his voice much softer and his angry expression gone.

'Is that an order from my alpha?' I asked sarcastically. He sighed and dipped his head.

'No. That is one friend asking another.' Arlo replied, reaching out and taking both of my hands in his. *Friend? In all the months that I had been here, I don't think I had ever heard him call me that.* I sighed once more and turned away from him, folding my arms across my chest defensively.

'I was going to say, that I never fell in love with you because of what you were. It was the person inside that captivated me. Although... right now... that person is far from the one standing in front of me.' I reached for the door and started to pull it open, when his placed him palm and pushed it shut once more.

'Please Lia. Don't leave. Not yet.' He whispered, leaning in closer to me. I felt his breath brush across my cheek and my heart started to race. *Why did he always have this effect on me?*

'Arlo, please, I can't do this. Not now.' I whispered, my voice trembling as I spoke. Arlo reached up and tucked a stray strand of hair behind my ear and rested his forehead against mine. 'I need to go and feed Pretty Girl...but I will call you later?' I pulled away from him and watched as his face fell in disappointment, but he forced a small smile and nodded. I quickly leaned forward and placed a small kiss on his cheek before sadly smiling up to him, in that moment I wished I could tell him how much I loved him, but I couldn't, not because I didn't want to, I just couldn't say it. I turned away from him and hurried out into the hall. I needed to see Pretty

Girl. She was the only one that could ease the pain of my broken heart. I fought back the tears and held my head up high. I couldn't let the other see me looking so broken. I knew what these wolves were like. The first sign of weakness and they would take me down.

Matt;

I glanced down to Piper as Amelia skipped away down the corridor, heading towards Arlo's office. I had never seen him look so angry. *And I hated to admit it, but I was scared for him. Amelia was not a force to be reckoned with.* I smiled to myself and shook my head.

'What? What is it?' Piper whispered, grabbing my hand and pulling me out into the hall. I sighed and shook my head.

'It's Valentine's day, and I have never seen either of them look so angry at one another. Why is it only us that can see that they are destined to be together?' I mumbled, more to myself than to Piper but she answered anyway.

'Matty... look... I think that it is time that we just admit that they aren't meant to be. Arlo is imprinting on someone, who isn't Amelia. We can't keep forcing them together. I mean... who is it benefiting? Them? Us? Who?' She replied. I narrowed my eyes and glared at her playfully.

'Ok. Well... someone has changed their tune. I wasn't it only last week that you were saying that there is something special between the pair of them.' I retorted rolling my eyes. The sound of footsteps heading towards us, had us pressing ourselves against the wall out of sight. We watched in silence as Amelia hurried past us and out the main doors. I knew that look on her face. She was heartbroken but trying to conceal it. *She may have been able to fool everyone else, but not us.*

'What do you think happened in the office?' Piper whispered, looking from me, back down the hall and noticing as Arlo paced the length of the room his both hands placed on his head.

'I don't know. Let's go after her and find out!'

'For Goddess's sake Matt. Just leave her alone for a minute! If she wanted us there, then she would have asked.' Piper snapped.

What the hell was going on with Piper? She was never usually this... hormonal. I stared at her for a moment longer as she reached into her pocket and pulled her phone from within. I watched in silence as her fingers flew across the screen, the only sound the gentle clicking as she typed her words.

'Sorted.' She snapped, before turning on her heel and storming down the corridor. I hurried to catch up with her and we both walked out the main doors and into the cool mid-morning air. I had no idea what was going on, but even though she was going through intense mood swings, she was still one of my best friends and I loved her.

Amelia;

I stood in the stables gently stroking Pretty Girls mane, allowing her soft hairs to run between my fingers. I had always found it so therapeutic to just stand here and stroke her. Her soft rhythmic breathing, soothing even the worst parts of my broken heart. I closed my eyes as I tried my hardest to keep myself from imagining the life that I could have had; Me, Arlo and our child... I clenched my teeth and shook my head. *Great... and this was me not thinking about it.* I don't even know how long I had been down here. I had let Pretty Girl out for her run; watching as she danced around in the morning sunlight. She was such a special beast to me. And I knew that I wouldn't have made it through any of this without her.

My phone vibrated in the pocket of my jeans, stopping my dangerous trail of thinking and giving me something else to think about. I pulled it from my jeans and swiped at the screen waiting as it came to life.

Piper; Happy Valentine's day to you, happy Valentine's day to you, happy Valentine's day dear Lia! Happy Valentine's day to you! I love you!!!! Did you get my card? I couldn't resist, I got one for Matt too! :D What are you doing today? Me, Matt and Edward are going to the pub later if you fancy it?? Don't worry if you don't feel like coming but we will be there at 2! It's my day off so I'm making the most of it, we are going to get wastedddd!!! Love you xxxxxxxx

I rolled my eyes and fought the smile that I could feel tugging at my lips. How was I supposed to just up and leave these guys? Why did doing the right thing have to be so hard? With a heavily sigh I typed quickly, trying to act as normal as possible.

Lia; Happy Valentine's day you crazy lady! Haha I got you a card too! Great minds eh? Did you just say pub? Wasted? Hell yes, I'm in! I love you too! See you there xxxxxxxxx

I shoved my phone back into my pocket and turned back to Pretty Girl as she nudged me lightly with her nose. I had never noticed how purple her eyes had been before. As much as I told myself that she wasn't a unicorn, the more she showed me parts of her that proved otherwise. I sighed and pulled her head down to meet mine, before resting my forehead against her nose.

'Ok gorgeous girl. I better go and get myself ready. I have a date with my three-favourite people in the world.' I whispered, pulling back before kissing her softly. She shook her head gleefully and watched as I slowly left the barn.

After getting home and showering, I got myself dressed up in my favourite ripped skinny jeans and black high heels. Topping it all off a bright red, backless halter-top. I pulled my phone from my back pocket just as a message came through from Arlo.

Arlo; Ok… did our conversation this morning mean nothing to you?

Amelia; Chill out *alpha!* I am just meeting Matt, Eddie and Piper at the pub.

Arlo; The pub? That's why you missed lunch? Will you be back for dinner?

Amelia; What do you think?

Arlo; Will be there ASAP! Xx

I shook my head and suppressed a giggle before quickening my pace. I didn't want to get there and everyone else be slaughtered! *Was Arlo actually going to skip his duties to come to the pub?* As much as I was loving this new side of Arlo, I didn't want to get him in trouble. *But one night wouldn't hurt. Would it?* I grinned as I stepped foot into the pub and took in the smell of alcohol and food, I watched as a waitress walked past me with a tray of chicken and chips and my stomach rumbled a little too loudly, I was so hungry. *I knew that it was a bad idea to skip lunch. But I also knew that I needed this time with the people that I loved. My stomach could wait.*

I walked towards Matt's favourite sitting booth and noticed my brother and Piper kissing, Matt looked disgusted and his facial expression told me how relieved he was that I had arrived.

'Lia!' he cried loudly jumping to his feet before rushing over to me and pulling me into a bear hug, trying to get Eddie's and Piper's attention. He leant in a little closer, 'save me' He whispered, giving Eddie and Piper a bored side-eye glance. 'Are you okay?' he asked taking my hand and pulling me down next to him.

'Yeah I am good.' I smiled looking up at him through my eyelashes. while trying to supress a laugh. Matt sighed and crossed his arms against his chest, studying me suspiciously.

'No you're not... I know you too well... come on let's go outside and have a ciggy.' He said standing up, I looked back at my brother and Piper as me and Matt walked towards the pub door, they were both lost in each other's eyes and it was such a beautiful sight and yet my heart ached, I. *I couldn't help but wish I had that, I wish it was me that Arlo had imprinted with, and I wish I knew who it was.* Leaving knowing he was in love with a lovely woman who had a big heart and would protect him the way he would her would make going that much easier. 'Come on, spit it out, what's going on in that pretty head of yours?' Matt asked passing me a cigarette. I waited for him to light it for me before I started talking.

'I am trying... trying so hard to distance myself from everyone and yet I'm struggling so much, I'm coming across so rude and horrible and I feel awful. I don't want to leave you and Piper and Eddie... and I don't want to leave Arlo... but I have to. I think after today I'm just going to hide myself away until it's time for me to leave. I don't want to upset anyone in the process, but I have to be strict on myself.' I admitted before taking a long drag on my cigarette. Matt nodded his eyes full of sadness.

'I understand and I will support you if that's what you really want to do... but... we don't want you to distance yourself, it could be months before we find out who did those killings and now they have just stopped it's going to be even harder. There isn't any point in you becoming a recluse; Lia, not with your friends anyway...' Matt replied taking my hand.

'Matt I'm not waiting for them to find the killer, I'm going soon, I can't wait any longer an-' I stopped what I was saying as soon as Arlo walked into the pub garden, he looked down at my cigarette disapprovingly and then gave Matt a peeved off look. He hated me smoking, I don't know why though, it's not like I did it every single day, although with how I was feeling, that may just happen.

'I need a pint.' Arlo said walking past me and Matt and nodded towards the pub doors, we both followed Arlo in, and all looked up at Eddie and Piper, they were whispering sweet nothings to each other and I smiled to myself, it really was beautiful to see them so happy. Arlo ordered us all a new round of drinks and we all sat down, ready to relax and enjoy the rest of the day, but for some reason something felt off, I couldn't put my finger on it but an uneasy feeling was flooding through my body, I tried to shake it off and ignore it but...I just couldn't let it go. I glanced over to Piper and took in the blank expression on her face. She had gone from smiling loving to Eddie to looking confused as her eyes were glazing over.

'Hey baby, is everything ok?' Eddie asked, leaning in closer to Piper and checking her over. She shifted a little in her seat and smiled over to him.

'Of course. Everything is fine. Why?' She asked, glancing at him wearily as though she was a little uncomfortable. She cleared her throat a little uneasily and pulled her hand free from Eddie's.

'Baby, you're burning up. Please, talk to me?' My brother asked, his voice quiet and urgent. Piper jumped from her seat and pulled her long hair over one shoulder. I noticed that her skin was turning red, as though she had been sitting out in the sun for too long. She swayed on the spot slightly and downed the rest of her drink in one go.

'Piper? What is it?' I asked, jumping from my seat and hurrying over to her. She shook her head and stepped back, holding her hands up defensively.

'P-please. Stay back.' She cried, turning and fleeing from the room, rushing out into the cool February air. I rushed through the doors and watched as she swayed on the spot, swatting at her arms.

'Babe, please... wha-' Eddie started, but stopped rapidly as Piper dropped down onto all fours. He went to rush forward, but Matt grabbed his arm shaking his head.

'W-What? What is it?' I stammered, staring in confusion. Piper threw her head back and screamed, and I watched in horror as her bones snapped and popped and her skin rippled before my eyes. 'Is she... is she shifting?' I asked, my whole-body trembling from my fear. As if in answer to my question, red fur erupted from her skin, and her mouth and nose extended into that of a canine. Her teeth rattled before all stretching down into sharp points. Her dress exploded from around her, leaving nothing but tattered rags hanging from her body.

We all stood frozen from shock and stared at the beautiful red-haired wolf that stood shivering before us. Eddie stepped towards her slowly, holding his hands out in surrender, which only caused her to flinch.

'Baby. Please... its only me.' Eddie whispered, taking another step towards Piper. Her wide eyes darted from him over to us before she turned and fled from us. She moved with speeds unlike anything I had ever seen. Werewolves were fast, but she was faster than anyone. *Had she always been that fast?* I watched as Eddie chased after her, but by the time that he had taken a few steps forward she was already gone. He dropped to his knees and hung his head as he fought back the sobs that were threatening to escape his lips. *I had never seen my brother look so broken, and it killed me.* I hurried over to him and knelt beside him, pulling him into my arms and just held him as he sobbed. *Was this an adverse reaction to my blood changing her? Was this all because of me? What had I done?*

'Come on. I think we better go and speak to Tanya. She is going to totally freak out.' I whispered, rising to my feet and pulling Eddie to his. He kept his head down and never said a word. I didn't know what it felt like to imprint with someone, but I had heard stories about the way that the loss of your mate could affect a person. Even though Piper was not "lost" this was still a drastic change of things. And the not knowing would be breaking everything inside Eddie.

Arlo;

I stood there watching as Amelia paced back and forth. With everything that I had seen her go through, I had never seen her looking as stressed and worried as she did in this moment. She hadn't been right from the moment that she came back from Tanya's house. She never told me what was said, but whatever it was, was eating her up inside. And the thought of that killed me. I didn't understand. It was daylight. And not a full moon. *How the fuck did Piper manage to shift? Something really strange was going on around here.* First my fellow pack members are able to resist the alpha influence; which should be impossible. A Mutt and an Elite imprint? And now this… A werewolf shifting in the middle of the day. *It was strange. It seemed as though this all started happening around the time that Amelia came to live here with us at the mansion.* But how is any of that even possible? She is just a werewolf like the others… the only difference is that she cannot shift yet. I suppressed the growl that was threatening to escape my lips and clenched my hands into tight fists. The more that she paced up and down the more agitated I was becoming.

'Lia, please, just… stop a minute.' I begged, taking a hesitant step forward. Her eyes were glazed over as if she were lost far away in thought, and her hair stuck out from her lose ponytail at odd angles. I had never seen her look so… dishevelled. I watched as she continued to pace back and forth, not answering my question. I called to her again, this time a little more assertively. 'Lia!'

'What?' she snapped whirling around to face me. The blank stare had turned to that of anger and she stood clenching her teeth glaring at me.

'You need to rest. All this pacing is not going to do you any good. Especially after...'

'Well... you need to send your best trackers out to find her instead of standing there pestering me!' She shouted, tears filling her eyes.

'Look... it's not as easy as that. I can't just...'

'Yes, you can! You're the fucking alpha for goddess' sake! So, man the fuck up and start acting like the alpha you always bang on about being!' I paused for a moment, staring at her with my mouth hanging open. *What was happening here? I was confused.* I shook my head and sighed, letting her comment slide as I stepped toward her once more.

'Please. Just try and calm down. I don't know what is happening here. And right now, I don't care. All I care about is that you try and chill out because all this stress isn't doing you any good!' I whispered, trying to keep my voice low and calming. Her eyes still raged with anger and she stepped back away from me before continuing to pace the entirety of the living room. There was nothing that I could do to stop the anger spilling out of me, and before I had a chance to think the words left my lips. 'Amelia' I roared, lunging forward and latching on to her wrist. In the blink of an eye she spun around to face me and left me staggering slightly as her palm connected with my cheek. I caught myself mid stumble and lunged forward, grabbing her by the throat and slamming her into the wall. We stood there in silence for a second; *although it felt like an eternity*, and I watched in amazement as her emerald eyes began to shimmer. It was unlike anything I had ever seen and almost hypnotic.

Amelia;

'Amelia!' Arlo roared, lunging forward and latching on to my wrist. I was so lost in my thoughts and worrying about Piper that

I lost complete control of my actions. I spun around to face him, slapping his cheek with all my might. I hit him so hard that he staggered back slightly before righting himself and grabbing me by the throat and pinning me to the wall. We stared at each other in silence for a moment and I watched as his eyes turned black, *something I had never seen them do before,* and if caused a shudder to ripple through my entire body.

'Don't you ever fucking hit me again.' He growled, the words coming out angry and desperate. I tried my hardest to fight the urge to kiss him, but it was no use. I leaned into him and our lips connected. I felt waves of desire rippled through me as our kiss deepened and turned from passionate to desperate.

I poured all my anger, frustration and worry into the kiss and felt as Arlo's touch melted it all away. His hands grabbed at my top as he pulled it over my head, and I was powerless to stop him. *Not that I wanted to.* His hands travelled up my bare stomach, leaving a trail of goosebumps across my skin as he slipped his hand into my bra and pressed his mouth to mine once more. I dug my fingers into the bare skin of his back, dragging my nails down as his kisses moved to my neck. I slipped my hand into his jeans and felt him stiffen under my touch. His breath became ragged as I slowly rolled my hand up and down his shaft, causing him to thrust into my movements. His grip tightened on my breasts before he pulled his hands away purposely ripping my bra from my chest and tossing it to the ground in tatters. I smirked as his eyes fell down to my bare chest and he throbbed in my hand once more. I pulled my hand from his boxers and yanked at his jeans, sending the buttons shooting off and skittering across the hardwood floor. I dropped down to my knees and took all of him in my mouth. His hands ran through my hair, pulling it free from the loose ponytail and causing it cascade down my back. I slowly eased him from my mouth, making sure that my tongue ran all the way to the tip of his shaft and slide over the head causing him to groan softly. He pulled me to my feet and pushed me over the arm of the sofa, kicking my legs open and sliding my jeans down to my knees. Without a moment's hesitation he thrust himself inside me causing me to cry out in pleasure. He slowly eased himself out before slamming back into me, he continued this rhythm of slow thrust, causing my knees to quiver under the pressure.

I dipped my back and met each of his thrust with one of my own, causing him to speed up. His movements got faster and harder and I knew that he was reaching his climax. I felt that familiar tightening in the pit of my stomach and knew that I wouldn't last much longer. I thrust myself back on to him making him pound me that little bit harder. Arlo increased his speed and growled as he finally released himself inside me. I felt as he pulsed inside me, causing me to cry out as my orgasm took over me.

Arlo leant over and placed his head on my back, panting breathlessly before slowly sliding himself out of me. I rose to my feet and turned to face him with a smirk.

'Oh, you think that it's over?' I asked mischievously. He raised an eyebrow and shook his head.

'No chance.' He growled, picking me up as I wrapped my legs around his waist. I bit back the groan as he slowly entered me once more, slamming me against the wall. He kissed from my ear down my neck, teasing me all the more as he continued lower. He kissed down my breast and stopped at my nipple before sucking it into his mouth and biting it lightly. I threw my head back as waves of pain and pleasure coursed through me. And I was taken by surprise as he rose back up to face me and slammed into me hard. I gasped loudly as pleasure overtook all my senses, I rolled my head forward and bit the crook of his neck, which only seemed to encourage him more. Arlo twisted us around and we both tumbled to the floor. *Luckily our werewolf resilience made it feel like falling on a soft mattress.* And that was where we stayed; getting lost in one another. I was grateful that he was able to make me forget everything. Even if this was a temporary reprieve. I was still grateful.

The sound of the haunting lullaby filled my mind and was growing louder with each passing second. The words taking over everything else until there was nothing else that I could do but open my eyes. I sat up with a start, panting for breath and looking around the room groggily. *When did we fall asleep?* Arlo and I were a tangled mess together on my living room floor, laid upon the fluffy rug and covered with a sheet. I motion of me sitting up woke him with a start. He stared up at me with one eye open as he tried to adjust to the morning sunlight.

'Lia? Is everything ok?' He asked me, sitting up and rubbing his eyes. I turned to face him and allowed my eyes travel over the entirety of his naked body before glancing back out the window. I tilted my head to the side and listened for a moment, holding my breath. 'You're starting to freak me out.' He added, shifting for-ward, and placing his hand on my arm. I reached over and grabbed my t-shirt and jeans from the floor and pulled them on, jumping to my feet, snatching some clean clothes and running out the front door. I heard Arlo shuffling around behind me, but I didn't hesitate. I ran out into the cold morning air and watched as a bruised and naked Piper limped back towards us.

'Piper!' I cried, pulling her into my arms and sliding the baggy t-shirt over her head. 'Where the hell have you been? We have been so worried about you!' I held her steady as she stepped into the jeans, before putting her arm over my shoulders and walking her back to her mother's house. I knew that Tanya and Eddie would have been awake all night worried sick. We turned and watched as a shirtless Arlo came running out the door towards us. I bit my lip as I took in the sight of him with nothing but jeans with no buttons. He was barely able to hold them together, giving me the occasional peek that he had no underwear on. My cheeks flushed and I shook my head. My main priority right now was Piper. I needed to get her home.

24

Before we made it to the front door to Pipers house, it flew open. Crashing into the stone wall beside it. Tanya rushed out towards me and Piper, her hair was falling out of the loose bun on her head and her face drained of colour, it was clear to see she had absolutely no sleep the night previous, but the relief on her face when she saw her daughter was heart-warming. My brother followed close behind her and ran straight to Piper, pulling her into his arms as he breathed a large sigh of relief.

I stepped aside and watched as he covered Pipers face and head in kisses, before holding her out at arm's length and checking her over. The blood that had been scattered over her body was beginning to seep through the light denim jeans. Clearly, she was wounded.

We all scurried inside being sure not to draw any attention to ourselves but before I stepped into their house I turned around to see if I could see Arlo; but he wasn't anywhere in sight, I bit the inside of my cheek and turned back towards the front door, I wondered if he would be with us all shortly... after he found himself a new pair of jeans.

I followed Tanya and Piper into the living room whilst Eddie hurried into the kitchen to make Piper a drink; she looked exhausted and probably hadn't eaten or drunk anything since she had left the pub.

'Here lay down darling.' Tanya whispered helping Piper onto the sofa, pulling the throw from the back of the couch and draping it over her. I smiled and watched as she fussed over her daughter, plumping up the cushions, making sure Piper comfortable. *Piper was so lucky to have a mother that loved her so much, it was something that I wanted so much. To be with my mum and to be held by her was one of my biggest wishes and yet it was one that would never come true.*

I sat on the armchair opposite the settee and allowed my mind to wonder for a minute. How did this happen? Was this my blood that did that to her? And if so, how? How could my blood change hers and change what she could do? *And how the hell did it help her shift in pure daylight and yet I couldn't even shift?* I was broken out of my thoughts by the sounds of Tanya's voice, she had a lot of questions to ask and Piper didn't seem to want to talk, she looked like she wanted her bed.

'W...where did you go?'

She looked up at her mother and shrugged. 'This is the thing; I am not entirely sure where I went. All I know was that I ran and ran for miles. I could have been circling the woods or I could have gone further, I remember bits, it is slowly all coming back to me, b...but my head is kind of fuzzy.' She replied rubbing her eyes and staring into space as though she was racking her brain for the memories of her shift to come back.

'Okay... so you think you were in the woods, and is that the only place you remember being?' Tanya asked with concern *and we all knew why she was worried,* if Piper had gone in someone else's territory there would be a major problem. If she had stumbled into another pack's territory, they would instantly think that she was a threat. Especially if they could sense the abnormal blood that was in her system. *I wasn't sure how much about that that Tanya knew, but I guess now wasn't the right time to talk about this.*

Piper looked exhausted. Although she had shifted before, this time was completely different. Werewolves only change during the period of a full moon. *Who knew what trauma and stress her unintentional shifting had done to her body?* It is not natural for anyone to shift without a full moon let alone in daylight! And it isn't natural to lose your memory when you are in wolf form. *So far, she hasn't been able to tell us much about what happened while she was away.*

Piper would not have been in her right mind for a while so she could have done anything and as a pack; we could all be in trouble. *So why wasn't Arlo concerned? I know he was confused by the whole thing and I know he was worried about Piper... but why didn't he send out his trackers to find her?* Piper nodded and looked from her mother to me.

'I remember running for what seemed like minutes, and everything around me was passing by in a blur. I mean... I don't think I have ever moved so fast. And the adrenaline that rushed through me was like nothing I have ever felt before, not even on a natural shift, but it turned dark really quickly and then I realised I had been running around the woods for hours. I stopped to have a lay down, but I saw a blue glow out the corner of my eye, I haven't ever seen anything like it, it was beautiful and it sparkled a little under the moon; in all honesty... it looked like a tiny blue flame hovering in the darkness, but I didn't know what it was... I... I can't remember.' Her voice trailed off and she stared out of the window, as she seemingly got lost in her memories of the night.

Eddie walked into the living room with a tray of drinks for us all, he had made Piper a cup of tea and some toast and seemed rather proud of himself. *My brother had never cooked a thing in his life, let alone picked up a kettle!*

'Honey? What do you mean? Are you sure that there were... blue flames?' Tanya asked, sitting on the edge of the sofa, taking Pipers hand in hers and giving it a reassuring squeeze. Pipers gaze still stayed fixed on a spot on the wall, before she slowly turned back to face me.

'It... it was talking to me.' She paused for a moment and closed her eyes. 'No... not talking. It was... singing?' She added shaking her head. Piper kept her eyes locked on mine as though she were waiting for me to have the answer. *But I didn't. If I was honest, I didn't have a clue what she was talking about. And I was starting to fear that my blood was slowly driving her insane.*

'Wisp.' A deep voice came from behind me, causing me to flinch and spin around on the spot. The moment my eyes met those golden pools of amber I felt my insides melt to goo. I glanced down at Arlo's and noticed that he had gone back to his room and got clean jeans; that had all the buttons on, and a clean shirt. *Was it wrong that a small part of me was sad about this?* Arlo stepped closer to me and slipped his hand into mine. Before I had a chance to say anything, Piper whirled around to face us.

'Wisps' She cried excitedly, her hazel eyes widening. 'It was a Will-o'-wisp!'

'A wisp?' Tanya repeated looking from Arlo, to me and then back to her daughter. 'Piper; darling, are you sure you saw a will-o'-wisp? They are extremely rare and only show themselves if they are trying to communicate with someone. And that's usually something that witches deal with. They don't make themselves known to werewolves, a-and I don't know anyone who has ever actually seen one.'

'Mum it was a wisp!' Piper snapped angrily, her eyes narrowing at her mother as a low growl rumbled in her chest. *We all gasped, the unbreakable bond between my best friend and her mother was something that everyone had envied. Piper would never speak to her mother this way... well, the old Piper wouldn't. What have I done?*

'What is a wisp?' I asked, looking around the room before taking a sip of my tea.

'A wisp is a spirit that hasn't passed over yet. When someone passes away; depending on what sort of life they have led and depending on their actions the spirit either goes down to the realm of no return. Or they are welcomed with open arms to the heavens to live in the glory of their gods... ours being Selene. But a spirit who has led a good life of many great deeds has the choice to go to Selene's kingdom and live in enteral paradise... or the spirits that have unfinished business are left to live on in the realm between realms, waiting for the task that they had been sent to do. They appear in the form of wisps and try to give you a message, lead you to some place to show you something but again...they are very rare. And I don't think I have ever heard of them appearing to werewolves, especially while they are in wolf form.' Tanya explained. I looked at Piper as she eyed me anxiously, I was fascinated, and I wanted to know more, but there was still that part of me that felt that I was to blame for all of this. We needed to know more about my blood and what it did to people. *I just hoped that Arlo wouldn't find out that this is to do with me. At least not yet. I don't think I could take it if he started looking at me like the freak that I was.*

'I am so tired...I need to get some sleep, but would you guys mind if Amelia helps me up to my room?' Piper yawned stretching out her arms.

'Of course, I will run you a bath babe and then you can have a long sleep and talk to us about it all later.' Eddie smiled as he walked out of the living room. Tanya looked disappointed but nodded at Piper. 'Arlo, may I speak with you please?' I helped Piper to her feet just as Arlo crossed the room and took a seat beside my best friends' mother. We started making our way up the stairs when I could hear the pair of them talking, I couldn't make out the words that they were saying, they were whispering so low that even my wolf hearing struggled to pick up what they were discussing. I shook my head and turned all my attention to my best friend, who was surprisingly walking a lot better since getting back to the mansion grounds. I nudged her bedroom door open with my foot and closed it behind us, turning to Piper and offering a wry smile.

'Is everything okay?' I asked anxiously.

'Yeah I just wanted to talk you alone, I know what my mum is like and she will try to debunk my wisp sighting.' Piper groaned looking more than unimpressed over her mother's doubts.

'Well I believe you and I am curious to know what happened.' I smiled picking up a hairbrush to brush out the matted knots that had formed in her auburn hair.

'So, this wisp kept floating around me and it was whispering something, but the whispers were so soft and fast, that I couldn't work out what it was saying and then when I actually listened to it, I realised it was singing. Anyway, I followed it and it led me away from the woods and past an abandoned cottage; which I didn't even know existed but I stopped when it wanted me to follow it to Willow's creek' I carried on brushing through Pipers hair, becoming more and more intrigued.

'What is Willow's creek and why did you stop?' I asked.

'Willow's creek is a place where witches live and us were-wolves and witches do not get on, we despise each other and if they ever saw me on their land they would curse me and to make things worse, the wisp wanted me to follow it to the castle where a really powerful witch and his grandson lives... I would be dead if I was seen.' Piper said glancing over her shoulder, she was checking to see if her mother or Eddie were listening in.

'I don't understand. How do you know all this about the witches and there being a man and his grandson living there? If none of us knew that this place was around here, then how do you know that?' I asked, not able to contain my confusion. Piper paused for a moment and tilted her head to the side as though she was trying to hear something that she didn't quite understand. *Was she actually losing her mind?* She cleared her throat and sat up straight, shrugging.

'It told me. That wisp. It was hard to make out a lot of what it was trying to tell me, but every now and again something would come through clearly. I remember it telling me that. And there was something else that it wanted me to do. But for the life of me I can't remember what it is.' Piper replied with a soft sigh. I bit my lip as hundreds of questions swirled in my head.

'So, you said that it was singing to you? Do you remember the words? Or perhaps the tune?' I asked hopefully. Piper opened her mouth to answer when her face fell.

'Sorry Lia. It's like it's there, right on the tip of my tongue, but for some reason, when I try and focus on it, it just escapes me.' She answered sadly. I offered a slight shrug and smiled.

'It's alright. It's not important. I just thought that if we knew the song, we might be able to work this all out together. But I am sure that when the time is right it will all come back to you.' I answered kindly, giving her shoulders a gentle, reassuring squeeze. I cleared my throat and glanced over my shoulder.

'So, wait a minute. I thought that they said that Wisps were good spirits? If witches are werewolves truly are at war like everyone says they are, then why would it lead you there?? Why would one lead you to a place that is dangerous for you?' I whispered looking at Pipers reflection in the mirror.

'I don't know; Lia… but this wisp… it wasn't bad, it was… I can't explain it… it made me feel at peace when it was with me and I didn't feel as though it wanted any harm to come to me and that's why I followed it. I stayed behind some tree's and looked around when it was clear of witches. It was showing me the castle, I still don't understand why… but I want you to help me work it out.'

I nodded my head in amazement, something amazing was happening to Piper, she was so lucky to see a wisp and if she needed my help to find out what it was trying to tell her then I was in, this was going to be astonishing. I could feel it. 'Lia… I need to speak to Arlo though…' Piper said with a panicked expression on her face.

'Okay… why are you getting worried about that… are you okay?' I asked concern filling my voice. Piper turned to look at me, her face said it all, she was in trouble. 'What?' I asked.

'So, when I was looking at the witches' castle, I heard someone talking to someone else, so I ran away, but in my panic, I ended up going into another packs territory. I saw the brown wolf that we have all been seeing on and off. And he growled at me, so I apologised and ran away but one of his mutts followed me, we got into a fight and he threatened to cause trouble for our pack.'

'Hold on… did you say the brown wolf?' I asked, a smirk filled my lips.

'Yeah… why are you smiling… this isn't funny; Lia.' Piper sulked scolding me.

'Pipe's we don't need to say anything to Arlo, I can talk to the brown wolf, he isn't as bad as I thought and if he wanted to hurt us before then he would have.'

'But we have never been in his territory before, he might be different this time, he looked furious.' Piper panicked standing up and walking to her bedroom window.

'Listen, have a bath, get some sleep. I will go and talk to him okay. But do not say a word to anyone. Especially Arlo. Let me worry about that when the time comes to it.' I said before pecking her on the cheek and heading back towards the door.

'Lia; please be careful.' Piper whispered.

'Hey, if my blood can turn you into a werewolf before a full moon, heal you and give you super strength and super speed, then imagine what I can do.' I grinned before walking out of the room. It was true, if my blood gave all these amazing new abilities to Piper, then surely, they would be even more incredible for me. *The only problem was, I still couldn't shift.*

I tiptoed down the carpeted stairs being careful to miss the squeaky stairs beneath me, I did not want Arlo or anyone to hear me leaving the house and I knew he would follow me. I jogged across the landing and quietly opened the front door. *I was going to find the brown wolf; even if it meant going into his territory.*

I closed the large iron gates behind me and Pretty girl before glancing back at the houses and mansion, Arlo hadn't followed me and I could breathe a sigh of relief, he would hit the roof if he knew what I was doing. Pretty girl walked by my side, nudging my face every now and then, I admired her beautiful eyes and smiled.

'You are such a beautiful girl.' I soothed rubbing my hand down her silvery grey hair. Before we knew it, we were walking past the abandoned little cottage that Piper had mentioned seeing, but this time smoke was coming out of the chimney. *Someone must live there. But who?* I was about to go and investigate when I heard the familiar tunes of the lullaby, I stopped in my tracks and looked around, the singing was much louder this time and I was sure it wasn't in my head. I looked at Pretty Girl whose ears were now pricked up.

'You can hear it, too can't you?' I whispered amazed; she was the only other thing that could hear what I could. I looked around again and noticed a Large Willow tree, I had never seen one as big as this, it was stunning. 'Come on; Pretty. We will wait here for him.' I said trying to distract myself from the alluring voice around me. I leant against the tree and closed my eyes; trying to relax myself and listen to the lullaby more intently. The words filled my ears.

When the Dark Moon meets its peak,
There's a brother who is your destiny
Hide, my child, safe and sound,
As in this brother, your destiny is found

In the Moonlight, she will show you,
All the questions, that were kept from you,
Go in search until she's found,
Resist the evil all around.

When the Dark Moon meets its peak,
There's a sister who is your destiny
Hide, my child, safe and sound,
As in this sister, your fate is found.

In the Darkness, he'll show you,
All the answers, that were kept from you,
Go in search until he's found,
Resist the liars all around.

Yes, you will speak to those who'll hear
And in your words a sadness flows
But can you brave what you most fear?
Can you face what the Dark Moon shows?

When the Dark Moon meets its peak,
There are the siblings, and their destiny
Come, my children, homeward bound
When all is lost, then all will be found.

I opened my eyes just as the lullaby stopped and looked at Pretty Girl, she was beginning to become anxious and started pacing up and down in front of me as though she was trying to protect me from something. This was the first time that I had ever heard the lullaby fully while being awake. And even though I had just heard the words it was as though my brain couldn't retain it.

'What is it girl?' I asked trying to calm her down, and then I heard him, I looked in the direction the rustling was coming from and stared trying to see him as he came out from behind the tree.

'I have been waiting for you.' I called walking in front of Pretty girl who was now snorting and her tail swishing from side to side in fast motions. She was nervous and I didn't blame her, after that time in the woods when he chased us, I thought he was dangerous and a threat to us too, but for some reason although he looked vicious; he wasn't and I just had a good feeling about him. 'It's okay girl, he won't hurt us.' I whispered looking back at her eyes which were more like a violet colour than the grey they were before. The wolf slowly stepped forward his green eyes darting from Pretty girl to me, he was as nervous of her as she was him. 'I am here because of what happened yesterday, the girl who accidently went into your territory.' I said.

'I know why you are here and consider it forgotten, but make sure it does not happen again.' He said his eyes falling to my leg, my eyes followed his gaze and I noticed a blood coming through my light blue jeans; *I must have cut myself at some point.* I thought, looking back up at him. 'Your friend, her blood... it is unusual; it smells similar to yours... is that why she can shift as and when she wants to?' he asked. I shook my head and sighed.

'Not as and when she wants to, but it did happen yesterday in broad daylight and not under a full moon.' I admitted. 'And yes, I think it's because of my blood.'

The wolf took a hesitant step towards me before looking up to make sure I was okay with him edging closer, I smiled and nodded. 'Interesting.' He mumbled under a deep growl after sniffing at the blood on my jeans. 'You are something special... but a mystery.' He continued. I raised my eyebrows and nodded in agreement.

'A mystery I am, but I want to find out why.'

'I am sure you do, and I hope that I would be able to help you do that. Amelia is it? I don't want you to ever be afraid of me, I will never hurt you or your friends... or your unicorn. You can always talk to me; I know when you are near so just wait under the Willow tree for me.' I smiled at his words, I knew he wasn't a bad werewolf and there was something familiar about him, he made me feel comfortable… something only a select few could do.

'Thank you so much.' I smiled looking down into his eyes and then I realised something. 'I don't even know your name?' He chuckled and then sat in front of me.

'It is William.' I nodded at him and looked around at Pretty Girl.

'Pretty girl; this is William and William; this is Pretty Girl.' I froze as the brown wolf's fur raised on his back and he sniffed the air.

'We have company.' He growled angrily. I turned to look in the direction he was facing; *Arlo*!

Arlo;

I stepped though the line of the tree and locked eyes with the familiar brown wolf. Anger surged through me as I turned my stare from him to her. *How could she have been so reckless? She knew that there were killings happening and we still hadn't caught the culprit. At currently, the brown wolf was top of my suspect list!* I glanced over to Pretty Girl who was eyeing me cautiously. She had always been so good with knowing when Amelia was in danger. So why wasn't she bothered now? I strolled forward, grabbing onto Amelia's arm and dragging her behind me. The brown wolf jumped back and lowered his ears to his head letting out a warning growl.

'Get back to the mansion. I will take care of this!' I snapped, my anger flowing with every word that I spoke. Amelia barged past me, with more strength then I knew she had and whirled around to face me. I turned my attention from the brown wolf to Amelia.

'What the fuck do you think you are doing?' She shouted; her face contorted with rage. The unknown wolf straightened itself up once more and slowly made its way to stand beside her. 'Who do you think you are? Coming out here and acting all threatening.'

'I am your fucking alpha Amelia. And I am only here to ensure that you are not in any danger. You know how reckless it is to just wander out into these woods alone!' I shouted, trying my hardest to get my anger under control. The wolf growled once more, and I turned my stare down to look at him.

'No, it's ok. I promise.' She said, glancing over her shoulder and looking to him. *Was she communicating with this wolf? How is that even possible? Firstly, she was in human form, and secondly, he wasn't a part of our pack!* I turned back to face her; the confusion clear on my face when the brown wolf stepped forward snapping its jaws. In that one action I knew that there was something going on here... Amelia wasn't in any danger from the wolf. He only started growling and snapping his jaws the moment that I came out. Was he... was he protecting her? That was very unusual. I could sense that he was clearly the alpha to another pack. So what did he want with Amelia? *Wait...* Those eyes. I knew those eyes. There was only one other person that had eyes as green as those. And she was stood beside the unknown werewolf.

A million thoughts rushed through my head as I tried to make sense of everything. She looked nothing like the rest of her family. She was always the odd one out. No one remembers Molly being pregnant. Her strained relationship between her, her "father" and "brothers". I stepped forward hesitantly once more and the wolf let out a low growl again. I stepped back holding my hands up in defence.

'I don't mean either of you any harm.' I said, keeping my voice low and calm as I slowly dropped down onto my knees. I closed my eyes and tried my hardest to call out to this wolf. To see if there was a way for me to communicate, but it was useless. I opened my eyes just as the wolf pushed his face into Amelia's hand, causing her to turn around to face him.

'Thank you so much William; I can assure you that I am safe. Go back to your pack. And I hope we get to speak again soon.' She paused and bent down, leaning in placing a gentle kiss on his muzzle. She gave the top of his head one last scratch before he turned and disappeared into the forest. Amelia stood staring after the wolf, and I could already tell that she was about to cry. I stepped forward and placed my hand on Amelia's arm.

'Lia... I-'

'Fuck you Arlo!' She shouted, pulling away from my touch and storming back towards the mansion, barging me out of her way once again. Pretty Girl cantered over to her, walking so close that they were touching. *As much as her defiance angered me as an alpha, there was something about it that aroused me. Why did she have this effect on me?* Anyone else acting in this way would have them on the verge of banishment from the pack. But there was something different about her. The fact that my alpha influence had no effect on her intrigued me more than I cared to admit. With a heavy sigh, I turned and slowly followed her back to the mansion, making sure that I gave her space.

Amelia;

Who the fuck did he think he was? He always treated me like a little fragile doll that needed protecting. But he was wrong. I didn't need his protection. I was capable of looking after myself. And there was something about William that just felt so… familiar. So natural. I bit back the growl of frustration that threatened to leave me and turned to look at Pretty Girl. She turned to look at me and gently nudged me with her nose; her way of letting me know that she would always be there for me. There was just so much that I didn't understand right now. And I had the feeling that William would be able to answer some of them. *Or at the very least point me in the right direction to find those answers.*

I could hear Arlo following slowly behind us. I know that I shouldn't have spoken to him that way in front of another alpha wolf, but I couldn't help it. Who knew what I could have learnt if Arlo hadn't of turned up? I shook my head and pushed on that much faster, just as we crossed the iron gates of the mansion grounds. Pretty Girl followed me all the way to my front door before galloping off back to her stables. I turned and glanced at Arlo once more as he stood staring at me from my front gate, I slammed the door shut before he had had a chance to say anything. I wasn't ready to talk to him. And I had nothing to say.

Arlo;

I knew that Amelia and Piper were hiding something from me. I was their alpha for fuck sake. I was supposed to be the one that knew everything. And to find out that it was my mother that had asked for me not to be told was just infuriating. Well, if no one was going to tell me anything then I was going to find out for myself. And after everything that I had seen in the woods, I knew there was something not right with Amelia. And I was going to find out what that was.

I waited until Benjamin's office lights went out, and I listened as he closed and locked the door before heading out and making his way home. As soon as I thought the coast was clear I crept from my concealment and quietly made my way over to his office.

I twisted the door handle and felt that it was locked; *I know that I heard him lock it, but I was still hopeful!* So, with a heavy sigh, I tightened my grip and twisted that much harder. I heard the lock snap and I slowly opened the door. The room was in darkness and I knew that I needed to make sure that I remained unseen. I pulled my phone from my pocket and turned on the torch. The light seemed overly bright in the darkness, but I was certain that it was just my paranoia getting the better of me. I hurried over to the computer and wiggled the mouse, watching as the screen sprang to life. The log in box flashed before me and I closed my eyes. *What the hell was the password? I was certain that I knew, but I couldn't for the life of me think of it.*

'Think god dammit!' I muttered angrily to myself, clenching my teeth and closing my eyes once more. My mother was the one that was in charge of the medical ward, so she would be the one that created the password. I stood up straight as a thought suddenly hit me. What are the most important things in her life? Me and my father. So let's start with that. *Now I just had to hope that there wasn't a limit on how many tries you could have with the password.*

I lost count of how many passwords I had tried, and to my relief there was no limit on the attempts. I had tried everything that I could think of. My birthday, my father's birthday. Our birthdays combined. Our names, forwards and backwards. After that I decided to try any word that came into my head. I knew that I should have been focusing but I was beginning to become disheart-ened. I was about to give up when I thought I would try one more thing. "*Amelia-May Beth Hunt.*" I don't know why I would think it would be her full name, but hey, I remember she told me it once and my mother has always had a soft spot for her. I typed the name and hit enter, when to my surprise I was in!

I scanned across the screen, trying my hardest to work out what it was that I was looking at. Although I was pretty good with computers, this operating system was completely knowing to me.

I followed the links and searched through the files until I came to her name. I doubled clicked the folder and watched as her complete medical history appeared on the screen. I thought that the first time that she had come to the mansion was that day on her eighteenth birthday? But her medical records went all the way back to the day that she had been born. *So, why didn't I remember her? Surely, I would have done. I would have been ten at the time, so... why are there no memories of that?* I shook my head and scrolled to the bottom of the page, it was all here, the day that she was rushed in when I found her, the day that Lori put her in here and when she had her... I closed my eyes and I fought through the tears that threatened to fall. *I knew that she wasn't destined to be mine, but, why did the thought of her losing that child destroy me?*

I turned my attention to her personal details, all the stand-ard doctor stuff that defines who we are... and everything looked normal. There was no explanation for why she couldn't shift and other than that her incredible speed healing fixed everything that was wrong with her before she needed treatment. I plucked my phone from the desk and snapped some photos of the screen before closing Amelia's medical files and scrolling through to Pipers. Maybe there was something here that would answer a few questions. I waited patiently as her file opened, seemingly taking forever, until it was there on the screen. My eyes scanned the page and I noticed something that was strange. There had been a change made to this file recently. I locked my eyes on the blood group. ABO positive... That was impossible. Werewolves all had O nega-tive blood. It was a biological fact. And secondly, there was no such blood group as ABO positive. I snapped a few more picture of the screen, before tucking my phone back into my pocket and closing down the computer. I needed to make sure that there was no evidence that someone had been here. I turned and slowly made my way back to the door.

Then I felt it. Like a prickling sensation down the back of my neck. There was something that I was missing. I don't know how I knew; *I just did.* I sighed and turned back to scan the office when my eyes locked on a large filing cabinet on the other side of the room. It looked as though it needed a key to open it, but I had, had enough practice unlocking doors with my trusty pen knife when I was a kid. I hurried over and pulled my pocketknife from my hoody and carefully slid it into the lock. I jiggled it about for a few seconds until I heard the familiar click. *I was in!* I opened the drawer as carefully as I could, trying my hardest to make sure that it didn't squeal from the movement. I glanced into the open drawer and to my surprise it was empty. Except for one manilla folder, carefully placed on the bottom.

The sound of footsteps snapped me from my hesitation, and I grabbed the folder and tucked in into my hoody before pressing myself in the tight gap between the cabinet and the wall. The door to the office opened a little wider and the light from the hall flowed in, illuminating the office dramatically. I knew that I wouldn't get in trouble for being here. But if my mother found out that I had broken into hers and Benjamin's office she would go mad. Especially as I am stealing folders.

'H-Hello?' One of the nurses called, hesitantly stepping into the room, looking around cautiously. I held my breath and waited for her to leave, praying that she couldn't pick up my scent. She took another hesitant step into the room, when her pager clipped to her belt bleeped causing her to squeal. She grabbed for the small device and punched a few buttons before sighing, pulling the door closed behind her and rushing down the hall.

I stood in silence for a few more seconds, using my heightened hearing to hear the rhythmic beating of her heart disappear into one of the rooms and leave me alone once more. Without a second of hesitation, I dashed forward, tucking the manilla folder into my hoody and pulling my hood back over my head. Before following the quiet darkened halls back to my office.

I threw the door open before hurrying into the office and slamming the door behind me, rushing over to my desk and pulling my phone from my pocket once more, swiping at the screen. I pulled up the pictures of the medical files that I had snapped and sent them to the printer. I needed to be able to cover all angles at once. Something has happened to Amelia and Piper that day in the hospital, and I was going to find out whether people wanted me to know or not. I paced back and forth across the room as I waited for the documents to print before snatching them up from the paper tray and dropping down into my desk chair and spreading the papers out across the smooth surface.

I knew that something had to have changed Pipers blood type, but the last statement on her medical record that she was kept in overnight for severe wolfsbane poisoning. There were Elites out there that were powerless against that drug. And from these readings, Piper had a hell of a lot of it in her system. *Could that have been what had, had this effect on her blood?* But that doesn't sound right. Wolfsbane kills our kind. That is what we are always taught, and I have seen the effects of the poisoning myself. I continued reading over the documents, switching from Piper to Amelia, back to Piper... but there was nothing that seemed to give the answers!

I let out a low growl of frustration and turned away from my desk closing my eyes. I needed a second to think over everything that I had just read. *There had to be something there that shed a little light onto all of this. It was as though the answers were right in front of me, but just out of my reach.* I turned back to the papers and scanned over them again but, it seemed that the harder I stared at the pages before me, the less I noticed. The less I understood. It was as though every word on the papers were merging into one. With a heavy sigh I dropped my head into my hands and scrubbed my eyes angrily. *Why wasn't any of this making sense? I was the alpha of this pack, yet I seemed to be one of the only ones that didn't have a clue what was going on!* I slammed my palms onto my desk and rose from the chair heading towards the door when something fell to the floor, dropping the contents from within.

I glanced over my shoulder and remembered the manilla folder. *How had I even forgotten about that? I had risked so much to get it, and then it was as though it completely slipped my mind.* I reached for the folder when I noticed two names written on the paper sticking out from within. *Amelia and Pipers!* I pulled the pages from the wallet and placed them on the desk as I scanned over them.

'T-this is impossible. What does all this mean?' I muttered to myself, as my eyes darted back and forth. The words that I was reading were barely registering in my brain. None of this was possible. But at the same time... it now all made perfect sense. *Of course!*

Amelia;

I sat on my sofa staring down at the envelopes with all my friend's names on them. I had written a letter for each of the people that I loved the most in this place, because I was too much of a coward to tell them goodbye to their faces. This was it. Tonight was the night that I was leaving. I hadn't given myself enough time to think it through fully. But I knew that the longer I remained here, the harder that it was going to be when the time came to leave.

My time here with the pack had been eventful to say the least, and I couldn't wait to get away. However... part of me would die the moment I left here. But I knew that that was what I was going to have to do. I felt the familiar burn of unshed tears sting my eyes and tried my hardest to get my emotions in check. Once I left this place, I would become a Deviant. So I needed to toughen the fuck up and prepare myself for the outside world. A knocking at my front door had me snapping from my deep thoughts and before I had a chance to get my brain to catch up with my actions, I was already opening the door. I blinked in surprise and took in the tall, dark handsome figure stood before me. *Ethan.*

'Hey beautiful. How are you getting-' Ethan started, stepping around me into the house and noticing the letters that were neatly laid out on my glass coffee table. 'What is this?' he asked, he tone full of hurt.

'Ethan, I...' I paused and followed his line of sight and realised that he had found his letter. I closed my eyes as a single tear escaped and rolled down my cheek. 'Look, I wanted to tell you all. I wanted to be the brave one that could pretend that I didn't give a shit and walk away from this place forever. But... I can't.'

'Lia... I am coming with you.' Ethan replied, stepping forward and tilted my head up to meet his eyes. 'I told you that I would do anything for you. And I meant it. I will relinquish my place in this pack, and we can leave together.'

'What? No! Ethan, I am not letting you become a Deviant because of me. You have a place in this pack. Your family are well respected. Think of the effect that it will have on them if their only son leaves? Especially if their only son leaves to become a fucking Deviant! And what about Hannah? You can't leave your girlfriend! It's not happening!' I scolded, stepping out of his reach and folding my arms across my chest.

'What? Lia... this is not up for discussion. I am coming with you and I ended things with Hannah.'

'And why the hell would you do that Ethan?' I retorted.

'Because... I am in love with you Amelia. I want to spend the rest of my life with you. And if that means that we live on the run as Deviants then so be it.' I sucked in a gasp as his words hit me like a ton of bricks. 'I mean it Amelia. I love you. And to prove it...' He paused as he dropped down onto one knee pulling a ring from his pocket. 'Amelia-May Hunt. Will you marry-'

'Ethan... stop!' I whispered, closing my eyes as dread filled my chest. 'Get up. Don't do this.' I said, trying my hardest to keep my voice strong.

'But...'

'Just listen to me. The reason that you cannot come with me is because...'

'Because you are in love with Arlo.' He answered for me. I

paused. *That was not the answer that I was going to give. But at the same time, I knew it was true.* Even though I knew it wasn't a question I nodded anyway.

'But that's not to say that I don't love you. I do. Just... not in the same way. You have a special place in my heart Ethan. And I don't think that there is anyone else that I could ask to do this for me.' I paused as a single tear rolled down his cheek. I wiped it away with my thumb and pushed myself up onto tip toes, kissing his cheek lightly. 'I need you to stay here and make sure that Piper, Matt and Eddie are safe, and you are going to need to be the one the deliver these letters for me.' I pulled away from him and gathered the envelopes up into my hands and gave them to him. We stood in since as he flicked through them all.

'Lia, there are letters here for half the pack...' He paused for a second longer then nodded. 'I will do it.' He turned back towards my front door and glanced over his shoulder one last time. 'But I will not be the one delivering this one.' He placed an envelope of the desk by my front door, propping it up on the lamp. 'I think that you need to talk to him. You need to be the one to give this letter to Arlo.' He pulled the door open and a flurry of cold air billowed in around us.

'Ethan... I...' I stepped forward reaching out to him but faltered. I glanced back at me once more with tear filled eyes.

'You are the only woman that I have ever loved Lia. And I am pretty sure that I will never love anyone as much as I love you. I hope that you are happy wherever this journey takes you. And... above all else... stay safe. I love you.' He jogged back to the open door and pulled me in for one final kiss. It was full of passion, love, hurt and finality. Ethan pulled back without meeting my eyes, turned and disappeared into the darkness leaving me broken and alone in my house. I pushed the front door closed and dropped back against it, allowing all my hurt and sadness to leave me in a rush. *I could have got Ethan to come with me. But I couldn't do that to him. He deserved better. He was going to find better.* The tears rolled freely, pooling on my chin before dripping down onto my bare leg. I'm not sure how long I had been sat there crying, time had seemed to lose all meaning. It could have been minutes; it could have been hours. But I knew that Ethan was right. Arlo deserved more than a letter telling him that I was gone. I would go and speak to him face to face. It was the least that I could do. I pulled open the door once more and rushed out into the cool night air. I was still in my vest top and short, short pyjamas, but I didn't care. I ran barefoot up the path towards the mansion.

25

'Yes I know what time it is! Get here, *now!*' I snapped, ending the call with Piper and slammed my phone down onto the desk before glaring at the family portrait on the wall. Other than the fact that I looked like a moody teenager, we were such a happy close family. *When had all of that changed?* My office door opened, and my mother walked in; I had called her before Piper, telling her that I needed her in my office immediately. She walked into the room flashing her famous warm smile. She took one look at my scowl and knew that something was wrong. She came a little closer to my desk and noticed the medical files spread across the tabletop.

'What is this?' She asked, her voice turning colder than that of what I was used to as she raised her angry gaze from the table to me. I climbed from my seat and stood behind the desk, staring into my mother's eyes silently. I clenched my jaw, causing my jaw to flex, when a knock at the door brought my attention from my mother, I glanced away from her as I called for the person to enter. Piper's auburn hair rounded the corner before her face broke out in a beaming smile. She took one look at my mother standing in the corner and her smile faltered. *She knew that something was wrong. But it was too late now.*

'I-is everything alright?' she asked, looking between me and my mother. My mother's eyes widened as she jerked her chin to-wards my desk and Pipers eyes widened in shock. *So they had been keeping something from me? Both of them!*

'I know everything.' I growled, pacing back and forth in front of my mother and Piper. They glanced at one another nervously but remained silent. 'And what I really want to know, is why neither of you thought that it was important enough to tell me?' I continued, trying my hardest to get some control over my anger, but it was no use. It was as though the flood gates to all my concealed emotions had broken, and now all that anger was coming out in a rush. 'Answer me!' I yelled, spinning around to face them. I locked eyes with Piper who stood there and glared at me.

'It wasn't as simple as that.' Piper said, her voice low, but holding a courage that I had never seen in her before.

'Neither of you thought to tell me that Amelia's blood is the key to us being resistant against wolfsbane? Do you not understand how much of an edge that would give us over all the other packs out there? And what about these murders that have been happening? Do you not think if I had found out about this sooner then we could have at least found out what it is that has given Amelia what she needs to be around Wolfsbane?'

'How do you even know any of this?' My mother asked, a sharp edge to her tone as she crossed her arms across her chest. I reached into my top drawer and pulled the manilla file from within, before dropping it on the desk.

'Want to start talking mother?' I asked maliciously. My mother's jaw flexed, and I knew that she was pissed. But I didn't care. I should have been given these answers from the very beginning.

'I am speaking to you; I demand an answer.' I bellowed, causing them both to flinch.

'You may be the alpha Arlo, but I am still your mother. And a respected elder. You do not speak to me in this way. And as for Piper. I was the one that asked her not to tell you.'

'And why shouldn't I be told? Something like this is huge mother! If we had known about this sooner, we may have been able to prevent some of these deaths from happening.' I snapped.

'And that is why I never told you! You think that I was going to just stand aside and let you use my best friend as your little fucking lab rat?' Piper screamed, lunging forward and slamming her palms on my desk. The wood beneath her hands cracked from the force but she didn't stop. 'You know what *alpha;* she deserves so much better than you. You're nothing but a pathetic user!' She continued. I tensed at the choice of words that she had used. The way that she had called me alpha. The only other person that said it in that way was... *Amelia.*

I shook my head and turned back to Piper and noticed that her eyes were beginning to take on the tell-tale glow that she was about to shift. *I knew that if I didn't calm her down now then there would be nothing to stop it. And who knew what effects this was having on her psychologically? The last thing that we needed right now was a feral, pissed off Piper tearing through our little community.* I caught my mother's eye and she put her arms around Pipers shoulders, calming her instantly.

'It's ok dear. Please try to keep calm. Remember that we are not entirely sure what effects that this is having on you.' She whispered softly. Piper nodded her head but refused to take her eyes from me. And they still held that slight shimmer.

'What is happening around here? I asked, feeling more than a little defeated.

'Do you not see how important that this is? I knew that your feelings for Amelia would cloud your judgement. She could be the key to us surviving. She could be the one that changes everything. Do you not see that?'

'Of course I see that. Why do you think that I am so angry that you never told me any of this?' I shouted in reply.

'The less amount of people that know the better. If anyone else found out about this... we don't know what they might do. Would they try and take her for themselves? Or would they kill her? Don't you see... she is our ultimate weapon.' My mother said, this time her voice a little softer. I stood in silence for a moment, think-ing over this new information.

'You're right. Of course, yes. Who else knows about this?' I asked, looking from my mother to Piper. Piper shrugged and turned her face away from me angrily and my mother smiled.

'Benjamin, Tanya, Piper and I... and now you. Not even

Amelia knows this yet. She knows that her blood is special and that it can heal. But she does not know how important to us her blood truly is. Our ultimate weapon.'

'Agreed. Piper would you mind keeping this to yourself? I am asking as a friend and for a friend... that is not an order.' Piper nodded with an unimpressed sigh. 'Good. So, now we just need to make sure that our "ultimate weapon" is kept safe and well hidden.' I said with a sigh of relief.

'Is that all I am to you people. A fucking weapon?' Amelia cried, causing us all to spin around to face her. Her face was pale, and tears fell from her eyes.

'Amelia... wait...' I called stepping forward just as she stepped back. 'Please... I can explain.'

'Fuck you!' she screamed. Stepping back and fleeing from the office. I hesitated for a second as all the lights in the room began to flicker. I glanced over to Piper and my mother who looked as equally confused as me, before dashing after her. By the time I caught up with her in the main hall, the entire pack had gathered around the stairs. Amelia was crying and trying her hardest to fight her way through the crowd, but it was no use. She couldn't get through. *Why had they all come out? What had brought them all in at this time of night? Had they heard the commotion?* I glanced over to the door and saw Charlie leaning against the doorframe smirking, with his arms folded across his chest. *I should have known.*

'Amelia... please wait.' Piper called, running past me and running over to her friend. Amelia shoved her away, causing Piper to slide back further than what she should have done. *Amelia had barely touched her, so what caused her to fly back like that?*

Amelia;

'Get away from me. All of you.' I screamed, spinning around to face the people that I believed I could trust. My heart was racing, and it felt as though my throat was closing up. *Why would all these people betray me in this way?*

'Move. Get out of my fucking way!' Came a familiar voice. I

glanced over my shoulder and noticed Matt literally throwing pack members out of the way to reach me.

'Was you in on this too?' I growled, stopping him dead in his tracks.

'Lia… I have no idea what the fuck is going on? Am I in on what?' He asked, looking from me to Arlo and Piper. I shook my head and stepped back just as Arlo reached out and took my hand. I wrenched it free from his hold and slapped him across the face.

'Don't you fucking touch me!' I screamed. I glanced down at my wrist and noticed the charm bracelet that he had bought for me and snapped it from my wrist, causing the charms to scatter across the floor noisily.

'All this time Arlo. All this time I have been wondering what was wrong with me. Wondering what my role in this pack was… and now I know.' I whispered, tears rolling down my cheeks and pooling at my chin. I never looked up, but I heard him slowly walk towards me.

'Lia, please, listen to me…'

'Don't call me that!" I snapped, turning my glare towards him, causing him to freeze on the spot. The look of hurt that crossed his face felt like a stab to my heart, but I was not going to back down. *He knew how desperate I was for answers and did nothing.* 'Was that your job *alpha?* To get close to the lab rat. Was fucking me including in all of this? Or was that just for your own thrills?' I screamed. The sound of someone gasping had me glancing over and locking eyes with my father. His eyes were full of rage, but for once it wasn't directed at me. I followed his line of sight to Arlo who had a blank expression on his face.

'Look, I know how this looks… but…'

'I don't want excuses Arlo. I want answers.' I cut in, my voice hard and emotionless. I couldn't allow myself to succumb to the true feelings that were raging within. I could feel my heart pounding in my ears, and I felt as though I was going to pass out. Arlo cleared his throat nervously and glanced around at the rest of the pack.

'Can we please talk about this back in my office? We do not

need an audience.'

'Why? Because now they can see what a true scum bag their alpha is?' I screamed. Arlo sighed and glanced over to his mother, who was stood pale and emotionless staring at the scene playing out before her. 'Oh... now it all makes sense. You were in on it too!' I said, a humourless laugh escaping my lips. Marie's eyes widened as she shook her head.

'Amelia... no. I...'

'That's why you gave me the room next to him... wasn't it. So that he could keep his eye on the little ultimate weapon. Let me guess... it was you that encouraged him to spend all that time with me. Did you also put him up to asking me to join you guys in the Luna's seat at mealtimes?'

'Amelia... I know that you are hurt right now but...'

'Save it Marie.' I snapped, cutting her off and glaring at her in disgust. 'You make me sick. All of you.' I spun on the spot and began making my way back towards the main doors. The sea of pack members parted, creating a divide for me to pass through. All staring at me with a look of amusement, shock and horror. Arlo grabbed my hand once more, this time a little more forcefully pulling me back around to face him.

'I should have told you the truth.' He answered, his voice low and filled with pain. I gulped down a deep breath as a new wave of tears washed over me. 'But...

'Why didn't you tell me Arlo? How could you have done that to me?'

'It's because I-'

'I gave you everything. I gave you the one thing that I can never get back. I even thought that I was going to give you my heart. I knew that you were feeling the beginnings of an imprint, and I knew what I was doing. But... I just thought that you could have at least been honest with me.' I cried, dropping my face into my hands and sobbing uncontrollably. Arlo closed the distance between us and pulled me into his arms; I know that it sounds strange but, in that moment, I thought that I could feel a tiny part of his heart break too.

'Lia, I never told you because I... I love you.' He whispered, his voice trembling as he spoke. And I felt a warm tear drip onto my forehead. I jerked my head back and stepped out of his embrace. Why was it that the three words that I wanted to hear more than anything just made me hurt more? I shook my head and stepped backwards, holding my hands up defensively. It was only then that I noticed the rest of the pack were closing in around us. Some with looks of curiosity on their face, some with concern, and some that were smirking. I grit my teeth and shook my head again, this time more forcefully.

'Get away from me.' I whispered, my words seemingly stunning Arlo.

'Lia, I just... I just said... I just told you that I am in love with you' He repeated, reaching out for me once more.

'I said, get *away from me!*' I screamed, this time throwing my arms down at my sides, allowing my anger to explode out around me. The lights overhead began to flicker, and the framed portraits on the walls began to shake. The sound of breaking glass filled the quiet of the room followed by the sounds of people screaming out in fear, which all ended with an almighty crash. Louder than anything that I had ever heard before.

I opened my eyes and looked at the devastation that was laid out before me. The entire pack lay on the floor, some staring at me speechlessly, others scrambling to get away from me as fast as they could, with others clutching at open wounds on their bare skin caused by the torrent of falling glass. Every window in the main hall had shattered and the crystal chandelier had fallen from the ceiling. I felt my breath catch in my throat as my fears and anxieties crashed down on me.

Without a moment's hesitation, or stopping to check that everyone was ok, I turned and ran out of the mansion, needing to be free of this place I know that I had tried escaping many times before, but this time was different. I would kill if I had to. I just needed to be free. I burst through the main doors and ran out into the darkness. I guess all the training that Matt had been giving me was paying off. I remember last time I tried to run this my legs gave out and my lungs were burning, but this time, everything was different. I noticed that the trees and houses were beginning to whizz past me in a blur and the cool night air slammed into my bare skin, leaving me feeling free. I was so caught up in that moment that I never noticed the dark figure lurking in the shadows of the canopy of trees.

In the blink of an eye, the shadowy figure lunged forward, slamming into me with so much force that it knocked me to the slightly dampened earth. I rolled over the ground a few times before finally stopping on my back and staring up at the stars above me, panting breathlessly; the tackle winding me.

'You thought that you could just turn up here and ruin everything? Everything that I have been working for?' The familiar voice asked menacingly from the darkness. I knew that voice. Why did I know that voice? I propped myself up on my elbows and was surprised at how easily I could see into the darkness. Charlie was crouched beside me, a look of disgust crossing his face.

'C-Charlie? What are you doing?' I asked, disorientation and confusion causing my voice to wobble.

'I am here to make sure your time at ruining my life is over. Do you not understand how disgusting it is to have to be associated with someone like you?' He sneered, turning his nose up in disgust.

'I-I don't know what you are talking about!' I stammered, shaking my head and slowly crawling backwards. My brother leapt up to his feet, and in one swift movement, kicked my arms out from under me, causing me to slam back down to the ground.

'A disgusting half-blood like you. We are pure bloods through and though. And you can't even shift. Have you not wondered why father always kept you hidden away in that cottage? Too ashamed to be linked to the likes of you.' He continued, circling me like a shark following the scent of blood on the waves. I tried to prop myself up once again, but Charlie moved forward, placing his boot on my hand, pressing down with all his weight. Pain burned through my fingers at the force of being crushed, and I bit my lip to stop myself from crying out. His other foot raised into the air before coming down on my face with a sickening crunch.

My head jerked backwards, slamming into the ground, a sharp pain erupting down my neck. Warm blood gushed from my nose, and I could feel it running down my face and pooling in my hair. In one swift motion, Charlie place a foot either side of me, giving my fingers once last stamp before dropping down on top of me, straddling me.

"Please? W-Why are you doing this to me?' I sobbed, pain flooding through me from the slight motion of talking. I tried to struggle out from underneath him, but the world was spinning around me in a blur. I was obviously suffering from some kind of concussion. Charlie threw his head back and laughed into the nights air, his breath coming out in clouds in front of him. He turned his stare back to me and grabbed my throat my both hands, squeezing with all his might.

Ethan:

I ran from the main hall as soon as Amelia had left and noticed the way that Charlie and already slipped out moments before the chaos. I never trusted him, and after seeing the smirk on his face while all of the drama was happening just went to show how untrustworthy he truly was. I needed to make sure that she was ok. I didn't care about what had just happened back there. I didn't even care about what she really was. I loved her and nothing that she could do or say would change that.

I ran out into the cold night air and could see Amelia's silhouette running towards the main gates. I needed to reach her. I pushed myself as fast as I could and slipped through the gates just in time to see Amelia tackled to the ground in a small clearing a few feet from the entrance. She hit the ground hard and rolled a few times before stopping on her back and staring up at the sky. The shadowy figured loomed over her. I couldn't make out what they were saying but everything in me was telling me to remain unseen. I lowered myself down into one of the bushes, making sure that I was silent and hidden. And watched in horror as the figure's foot slammed down into her face, filling the air with a sickening crack. The scent of Amelia's blood filled the air and I knew that I needed to do something. Her attacker stepped to the side and I caught the briefest glimpse of their face. *Charlie.*

He stood either side of her, stepping on both of her hands at once causing her to cry out and that was when I knew what needed to be done. As quietly as I could, I ran back into the mansion grounds and ran toward the stables. I needed to set the unicorn free. She was the only one with the power to save her now. I was no match for an Elite. And I was especially no match for our packs Beta.

Amelia;

I felt the panic setting in as I struggled to get my breath. My eyes were bulging from the force of his hands and I felt as though my head was going to explode. A pressure began forming in my head and I kicked my legs out trying to get him off of me, but it was no use. He was too strong. I could hear my heartbeat in my ears once again, at first slamming hard, but gradually slowing down. The edges of my vision darkened, and I knew in that moment that I was going to die. I felt every muscle in my body tense unlike anything I had ever felt before, and a strange glow gently illuminated a terrified looking Charlie. I threw my head back and screamed, the pressure releasing me instantly. A force threw Charlie from on top of me, throwing him across the clearing, before slamming him into a tree. A sickening crunch filled the silence as he dropped down to the ground, groaning in agony. I climbed to my feet and looked down at my hands in awe.

Every pore in my body began to sting, and bones felt as though they were vibrating within. What was happening to me? A red-hot pain bolted down my spine, hitting my hips and causing me to buckle to my knees. A heat from within seared my insides, causing me to cry out in pain once more. I rolled onto my back and laid staring up at the beauty of the night sky, happy that the final moments of my life would be spent staring up at the magical array above me. The sound of running footsteps could be heard getting closer to where I lay, but I couldn't move. My body suddenly felt as though it had turned to lead, and I couldn't move an inch.

The footsteps grew louder, and I realised that it must have been the entire pack, and then the sounds of gasps filled the air. They had obviously just seen Charlie. Someone rushed over to me, dropping down to the ground and reached out for my hand, but it was too late. The burning pain had reached a level that was intolerable, and my back arched, snapping sounds filling the air.

'Lia its ok, just breathe, it will all be over soon.' Arlo whispered, leaning in close so that all I could see was those golden eyes staring down at me. My back arched once more, this time the burning spreading through my entire body, throwing me forward onto my hands and knees. I watched in horror as my fingers seemed to retract back inside my palms and my nails turn into claws and darkening. My knuckles popped up and my wrists bent in ways that seemed inhumanly possible. Pure white hairs began to sprout through my skin, slowly at first and then speeding up, spreading up my arms and down my back. My mouth and nose stretched out into one and my teeth throbbed as they extended and sharpened. I felt my shoes loosen, before falling off and just knew the same thing that happened to my fingers was happening to my toes. I closed my eyes tightly and clenched my teeth, riding out the burning pain as it intensified. For a brief moment I thought that I was about to pass out, and then there was a pop.

My clothes burst out into tattered rags around me and all the pressure that I had felt moments ago seemed to ease. I dropped down into the dirt; my eyes still tightly shut as I panted to catch my breath. Something was different. Every little sound that I heard seemed to be intensified somehow. I could hear the thumping of people's hearts. I could hear every whispered from around the pack. And I could hear Charlie.

'I t-tried to s-stop her. I j-just wanted t-to help.' He stammered, his voice sounding weak and feeble. My eyes flew open and I came face to face with the shocked faces staring at me. I turned my stare across each member of the group, finally stopping on my father. Before I could stop it, my lips curled back, and a low feral growl erupted from deep within my chest and everyone stepped back.

I finally stopped and looked at Arlo. His kind eyes filled with a look that I couldn't quite place. Was that fear? Concern? Panic? I shook my head and slowly began backing away from them. A shrill voice filled my ears, so loud that I thought my eardrums were about to burst.

'*Get her!*' Lori screamed, bursting her way to the front of the group and pointing at me. 'Look what she has done to one of our pack members. This goes against pack lore!' She continued, her hateful stare boring into me. The sound of fellow pack members agreeing filled the silence causing me to back away from them further.

'We don't know...'

'I know that you are the alpha Arlo. But look. See for yourself what she has done to our Beta. To your best friend!' She cried, turning back to Charlie and gesturing to the ground where he lay. Arlo closed his eyes and drew in a deep breath. Before turning his sorrow filled eyes back to me. I narrowed my furious stare at them all and shook my head, growling viciously once more. I snapped my jaws and turned to run. I moved at speeds that I had never moved before. I no longer cared if anyone was following me. I was not part of that pack. I knew in my heart that I didn't belong there. And I was finally free.

I ran as fast as my paws could take me. Not stopping at anything. This was a whole new world to me. Every sight, every sound, every feeling. It was all new. I don't know how long I had been running. I didn't care. I felt so alive. I ran beside a huge lake that separated the pack mansion from the rest of the world and stopped to drink.

I turned my stare down to the reflective surface and startled myself with wide shocked eyes. I had never seen another world look the way that I did. My green eyes seemed to sparkle, as though they held their own light. And my fur; although it was white, it shimmered in the dull light of the moon, looking just like that of a pearl. I shook my shoulders from side to side, and watched as the white seemed to reflect, blue, purple and green. I narrowed my eyes and nodded to myself before throwing my head back and letting my first howl rip through me. My sorrow filled cries filled the still night air, drifting off into the darkness.

Now, all I needed to do was follow this voice that seemed to be calling me. I wanted answers and, in that moment, I swore to the gods that I was going to get them!

Arlo;

I stepped forward and glanced over my shoulder to a bruised and bloodied Charlie. Something wasn't right about this entire situation. And I was going to find out what. I stared down at the tattered rags that had once been Amelia's clothes and noticed a white envelope sticking out from the remains of one of her pockets. I plucked it from the ground and saw my name written in her beautiful swirly handwriting across the front. I was about to open it when the sound of galloping hooves filled the night air. I glanced over my shoulder just in time to see Pretty Girl charging towards us. She got to the clearing and looked at me before whinnying away. She reared up onto her hind legs and let out a heart-breaking squeal. It was a sound unlike anything I had ever heard before.

I watched as the unicorn trotted around the circle for a moment, stopping at Charlie and kicking him in the gut with both of her hind legs. He flew through clearing and slammed into another tree with a crunch. He let out a squeal of pain and all it took everything in me to hide my smirk. I slowly made my way over to Pretty Girl and gently patted her neck.

'Go get her girl. Keep her safe.' I whispered. Her ears lowered for a second before she galloped off in the direction that Amelia had gone. I stood and watched as her silver shimmering body disappeared into the lining of the trees, the horn on her head glowing lightly in the darkness; just like it always had. I fought back the tears that were threatening to spill and stormed back towards the mansion. I needed some time to myself. I needed some time to understand everything that had just happened.

I entered my bedroom and slammed the door behind me, the letter in my hands burning my fingertips, *I needed to read this… now.* Despite everything that had gone on this evening, I needed to know what she was going to say to me. I needed to know some of the answers. I tore open the envelope and pulled the sheet of paper from within. My eyes burned as her familiar scent washed over me.

Arlo,

I have written so many letters today since getting back from the forest and yet, this one has been the hardest. There are so many things that I wanted to tell you, so many things that you have needed to know. I wish that I could have done that face to face but, I fear that my time is up.

Firstly, you just need to know how much I love you. I have done from the moment those golden eyes saved me back on that day in the forest, and you have no idea how much it kills me to know that you are destined for someone else. But… that is not the purpose of this letter.

I am leaving. I know that we have all known that this day was coming, but… it is time. The thought of leaving you and all the people that I love is heart breaking. But I know deep down that I am not where I belong. There is something out there calling to me. I hear it every day. I hear it every night. I have tried to fight it since the day I was born, but now it is time that I finally give in and go in search for who I really am.

I am sorry for all the pain that I have caused, as well as all the trouble that we have been through. And I am especially sorry that I was not strong enough to carry the child that would have been loved more than life itself. That will haunt me until the day I die.

I also think that it is time that we told you the truth. I have been asked to keep this to myself, but I think that you have a right to know. You are the Alpha after all. I need you to watch over Piper for me. I don't know what I have done to her but… she is changing. I am so sorry that I cannot be there to help her through all these problems that I have caused her, but now it is my time to go. If I had known that saving her life with my blood would change her… n… I still would have done the same. I need you to watch over her.

Protect her. And help her learn to control these new abilities that she is gaining. Between you and Matt I know that you will have her controlling herself in no time. I mean… if you could put up with my attitude then surely you could help her? And don't be mad at Matt. He knew nothing about any of this.

Speaking of Matt… guide him. Protect him. Love him. And for fuck sake find him a man; he deserves to be loved the way he loves all those around him. One that will love him for the truly beautiful soul that he is.

I can't say that this is forever, but I all I know is that if we meet again, in this life or the next, everything would have changed… except for one thing.
My love for you.

Goodbye my love.

Lia

xx

I dropped the letter to the ground as the tears flowed freely down my cheeks. *If she wasn't the one that was destined for me then why did it hurt so much?* I glanced down at the table beside my bed and stared at the framed picture of Amelia and me. We both looked so happy. Sitting in the pub and she demanded a selfie. I thought back to how I protested so much; but was secretly overjoyed that she wanted to capture that moment. The pain that ripped through me was unlike anything I had ever felt, and I needed this image to be away from me. *Right now.*

Without a second thought, I threw the photo across the room and heard it shatter as it smashed into the wall. I glanced up just in time to see the framed painting of the wolves from legend rock back and forth before tumbling to the ground and shattering on the floor. I let out a growl of frustration. *This was a family heirloom. One that was passed down from generation to generation, and I destroyed it.* I climbed to my feet and began gathering up the glass when I noticed a corner of material sticking through the frame. I plucked it from the ground and was amazed as it unfolded into a huge tapestry. The painting of the wolves held more than one image. *Was this the original prophecy? How had all of this fit into the frame?*

I raised it to my nose and sniffed cautiously and then it hit me. The distinct smell of a witch's magic. The writing that surrounded the images was unlike anything I had ever seen, and there was no way that I would ever be able to decipher it. But from the pictures it looked as though the prophecy was yet to unfold. I stared hard at the image and gasped. *No... It couldn't be.*

EPILOGUE

Lennox;

When the Dark Moon meets its peak,
There's a brother who is your destiny
Hide, my child, safe and sound,
As in this brother, your destiny is found

In the Moonlight, she will show you,
All the questions, that were kept from you,
Go in search until she's found,
Resist the evil all around.

When the Dark Moon meets its peak,
There's a sister who is your destiny
Hide, my child, safe and sound,
As in this sister, your fate is found.

In the Darkness, he'll show you,
All the answers, that were kept from you,
Go in search until he's found,
Resist the liars all around.

Yes, you will speak to those who'll hear
And in your words a sadness flows
But can you brave what you most fear?
Can you face what the Dark Moon shows?

When the Dark Moon meets its peak,
There are the siblings, and their destiny
Come, my children, homeward bound

When all is lost, then all will be found.

I opened my eyes and stared up at the ceiling above. This was getting ridiculous now. Every night for as long as I could re-member I had heard the same stupid song. Everyone word burning into my brain as though being stamped with a branding iron. I rolled over and grabbed for my phone. *3:30am. Brilliant. I hadn't even been asleep for an hour.* I rolled from my bed and dropped my phone back on the table and walked over to my bedroom win-dow, staring out at the sky above.

I flexed my fingers and summoned my magic to my palms, watching as the midnight blue mist danced around my wrist. I closed my eyes and shook my head, running through every spell I could think to try and get some sleep. A sense unlike anything I had ever felt rushed up my spine causing me to open my eyes once more.

The song… it was louder now. It seemed as though it was just outside my window. I looked out and peered into the darkness. A flash of white caught my eye. *What is that?* I pushed up onto my tip toes and leant a little further out, hoping to get a better line of vision. Whatever it was, it was moving fast. I sucked in a sharp breath, feeling as the icy air filled my lungs.

Was that a… a… was that a wolf?